Agave Revealed

Anna
La Fouge

Other books by Anna LaForge

The Marcella Fragment

Agave Revealed

by

Anna LaForge

Book Two of Maze

 Newcal
Publishing

Edited by John Feltch
Cover design and illustrations by Jeff Raby: Creatis Group
creatisgroup.com

Cover art: *Demon Seated in the Garden,* by Mikhail Alexandrovich Vrubel
[Public domain], via Wikimedia Commons

Newcal Publishing
newcalpub.com

Trade Paperback Edition
ISBN 978-0-9850168-4-5

All of the characters in this book are fictitious.
Any resemblance to actual persons living or dead
is purely coincidental.

This book is set in Palatino Linotype and is printed on acid free paper.

Again, for Bob

Only those capable of envisaging utopia will be fit for the decisive battle, that of recovering all the humanity we have lost.

Ernesto Sabato

Contents

Cast of Characters

The Council of Pelion:
    She-Who-Was-Meliope, Seventeenth Mother
    She-Who-Was-Hesione, Eighteenth Mother
    Prax, Commander of the Legion
    Kazur, Head Scribe of the Great Library
    Chryse, Instructor of the Maze, Member of the Hetaera Guild
    Ranier, High Healer of Pelion, healing partner to Nadia
    Nadia, High Healer of Pelion, healing partner to Ranier

Mission Helpers:
    Lukash, Searcher of Souls, mate to Selena
    Selena, Searcher of Souls, mate to Lukash
    Edothea, Master Teacher of the Hetaera Guild
    Timon, Master of the Guild of Players
    Flavius, Monitor of the Maze
    Strato, Head Trainer of the Maze

The Legion of Pelion:
    Hume, Commander of the Cavalry
    Spence, Hume's second-in-command
    Didion, Healer to the Legion Cavalry

Citizens of Pelion:
    Denassa, President of the Guild Assembly (A.T. 22-27)
    Reddin, Healing Practitioner
    Pasiphae, Co-Founder of the Guild of Printers, mother to Reddin
    Orrin, Master Teacher of the Hetaera Guild, brother to Reddin
    Tubal, President of the Guild Assembly (A.T. 45-50)
    Eluria, mate to Kazur

Agave:

    The Aeson of Agave
    Charis, slave to the Aeson
    Lillas, daughter of Charis and the Aeson
    Seth, nephew of the Aeson
    Scarphe, sister to the Aeson, mother of Seth
    Phoron, bondsman to Lillas
    Mia, slave to Lillas
    Olwyn, slave to Lillas
    Abas, slave to Scarphe
    Paladin, Captain of the Imarus Guard

Women and Men of the Maze:

    Thais / * Jarod of Lapith
    Charmian / * Stym of Lapith
    Valeria / * Altug of the Sarujian Mountains
    Phoebe / * Keret of The Flowering Lands
    Aethra / * Manthur of Endlin
    * Halys of Lapith / Dysponteus
    * Fenja of the Eastern Isles / Dorian
    * Gwyn of Cyme / Adrastus

[* indicates ernani]

Acknowledgements

Thomas Kyd and John Donne for the use of their poetry, dramatic ("The Spanish Tragedy") and metaphysical ("The Good Morrow"), and Dr. Barbara Traister, who introduced them to me. Jennifer Rockwood, friend and fellow walker, who introduced me to Stephen Sterns, who, in a single meeting, gave me enough insights and good advice to set me back on the path of writing after a too-long hiatus. Meghan Found, a trusted colleague, who reads deeply, wisely, and well. And lastly, to George Brashears, Eleanor & Bill Crum, and Keith & Lissa Parr, who contributed much appreciated financial support to this book through The Agave Translation Kickstarter Project.

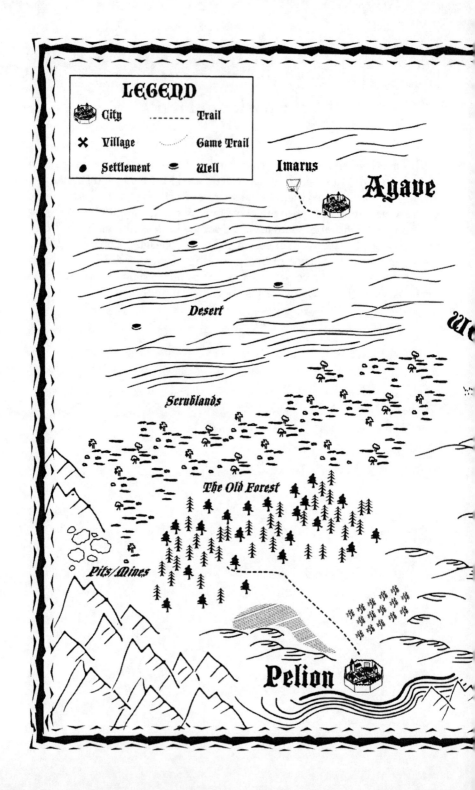

EASTERN LAPITH
River Tellas
Harvest Celebration
od's Lake
The Colony
TERN LAPITH
N
W
E
S
SOUTHEASTERN PROVINCES
Cinthea
Cyme
Cottyo

Agave Revealed

Prologue

The Second Day

HER SECOND AWAKENING came more gradually than her first. Moist air moved in and out of her nostrils, luring her towards consciousness with a fragrance from her childhood, one she hadn't thought to experience again in her lifetime. Honeysuckle, sweeter than sweet, floated on the scent of roses, the tiny star-shaped variety that climbed a trellis in her grandparents' garden.

Where am I this time, she wondered, before slowly, cautiously, opening her eyes.

Powder-white clouds skipped and skidded across a wide expanse of sky. A visual sweep of her surroundings found a lush landscape as deeply green as the sky was blue. No mountains, she thought, triumphant at this particular discovery. How she hated the idea of settling near the mountains shown her on that initial visit, imagining as she did their biting winds and stony soil.

"In your dreams you spoke a warning: 'We must grow food or perish.'"

For a moment she'd forgotten he was always present, linked to her consciousness asleep or awake, experiencing her dreams as she worried over the new world being prepared for her and other former residents of Old Earth. Dead Earth, she corrected herself, not without bitterness. A millennium might have passed, but for her, the destruction of her world was but a few days past and remained a raw-edged wound. True to form, he ignored her self-pity. Nostalgia held no interest for him.

"Orchards have been planted; also vines and groves. Streams abound, as does game in the hills to the east and the forest to the west of the valley in which we stand. Winters and summers will be milder than you remember, the seasons longer in their number of days."

She had not realized she was standing. Looking down, she stared at unwrinkled forearms covered with unspotted skin. When she made a fist, her bones did not ache, nor were her fingers disfigured by the osteoarthritis inherited from both sides of her family. When she ventured a step or two, her joints moved so smoothly they might have been oiled. What had they done to her?

"Improved your mobility and gave you another thirty years of life."

What for? What did this new world have to offer save years of untold labor, not to mention hardships of every kind? Food and water were just a beginning. What about fuel and clothing, sanitation, housing? And what of the babies? For, people being people, babies would follow. We must care for the children or we'll not survive as a species no matter what these aliens, these Sowers, do before they fly away to some other part of the universe, leaving us alone on a planet we cannot pretend to know as well as we knew Old Earth.

"The laws of gravity and thermodynamics do not change, nor do physics, or mathematics, or the principles of electromagnetism. We ask: would the duplication of Old Earth be your goal?"

And she knew in that moment, before the alien finished posing the question, that her answer was a decided "No!" There must be a different path, a different way of life for her species, for she would not knowingly participate in yet another destruction of her planet, even if it occurred thousands of years in the future. But how to go about it?

"We offer a different path."

Curiouser and curiouser, she thought. Like Alice, I find myself in wonderland. Tell me, Sower. Tell me how to avoid the mistakes of human history.

"We can make alterations to your genome, creating the possibility of shared consciousness."

She wrestled with it, trying to imagine how a population of telepaths could prevent humanity from destroying themselves through their own technological achievements. Could shared empathy be the answer? Certainly she could never cause harm to this Sower . . .

"Nor could I harm you. But this would be far more complex than the simple bond we share. In time, your descendants would be genetically linked to every living system on the planet. As these bonds multiply across the population, humanity working together as a single entity might influence the nature of existence itself."

How long, Sower? How long to become one with the world we inhabit?

"Fifty generations; perhaps more, perhaps less."

This was how a Sower thought. Not in years, but in generations.

Who am I to make this decision? Ask the others, why don't you? And while we're on the subject, exactly how many "others" are there?

"We communicate with all of you in your dreams. A few have been awakened, you among them. Like you, they thought of others before themselves. Also like you, they reject the old model."

Numbers. Give me numbers.

"You must understand, by the time we reached you, the few who remained had fled to the highest places on your planet."

He took her with him into his memories of the final days of her dying world: people scrambling to survive, the mountains shaking, paths crumbling underfoot, the thin air increasingly poisonous, the peoples' faces as they looked up at the ship hovering overhead, wondering if something so alien to their idea of what constituted a space-worthy vessel might actually save them from destruction. Despite their doubts, they lifted their children up to the throbbing light and jumped forward into nothingness, just as she had done, to be enveloped in tissue-like membranes rocking her to sleep. Sinking into unfamiliar smells and textures, she surrendered consciousness without even a thought of protest, so grateful was she to escape the horrors left behind.

Out of nine and a half billion people less than thirty thousand remained. On other ships, how many she could not guess, a few were awake, a tiny few who, like her, were being entrusted with decisions regarding the future of their race. As much as she would have liked to confer with them, she was prevented from doing so by the Sower, whose shared visions began to fade until the two of them stood where they had begun, near a grove of what she thought might be pear trees.

"You will never meet them, nor they, you. We will scatter your people, your books, and your music across the continents."

Like farmers sowing seeds—some landing on fertile soil and putting down roots; others thrown onto rocky ground that would not yield. Rough justice in this new Eden, she found herself thinking, aghast at the idea of being cast in the role of Eve.

Then, in a moment of clarity, she envisioned her future on this nascent world, building a community in this temperate, fertile valley with the Sower continually by her side, for she knew deep inside herself that he would remain with her until the moment of her death. Books would be her guide, hard work her daily companion, and the other survivors would call her . . .

"Mother."

The irony of it struck her hard, for she had never given birth, never longed for a child to call her own. She frowned; for it occurred to her there must be consequences to the choice she was being offered. Even as she formed the question, his answer came clearly, calmly into her thoughts.

"If you choose to bind yourselves to this world, you cannot be unbound. We will not be able to rescue you a second time."

A second chance for humanity. There would be no third.

Without explanation, the Sower burst into song, his eerily inhuman voice pitch perfect. The tune was unknown to her, but the lyrics, ah, the lyrics! Her trained ears identified Latinate roots and quickly settled on Occitan, an ancient dialect spoken two millennia ago in what was the Roman Empire before it became modern France. Tears stung her eyes as she listened to this folk song of indeterminate age, a shepherd's song, she discovered as she translated, sung on a lonely hill at nightfall, the sky splendid with stars, the night air soft and tender.

Her tears spilled onto her cheeks as she realized she was most probably the only person in the universe capable of understanding the language being sung. On Old Earth, this was her specialty, the study of ancient Indo-European languages, many of them extinct, most of them endangered. There were barely three thousand Occitan speakers alive the day the world ended. Now there was but one.

Judging the occasion merited a human voice, she spoke her choice aloud: "So be it."

As he had done the First Day, and would do every day of her life, the Sower sang the First Mother to sleep.

The Agave Translation

. . . *and so the days shall pass until the beast wakes, and lo, the land shall wither, even to the last blade of grass. On the anvil of the sun, two silver rings are forged.*

The prophet speaks, but only one shall heed his call. The flame of the west shall pass into the wet lands where it will not be extinguished. The candle of despair shall be lit, and yea, they shall be joined as no others before or after.

As the beast roars, so shall the people thirst, until their thirst at last is quenched. The staff lifts, falls, and lo, the earth rumbles and shakes. From the depths spurts forth the fountain from which all may drink. And all will drink.

One ring will pass away; one will abide with you forever.

Agave shall be translated and Pelion will wed.

Attributed to the Fifteenth Mother

Chapter 1

The Call

ENERGY SPRANG OUTWARD, fueled by her need, the words a simple incantation, a means by which she could more easily concentrate. As she summoned the full strength of her powers, it seemed that her sixteen forbearers leapt to her assistance. As their minds linked, her call grew in strength and clarity, diverging around her in concentric circles radiating outward, toward and beyond the enveloping gloom.

"My time approaches! Answer the call!"

Her mind cleansed of everything but the necessity of the call, immersed in the discipline of endless repetitions, she closed her eyes against the slanting sheets of rain slamming into the stone walls around her. The weather was raw; the winds brutal and unforgiving. When a gust rammed her against the battlement, she nearly lost her footing on the wet, slightly oily surface of the stones. Moving closer to the parapet, she clung to the glistening stones like a determined spider cut loose from its web.

Concentration broken by her near misstep, She-Who-Was-Meliope halted her summons, waiting, without much hope, for a reply. Made miserable by the cold and damp, she pulled the cloak closer around her head and shoulders and shivered. Her robes sodden now, her toes squelching inside her shoes and stockings, she would be forced to return to her tower chamber sooner than planned. A few years ago she would have greeted a winter storm with pure exhilaration, standing her post as stolidly as a sailor on watch aboard a wooden ship sailing the eastern seas. Now was not then, however, and she was tired, half-frozen, her crippled leg aching bone-deep from thigh to ankle. Reluctantly, she turned away from her view of the valley, hidden now by a dense fog, and edged along the walls until she reached the tower steps. Here a slight overhang offered shelter. Pausing underneath, both hands grasping the railing, she considered the city nestled inside the fortress walls on which she stood.

Not even the shroud of mist and clouds hiding the weak sun of winter could dim the glory that was Pelion. Despite the grey pall, the white stones and tiled roofs of the Sanctum and the Great Library rose gracefully above all other buildings, their heights dwarfing the low-slung roofs snuggling companionably against one another around the circular walls of the battlements. On the northern-most wall, the Maze was nearly hidden from view by low-hanging clouds, while the House of Healing, nestled in the heart of the city, was clearly recognizable with its atrium and interlocking arched corridors. She could see it all; the markets, guild shops, schools, residences, parks, fountains, and promenades. Even with her admittedly limited knowledge of architecture and design, she could appreciate the ordered vision of the city planners. The buildings were constructed over a period beginning some five hundred years ago—the Maze a mere seventy years old—yet each harmonized with the other, lending elegance to their studied simplicity.

As a child, She-Who-Was-Meliope knew every street, every byway, hawking her parents' fruits and vegetables so they might work without interruption in the orchards and gardens outside the walls. Her limp might render her awkward and ungainly in the closely planted rows of a garden, but on the streets she was confident, almost arrogant, as she pushed the two-wheeled cart before her, crying out her wares in a sing-song melody of doggerel rhymes that varied with each passing season. The hours just before dusk were her favorite times, the windows lit by flickering ovals of candlelight, the doors opening in answer to her call, throwing their ruddy gleam of hearth-fires into the rapidly darkening streets—here a woman anxious to obtain an extra measure of rice to stretch a meal for an unexpected guest, there a man hoping for a bushel of his favorite grapes so he might begin making the household wine. The people of Pelion were her business; even when she donned the black robes, that relationship never faltered—their streets remained her streets. The fact that she labored now to improve their lives rather than filling their stomachs bothered her not a bit. To others she might be the Seventeenth Mother of Pelion, but her own private vision of self remained Meliope, the crippled girl with the cart, limping through the evening hush that fell nightly on the great city, gazing on ruby hearth fires glowing from within.

To this day, she never failed to be amused by looks of consternation bordering on amazement when she corrected a Guild member's faulty location of a particular shop or trading house. How predictably ridiculous they are, she thought. The black robes make them uncomfortable, so for self-protection they find comfort in thinking of me as a recluse, completely removed from the world of the streets. Do they imagine I forgot all I knew from the day of my ascension? With a wry grin, she nodded her head in assent, answering her own question.

As her eyes passed over the domed roof of Guild Hall, her smile faded, the lines between her heavy brows becoming more deeply entrenched. Twenty-some years might have passed, but the memory of one particular defeat gnawed at her. That none of the citizenry shared her opinion was of little consequence. Born out of discontent, evolved from mistrust and suspicion, her compromise had kept the peace, although the fruit it bore remained as bitter as the crabapples that used to deck her cart—demanding repeated doses of sweetening to render their jelly palatable.

In the first years of her reign she was blithely confident of her call. Born into a family of farmers and produce merchants, she understood the Guild Assembly's exultation when one of their own became the Seventeenth Mother. Even if the guilds paid lip-service to the belief that each wearer of the black robes worked solely for the general good, in their heart-of-hearts they knew Meliope was one of them.

One of them, yet even so they forced her into a bargain for which there could be no satisfaction for either side.

It began, as all such affairs begin, on a day of seemingly perfect peace, a quiet afternoon in late autumn whose crystalline breezes and brilliant sunshine boded well for the farmers' first harvest. There was no warning, no hint of what might erupt when Edothea, Master Teacher of the Hetaera Guild and Instructor of the Maze, walked across the Plaza and up to the Sanctum doors to post the list of citizens accepted for Preparation. For forty years this ritual had been performed by the Instructors of the Maze, and for forty years there was always a small crowd of interested onlookers, mostly family members, gathered to support their next-of-kin—a daughter, son, niece, nephew, sister, brother—who sought entry to the Maze, hoping to walk the Path, eager for the blessing that lay at the end of that mysterious, yet beckoning, road. Although Meliope usually accompanied Edothea, her customary presence was made impossible by another duty, one that commanded the highest priority. In the narthex of the Sanctum, the Seventeenth Mother was interviewing a prospective ernani.

HE CAME FROM the farthest reaches of the eastern shore, making his way by a series of caravans that followed treacherous and unfrequented routes over the Sarujian Mountains, moving west across the great river Tellas and its many tributaries, and finally turned south to traverse the fertile provinces of Cinthea, Cyme, and Cottyo. Arriving that morning at the northern gate, his eagerness to see the city for which he'd risked his life not once, but many times, prevented him from changing his garments. His many-layered robes, once precious silks now ripped to tatters, were dyed ocher by the dust of his journey. Dirty toes peeked out through the rents in his soft leather boots. His bearded face, streaked with furrows of grime and sweat, was a study of confusion as he regarded her and the stern-faced Legionnaires who flanked him on either side. Brought to her directly from the northern gates, the posted guards obeyed strict orders that any outsider requesting information concerning the Maze be thoroughly searched, stripped of any weapons, and escorted without explanation to the Seventeenth Mother. Now they stood on either side of his chair, twin statues dressed in the rough garb of the Legion Infantry, suspicious of the newcomer and protective of the woman in black.

He made no motion at her approach, but sat frozen as she limped toward the high-backed chair she customarily occupied. Sending out a fragile tendril of thought, she sensed both his distress and the reasons behind it. After almost four moons of constant travel, he was exhausted to the point of collapse. His reception by armed guards surprised and unnerved him. His hands gripped the arms of the chair, his fingers seemingly embedded in the wood. She touched his mind more firmly now, her barriers protecting him from any knowledge of her contact, offering the simple suggestion that he breathe more slowly and begin to observe his surroundings. Almond-brown eyes lifted to study the slender columns of the Sanctum's cool, dim interior. White-knuckled hands flexed and loosed their hold.

Waiting for him to regain his self-possession, she found herself comparing him, this new-breed of ernani, with the ernani of old. The vast majority of the early ernani were men without ties to families or friends. Slaves, mercenaries, and even criminals, they were chosen (oftentimes without their consent) to experience a new chance at life within the thick walls of the labyrinth called the Maze. Illiterate, downtrodden, and ill-used by the world outside the fortress walls, they entered as slaves to emerge as educated and highly-trained men-at-arms. Joined to a woman of Pelion, most of these reclaimed souls entered the Legion, their mastery of different languages and knowledge of the outside world increasing their ability to protect their adopted home. Offered freedom and sanctuary for the first time in their lives, few (if any) strayed from the city. The ernani's lack of roots, combined with their mates' strong affiliations with Pelion, ensured that the city would prosper from a yearly influx of new citizens.

The fatigued, travel-stained man sitting across from her, his thickly-braided plaits arranged to reveal a single golden hoop hanging from his left ear, was something new, a so-called "pilgrim," voluntarily crossing many hazardous miles, his feet put on the long and weary path by the Third Wave of Searchers. After the long-promised first Transformation took place, the Sixteenth Mother opened wide the gates of Pelion, welcoming anyone who sought entry to the Maze. They arrived in a slow trickle of determined, curious souls, encouraged to begin their journey by the Searchers who roamed all parts of the inhabited world. Given the danger and rigor of travel through surrounding territories, the majority of pilgrims continued to be male. Unlike the original ernani, these men had not been rejected by the world outside Pelion, nor were they illiterate or unskilled. Like the one she now observed, they traveled on hope fueled by a dream.

Touching his mind again, she deemed him ready to begin.

"What do you seek, stranger-to-the-city?"

The words of the ritual were timeless, ingrained in her thoughts since the moment of her call.

"I . . . I seek the gift that was promised."

Meliope's lips curved into a smile. Relief flooded the face in front of her. He hadn't known what to answer, but the Searcher prepared him well, implanting a simple suggestion that sprang to the forefront of his consciousness at the proper moment.

"Do you understand that the gift comes only to those who walk the Path?"

She sensed his reticence, yet there was no rebellion here, only doubt. So many doubted, yet these were the ones who often proved the strongest candidates.

"I know nothing of this path you speak of, but I . . . I was told that in this place I would find a treasure beyond price."

"The gift is not given lightly. Not all who enter the gates are worthy. The Path is difficult, more difficult than the journey which brought you to Pelion. Body, mind, and soul; each will be tested in the time to come. Are you prepared to undergo such a test?"

When he frowned, she found herself grateful for his thoughtfulness. Too many rushed through the first interview, brash in their beliefs, confident as only the young are confident. She resisted the impulse to enter his mind and explore his doubts and fears more deeply. The rules were clear—ernani were not to be read. Her first touch was necessary to insure a successful beginning to the interview; once they began the ritual exchange, his mental privacy became sacrosanct.

"How can I answer your question without knowing what you propose? I'm sound of body, if that's what you ask, and I've studied with respected teachers in Endlin. As to my soul, I'm willing to learn of your religion. Certainly I worship no other gods."

"What have you studied?"

For once he spoke without carefully planning his response.

"Languages, history—anything to do with the old learning. My father told me about your libraries."

"Your father?"

His face alight, he edged forward in his chair.

"Nazur Kwanlonhon, Equerry of Endlin."

This was spoken with considerable pride.

"In his journeys as a young man, he met a traveler who told him something of this place. My father never mentioned his name, but I know he was a dark-skinned mute who traveled with a servant who translated his finger-speech. My father says he spoke more intelligently with his hands than most do with tongues and never wasted two words when one would do."

Inside she smiled at such an apt description of Stanis, well-known to her through his writings stored in the Great Library. This earnest young man piqued her interest as few did. Literacy among ernani was more frequent since Transformation, although a dedicated scholar remained a rarity. Still, he must understand that until Transformation, the books he coveted would remain inaccessible.

"Although you may continue your studies during Preparation, the Greater and Lesser Libraries may not be visited until you pass out of the Maze."

Her honesty was a blow, for the vision of the libraries sustained him for many a long mile. Sadly, he nodded his acceptance.

"There are other requirements. The gift will not come to you alone. In the Maze, two become one, and so you must be joined to a woman of Pelion. I must ask you now if you are willing to join with another to receive this gift beyond price."

A slight smile crossed his lips as he raised his hand to finger the golden hoop dangling from his earlobe. Beneath his skin, darkened to mahogany by constant exposure to the sun, she saw a flush rise along his cheekbones.

"I have no objections, although I wonder . . . "

Having heard his next question voiced by so many, sometimes asked with embarrassment, sometimes with dismay, she was grateful when this ernani posed it as delicately as possible.

". . . if I may choose the one with whom I'll be joined?"

His smile was self-assured; his gaze intent.

"The choice is not yours, although you may reject the one chosen for you. I can say no more of this, except to add that the woman may reject you as well."

It never occurred to him that a woman would be given equal power to choose or reject. His recovery was quick as she continued the ritual.

"These are the last conditions: you must pledge your intent to enter Preparation with the understanding that for five moons you will live and work according to our rules, accepting all our judgments. You may not leave the Maze for any reason, nor communicate with anyone outside its walls. You enter Preparation as you are born into the world, naked and alone. If you choose to leave, you may not reenter. Thus there can be no doubts, no second thoughts about this endeavor. You come to change your life. We will start you on the Path, but offer no guarantees of your success."

As the silence stretched between them, Meliope watched him consider the magnitude of his decision. He had been lured half-way across the known world by a Searcher's visions and the promise of knowledge. She denied him books, offering instead a woman not of his choosing and enforced isolation. Finally he spoke, a slight tremor running through his voice.

"I pledge my obedience to your rules."

"Then you are accepted into Preparation. The next class begins in three days. Until that time you will live in the Hall of Men. These guards will escort you there and remain with you until a monitor from the Maze arrives. We will not meet again until the day of Blessing."

Swallowing hard, he rose to his feet. Immediately, the guards closed in on him, flanking him on either side. He flinched, the whites of his eyes showing, and forced himself to relax. Meliope watched all this without seeming to do so, pleased that he was already adapting himself to the rigors of the Maze, for from this time forward, he would always be watched. Pulling herself to her feet, she posed the last question.

"How are you called, stranger-to-the-city?"

"Kazur of Endlin."

"Welcome to Pelion, Kazur of Endlin. May your path be joyous; your gifts offered freely, your journey quickly ended."

He extended a dirty palm. Studying his outstretched hand, she hoped her reluctance did not show. Adepts do not touch human flesh lightly, since to do so increases their ability to read thoughts and experience emotions. Especially sensitive adepts, foremost among them the Seventeenth Mother, were especially vulnerable. Adept healers receive a special dispensation that allows them to touch patients without prior permission; adept mates touch one another freely and often, since physical contact increases the strength of their private connection. Physical contact between adepts and non-adepts was strictly forbidden. For an adept to touch another adept without first receiving permission was considered a breach of propriety bordering on assault. Thus, the shaking of hands, or any such exchanges of welcome, farewell, affection, or respect, did not exist in Pelion. Meliope, who greeted ernani from the world over, understood that beneath these various rituals lay a need to establish and reinforce trust. Steeling herself, she placed her hand in Kazur's.

Underneath calluses that bespoke the hardness of his journey, his hand trembled slightly in hers. Gazing into those weary eyes, reddened and heavy-lidded from wind, dust, and endless miles of constant watchfulness against those who asked no better prey than pilgrims to Pelion, she experienced his bone-deep weariness. An unexpected surge of loneliness brought a sudden rush of salt tears to her eyes. Blinking them back, for they were Kazur's tears, not hers, she disengaged her hand and forced a smile.

"Rest, Kazur. You are safe from harm. Let others watch and worry. You must sleep."

He couldn't resist a question of his own.

"What are you called, lady?"

"I am the Mother of Pelion, the seventeenth of my line."

As he turned to go, he stumbled. When a guard moved to steady him, he did not flinch, but leaned heavily on the sturdy shoulder as the guard's arm wrapped around his waist, allowing himself to be led away.

Her lips pursed in concentration, Meliope considered this most recent of ernani. Tired as he was, he had already proved his ability to adjust, accepting new conditions as quickly as she made them. His were the qualities most prized by the Searchers: malleability and endurance.

Heartened by the entrance of yet another ernani in this year's class, her thoughts flew to Edothea, who must be alerted immediately since the name of another female candidate from Pelion must be added to the list. Making her way through immense inner doors of bronze, Meliope headed down the long hallway toward the southern doors that opened directly onto the city square, the northern doors reserved solely for entrances to and from the Maze.

Preoccupied with her news for Edothea, it was some time before she observed that no one was walking or meditating in this most favorite of Sanctum haunts, its enormous windows seeming to invite the elaborate formal gardens inside to mingle with the tiled floors and intricate mosaics of intertwined circles and spheres. Even stranger than the deserted corridor was the sight of the closed southern doors, which habitually stood open throughout the day. Concerned, she stopped and turned to face the northern doors, which, like every entrance and exit to the Maze, were guarded every hour of the day and night. When her sharp eyes found no familiar shapes in attendance, her heart thudded noisily inside her chest, to be joined by a sudden roar and an erratic beating against the wooden timbers of the outer doors.

Dragging her clumsy body down the corridor, her mind flew outside the doors, commanding Edothea to join her.

"Don't come out! They've gone mad and might hurt you, not knowing what they do!"

Through Edothea's terrified eyes Meliope saw the mob. Hundreds of citizens were gathered in the Plaza outside the Sanctum's southern doors. The ones closest to the steps raised closed fists against guards who had drawn their cudgels and were trying to fend the boldest ones off at the same time they protected themselves from rocks, firewood, coal and other assorted missiles being thrown at the closed doors. Individual screams of rage soared over a steady chant of "Open the doors! Open the doors! Open the doors!"

Edothea attempted to reason with the ostensible leaders of the group, but was inaudible in such a din. A hand appeared from nowhere and masses of Edothea's raven hair tumbled around her shoulders as her veil was ripped from her head. Still linked to the hetaera, Meliope felt her being shoved roughly to the ground, her palms and knees scraping on the paving stones as she tried to avoid being trampled.

Neither cowardly nor foolish, Meliope worried over what action to take. The attack on Edothea made her course clear. There had been no violent demonstrations in Pelion for almost three centuries. If it was to occur during her reign, her place was among her people. She would enter the fray and accept the consequences. Breaking her connection with Edothea, Meliope steadied her nerves, placed her hands on the iron handles of the heavy doors and wrenched them open.

The hinges creaked out a protest, the doors swung wide, and she planted herself between them on the top step, addressing the crowd in full Voice, her words and thoughts joined to welcome the wave of citizens who even now were poised to rush the guards and force their way into the most sacred space in Pelion.

"The doors are open, citizens of Pelion! Enter as you will!"

Murmurs of "The Seventeenth Mother!" quickly replaced the furious chanting. A growing hush spread outward until the plaza stood silent. As the crowd pulled away from the steps, Edothea struggled to her knees, her gown ripped at the shoulder, her lovely face marred by a bloody abrasion along her cheekbone. Wanting to assist the wounded hetaera, yet unable to break her concentration as she held this enormous group at bay, She-Who-Was-Meliope witnessed an elderly woman help Edothea to her feet, and having done so, calmly begin re-pinning her veil. That simple act of charity so moved Meliope that she was able to turn her outpouring of affection for this compassionate woman toward the crowd at large, filling their minds with her love for them. Other adept minds sought hers, the extreme focus of her concentration making it impossible to identify them all. Edothea made herself known, as did Prax, a young Legionnaire newly assigned to the Maze who took a stolid stance on Meliope's left. Once linked with her mind, they obeyed her silent commands.

"Purge yourself of anger. Control nothing; simply send a message of peace."

Meliope had no intention of trying to control the minds of the crowd. It would be unwarranted even if her vows did not forbid her to do so. The crowd's potential for violence sickened her, although, having been forced into action, she was almost relieved that the protest had occurred. This issue had been simmering for years; that it reached a full boil and finally overflowed was a welcome release of festering hostility.

"Is there one who speaks for you, my people?"

A rustle ran through the crowd as an imposing woman was pushed to the front row. Meliope knew her well—Denassa, a Master of the Guild of Goldsmiths, and current President of the Guild Assembly. During her five-year term as president of that ruling body, Denassa was in charge of every aspect of civic life in Pelion. An accomplished adept, she was tough, demanding, and completely devoted to her task of keeping the city strong, free, and self-sustaining. Much of the present discontent was due to Denassa's long-term plan for Pelion, for she knew firsthand the importance of adept citizens in all areas of healing, teaching, and trade. Meliope fought regularly with her whenever she was invited to sit at the Guild Assembly table. Today they would match wits for the first time in public.

"Speak, Denassa! What is the people's will?"

Meliope pitched her voice so as to reach every corner of the plaza. Denassa did likewise, her booming contralto echoing off the surrounding buildings in the hush of the afternoon.

"An end to Preparation!"

A quick murmur of assent rippled through the assembly, fading as Meliope quickly responded: "So be it!"

The adept minds linked with hers reeled. Before they could protest, she broke her connection with them. Denassa's shock rapidly turned to derision.

"You're bluffing!"

Prax's grip tightened on his cudgel. Meliope remained unmoved. Taunts meant nothing to her. The crippled girl who lived inside her had heard them all before.

"Am I? Think again. The Path of Preparation is a gift. If the people reject that gift, if they deny the worth of it, I will not gainsay them. I serve the people of Pelion. If this is truly their will, then I say again, so be it."

She lifted her eyes to survey the crowd. As she did so, a score of heads bowed and a sigh seemed to pass through the square. A man's voice rose to object.

"Denassa does not speak for me!"

Searching her memory, Meliope remembered his name. Jons, a wheelwright, he sat on the Guild Assembly as a representative of the Forge.

"If she does not speak for you, Jons, why are you here?"

"I came to see the list posted, for my boy was hopeful," his voice faltered before rising in anger. "It's all he's ever wanted! He's applied for three years and been rejected every time! When I saw there were only two men on the list, while sixteen women were chosen, I . . . I was angry!"

Another voice spoke out of the crowd, this time a speaker unknown to her.

"My nephew was interviewed five times by that woman," a long finger pointed accusingly at Edothea. "Each time she chose someone else to enter the Maze!"

Other voices raised to denounce Edothea, their words lost in a babble of hatred. The hetaera shrank against the Sanctum doors, her hands upraised to her bruised face. Over her shoulder, the list of names fluttered in the breeze.

Meliope raised her hands for silence.

"I share your disappointment that only two women were able to make their way to our city, but you cannot blame Edothea . . ."

Denassa interrupted her.

"Why must we share the gift with those not born-of-the-city? Hundreds of women have received the gift; a mere handful of men have done so. Each year, more and more women leave the city with their mates. With every departure we lose a couple who might serve the city."

Turning her back on Meliope, Denassa addressed the crowd:

"Let citizen join with citizen and forget these ernani!"

Shouted cries of agreement attested their belief in Denassa's solution. Saddened by their selfishness, Meliope considered her opponent. It was easy to accuse Denassa of being short-sighted, but how could she know that the Sixteenth Mother foresaw such a development and tried repeatedly to join couples native to Pelion, meeting failure in every instance? Reading through those records ripe with self-reproach, Meliope's heart ached for the thwarted hopes of the city-born couples and the unrealized dreams of her predecessor. Perhaps it was time to reveal what was hidden. The citizenry must accept the conditions under which she worked, even as she was forced to accept them.

"What you suggest was tried and proved impossible."

Denassa snorted her disbelief. A rush of sudden anger coursed through Meliope. To question her judgment was one thing; to insinuate she spoke an untruth was another. Her pride wounded, she lashed out:

"If you doubt me, read the records of Transformation! Do you think Edothea or I take pleasure in refusing so many worthy candidates? We would happily give up this painful chore . . ."

Before Meliope fully realized what she'd said, Denassa pounced. With a sinking heart, Meliope realized the price of her brief, but unforgivable, moment of pique.

"Then give it up, Mother! Let the people decide!"

The square erupted. A hundred voices took up the chant, pulsing in her ears, filling her with such regret that she closed her eyes against the proof of her ineptitude. She had hoped to sway them, to make them see the rightness of her labors, to turn them away from their selfish interests. They were her people, yet she was not blind to their faults. Pelion had flourished as a closed city for five hundred years. Distrust of the outside world was the price of such a sealed existence.

Opening her eyes on the triumphant crowd, she tightened her jaw, fighting to reclaim what little she could. She couldn't recall her words, but she could fight to correct the result of her error. Mob rule would turn the selection process into a shambles of power gone awry. No matter what the general opinion might be concerning the method of selection, she knew it to be fair and true. Edothea chose male and female candidates without regard to wealth, parentage, or frequent upheavals in Guild politics. In the twenty-six years since Transformation, with each Instructor of the Maze following the same careful guidelines, every couple composed of an ernani and a citizen of Pelion completed the Path. Somehow, Meliope must insure that the covenant not be broken.

Lifting her voice, she spoke the words that bound her to a choice not of her making.

"So be it, my people! Today I begin drafting legislation whereby male candidates may be selected for Preparation. Once they are approved by the High Healer and the Guild President, they will be submitted to you for approval." She paused, sensing the crowd's growing excitement, watching them shake their heads in approbation, their discontent turned to self-congratulation. At the height of their euphoria, she struck a blow for independence. "The class posted today will begin as planned and the Instructor will continue to select all female candidates."

Caught unaware, her scheme for controlling the entire process of selection crumbling in the face of Meliope's authoritative stance, Denassa called out a complaint unheard by the growing noise of the excited spectators. Meliope continued without missing a beat.

"The first Trial will be held next year in the tenth moon. On that day, the entire city will vote to select the male candidates and celebrate our thanks to the city we serve."

For the first and only time in her life, her leg obeyed her command that she move without awkwardness. As she turned, her gown swirled gracefully around her stout form. As she walked across the threshold, cheers and whistles filled the sunlit plaza.

Limping down the corridor of glass and stone, her sense of loss grew to such proportions that she found herself wandering not in the halls of the Sanctum, but down the paved streets of the city, pushing the vegetable cart in front of her.

Just as it had occurred on the day of her call, a chorus of whispers surrounded She-Who-Was-Meliope, spiriting her away into another realm, a place she recognized by virtue of inner sight rather than worldly eyes. There, she saw a group of black-robed figures standing on the dark vista of a place that knew no temporal time. On that darkling plain, the wearers of the black robes worked their magic with a gift given to them by the Sowers who rescued the survivors of Old Earth. Over the course of untold years, the Sowers searched the universe for a replacement planet, one with a golden sun and a single moon, and prepared it as a home for the survivors of a ruined world. Here, on this plain that was not so much a place as a state of mind, the consciousness of the First Mother lived on, as did the Mothers who came after, sharing an unbroken line of memory reaching back to the Days of Before.

As whispering became chanting, the circle of black-clad figures began to move, hands clapping low to the ground, feet stepping heel-toe, beating time as if the earth was a drum. More figures clad in hooded cloaks of many colors joined the dance, some of them leaping up, pounding the earth as they landed only to jump and jump again. In a circle they danced as the air vibrated with the rhythm of hands and feet until, as if with a shared exhalation of breath, the dancers froze, standing silently, waiting, it seemed to Meliope, for a response.

It came. Slowly, with a deep bass rumble, the earth beneath the feet of the dancers began to dance as well, the soil rippling wave-like across the darkling plain before gradually coming to rest again, silent and seemingly replete.

On the day of her call, kneeling beside the Sixteenth Mother's deathbed, Meliope took her first step into this inner world, understanding little save that she and only she, a crippled girl who hawked vegetables, could accomplish the next step of the Mission for which all Mothers worked. With that knowledge came pride, and as a decade passed, humility. A few moments earlier she stood dejected, alone within the hugeness of the Sanctum, certain she had failed her sixteen sisters. Now she stood on the darkling plain, beginning to understand that she had not failed. Not at all.

Something had shifted in the balance of existence, something extraordinary, so extraordinary that even now the plain hummed with a new energy. The murmur of individual voices hushed, blended, harmonized, until one unified voice emerged, assigning her a task:

"The earth has awakened! Forge the first silver ring!"

BLINKING SEVERAL TIMES to clear her eyes of the fog of old memories, Meliope turned her back on the raining world and began to descend the staircase that led from the battlements to her living quarters. It was a steep descent, so steep that she gripped the railing with both hands, moving her bad right leg first before pushing her hip far to the left to lift the good leg down onto the next step. By the time she had traveled half-way down she was panting, the unaccustomed strain on her muscles making her heart race and her legs ache. The pains in her chest had increased in regularity in the past few months, the expression on her healer's face silent witness to the fact that her time was coming to its end. It was for this reason she sent out this morning's call. After sixty-five years of ignoring the limitations of her body, it was time to acknowledge its frailty.

Hardening her will against any show of weakness, she took another step down. As she jutted out her left hip her bad leg collapsed beneath her, she lost her balance, and fell. Reaching for the railing, for anything that could save her from her headlong fall, she tumbled helplessly down the slippery stone steps, finally slamming against the closed door that separated the staircase from her tower apartment. For a time she lay still, sunbursts of pain exploding inside her closed eyelids, the only sound her ragged breathing. Bruised and battered, she attempted a slight movement, stifling a scream as broken bones ground against one another. Her right hip was broken; her left arm hung at a crazy angle. She sought to master the pain, running her mind through the concentration exercises learned as a child from her adept teacher. With a tremendous effort of will, she forced the pain away, pushing it deep inside the recesses of her mind where it crouched like a hungry beast, biding its time before the kill, ignored but not forgotten.

Her control regained for at least a little while, she rested her head against the rough timbers of the door and decided her course. She could use her last bit of strength to call for help or she could call again for her successor. She had not the strength to do both. It was a surprisingly easy choice. The link binding seventeen generations must not be broken. Closing her eyes, she began:

"My time is upon me. Answer the call."

She sensed a difference this time. On the parapet she'd struggled for concentration; now the power flowed out effortlessly. No longer diffuse, the call seemed directed, her mental energy traveling toward a distant point, relentlessly beckoning, pulling the one she sought closer, ever closer.

She dozed, moving in and out of consciousness. Minutes, hours passed. She lived without measuring time, lulled by the faces and voices of the whispering plain, trusting them to ease her passage.

The door opened and a brilliant rectangle of light illuminated her. A slight form knelt beside her, a troubled face gazing down on her broken body.

"Mother, it seemed you called me."

She's little more than a girl, Meliope thought, before batting that idea away. Be she girl, woman, or toothless crone, she alone had answered the call.

"I called and you came. We have little time. Take what I must pass on before I die."

Her breath increasingly labored, Meliope lifted her hand to touch that smooth-skinned face, her power leaping across the bridge from her fingertips to enter the mind of the Chosen One.

The girl's eyes widened with shock as the transition began. The still vibrant mind inside Meliope's dying body urged calm.

"There's no need to understand, simply accept. In time, your mission will be revealed."

Hard as it was to do, the girl held steady, her eyes shut tight now, suffering the onslaught of memories from sixteen forbearers. Then, as the last of the stored memories finished the journey across the bridge between Meliope's mind and that of the girl kneeling beside her, the Seventeenth Mother began what would be her final duty.

"Receive them now, my memories as Seventeenth Mother, for you are eighteenth in a line that must not fail."

Her mind stripped, her strength sapped, the pains in her chest returned, tearing at her with the claws of the waking beast. Gratefully, She-Who-Was-Meliope surrendered herself to darkness, whispering her last word, entrusting the completion of her mission to the Eighteenth Mother of Pelion.

"Lillas," she gasped.

Her heart bursting asunder, the girl with the vegetable cart breathed her last.

Chapter 2

The Betrothal

"ARE YOU COMING?"

One spoke with civility when one addressed a woman wearing black, but in Prax's tone Hesione heard impatience, frustration, and even, if she was honest with herself, a touch of dislike. Scurrying to mount, She-Who-Was-Hesione, the Eighteenth Mother of Pelion, guided her mare up to the front of the line. As Prax, the Legion Commander, had warned, nay, promised, their journey was a hard one, her muscles and joints resisting the arduous nature of this particular exercise after three years of relative disuse. Once she pulled up beside him, Prax threw her an appraising glance, grunted, and nudged his horse forward.

They departed Pelion's northern gate at dawn two days ago and now it was late afternoon. Sore as she was, she knew the reason for his haste and heartily approved his plan. They must reach the site before nightfall. Some things can only be faced in the comforting light of day.

It might have been a pleasant excursion if the circumstances which brought it about were not so grim. That an altered purpose for the same activity could create such a reversal of expectation, from the pleasurable anticipation of an activity she adored (namely, riding through a quiet wood on an autumn afternoon) to one of trepidation, was a problem worth pondering.

That became the substance of her reflections for all these long miles. Surely it should be possible to forget the reason for the journey and enjoy the journey for itself! Yet the more she strove to capture the lightheaded spirit of the latter, the more the former intruded, coloring every sight and sound. The leaves should have crunched comfortably under her mare's hooves; instead the sound of their destruction was a reminder that eventually their bright remains must crumble and decay. The array of colors from oak, ash, and maple made for a bold dance in which every leaf participated, even to the moment of their *coup de grace,* at which time they began a final pirouette, descending to the earth below. As each leaf tumbled down, the newly bare branches became incapable of producing a sense of movement or the accompanying sound of wind through leaves. Implacably, the studied neutrality of the natural world, its cycles accomplished without forethought or regret, was reinterpreted by the fluctuations of her mood.

Her inability to find solace in her surroundings was annoying, so much so that she compensated for her self-induced melancholia by kicking the mare into a trot, leaving the others behind, mouths agape, faces classic studies in confusion, for who could say the Eighteenth Mother shouldn't trot if she wanted to? And who would possibly be brave (or foolhardy) enough to stop her?

The rollicking gait of the rangy mare, together with a breeze that lifted her veil from her shoulders and sent it streaming in a wide half-circle behind her, inspired her to yet another private revolt, and soon the mare was cantering, responding to a second nudge from an insistent leather boot. Looking back over her shoulder, she could see Prax motioning the others forward at a quicker pace and guessed he was distinctly annoyed.

Why had he fought so hard in Council to prevent her presence here? Perhaps he questioned her ability to keep up, though he knew she had ridden almost from birth, a requirement for the daughter of a Legion Cavalry officer and his mate, a distinguished horse-breeder who was primarily responsible for the introduction of imported Lapithian bloodlines into the herds of Pelion. The mare Hesione rode today was a product of her mother's farsightedness, for the small, sturdy horses of Pelion benefited from the influx of Lapithian stock, gaining speed and stamina while retaining their native surefootedness suitable to hilly terrain.

The path they followed was an old one, worn down by countless patrols monitoring the perimeters of Pelion. She welcomed it as an old friend, no less welcome because that friend's face reveals the wear and tear of life's demands. By the time she was nine she knew the hills surrounding the city more completely than she knew the pattern of avenues and promenades within the fortress walls; in her fifteenth year she traveled to the outskirts of the patrolled area, seeing with adolescent eyes the realities of a world that was not Pelion. Even at fifteen, and with an ever-growing sense of gratitude, she knew the reason for the dour expressions worn by veterans of the Legion.

Here she was again, thirteen years since her last sojourn to the northwestern boundaries of Pelion's territories, traveling with an armed contingent of twenty men, cantering toward the problems of the outside world, knowing deep inside, in the places she allowed none to enter, that these problems could no longer be ignored.

She always feared that her three-year tenure as the Eighteenth Mother had been deceptively easy. The comparative smoothness of the transition from her predecessor to herself was more traumatic for her family than for the city, the guilds, or the Council. It was difficult enough for her athletic father and energetic mother to adjust themselves to a daughter who was a literary scholar; to envision their twenty-five year old girl-child wearing black robes bordered on the absurd. In a rare moment of contemplation, her notoriously pragmatic mother confessed her complete bewilderment at her daughter's elevation to the highest office in the land.

"Hesione, this whole thing is beyond me! A scholar, yes, but a Mother . . .? What do you possibly know about governing a city? I fear there's little enough on that subject to be found in your beloved books."

With a helpless shrug, her mother kissed her, grabbed a scarf for her hair and her ever present quirt, and ran off to the breeding stables, no doubt as anxious to oversee the activities of her staff as she was grateful to escape the bewildering task of mothering a grown daughter. Watching her mother's strategic retreat, a half-smile hovered about Hesione's lips. Single-handedly her mother had changed an entire breed of domestic animals, monitoring their progress despite failures and setbacks, making her decisions as best she could with the information available, planning not for tomorrow's foal, but for the progeny of three, five, or seven generations in the future. It never occurred to her mother that the difficulties she faced were as daunting as those facing her daughter.

Thankfully, her mother's fear was for naught. Indeed, there were books, seas of books. Some were precious volumes of velum and parchment, so ancient that few understood their language, their wisdom lost in the years of before, unknown and unread except by a tiny group of stubborn scholars who insisted that their knowledge be reclaimed. Then there were the books carried by the faithful as they founded the city, some collected by the Sixth Mother's dictum that the old knowledge must be gathered and treasured; others sent by the First and Second Waves of Searchers as they wandered unknown lands, passing on their precious discoveries even as they remained far from the city they served. Many were damaged—faintly printed letters on rotting paper that crumbled at the touch of human hands. Even more were unreadable, their formulas, designs, even the purpose of their writing, lost with the technology of the Earth that had once been their home.

Yet each was a treasured presence in the Great Library of Pelion, duly catalogued, shelved, copied and restored by eighteen generations of librarians, scholars, and scribes. These were the ones who garnered Hesione's respect: a cluster of scribes, hunch-backed, squinting in the dusty air of the library, their sleeves stained black from the endless outpouring of ink necessary to copy hieroglyphics for which there was no longer any key of reference, but copied all the same in the hope that someday that key would be found, and with it, the lost knowledge that might in some way enrich their lives. For the Great Library of Pelion was not a monument to the past, but a guardian of the future, a future for which Hesione worked.

Important as books might be, they couldn't provide a sense of purpose. For the thousand days since her call to office Hesione read, studied, memorized, and questioned. Members of her Council, some of them retained from her predecessor's advisory group, were unfailingly polite, informative, and decidedly disengaged. That they were watching and waiting for a sign from her was clear, but until three days ago, she'd been adrift in a sea with no stars to steer by. At last, she had hope that a sign was nearby, waiting for her in the deep shadows of this old forest, a sign that would give her life and the lives of others who served the city, substance and meaning.

The path before her was dwindling now, the trees thicker, shadows more prevalent than sunshine. Before Hesione could pull her up, the mare slowed her pace, influenced, no doubt, by Hesione's growing reluctance to view what lay before them. Her saddle creaked as she turned to view her companions. As she'd predicted, Prax was out in front, his bald head reflecting the dapples of leaf-filtered light. As he approached, he called out to her, his voice raspy and harsh as it broke the silence of the forest.

"I see you haven't lost your ability to sit a horse."

"What remains to be seen is if I will ever walk again."

She tried to sound prim, for it was decidedly difficult to be the Eighteenth Mother around Prax, a stern man of seemingly little humor. His belly-deep guffaw broke through her reserve and she added her laughter to his, grateful that at least one person in the patrol was not awed by her presence.

As the others gathered around, she saw the entire company exchange uncomfortable glances. It was odd enough that a Mother had left Pelion, an event unheard of in their lifetimes; doubly odd that she could ride as well as any of them. The added factor of the Legion Commander actually laughing with her strained their credulity.

Lukash, on the other hand, seemed for once to be pleased with her, his dark face relaxing its stern lines and a shy smile revealing white teeth and pink gums.

"If I may say so, Mother, it's gratifying to watch you run free. No one knows better than I how tiresome the city can be after a life lived outside its walls."

Hesione heard the weariness beneath the compliment, but cloaked her concern by flashing him a quick smile. Lukash was aging badly, the death of his mate three months ago taking its toll, sapping his vitality as well as his adept abilities. This was the sad reality of transformed adepts, and one that was only gradually being studied by the caretakers of the Maze. Lukash was one of the first males of Pelion to be mated with a female ernani, entering Preparation only eleven years after the first Transformation. For thirty-eight of his fifty-nine years, he lived with his mate, working side by side with her in the outside world, sending others like themselves to the sacred city.

Hesione had only known this Searcher of Souls for a few months, but she had done meticulous research on the writings of Selena/Lukash. Once they were joined in the Maze, they followed in the footsteps of Lukash's mentor, the great Stanis of Pelion, and became specialists in the new field of transformed adeptness.

Pelion was founded by what were now called "natural" adepts, people born with the gift of receiving and sending their thoughts to others. Writing as members of the first generation of "transformed" adepts (adult couples who had gone through Preparation and duly received the gift), Lukash and Selena's reflections were highly personal and inarguably subjective, yet within them Hesione found much worthy of admiration. Their studies were exhaustive, for they interviewed and recorded conversations with hundreds of transformed adepts, their travels allowing them to crisscross the vast lands outside Pelion, finding couples who chose, for one reason or another, to leave the city and return to the lands of their birth.

Sadly, their observations and theories were one of the reasons for Lukash's recent return to the south, for they had predicted as early as fifteen years ago that the death of either transformed adept had a degenerative, crippling affect on the one left behind. After receiving news of Selena's death (and at Hesione's personal request), the Council invited Lukash to Pelion as a consultant within the Maze, offering him complete access to all Records of Transformation.

His initial reaction to their offer was wary, almost suspicious, but once arrived, he settled immediately to work, his shy, self-deprecating nature winning him a place in Hesione's affections. Much to her surprise, he didn't return her overtures of friendship. At first she interpreted his reticence as the normal reaction a citizen of Pelion had to the black robes; lately, she'd felt his eyes following her, his gaze a kind of judgment, and one Hesione guessed was not wholly favorable. There was never any cause to enter Lukash's thoughts, and he'd certainly never issued an invitation for her to do so. Even so, his disapproval nagged at her, causing her to wonder how she'd failed him.

Prax interrupted her thoughts by extending his right arm off to the left of the path they followed, his thick forefinger pointing out a stand of birch trees. With that gesture all traces of humor were wiped from his flexible, homely face, and the imperious tones of command replaced those of good humor.

"This marks the end of our territory. Here we leave the path. "

Turning slightly in his saddle, he addressed the four bodyguards chosen to accompany them past the borderline. They snapped to attention, one of them actually reaching for the hilt of his short sword, only to stop his hand a mere inch away from the weapon before noticing Prax's rapt stare of disapproval.

"The district patrol should have cleared the area this morning, but we all know the risks involved, and I'll take nothing for granted this far out. The trail narrows up ahead, so we'll proceed in single file. I'll take point, Decon behind me, Lukash next, Mother between Spence and Rafe, Hume to protect the rear."

Prax paused, his eyes narrowing. The four guards seemed not to breathe.

"Each of you is a volunteer, and it occurs to me that you might harbor some grand notion of fighting to the death for her." Indicating Hesione with a jerk of his head, he ignored her dismay. "Let me be absolutely clear: at the first sign of trouble, whether a snapped twig or a flushed field mouse, you are to grab her reins, pull her horse around, and run like hell back to this point, calling for help the entire time."

With a sharp jab he indicated the remaining riders who waited obediently for their orders. "You will post scouts and stay mounted, ready to ride hard if you're summoned. You serve as our insurance that whoever's out there will be unpleasantly surprised if they choose to take on our five swords."

Smoothly, Lukash corrected him.

"Six swords, Commander."

After a slow, silent appraisal of the older man, Prax nodded, and Hesione felt the tension between them (for Lukash's presence in the patrol was Hesione's idea, not Prax's) ease somewhat.

There might have been a measure of comfort in Lukash's offer (for it was his first indication of any regard for her), if Prax's orders to his men hadn't accused her (without saying so directly) of putting him in an untenable situation, namely, to protect the Eighteenth Mother of Pelion in a place where the Legion maintained a fragile foothold with no rights at all. Still, he was Prax, the son of a pre-Transformation ernani and a woman of Pelion, a transformed adept twenty years her senior, a man in whom she had every confidence, even though she'd recently defeated him in a heated Council debate over this exact issue. Though he might question her demands in private, he would guard her with his life and that of everyone in his command.

"If we're clear that the only heroic action I'll tolerate is a hasty retreat, we'll proceed."

When five sets of eyes blinked their acceptance, Prax switched to inner speech.

"No more talking. The horses make enough noise as it is."

Hesione foresaw his tactic, for she had suggested that no spoken words be overheard once they left the boundaries, but Prax's lightning-fast shift was unannounced and caused a jolt among the rest of the group. Just as quickly, she felt his delight in taking them unaware, an adept school-child prank Hesione had been known to practice in her early days, but had not witnessed since. Quelling her mirth, for she was seeing a side of Prax that never emerged in the Council meetings, she waited until Spence took his place in front of her and proceeded forward at a sedate walk. Prax's silent commentary accompanied them from time to time.

"We'll turn due north again at that beech tree, then west after we ford a small stream."

The stream crossed in due order, they progressed silently, the low-hanging branches and thick undergrowth pulling at their cloaks. The trail continued to narrow, and finally disappeared entirely. Hesione kept her attention on the rump of the horse in front of her as they moved around trees, following Prax's lead as he navigated a path he had never trod. Once the Council decision was made, he'd read the memories of the scout who reported the discovery. Prax's eyes focused on his surroundings, matching the picture in his mind with the woods around him, his inner thoughts floating around the scout's report. On impulse, Hesione detached herself from the group, and letting the others remain connected to the outer world, followed Prax into the scout's memories . . .

HER FIRST IMPRESSION was unsettling; by the time the scout was interviewed a full day had passed, but the passage of time didn't lessen the emotional jangle in his mind. This scout was obviously seasoned—he knew the woods well and chose a small clearing marked by a tree felled from rot to relieve himself. His mind was on the task at hand, and once he finished, he swung his eyes over the area as his hands worked busily at his buttons. The sun was at a low angle and he might have missed the gleam of metal if he had not bent down to pick off a burr that had worked its way into the rough fabric of his breeches.

His instincts heightened as she felt his first rush of fear. His companions were off to his right, but metal equaled weapon and this western province had long been the most dangerous patrol duty a Legionnaire could draw, its thick woods providing ample cover for anyone in hiding. Quickly dismissing his sword, which might ring if he unsheathed it, he slid the knife from the back of his leather belt, and called silently for aid, every muscle tensed to run, his eyes searching the undergrowth for likely hiding places, measuring the distance between his position and the stump of the felled tree. Inching his way toward the stump, his fear mounted.

Hesione heard with him the scream of a scolding jay and the unmistakable thump of a hare. Like the scout, she readied herself for attack, but the bird did not rise in flight, nor did the hare burst from its thicket. His breathing slowed as he heard the faint jingle of bridles behind him, a sound that signaled his companions' arrival. Hesione experienced the scout's relief. As his patrol circled him, he fell to one knee and began pushing aside the leaves surrounding the shining metal.

Smell, rather than sight, warned him what he had found. The grave was shallow, a light covering of dirt and leaves lay on top of the remains, the odor of decay promising not fungus and leaf-mold, but rotting flesh. His stomach turned as he identified the scent, but he had carried too many dead companions back to Pelion to be put off by smell alone, and he settled to the task. Only when he uncovered more of what lay hidden did his revulsion turn to outright nausea, and closing his eyes, he retched uncontrollably, not ceasing until a friendly hand descended on his shoulder . . .

"THE EIGHTEENTH MOTHER, Lukash, and I will dismount. Guards, stay on your horses, maintain your connection, and keep still. If you see or hear anything . . . ," the Commander's inner voice emphasized the last word, *". . . anything at all, warn us silently."*

When Prax's hand grasped her right elbow, Hesione realized she was shaking. It was one thing to know; another to witness. He led her toward the felled tree and the cleared area around the stump. Lukash moved forward more quickly than her, gasped, and lowered his grey, close-cropped curls until his chin met his chest. His silent cry echoed in the chambers of Hesione's mind.

"Waste . . . waste . . . nothing but waste!"

Thrown haphazardly into a single shallow grave, one body lay face up, the other two face down in the damp dirt. Hair and limbs intertwined in a grotesque arrangement that suggested nothing so much as a child's dolls discarded in a fit of temper. Three shades of brownish-red hair, ranging from chestnut to copper lay tousled across pale flesh, the unbound strands matching the dried blood that had spurted from their sliced throats. All three were naked, although for some reason, probably a guilty afterthought, their killers had tossed their clothing on top of them before throwing on a thin layer of dirt. Hesione closed her eyes for a moment, swallowing her gorge before addressing Prax.

"Please remove the clothes."

He stiffened for a moment, his distaste for the task apparent, before moving swiftly to execute her command.

They're young, Hesione thought, no more than twenty.

She could see them clearly in her mind's eye, their breeches, blouses, and cloaks chosen for serviceability rather than beauty, their shoes sturdy and well-made, their hair wrapped in scarves or swathes of cloth to help disguise their gender. They might be sisters, cousins, or simply strangers who decided three traveling together would be safer than one going it alone. The bruises and scratches covering them were proof that they struggled with their attackers, fighting with knives perhaps, although no weapons were found. She wondered briefly if they might have saved their lives if they submitted to rape. Sadly, she dismissed the thought. The bruises and bloody scratches on their loins and thighs gave silent testimony of their tormentors' brutality. Yet somehow she was sure that rape was not the only motive.

"Why kill them, Prax? Why not sell them into slavery?"

He was silent for a long time, his mind active in inner recesses as he sought to answer her. She chose not to follow him, waiting patiently as he formulated his response, marking the thoroughness with which he faced every duty.

"Since the early days we've had no use for this land—it's too hilly for agriculture and offers no grazing. We patrol it, of course, but most of our force remains in the south and southwest. From time to time we'll give the area a good going-over—cleaning out a robber's den or a slaver's stronghold. On the whole, mass attacks have seldom originated here. The ground's not good for full-scale battle, and even though the woods offer cover, it's easy to become lost or taken by ambush. It's only lately that there's been activity."

There was more, but he was working slowly, his thoughts clear and neatly defined.

"We know that greater numbers of ernani are coming every year. We can also surmise that the pilgrimages to Pelion are attracting more attention. For five hundred years we guarded our privacy. In the last fifty, we've lost our anonymity. The Searchers practice discretion and only approach the best candidates, but word has spread and the vultures are gathering."

His next thoughts were colored with regret and deep sadness. Evidently this was not the first time Prax had seen such a sight.

"They're such easy pickings, either for their valuables or their worth as slaves. They travel alone, or in small groups, and this approach from the northwest seems a likely route south since there's ample water, firewood, and game. What they don't realize is that any raider or slaver worth his hire can locate them with little or no effort—spot a campfire at night, travel quickly and quietly to the site, and catch them while they sleep. If they'd come across the scrublands, we'd have spotted them on more open ground and provided safe escort."

"You've still not answered my question."

Up to now he'd been using the tones of teaching, filling in the details of a situation she was just beginning to understand. At her reminder, his calm was replaced with anger, although she couldn't decide whether its target was her or what lay before him on the blood-soaked earth.

"I'm not sure I know the answer."

He was hedging now, trying to control his rage. With a sudden rush of courage, she decided to risk its release. Her ignorance had been protected too long. If Prax's anger was directed toward her, so be it.

"Nevertheless, you have a good guess, and because of that guess you tried to prevent me from coming. Tell me, Commander! It's your duty and I demand it of you!"

Never in her life had she spoken so strongly to a single living creature. Prax seemed as startled as she felt. Then, all at once, his barriers dropped, sending out thoughts that pulsed with fury; anger at himself and his inability to protect everyone who sought refuge in his city, at the woman beside him whose inexperience and naiveté were a constant source of irritation and annoyance, and most of all, at a world which held so little regard for the well-being of three young women. If he had spoken aloud, his lips would have curled in a snarl of outrage. As it was, they were pressed together into a narrow line, the skin white around his mouth.

"The rapes are a studied insult; the killing is a warning. Agave is hungry, endlessly hungry, and every person who eludes its grasp is a threat. Pelion is known, watched, and hated. We used to buy slaves there, freeing them, of course, but still we fed their coffers. Now men and women come to us of their own free will, many of them escaped slaves, and to their mind we're robbing them. It's no accident that we found the grave. They intended us to find it. We have no way of knowing if the women's goal was Pelion, but whether it was or not, their deaths are a notice." He paused. *"A notice that we're trespassing and trespassers are not allowed."*

"But you've no proof."

Prax shrugged and shook his head.

"There's never any proof."

Once she accepted his anger, she let it pass over her, choosing to focus instead on his argument. If he was correct, there must be some way of discovering the women's final destination and the attackers' point of origin. Her eyes searched the bodies for clues, trying to avoid the naked thighs and loins, the breasts smeared with dirt mixed with gore. Then she saw it, the same gleam that had alerted the scout. A wide band of silver circled the middle finger of an outstretched hand belonging to one of the down-turned bodies, her nails black with the blood of the man she wrestled with. The ring was vaguely familiar to Hesione from her studies of the Records of Transformation, for she regularly reviewed the customs and backgrounds of each ernani who came before her in the Sanctum. Then she remembered. It was a betrothal ring from the western lands, given by a mother to her daughter, worn on the second finger until a woman gave her promise to her mate, at which time it was transferred to the third finger, where it was worn until death. Neither of the other women wore one, suggesting they were either former slaves or from more distant lands.

"Why did they leave her ring?"

Prax was instantly attentive, his anger forgotten as he reproached himself for not pursuing such an inquiry himself.

"There was a woman from the west in my class in the Maze. She wore a ring like that and told us that to remove a woman's betrothal ring without her consent would bring bad luck. There's no other reason for not stealing it. Anyone not familiar with local customs would have chopped off her finger without a second thought." He smiled at Hesione, his admiration genuine. *"There's your proof, Mother. The attackers were undoubtedly from the west."*

Lukash had stood silent for so long that Hesione started as he moved forward to the grave. Kneeling beside the hand with the silver ring, he lifted the down-turned head of chestnut hair. After brushing aside the hair to reveal a face, he raised his head so as to address Hesione. His lips moved as he formed the words in his mind, although no sounds emerged.

"I remember her. She's from a village three days north of Agave. Selena and I rested one day at her family's farm and she brought us fresh milk and a loaf of newly-baked bread. She'd just turned twenty and despite her lack of education, she was forthright and curious about our travels. I remember our joint impression that she was all we could wish for, compassionate and unafraid."

Lukash's mind flinched at the initial mention of his mate. Then, much to Hesione's surprise, she felt him open an internal door and welcome Selena in, a grey-haired woman with serious brown eyes, her lined face softened by a smile as she put a motherly arm around the chestnut-haired girl, leaning her wrinkled cheek against the softly curved shoulder of this prospective ernani.

"Selena struck up a conversation with her immediately. Soon they began talking of women's private matters and at Selena's request (for the girl was wary of me), I left them. That night, Selena lay in my arms and told me this girl was unhappy, even wretched. There were few men of her age to choose from and none were to her liking. Selena planted the thought within her, a simple suggestion, she told me, that if none were worthy of her, one might be found in Pelion, and that with him would come a gift, one that would change her life, as Selena's had been changed."

Nodding, Hesione broke her connection with both men and turned away. She wandered around the clearing somewhat aimlessly, feeling Prax's anxiety increase, his head moving nervously around the clearing as if he scented the air.

With a sudden flash of insight, she knew why she had come. It was not some foolish whim, this desire to visit the western boundaries of Pelion. She had been sent.

"Prax, put on your gloves and remove the ring."

Her request caught him off-guard, but with an encouraging smile she continued to reason with him as he knelt to begin the dreadful task.

"You asked me in Council why I was so insistent—why I was unwilling to let you visit the site and then glean what I desired from your mind. Here is the reason, Prax, for this ring is necessary now. I must claim it before the patrol burns the bodies and I say the rite of passing."

She felt his immediate resistance to her plan, but continued to oppose him, refusing to let his fears for her safety affect her judgment.

"I know they are not citizens of Pelion, and so the rite is unnecessary. But now we know their destination, and tomorrow or the next day they would have stood in front of me on the pedestal, three female ernani, untold riches brought to us by Selena the Searcher, and I would have welcomed them to the Maze. So, alert the full patrol. Here we will honor them, these women from the west who braved these sullied lands to cross our borders."

As she paused, he turned to her and placed the silver band in her outstretched palm. At the touch of her bare flesh on the cold metal, Hesione winced, hearing the girl's anguished moans as her life's blood coursed down her bruised and battered body; her death rattle as she closed her eyes and breathed no more.

Prax clasped his arms across his formidable chest, his jaw clenched tight.

"If we fire them, the smoke will attract every outlander for miles in all directions. It's senseless, Mother, to risk so much for the veneration of so few. We've been given a warning. This is not our land. To claim it as such might mean war."

Locking her eyes with his, she addressed him in full Voice, bending his mind to her will, his eyes reflecting the blaze within her own.

"And so we declare war today, Commander! These women's lives will not be ignored or brushed away, explained as the sad reality of a system we support by our inaction. I, the Eighteenth Mother of Pelion and Keeper of the Flame, announce that today begins our war, not a war against a people, or a war for new territory, but a war against a way of life that ends in waste which we will no longer tolerate. If we cannot be reached by ernani, by all ernani, women and men from each point of the compass, then the gift the Makers gave us is doomed to failure. This is, and always has been, the mission of Pelion, and I, for one, will not gainsay it. What say you, Prax? Will you be my Commander or no? Will you wage war with me?"

Her image was reflected in his clear hazel eyes, a woman of indifferent face and figure, black robes dusty and ill-kept. What must he think of her, this worldly man who rose from the ranks to the highest level of leadership? She was the youngest woman to wear the black robes in living memory, a scholar unskilled in anything but her own narrow fields of interest, a natural hermit who asked nothing else of life but a book, a chair, and light by which to read, a novice unsure of her new duties, the daughter of a man who never aspired to anything higher than the regular Calvary and a woman who raised her as a recalcitrant foal, with much love, but little understanding. Chastened by the unflattering portrait she'd just drawn, Hesione retreated, only to feel a leather glove grasp her hand.

Prax knelt at her feet, his rough brown cloak matching the dead leaves on which it rested, the bronze clasp at his throat the only decoration that broke the severe lines of his regulation garments. He spoke aloud, his eyes shining with excitement and pride.

"I, Prax, son of a slave from Agave and a woman of Pelion, pledge myself to you. I will wage your war with every skill I possess. Together, we will bring the west into the fold."

Another voice took up her challenge. Lukash, too, knelt among the leaves.

"I, Lukash, son of parents long dead, enslaved by Agave, freed by Stanis and transformed within the Maze, pledge myself to you. I, too, will wage your war against a city that has wronged too many sons and daughters of the west."

Looking down at their eager expressions, the pleasure of their approval and support faded as quickly as it arrived.

War. It was a man's word, yet it sprang naturally from her lips. What did she know of war? Sifting through her memories of hundreds, even thousands, of books, every reference she could recall was associated with images that sickened her. She reverenced life. How could she be associated with a word that gave license, even sanction, to acts of violence? Add to this moral horror the fact that nowhere in the litany of battles and sieges, trenches and pogroms, campaigns and slaughters, could she find a war waged by a woman. Women had ever been the victims of war; never its practitioners . . .

A presence she had felt only once, at the moment of her call, addressed her:

"It will be a war like no other, for we cannot fight it openly, nor can we fight with angry hearts. We must be like the lambs among the wolves, prudent as serpents and wise as doves."

There could be no thought of questioning this presence that spoke with the voice of wind through leaves and water flowing in brooks and rivulets. No longer unsure, her fears forgotten, Hesione embraced the vision shimmering around her. A circle of figures surrounded her on an unlit plain, faces indistinct, black robes fading into the surrounding darkness. Hesione surrendered herself to them and their thoughts became as one.

She was no longer on the whispering plain. She stood again in the wood, alone this time and unafraid. A plume of smoke rose from three bodies arranged on wooden pyres, the flames high and glorious in their colors, a match to the forest attired in its autumnal best. As the smoke rose, Hesione rose with it to high above the forest floor, turning her gaze to the west, her eyes those of eagles and hawks. There, outlined against the horizon on a desert plain marked by deep quarries and pits, lay the city of slaves, its sandstone walls burned orange by the glowing stone of the sun. From within its walls she heard the din of madness, of unrestraint, of greed and the agony of those who paid the price of that greed. Hesione regarded her opponent steadily as it sulked in the distance, marking its strengths and weaknesses, memorizing her antagonist as it sat ignorant of the battle which began today.

Satisfied, she opened her eyes on the waking world. Prax and Lukash remained kneeling in the dirt, their attention fixed on her, their eyes wide with wonder. Unembarrassed by their worshipful attitude, Hesione placed the dead woman's ring on her middle finger. She had decided not to mate; now she reversed her decision. I have chosen my mate today, she thought, and when Agave weds Pelion, I will place this ring on my third finger and wear it until the end of my days.

Lifting her hand to the west, the Eighteenth Mother of Pelion faced her promised bridegroom and sent out her call. Sparks of brilliant light flew from the silver band, flashing out a warning to all who would deny her will.

"We are betrothed, you and I! Wait for me, Agave, for surely I come!"

And the whispering voices of all those on the plain added their pledge.

"Yea, surely we come!"

Chapter 3

Imarus

DISMISSED BY THE wave of a perfectly manicured hand, the serving girl took her leave, pausing to close the gauze curtains behind her. As the faint pad of bare feet on marble faded away, Charis leaned her smooth elbows on her dressing table and regarded her reflection. The summer had been beastly hot, the sun blazing down with perfect indifference on the parched land. Each morning and evening she took a cooling bath, letting the water trickle down her back and between her breasts, anything to combat the heat-induced fatigue that left her limp and lifeless, unfit for anything except napping. Even with her still-damp skin draped in a thin, almost transparent robe of feather-weight silk, she was uncomfortably warm. Picking up a cloth, she blotted the beads of perspiration anointing her brow and upper lip and began to apply her cosmetics. There was a time when she'd faced the world without them. Those days were past.

"You are a tool, my child, a vessel to be filled with the hope of the future. Place the secret deep inside you and examine it rarely. If you dwell on it too often, I fear unhappiness will be your reward. Find delight where you can, Charis; there is little enough of it in the world."

"You are a tool," Charis told her reflection, and began to line her eyes with the kohl that arrived regularly with the eastern caravans. "You are a vessel," she chanted, brushing the powdered henna lightly over her cheekbones, the tips of her breasts, and the arches of her feet. "Find delight," she ordered herself, and smoothed the pale pink wax over her lips. Placing the containers and brushes in careful order on the marble block, she selected a soft brush and began polishing her hair, running the bristles through the long tail of fine, perfectly straight hair that shone blue-black in the filtered light of the slatted wooden blinds. Satisfied that each detail was perfect, she rose from the plush ottoman and moved to her wardrobe to select an appropriate gown. As she moved away from the glass, her reflection caught her eye. Pausing, she studied the dark-haired stranger who stared solemnly back at her.

Was it possible that the mature woman she beheld was the young girl who dreamed of adventurous deeds and a measure of fame? Who imagined having a ballad composed in her honor, of generations of musicians singing her name long after her bones were burned to sacred ash? What a silly little girl you were, she scoffed. How naive to imagine you could make a difference in the world! Don't you know the world makes short work of dreams? That it feeds on the remains of foolish ideals? Impossibly blue eyes stared back at her. Disgusted, Charis turned away, attending to matters of dress.

The gown of indigo silk she chose was embroidered with tiny silver fists, the heraldic emblem of the Aeson of Agave. She had long grown accustomed to the crest, which decked every garment, every rug and wall-hanging, every belonging she touched. The Aeson was generous, had been generous since their first meeting. Daily, he showered her with delicacies, his wealth and prestige unequaled in this desert land. He had given her everything; everything, that is, except the thing she wanted most.

Throwing on the gown, she wrapped it around her waist, noting as she did so that the indigo color darkened her eyes until they exactly matched the fabric. Carefully she draped the gown so it hugged her shoulders and accentuated her breasts. Then, walking back to the dressing table, she picked up a hammered silver ring. The Aeson's thoughtfulness extended to having one crafted in both silver and gold, so that they might match the elegant fabrics he chose for her. They were her idea, not his, for he hated them, and had gone so far as to beg her not to wear them. But, for the only time in their lives together, she disobeyed. Her refusal hurt him, as she had intended, for she knew him better than anyone. As proud as he was stubborn, he never repeated his request. Every morning she clasped a slave ring around her neck. Every evening he removed it.

The perfect stillness of her chamber was broken by a familiar cry and her daughter burst into the room, tossing aside the curtain with a sun-tanned arm, her face glowing with youth, heat, and a supply of energy so boundless that it never failed to overwhelm her mother.

"Father said I could go, and he wants you to come, too! Oh, mother, aren't you excited? It's by far the most talked-about topic in the palace! Seth is furious. I can always tell. He pursed his lips in that hideous way of his and said something snide about `dangerous precedents'"

In the span of this rambling discourse, the girl flew about the room, making a quick inspection of the wardrobe, opening a blind to survey the gardens below, and finally settled cross-legged on the ottoman, where she rifled the top of the dressing table, opening bottles and boxes, inspecting the lotions and salves, spreading disorder and chaos wherever she roamed.

Sighing, Charis held her tongue, watching as the girl bent her head to sniff a box of powder. The resulting sneeze, and the curse that followed, would have made Charis' serving girl giggle behind her hand.

"Lillas, you must compose yourself! Your hair is a disgrace, although not so disgraceful as your language. Sit quietly for a moment and tell me about this new adventure while I work through the tangles."

Oblivious to her suggestion, the rampage at the dressing table continued unabated, the girl mouthing an endless stream of invectives against Seth, her voice shrill with dislike, until Charis could stand it no longer. Clamping a hand on either shoulder, she gave the girl a shake and was rewarded with immediate silence and a fretful pout.

"I can stand your rowdy ways and frightful language. I can stand the fact that you ride and hunt and gambol about, dismissing your tutors and insulting your slaves. I can even stand the fact that you avoid me. But I will not be ignored in my own chambers!"

Two sky-blue eyes looked back at her in the glass and blinked rapidly for a moment. A sun-tanned hand stole up to rest on top of hers.

"I ask pardon, mother. I know I'm noisy and difficult to love . . . "

Charis couldn't bear to hear the sentence completed.

"You've never been difficult to love. Difficult to live with. Never difficult to love."

The girl's eyes widened and softened, her lips curving up into a shy smile. Charis saw her departed youth reflected in that face, the cheekbones, brow, and jaw line a perfect copy of her own. Her father's contribution could be found in her light-brown mass of wavy hair and sun-touched skin that browned easily without burning, but her face was pure Charis—a face that could have been chiseled in marble, so distinctive was its haughty nose, full lips, broad forehead and wide-spaced eyes. She's not quite old enough for her face, Charis decided. The features are too distinctive for one so young, and almost overpower her. Still thin as a reed, she needs a woman's roundness to complete the promise of the curves and hollows of cheeks, neck, shoulders, and breasts. Charis' thoughts were interrupted by her daughter's question.

"What makes you think I avoid you?"

Charis busied herself with the comb, pulling out her own dark hairs before she attacked the nest of tangles and snarls falling in obstinate abandon over the girl's shoulders.

"Because it's true."

Starting from the ends, she worked the comb gently through the tangles, refusing to continue a conversation guaranteed to bring pain to them both.

"It's not true."

Under the sound of Lillas' protests lay guilt. Charis maintained her silence. She would not be the first to break the peace, uneasy as that peace might be.

"It's just that you . . . well, you make things hard sometimes, and I . . . I wish . . .," she paused, flushing as Charis' refusal to speak began to annoy her. In the face of her mother's continued silence, Lillas, never one to hold her tongue for long, blurted out the truth.

"I wish you'd be more . . . more agreeable!" complained this pampered princess of Agave. "Father doesn't treat you like a slave, you do it to yourself! You keep to yourself, you never gossip or take meals with the other women, and you insist on wearing that stupid collar even when Father asked you not to! Frankly, mother, sometimes you embarrass me!"

The comb frozen in mid-air, Charis closed her eyes against the tears fighting to escape her tightly-squeezed eyelids. They prepared her for humiliation, indifference, and loneliness; no one ever bothered to mention that her child would despise her. For a moment she thought she would explode and tell this overly-critical child exactly what she had endured for her sake, informing her in no uncertain terms of twenty years of sacrifice. But they had trained her well, especially the woman in black, so she bit back the words, controlled her breathing, and considered her reply.

"I'm sorry if I embarrass you. It's true that your father doesn't treat me as a slave and never has. He honored me by accepting you as his free-born daughter and I serve him as faithfully as I am able."

Despite her efforts, her voice hardened. For a moment she feared the force of her bitterness might crack the mirror.

"Don't forget there is a profound difference between serving someone because you choose to do so and serving someone because you must. I am in Imarus because I was purchased in Agave. If I choose to wear a collar to remind myself, your father, and everyone who sees me that I am his property, that is my right, my only right, and I will continue to do so." She rushed on, unable to prevent herself from speaking despite the possible consequences to her relationship with her daughter. "If you find my behavior objectionable, I suggest you practice your free-born rights and request that I be sold."

Her face having lost all color save for two red spots burning on her cheeks, Lillas jumped to her feet and strode toward the door, her back ramrod straight, her chin lifted to an impossibly high angle. Reaching the curtain, she spoke without deigning to turn her head.

"The carriage leaves in an hour. Be on time."

As Lillas sailed out of the room, Charis sank onto the ottoman. She had not meant to hurt Lillas' feelings, but to be rejected by her own child was too much to be borne. Ah, my daughter, how truly I am repaid for my ambition!

They had forgotten her. Of that she was sure, the ache of their betrayal a constant companion. Caught in a mire of plans gone awry, her attempts to contact them to no avail, she was beginning to lose control, the cool, clear-headed control they had schooled her in. That they would cast her aside was barely acceptable; that they could abandon Lillas was eating away at her, making her prone to mistakes, misjudgments like the recent quarrels that were slowly pushing Lillas away from her.

Lillas, the only fruit of her body. Lillas, the only child of the Aeson and a favorite in the palace and the city. Good-natured, exuberant, a natural mimic and a prankster, her exploits kept the palace humming. Her only faults were a hasty heart, an explosive temper, and her refusal to regard slavery as anything other than the traditional and comfortable right of every member of the nobility of Agave. She had visited the markets before, but what affected Charis to the point of nausea and acute abiding horror was brushed off by Lillas as a regrettable, but unavoidable, economic necessity. The business of Agave was the buying and selling of slaves, a service no other city offered. If certain owners mistreated their property, it was unfortunate, but certainly not something the Aeson could control. If their family didn't control the market, they pointed out reasonably, someone else would. Their plucked eyebrows lifted in righteous indignation, they would assure you that certainly no member of the royal house had ever dealt cruelly with a slave. Charis had lived with their self-righteous attitude for too long, finding it as repulsive today as it was twenty years ago.

The Seventeenth Mother's last words to her were cautionary. "Examine it rarely" meant "Don't dwell in the past." Understanding the reason behind this admonition, Charis obeyed, until today. Now, in this hour of inactivity and mind-numbing heat, she would examine her past, seeking a way out of the trap in which she found herself.

Twenty years ago, she had been exactly. . .

"TWENTY YEARS OF age on the eighth day of the sixth moon."

A pen scratched out her answers on a creamy sheet of unlined paper. The writer's hands were beautifully cared for, the elegantly tapered fingers tipped with oval nails buffed to a high sheen. Her handwriting, too, was flawless, the letters slanted in a perfect procession of alternating curves and straight lines.

"Are you a virgin?"

"Yes, lady."

Another careful line was added to the sheet. The next question was more disconcerting.

"What have you to offer the House of Hetaeras?"

"I . . . I've been told that my appearance is pleasing . . ."

"Yes?"

". . . and I wanted to . . .," Charis took a deep breath before stammering out the truth, ". . . to share my gift with others."

She waited for the woman to inform her, in no uncertain terms, that she was insufferably egotistical. Instead, the coronet of thick braids lifted and Charis was caught by eyes so piercing that she didn't notice their color or the features of the woman's face. Winding a strand of her hair around her forefinger, a nervous habit she would never outgrow, Charis managed to hold the woman's gaze. Her expression softening, the interviewer began to speak, her voice lacking the brusque edge it held during the long list of questions.

"It occurs to me, Charis, that given your beauty, which is considerable, you've had ample opportunity to share your gift with others, yet it seems you've chosen not to do so. Why is that?"

Since it was exactly this question that brought her to this interview, Charis didn't need to prepare a response.

"It's not just a question of joining. I've no qualms about losing my virginity. It's a silly dream, I know, but I've always wanted to make my beauty count." Heartened by the hetaera's interest, she began to elaborate. "You see, I've no other real gifts. I was an indifferent student, I've no particular craft at which I excel, and I'm hopeless with artistic pursuits. Over the past two years I've tried several apprenticeships, but none suited me. I was afraid to come here, but finally there seemed nothing else I could do, nowhere else I could go."

"What did you fear?"

Charis wound the hair more tightly around her finger.

"I was afraid you'd tell me beauty isn't enough."

"That's true."

They didn't want her. She'd been right to expect rejection. What had she been thinking? The Hetaera Guild was one of the most difficult to enter for both women and men, its prestige matched only by the House of Healing. The apprenticeship alone was five full years, compared to three in the craft guilds, and four in the Halls of Art, Architecture, Music, and Theatre. What was she going to do now? Charis rose and started for the door.

"Wait." The woman's smile was sunny as she motioned for Charis to resume her chair. "Tell me more about this silly dream of yours."

And so she entered her apprenticeship and came to live at the House of Hetaeras. She'd been uncertain what to expect, but even so, every day held a surprise, a challenge, and she found contentment and self-confidence for the first time in her life. Her fellow apprentices welcomed her as warmly as had Edothea, the woman who chose her as a fit member of the guild. All too soon, she began to connect this warmth, rather than physical beauty, with those selected for membership. Edothea's first lecture to the assembled novices neatly defined their method of study, their purpose, and the ethics of their craft:

"There are many misconceptions of what we do here, but I will describe it for you in a single sentence: We celebrate the body. Please note I did not say, `We worship the body.' This is a fine distinction, but one you must examine closely in your studies and in your hearts. If we worshipped the body, these halls would be filled with the most perfect specimens of human anatomy now living in Pelion."

A self-conscious ripple of laughter washed over the classroom.

"If you but look around you, you'll see that this is not the case. In your interviews you were asked an identical set of questions. Of the eighty-five applicants for this class, only nine of you convinced me that you revere your bodies as gifts and want to understand and teach others how the act of joining enriches our lives."

"Your studies in the first year will be three-fold. To begin, you will study male and female anatomy with a teacher from the House of Healing. Since all aspects of sexuality are of interest to us, you will study fertility, conception, pregnancy, and childbirth, as well as methods to ensure and prevent pregnancy. Remember that at the same time you study, you are also learning to teach, for a major part of our work occurs in counseling sessions. Our members work regularly with the pre-pubescent, the adolescent, the mature, and the elderly, concerning all matters connected to the body. You must be able to describe fertility cycles to a girl as well as providing explanations and reassurances to a boy whose dreams, and his body's response to those dreams, disturb and frighten him. Since we also counsel mated couples, you must learn to maintain tact and compassion while speaking of intensely private, and sometimes painful, matters."

"Next, your body is your instrument and must be trained as well as your minds. You will each keep a journal during your first year so as to reflect on your development. We have an extensive gymnasium and trainers who will help you keep yourself strong and supple, plus experts in movement who will teach you fluidity and poise. Women must keep rigorous records of their monthly cycles and each of you is expected to maintain a high degree of perfection in your personal grooming habits. This does not mean cosmetics, wigs, or heavy dousing of perfume. It does mean cleanliness, attention to your unique physical attributes, and the development of a quiet, and very personal, sense of beauty."

The lecture stopped. Charis lifted her eyes from the notes she was frantically scribbling. Her eight compatriots likewise dropped their pens, their attention riveted to the woman at the lectern.

"For the last area of study, I will be your teacher. I am a Master Teacher of Joining, and with me you will study the artistry of your craft. You will learn to share your body with others with joy, grace, and skill. We will study all manners of positions and techniques to excite and extend the pleasure of man and woman. Part of your studies includes the detection of sexual dysfunction. Impotence, sexual fears; for all of these we will discuss methods and treatments."

For the first time, Edothea's face grew stern.

"Lastly, and in some ways most importantly, you and I will consider the ethics of our profession. Eroticism is a powerful drug. You will discover for yourself the difference between using your gifts and exploiting others with those same gifts. For this reason, all your joinings will be assigned, planned, and discussed in detail with me in private sessions. Your partners in these sessions will be full members of the guild. None of these joinings may be discussed among yourselves. There will be no exceptions to this rule."

There was slight rustle of movement among the others. Charis guessed they shared her relief. Edothea's rule would allow privacy and the ability to experiment without fear.

"And so I welcome you, apprentices, as you begin to study this most ancient of arts."

Her training was everything Edothea promised, with one important exception. Three moons passed and Charis excelled in her studies, but the expected first joining never occurred. Since the topic was a forbidden one, she couldn't question her classmates, yet it was becoming increasingly clear, from random comments and observances made in class, that the others displayed firsthand knowledge denied to Charis. Worried that for some reason she had displeased Edothea, she doubled her efforts, with no result. At the end of the fourth moon, she made an appointment to discuss her plight.

Welcoming her into the office, Edothea indicated a chair to the right of her desk. Attempting to be as graceful as her movement teacher demanded, Charis sat and arranged the folds of her gown. As she raised her head to address her teacher, she heard the door shut behind her and found herself alone with the Seventeenth Mother of Pelion.

Hetaeras were trained to approach every situation with aplomb. Even so, a gasp escaped her as she took in the black gown. No one else in the city wore this color. Awestruck, Charis searched for something to say, anything that would cover her shocked and impolite reaction to so great a personage.

Ignoring Charis' flustered state, the Seventeenth Mother began the conversation.

"I've been waiting for you."

Her manner was friendly, matter-of-fact, as if she met daily with apprentice hetaeras and enjoyed those meetings immensely.

"W . . . w . . . waiting?"

"Despite my impatience at meeting you, I was impressed by how long it took you to question Edothea's judgment. Humility is a much undervalued trait, in my opinion, especially among the young."

Dumbfounded, Charis stared at her. Why would the Seventeenth Mother of Pelion possibly want to meet her? The woman's eyes twinkled.

"It's always a shock to come face to face with the most feared person in Pelion."

When a genial laugh escaped her, Charis relaxed. This woman might be all-powerful, but she possessed a rare sense of humor and a down-to-earth quality that inspired confidence. In any other garb she would be taken for a farmer or a gardener; someone who reveled in growing things.

Charis chanced a reply.

"I don't think you're frightening."

The woman's eyes glowed in appreciation.

"I'm glad of that. Most people never realize there's flesh and blood underneath these robes. But, enough self-pity!" she chuckled. "As you've probably guessed, I'm not in the habit of visiting apprentice hetaeras. Your case was brought to me by Edothea, who, although you may not know it, is a former Instructor of the Maze."

The Maze. Charis knew of it in a second-hand sort of way. After a screening process, selected citizens of Pelion might enter the Maze and undergo Preparation. Once there, they were mated to a foreigner, someone from the outlying lands. There was even a rumor that their joining resulted in some kind of advanced mental abilities. It was all rather vague and not particularly interesting to Charis. She'd never met anyone not native born, and as to becoming an "adept" (she remembered the correct term from a recent class), she wasn't quite sure what it signified. Most healers were adept, and others as well, she supposed, but having never known anyone with this particular talent, she had no desire to seek it for herself. She decided to be frank with the Seventeenth Mother and prevent any waste of her time.

"If you're considering inviting me to enter Preparation, I think I should tell you I've no vocation for it."

If she'd thought the Seventeenth Mother might be disappointed, or taken aback by her forthrightness, she was mistaken. If anything, the woman's round cheeks flushed a deeper shade of pink, her lips curving upward into a happy smile.

"My proposal doesn't concern Preparation. However, before I share it with you, it might be helpful if I provide you with a short history."

Charis shifted uncomfortably in her chair. History, in her opinion, had been purposefully invented to bore students. The woman chuckled again.

"Not the history of the classroom, Charis, but the story of living, breathing people."

The Seventeenth Mother seemed to be waiting for permission to continue, so Charis inclined her head. At her signal, the woman leaned back in the chair, rested her fingertips together, and looked out the window to her right, seeming to bask in the warmth of the afternoon sun flooding the room.

"Pelion has come to a crossroads of sorts. We've fortified our city to the point that we've become, for lack of better words, stagnant, in-bred. Our walls encourage indifference toward what exists beyond them, offering an impression of security that is ultimately false. The time has come for us to emerge from our cocoon. To do that, we must send our best and brightest out into the world."

"For several years now, I've been looking for a young woman of very particular talents. Now, I don't meet many young people in the normal course of my days, with the exception of the ernani in the Maze. For that reason, I asked several friends to assist me in my search, one of them being Edothea. There are many qualifications for this young woman, but the most vital one is that she believes that an individual can make a difference in the world; that a person is the sum of the actions they perform with the gifts they are given." She paused, searching her memory for a moment. "I believe the expression you used was 'make my beauty count.'"

Startled, Charis looked into eyes that were now absolutely intent on her, drinking in her expression, measuring every response, every breath, every thought.

"Here's my question. You called your dream 'silly' when you described it to Edothea, but to me it's not silly, but achievable, although it will be dangerous and lonely work. Are you willing to put your beauty to use in order to accomplish something that might change the world?"

"I . . . I . . . I'm not sure I can answer without knowing more about the plan."

She was playing for time, but the Seventeenth Mother would have none of it.

"And I'm not sure how much more I can safely tell you."

The Seventeenth Mother rose from behind the desk and moved slowly around it, her movements marked by a distinct limp that made her ungainly on her feet. She stood an arm's length from Charis, but refrained from physically touching her; only her eyes spoke her need.

"I don't mean to intimidate you, but I want you to understand the weightiness of my request. I've searched for years, and you're the only one who has every attribute necessary, the only one I've ever approached. I've come to believe that you have been chosen. Having been chosen, it is time for you to choose. Do you have the courage of your convictions as you described them to Edothea?"

As the Seventeenth Mother spoke, Charis began to tremble. Was it possible that she actually was as special as she'd always fancied herself to be? Had she indeed been chosen, and was this her destiny, to serve her city as no other woman could? Might her name live after her, celebrated in verse and song?

"Yes, Mother. I'm willing."

MEMORIES FADED AT the sound of a cleared throat and a half-whispered entreaty.

"Charis?"

In all these years, he'd never invaded her privacy. He purchased her on the block for two hundred pieces of gold, yet he waited outside her door, the ruler of all Agave and its environs, begging permission to enter her chambers.

"Come, my lord."

As the curtain parted, she saw his figure outlined against the harsh sunlight of the outer hallway.

"I wanted to speak to you before we leave for the city."

"Of course, my lord."

In the few moments it took him to cross the room and sit on the edge of the extravagantly bedecked bed, she could see his tension. Fifteen years her senior, he gave the impression of a much younger man. To be sure, there were gray hairs mixed with those of gold, and his skin was lined around the eyes and mouth, but there was no trace of a paunch or stiffening of the legs that usually accompanies a man of over fifty years of age. His tension showed in the set of his shoulders and the worry lines between his sandy brows. Moving quickly to the bed, she knelt beside him, massaging his neck and hearing his grateful sigh.

"I've quarreled again with Seth, but this time Lillas came between us. It was ugly, far uglier than it's ever been."

"What did she say?"

Upset as he was, the shadow of a smile passed over his face. Lillas was the Aeson's delight, his indulgence of her a major reason for the wildness of her ways. As she grew to womanhood, she had come to symbolize a freedom from restraint he had never experienced.

"She says the things I've longed to say, but never had the courage to put into words."

Charis translated.

"So, she informed Seth that although he may be your nephew, he is not yet the Aeson. And I would guess, knowing Lillas, that she said it publicly, loudly, and as insultingly as possible."

He pulled her into his arms, tracing her face from forehead to chin with a single finger.

"She's your daughter as well. We're both responsible for what she is."

Charis looked up into adoring eyes, feeling some of the bitterness of the day fade away. He continued to caress her, running his palm lightly over the crown of her head, and she welcomed his touch. He had always been this way with her, even from their first night together, for he was exactly what Charis had been promised . . .

STANDING SHACKLED ON the raised platform, petrified that he might have her stripped and handle her in front of the stinking crowds who screamed profanities and lewd suggestions, she felt a hand pull aside the veil of her hair. A deep voice spoke with the soft, sibilant accent of Agave.

"Don't be frightened, blue-eyes."

He was a hands breadth taller than her, his light brown hair and beard arranged in the fashionable ringlets of Agavean aristocracy. Somewhere she found the daring to address him, remembering the Seventeenth Mother's comment that although he rarely purchased slaves, he was known to value spirit in those who served him. Her beauty kindled his interest; her courage must make that interest grow.

"I'm called Charis, lord."

A particularly loud obscenity floated up from the crowd below. He frowned, distracted for a moment. She'd been standing here since noon, waiting for his carriage to pass through the square, enduring the stench of excrement, vomit, and unwashed bodies. Her caretaker, Timon, allowed no one to touch her, pleading the excuse of a contract already made although as yet unpaid. Still, the crowd continued to grow around the platform, lured by a slender figure arrayed in spotless white, her unbound hair hanging in a dark cloud to her waist. As the Seventeenth Mother predicted, it was the crowd who brought him to her. Stopping the carriage with an uplifted hand, he bounded up the steps two at a time. The crowd subsided as soon as he was recognized. As he approached Charis, pandemonium broke out again, some of the more daring ones climbing up onto the platform, to be hurled roughly to the ground by the disguised Legionnaires who guarded Charis by day and by night.

As he turned back to her, she was aware that his gaze was traveling over her body. The gown was designed to draw the crowd's attention by promising much and revealing little. She understood the risk taken by its selection, for crowds had been known to attack the human wares that stood helplessly bound by chains. Her relative composure was made possible by her trust in the guards she'd trained and traveled with during the past moons. All of them were friends now, their concern for her evidenced by the swords they held unsheathed, their faces grim, their lips drawn back into snarls as they surveyed the rabble who howled and licked at her feet; a pack of wild dogs held at bay by their fear of metal and the brands of fire burning in the Legionnaires' eyes.

A faint smile hovered around the Aeson's lips.

"The color of your gown announces to all that you are, as yet, untouched. Yet dealers have been known to put a white dress on any woman of exceptional beauty. Does the gown speak the truth?"

It was for this moment that Edothea denied Charis her first joining. Virginity was not a highly-prized commodity in Pelion since all children were welcomed into the world regardless of their parentage, just as all children inherited equally, regardless of their gender or the order of their birth. In Pelion, Charis' virginity was neither an asset nor a detriment; merely a choice. But Agave was not Pelion and the man who stood before her had never fathered a child. He was known to be sexually active since the age of sixteen, but in all those years, none of the women in his household had ever borne a child of his body. For him to accept her child, the child for whom all this was dared, he must be assured that he, and no other, was the father.

"Yes, my lord. I am untouched."

Even if he didn't believe her now, the bloodied bedclothes would prove her honesty in the morning.

He turned to the dealer, transforming himself into the Aeson of Agave. His tone was imperious, his words abrupt; his manner allowed none to brook his will.

"What is her price?"

Timon the slave dealer bowed and fawned, his eyes busily calculating the price, a brilliant actor cast in a perfect role.

"It's not just the matter of price, great lord. It seems, ahem, it seems that another has bid for her, although we have not as yet completed the sale. Perhaps another . . . ?"

His filthy hands indicated the other women arranged around the perimeters of the platform. A round of giggles passed through them as they eyed the Aeson. No one would have guessed that each of them wore a dagger strapped under her gown, and that they, like the Legionnaires, had sworn to protect Charis until she was safely placed in the Aeson's carriage.

Irritated, the Aeson glowered at the slave dealer, his desire for Charis all the more pressing because another claimed her. Untying a purse from his belt, he tossed it into the air. Timon dove unashamedly to catch it before it landed on the platform.

"I trust this will cover her price, as well as your time and trouble in arranging another suitable purchase for the first bidder."

Timon's hands trembled as he counted out the coins, his tongue darting out from time to time to lick his lips. Without waiting for an answer, the Aeson began issuing commands.

"Unshackle her. I'll expect her bill of sale in my secretary's hands tomorrow morning." He turned to address her, and again, his voice was soft and low. "My personal guards will escort you to the carriage. All your needs will be taken care of at my palace in Imarus, which lies to the northwest. I have further business in the city this afternoon, but will return to you by evening."

She nodded, acknowledging his promise without comment, and his hand crept up again to caress her hair. As the chains were unlocked from her wrists and ankles, her situation was transformed from plan to accomplished feat. In another moment she would be separated from her companions and protectors, completely alone in a foreign world, her life and well-being intricately woven around the man who stood in front of her. Panic rose, and then, above the roar of the crowd, she heard the voice that would often drift toward her out of the south.

"I would not send you there without ample cause, my child, or without careful regard for your safety. We have studied him for years, and although many in his family are corrupt, he is kind to all and generous to a fault. I cannot promise that he will take you to his heart, but I know he will not mistreat you. When the child comes, you will bind him closer to you than before."

"How can you be so certain there will be a child?"

The Seventeenth Mother laughed softly, her eyes alight.

"Because she dances in my dreams, a being of endless possibility, for she is the hope on which history is hinged. You will call her Lillas: 'light that flickers like a flame.'"

"WHAT DREAMS FILL your eyes?"

The Aeson's question brought Charis back to the present moment.

"Dreams of past and present, my lord."

"Which do you prefer?"

"Dreams of the future, of things yet to come."

He hugged her tightly for a moment, glad of her answer, and then rose from the bed, straightening his sumptuous robes. He held out his hand to her, helping her rise to her feet.

"I would prefer to linger with you, blue-eyes, but we must not let Seth and Lillas ride in the same carriage unattended."

"You never told me the subject of the quarrel."

"It seems there is a prophet who attracts great crowds in the city. Seth fears his predictions will create riots of dissatisfaction. Lillas, on the other hand, has heard him speak and believes his visions to be true."

"Where does he come from, my lord?"

The Aeson frowned, looking every one of his fifty-five years.

"From a place that is becoming more of a problem with every passing year."

"What place?"

"Pelion."

Chapter 4

Sacrifice

AGAVE WAS A marketplace like no other in the world. Other squares bustled as did this one, vendors hawking their wares, prospective shoppers strolling from stall to stall, lured by the ever-present hope of a better product for a more reasonable price. There were even smiles to be seen on certain faces, for it is undeniable, this mutual delight generated by commercial exchange, an enterprise which tests the wit and mettle of buyer and seller alike. To strike a bargain, settle a price, come to terms without rancor or regret, and then to walk away from the completed transaction, confident that both parties have benefited, these are the joys of trade.

Arm in arm with Selena, Lukash passed through village and town squares the world over, lingering at certain stalls, ignoring others, savoring the sensory delights on display to buyer and spectator alike. With Selena by his side, he reveled in the purplish splendor of onions set beside the deep summer green of leeks and cabbages, their colors magnified by two sets of eyes that saw as one. Together, they inhaled the sharp fragrances of eastern spices and the heady perfume oils distilled by the flower merchants from the lands of legend far to the south. Every market had its own distinction, a flavor, if you will, that spoke of life and craft and even a certain rarified aesthetic. It was Selena who honed Lukash's appreciation of such things. She, who saw with clarity unmatched by anyone he had ever known, taught him that as a people live, so do they create goods and products, and that nothing so marks a peoples' character as the way they engage in commerce.

Over years and leagues of travel, it became a game between them. Her dark eyes announcing her challenge, she would select an item from a booth or counter and place it in his hands, demanding silently that he tell her of the people who had grown or formed it. Sometimes with suspicion, sometimes with pride, the ever-watchful vendor would scrutinize Lukash as he slid his hands over the object, gauging the type of life necessary to produce it.

Once, in the village of Cinthea, she handed him a piece of lace, its lattice-work pattern of swirls and scallops so intricate that the eyes lost their way among its convolutions. He was hard-pressed to answer her, other than to suggest a love of detail and an exceptional amount of leisure time, for he

guessed that many hours of work would be necessary to produce this scrap
that fit neatly into the borders of his open palm.

Taking the lace from him, Selena stroked it lightly with a single finger.

"It speaks of so much more. Only small fingers can work so involved a
design; thus it is a woman's craft. Yet the pattern is far too difficult for a
young girl to invent or execute. An elderly woman made this, and judging
by its price, a woman who is cherished for her skill. She sits in the sun, its
warmth penetrating her bones and warming her joints as she works patiently,
her failing eyes unnecessary as her fingers work by touch alone, knotting
and tying threads. In Cinthea, elderly women are treasured; not burdens to
be cast aside, but valued for the experience that age alone can bring."

So Selena envisioned the world—each market, each ware, a microcosm
of human processes. Together, they made the world their text, reading of
lives lived in harshness and abundance, leisure and unending toil, grace and
futility.

With Selena's passing, he lost the perceptions which made their chronicles
possible. Without her, he was a scholar without a subject. Try as he might,
he could sometimes regain a glimmer of their former association, but to
recapture the uniqueness of her vision, the keenness of her insights, was
hopeless. The loss of her made the world, once intelligible, suddenly
impenetrable. And thus he finally came to the only market he and Selena
never visited. He came to Agave.

It was no plan of his that he came to be here on this sun-bleached day
in late summer, yet he came of his own free will. For fifty years he avoided
this place, taking detours of days and weeks to avoid its boundaries, Selena
understanding without need of spoken word how deep was his need to
bypass even the remotest reminder of the brutalities visited upon an enslaved
orphan child. Yet after a single conversation with a woman barely half his
age, whose knowledge of the world came solely from books and who had
never traveled farther than a three-day journey from the city of her birth,
Lukash returned willingly, even thankfully, to the city of slaves.

"LUKASH?"

In the few seconds necessary for his eyes to adjust from the tiny script
he was attempting to decipher to the pale face whose veil surrounded her
like a halo painted in blackest hues, he felt an involuntary smile tug at the
corners of his mouth. This Mother was unlike any he had ever known.

At twenty-one years of age, he was welcomed into the Maze by the
Sixteenth Mother, known to all as "The Beloved," although, to Lukash's
knowledge, no one was ever so disrespectful as to use that title to her face.

She must have been nearing her seventieth year as she greeted him at the altar. Lukash remembered her as a woman whose wrinkled skin did nothing to diminish the beauty of her appearance.

Her successor, the Seventeenth Mother, apple-cheeked and robust despite her distinctively awkward gait, had a maturity about her even from the beginning of her reign. This one, this new wearer of the black robes with her smooth skin and sharp eyes, would likely be called "mother" by a child of no more than two or three years of age.

"How may I assist you, Mother?"

An answering smile tugged at her lips as she pulled back a chair and seated herself companionably by his side. The late afternoon sun was diffuse in the Great Library; most scholars chose the brighter morning hours for their work. In point of fact, the reading room was empty but for Lukash, the Eighteenth Mother, and a librarian working at the files near the entrance. This alcove was his special province. Since his duties for the Council gave him access to works unavailable to others, he studied in near isolation. After a full year since his return to Pelion, he had little more than a nodding acquaintance with his fellow scholars. The novelty of having someone engage him in conversation was unexpected, and, he reflected, surprisingly welcome.

"Why do you think I want something from you? Is it beyond the realm of possibility that I came here for an entirely different purpose?"

There was always an element of debate in her conversation. Prax had conveyed something of her history, yet even without that basic information, Lukash believed he would have been able to guess her academic background. Rising to her challenge, enjoying the opportunity for unaccustomed repartee, he answered her point for point.

"My deduction comes from several observations. First, although you often visit the Great Library, you rarely enter this particular room. Secondly, if you intended to work here, you would be carrying a tablet and pen. You have neither. And lastly, if your intention was simply to greet me, I would not have heard hesitation in your voice."

"Hesitation?"

Her eyes widened as he explained his logic. Now they narrowed, a tiny crease appearing between her eyebrows.

"Hesitation, a trace of worry; I can't be exact. Certainly it was more than a simple greeting."

"I hope others don't read my intentions as easily as you."

Without further ado, she reached into one of the deep pockets of her robes, producing a single piece of water-stained parchment that had once been folded into a letter. Bits of wax still clung to the broken seal. Smoothing the folds, she spread it out on the table before them, and, with a simple gesture, invited him to read.

As was his custom when working with documents, he first considered the nature of its writing. The letters were formed in a simple, almost child-like script. People accustomed to many hours of writing longhand tend to blur or elide the formation of individual letters, with the result that their handwriting achieves individuality, becoming further and further removed from the formal loops and curlicues drilled into them by their teachers. Judging from their careful formation, Lukash deduced that the writer was schooled, but not a frequent user of a pen.

The message itself was brief:

> The time approaches, yet I have no word from you.
> Have you forgotten the "light which flickers like a flame?"

There was no date, no addressee, and no signature; twenty words written by an anonymous person pleading for present action. The Eighteenth Mother, who continued perusing the document, fiddled nervously with the silver ring, turning is round and round on the middle finger of her left hand. Three moons ago he had seen her power revealed at the gravesite of three women from the west. Kneeling at her feet, he offered her his services. It was time to make good his word.

"What does it signify, Mother?"

He had never appreciated the strange quality of her eyes. Neither large, nor heavily lashed, they possessed none of the popular requisites of beauty, yet they were oddly compelling, as if one could enter their grey-green orisons as one entered the shallows of the sea, and this done, be lured to swim into deeper and more dangerous waters. With an effort, he pulled himself away from such ominous musings so as to concentrate on her answer.

"In truth, Lukash, I have no idea."

Turning the paper over, she pointed to a single word; in the same hand was written "Mother."

"I received it three days ago by way of an ernani, a woman who came via caravan from the west. Strange isn't it, so many women trying to reach us from the west in the past few moons? This one arrived alive." Her next words were laced with irony. "Is it coincidence, Lukash? Or do you believe, as I have come to believe, that no such thing exists?"

"What did the ernani tell you?"

She shook her head.

"Nothing. And she won't be able to reveal anything else to us for a long time."

Lukash had been puzzled by the letter. He was even more mystified by the Eighteenth Mother's air of hopelessness. Leaning back into the chair, resting her head against the rungs, she resembled a child returning indoors after an afternoon of strenuous play.

"Can't you guess, Lukash? Surely you remember the first rule! Once accepted into Preparation, no ernani can be read. And, sadly, the woman said nothing of this note until the day of Blessing. If all goes well, she will be transformed in five or six moons. Until then, I have a note written in a code I cannot break, and am forbidden to read the thoughts of the one who may hold the key to its meaning."

"Then we must decipher the code as best we can."

"I've tried everything! The parchment holds no information; many moons have passed since the writer held it. Other hands have touched it since, blurring my attempts to trace its source."

"Three years in the black robes and already you rely on your powers instead of good common sense. It is often so with born adepts. We who come late to the gift tend to put our trust in observation."

"Do you rebuke me, Searcher of Souls?"

Her smile belied the formality of her address. With it, he sensed the return of her good humor.

"Let us study it together. Brought out of the west by the hand of an ernani, yet the writer was either schooled within this city, or taught by someone from Pelion. Note that the writer has more than enough space to write a longer message, but chose to write two short sentences. Thus, we can guess the sender feared to write more in case it fell into the wrong hands."

Nodding at his side, the Mother picked up his train of thought.

"There is danger here, and a clear note of begging mixed with reproach. Someone believes themselves abandoned and thinks I am to blame for their condition."

"Have you considered the placement of the quotation marks? Why would that particular phrase be so designated?"

"A password, perhaps? A place? A name?"

Frustrated, Hesione scraped the chair on the stone floor as she pushed it back and began to pace back and forth behind him, turning the ring around and around, her thoughts twirling with the silver band.

"Nothing! Nothing! I've gone over every document since my ascension. You have some knowledge of the plans begun since the attack in the woods. My war with the west is just beginning. Not even Prax, my strategist, can make sense of this!"

"Perhaps the sender does not accuse you in particular."

The pacing stopped and she closed her eyes.

"Of course, of course!" Her lids flew open again. "Not me, but another who wore the black robes!"

Lukash returned to the parchment.

"Although I've spoken and written your language for fifty years, it's not my native tongue. Let's assume the phrase in question is, as you suggest, a proper name. How would it best be translated?"

Pursing her lips, she considered his question.

"Lil-li-las, I suppose; Lillas for short." A startled gasp escaped her. "Lillas!" she repeated. "The Seventeenth Mother whispered it as she died. Afterwards, I asked everyone what it meant. No one knew."

Lukash straightened in his chair.

"I know," he said quietly. "Selena knew."

Her hand reached out to touch the sleeve of his robe, inviting him to share his thoughts. Since the loss of Selena, he had used his gift rarely, if at all.

"Take me with you, Lukash. I'm not Selena, but I will be your good and faithful companion. Help me find the 'light that flickers like a flame.'"

Lukash sighed and closed his eyes.

AT FIRST THERE was nothingness, a kind of floating in a place without light, sound, scent, touch, or smell. After living so long in the realm of the senses, he became increasingly disoriented, no longer sure where his body began and where it ended. When panic set in, he struggled, to be enfolded more tightly, like a fretful child being wrapped in a blanket and rocked softly in his mother's arms. In time, the darkness grew more familiar, more inviting, the demands of the waking world fading, receding, as she led him on, deeper and deeper into the reservoir of his mind. How long they traveled, he never knew, for time, that tyrant of human experience, wields no power here. Here were no endings. Here chronology held no sway. Here he became the essence of Lukash, and in so becoming, found the place he had tried to reach so many times since Selena's passing, the place they lived together as one being, a place he resolved never to leave. Here lived Selena; here he would stay.

"Not yet, Searcher. Soon, but not today. Take me to the place and time we seek."

Despite her assurances, he loathed the idea of leaving. Then, remembering that the memory he sought would include Selena, he surrendered himself to the Eighteenth Mother's will, taking her back through the years, searching through the chambers of his memory for the correct place and time. At last he found it, the door swinging open at his command to reveal a vista of desert flatlands shimmering under a harsh midday sun. As he entered, Selena's arm grasped him around the waist. At the welcome feel of her body leaning against his, he gave himself up to memory, no longer aware of the one who accompanied him . . .

* * *

AS TEARS GATHERED in the hetaera's eyes, a shudder ran through Selena, whether of foresight or commiseration, Lukash never discovered.

"My thanks, Searchers, for your company. You've been a comfort to me on our travels."

She was, quite simply, the most beautiful woman Lukash had ever seen, this apprentice hetaera with indigo eyes fringed with coal-black lashes, her eyebrows shaped like black swan wings rising to take flight on a moonlit night. The entire company was in love with her beauty, thought Lukash, which she wore lightly, like a feathered cloak resting on porcelain shoulders. Now it was time for them to part, for Selena and him to turn south, while the hetaera continued west. Neither he nor Selena knew what fate awaited her in Agave. From the first, neither of them wanted to know.

They had been summoned to the Seventeenth Mother's tower chamber two days before their regularly scheduled departure for the southeastern provinces. It was an uncomfortable meeting for all concerned, the Seventeenth Mother aloof and uncommunicative as she ordered them to cancel their plans and join a caravan bound for Agave. Before Lukash could protest, she silenced him with a curt command.

"Obey my will in this. I know your custom of avoiding Agave. For this reason, I give you leave to depart the day before the others enter the city."

Selena spoke up, clearly and crisply, as was her manner when she was angry.

"Will you tell us the reason for this journey, so that we may better serve you?"

"You accompany an apprentice hetaera who has never ventured beyond the city walls. Her mission is not your affair. She is not adept and you will on no account enter her thoughts. It is a large group: twenty Legionnaires, seven women, a healer, a member of the Players Guild, and the hetaera."

"Are we to serve as guides, then? Surely there are others more familiar with the route. Certainly there are others more willing to obey."

Selena's coldness matched the Mother's severity. Having served the interests of Pelion for her entire adult life, in her heart of hearts, Selena remained an ernani. Mindless devotion did not impress her, nor did time-honored rituals. Others bowed to the black robes by habit. Selena served the individual who wore them by choice. No one patronized Selena, nor did anyone order her about. Lukash readied himself for the worst.

Perhaps the Seventeenth Mother sensed she had met her match; perhaps (and this was the explanation Lukash preferred) the strength of Selena's resistance made her recall the magnitude of what she asked. Whatever the reason, she limped over to her desk, her gait more awkward than usual (proof, Lukash remembered thinking, of the extent of her fatigue), eased herself into a chair, and, after considering them both for a prolonged, tension-filled moment, said:

"Clearly, you think me a tyrant. Perhaps I am. Know this: I would not involve you if so much was not at stake."

It was nothing less than a masterstroke, Lukash thought later, a testament to the Seventeenth Mother's considerable powers of persuasion. Despite her physical exhaustion, despite the failure of her initial strategy, she conceded the loss of the first round without forfeiting the match. Mounting a rally, she switched tactics, her apology geared to placate Selena even as she restated her position. It was at this point that Lukash resigned himself to the inevitable. Selena, however, remained unconvinced.

"If so much is at stake, why not choose someone better suited to the task? We are not tour guides. Let us do what we do best."

"That is my intention," the Seventeenth Mother countered swiftly. "She has guides and guards aplenty. What she needs are companions."

At this point, she stopped fencing with Selena. Beneath the earnestness of her plea, Lukash sensed something akin to desperation.

"Both of you have spent your lives helping ernani find their way to Pelion. The hetaera needs help just as the ernani do, but in the opposite direction. Smooth her way to Agave. Keep her active; tell her stories of your travels, of people and places unknown to us citizens of Pelion. At all costs, prevent her from brooding. It might seem a small service to perform, but it is vital."

Selena's reply, when it came, proved that she, like Lukash, had bowed to the inevitable. Unlike him, she had also leapt ahead.

"You will tell us nothing more?"

"Secrecy is essential to the success of this mission."

"You are afraid for her, so afraid that you deny her a name."

"She can have no name to any of you."

"What should we call her, then, when we depart and she journeys on to the city of madness? When we think of her, as no doubt we will, what name should we use? For if she is in as much danger as you believe her to be, she has need of our thoughts."

Lukash strained to hear the soft mumble of the Seventeenth Mother's lips.

"Think of her as the mother of Lillas."

LUKASH OPENED HIS eyes on the reading room, which had darkened considerably since the Eighteenth Mother linked her mind with his.

Her soft, musing voice floated across the quiet of the dusky room.

"In my reading, I came across a reference that has haunted me ever since. A romance, as I remember, which described slaves who wore rings of beaten metal around their throats. Did you ever see such a thing in Agave?"

Troubled by this gap in logic, he shook his head. With a strange smile, one that mingled happiness and regret, she patted his sleeve.

"No matter, Lukash, no matter."

She sat for a long time in quiet reflection, regarding her hands outspread on the table, white and still and no longer busy with the ring. At last, she turned toward him and this time he experienced no urge to smile at her youth. She needed him. For what purpose, he did not know, but green eyes like warm seas warned him that her need was great and the danger even greater.

"I cannot see everything yet, but this I know. Your role is cast, for you are the link between past and future. Finish your book, Lukash, for time grows short."

She rose, and it seemed to Lukash that she had grown taller, more substantial; a woman of uncommon dignity rising to face the unknown.

"Truly, you must finish the book. When you write the last word, come to me. Together, we will write the words of dedication."

"I'm dedicating it to Selena."

"Who else, Lukash?" she replied softly, then again, "Who else?"

There was no one else, nor would there ever be. This Lukash knew, had always known. Something inside him, grief with its razor-sharp edges, began to dissolve. He raised his gaze to meet that of the Eighteenth Mother.

There was no hint of green in her eyes now. The sea was grey under a leaden sky.

"You will write with ink. I will write with blood."

"My blood?" he asked, although he knew the answer and accepted it with neither fear nor rebellion. So be it, he thought, peace flooding his mind for the first time since the death of Selena.

"Finish the book, my friend. All things come to an end. Our task is to find contentment at their closing."

THE LAST WORD written, Lukash began his final journey, returning from whence he'd come. The route of his life was circular, these last faltering steps leading him toward a promised beginning.

He arrived at his accustomed place in the market, settling his bill at the inn, avoiding the curious questions of the innkeeper, a gregarious woman who prided herself on the fact that she knew every merchant and every stall. In any other city, she could have given directions to the booth offering the plumpest raisins or the tastiest figs. In Agave, her knowledge was of another sort, for she directed guests of the inn to stalls where human flesh was sold. Within its wind-blasted sandstone walls the world gathered to do business, selling the helpless, the luckless, and the unfortunate without qualm or question; the only market on earth where Selena's game foundered and came to naught.

Children stood bound on the platform behind him, their faces solemn, unaware of why or for what purpose they had been brought here, but hopeful, as children are always hopeful, that if they behaved, if they did everything required of them, somehow the nightmare would cease, and they would be snatched up into their parents' arms again, the world made suddenly right. There was mercy to be found in the fact that they didn't know, couldn't imagine, what lay before them. With every passing hour, another small set of wrists bound with hemp was sold in the marketplace of Agave.

So he had stood so many years ago, frozen by the owner's threats, his legs trembling under him as he looked down on more people than he dreamed existed. Fifty years had passed, yet his fear of Agave continued unabated. A free man, a scholar, someone who had traveled the wide expanses of the world and known responsibility and power, he trembled as surely as if he stood alone on the block, his worth measurable by a few grimy coins that would never cross his palm.

Delving inside himself, putting aside the constant roar of the endlessly milling crowds, he took the steps necessary to achieve tranquility. Before he could tap that place, heavy footsteps descended the stairway leading to the platform. A slave dealer approached him, his sun-burned forehead creased into a frown.

"A word with you, prophet. I've let you preach here because you draw crowds, but I think it's best if you're off. Some of my neighbors complain that you're bad for business, and though I don't particularly agree, I can't let you come between us. After all, business is business."

This was delivered with a half-smile and a shrug. He was not a particularly cruel man, this seller of children. In the weeks he'd preached here, Lukash had seen no child starved or ill-treated, yet as the slaver would have freely admitted to any questioner of his motives, he was a man of business. Keeping his merchandise fed and watered was not a matter of charity, but common sense. To such a man, profit was the only possible motivation for good work.

"I understand, citizen. I'll not come back tomorrow, but could you possibly consider letting me speak today?" To counter the slaver's deepening frown, Lukash added the extra motivation necessary to achieve his goal. "It's rumored that the Aeson and certain other residents of Imarus will be in attendance."

The frown smoothed, turning into a genial grin.

"Well, that changes everything! Use my steps and welcome!"

As the slaver turned to remount the platform, Lukash sensed him considering the status that might result from such an encounter with the ruler of Agave, as well as the profits engendered by making his stall the focal point of the entire marketplace.

"One more favor, if you please. Could you point out the Aeson's entourage to me? I'm a newcomer to the city, as you know, and I've never seen them before."

Stopping half-way up the steps, the slave dealer leaned against the wooden railing and, dipping a ragged-edged square of cloth into a tin bucket reserved for the slaves' drinking water, wiped his face and ears. A satisfied grunt greeted the cooling relief of liquid against parched skin. It had been a long dry summer; water rationing measures went into effect a fortnight ago. Although rich in the human resources that were its primary export, Agave's natural resources were limited to its quarries and mines. Water had to be transported to the city from rivers far to the northwest. As the drought deepened, the cost of water doubled, then redoubled. It was hardest on the slaves, many of whom were allowed less than a cup a day. This dealer was more generous, although he never offered Lukash so much as a sip of water, his generosity, it seemed, confined to those who could turn a profit. Wringing out the cloth over the bucket, careful that not a drop be wasted, the slaver considered the black man sitting below him on the stairs.

"You say you wouldn't recognize them, prophet, but Lady Lillas has been here on several occasions."

Fighting his impulse to rejoice, Lukash let an expression of confusion pass over his face.

"I never knew. Is she a lady of remarkable face or figure? If you describe her, I might be able to place her."

A chuckle announced that his ploy was successful.

"Remarkable face or figure? No, prophet, or at least her looks aren't the first thing that comes to mind. She's a handful, though, and no mistake."

"How is that?"

Lukash could tell the slaver was intent on spinning a tale, one he had told many times. It took no effort to appear interested. He spoke the truth when he said he knew none of the royal family by sight. Each day he scanned the faces of the crowds, hoping she listened, speaking to her alone.

The slave dealer squatted down on the steps and placed the handkerchief on the top of his head, shielding his bald spot from the punishing rays of the sun. His eyes squinted against the glare and the clouds of dust that were ever present in this desert city, he began.

"There's little love lost between Agave and Imarus. The Aeson may govern the city and handle foreign trade, but we don't forget that it's our taxes that let his relatives live in that marble palace of his. The current Aeson is fair

enough, and allows us a good profit, but his heir, Lord Seth, is . . ." the slaver
lowered his voice, surveying the neighboring platforms before continuing,
". . . downright greedy. As bad as this summer is, three summers ago it was
worse. Water costs are always high, but that summer Lord Seth took it into
his head to add an extra tax on top of the water rates. He said it was to
discourage waste. We knew it was to fill his coffers."

Pausing, he adjusted his head-gear before leaning back against the tread
of the step above him.

"It was the seventh, no, the eighth moon . . . that's right, three years ago
exactly! Lady Lillas doesn't normally come into the city alone, but that day
she came to pick up a newly-purchased household slave, a healer, I think.
Anyway, the crowds were thick, hot, and thirsty, and some of them made
trouble for her, blocking the progress of her carriage. There she was, a mere
slip of a girl, being harassed and cursed by a decidedly nasty bunch. What
do you think she did?"

Lukash knew better than to attempt a guess. This tale was well-rehearsed.
Any deviation from its flow might annoy the teller.

"She stood up in the carriage, bold and sassy as could be, put her hands
on her hips, and yelled out to the crowd, 'What exactly is it that you want?'
Can you imagine such a thing? I'll never forget it as long as I live! Now there's
a girl who knows what she wants and how to get it!"

The speaker chortled to himself, slapping his thighs in pure enjoyment.
Lukash nudged him a bit, encouraging him to proceed.

"And then what happened?"

"Why, they told her, of course! Told her how expensive water was and
how little actually came into the city. One man spoke up, saying that if they
stopped watering the gardens of Imarus for two days a week, there'd be
water enough for a hundred more households. You know what she did,
prophet?"

Lukash indicated his ignorance with a quick shake of his head.

"She listened, truly listened! Even asked questions about rates, the extra
tax, and the rationing procedures. By the time it was over, she'd charmed
the crowd out of its rage, why, none of them would have hurt so much as a
hair on her head! But that's not the best part."

He shook his head in wordless admiration.

"The best part is that she did something! Two days later the extra tax was
dropped. A week later, rumor had it that the gardens of Imarus were burning
up. In another week, the city's reserves were full to bursting. She's someone
to reckon with, is Lady Lillas."

When a sudden noise drew his attention, he peered into the milling
crowds. Jumping to his feet, he folded the now dry handkerchief and replaced
it in his pocket.

"There she is now! Lady Lillas, her mother, the Aeson, and Lord Seth. You spoke the truth, prophet. They're heading this way and no mistake!"

Lukash's request for the slaver's help in identifying the Aeson's carriage proved unnecessary. Screams and shouts announced his presence as clearly as trumpets and tympani. Hurriedly, Lukash mounted a few more steps, and from that vantage point, marked the carriage's approach. An escort of uniformed guards led the way, their leather vests appliquéd with the fist of Agave, their iron helmets and nose guards reflecting the harsh sunlight and causing dapples of light to dance over the tumultuous crowds. They did not so much pass through the crowd, as lead it toward Lukash. His first few speeches were ill-attended, unheard by anyone not directly in front of him as he strove to project his voice over the never-ending din of the marketplace. Lately the crowds had grown, and with them, his confidence. Today would be the largest group of all, several hundred following the Aeson to view the prophet some called mad.

At the signal of an uplifted hand, the carriage halted, allowing Lukash a good view of its occupants. With a single piercing thought, he commanded Charis' attention. After her initial shock of recognition, for he was greatly changed even if she was not, relief and then thanksgiving flashed across her features. Now he had eyes only for the girl. The moment he saw her, her head thrown back in laughter at some jest thrown up to her from the crowd, her hand rewarding the jester with a spray of coins, he knew he looked on the future.

"Have you a name, stranger?"

An older man with a stately bearing addressed him, his voice that of one born to command and accustomed to instant obedience.

Lukash smoothed his robes, readying himself.

"No name of importance."

By refusing to employ an honorific, Lukash earned the older man's enmity. No matter, thought Lukash. I speak not to him, but to the girl.

"I am the Aeson of Agave. Do you know what that means?"

"Titles of this world are not my concern. I speak of another world, where titles will be of little use."

A ginger-haired man seated directly across from the Aeson spoke up, his pale, cold eyes glittering with suspicion and distrust.

"Where exactly is this other world? Pelion, perhaps?"

"You name Pelion, not I. The world I speak of exists not in another place, but another time, and that time approaches. For that reason I have come, to make clear the path to all that is promised."

Lukash was warming to his task. As the Eighteenth Mother promised, the words came easily. Opening the passages of his chest and throat, he let his breath flow freely, feeling the resonances of his voice in his forehead and cheekbones. The crowd began to quiet as he spoke, the chaos of Agave hushed by the presence of a single man. As the power grew within him, he began using the Voice, sending out his message on a grand scale, the crowd hearing his words with minds as well as ears.

"As was promised long ago, the path to blessings unimaginable is open to all. Agave must join in the transformation of humanity. Are there any among you who thirst for freedom, for knowledge, for a gift of untold worth freely given?"

A raucous cry interrupted him.

"The only thing I thirst for is water!"

Rough laughter and shouts of agreement threatened his concentration until, without warning, and with no effort on his part, another presence joined him in the marketplace. The words forming on his lips were not ones he had rehearsed. Even as he pronounced them, he recognized the weighty sound of prophecy. His role of prophet was no longer a sham.

"Then your thirst shall be quenched! And this shall be a sign unto you. As you thirst, so shall the waters rise. The staff lifts, falls, and lo, the earth rumbles and shakes. Brooks, streams, lakes and rivers shall be as nothing to the force of this fountain, and from its bounty, all may drink. And all will drink, for Agave shall be translated!"

With no thought but to obey the presence that drove him, a prophecy directed to all became focused on the girl, who rested her chin lightly on her hands, her eyes bright with interest, and more importantly, belief.

"Let nothing hinder you! No tie, no pledge, no duty, however strong, must prevent the seeking of the gift. Trust my words and begin the journey. All who seek will find!"

As Lukash drew his next breath, he realized the presence had disappeared. A moment ago he was a fearless, divinely-inspired prophet. Now he was simply Lukash, an elderly man grown tired of life.

A sharp gesture from an uplifted hand drew his attention back to the Aeson's carriage. At that moment, an arrow pierced his throat. Choking for lack of air, gagging on his blood, Lukash was falling, tumbling headlong down the steps to rest on sandy soil.

In the final moments of his life, he looked up, past the blur of faces gazing down at him, toward the blue-white haze of the summer sky. Everything grew white and blessedly silent, the crowd milling around him, their mouths working, producing no sound, the color leeched from their faces, their garments bleached bone-white by the fierce summer sun.

Somewhere beyond that vast complexity of whitened silence, Selena waited, ready to guide him to the place where she dwelt. Eager for an end so as to achieve a new beginning, Lukash turned away from the waking world, offering up his last and greatest gift to the city he loved.

Chapter 5

Flight

"I TELL YOU I saw Seth signal the archer! Why won't you believe me, mother? And why do you defend him? You know what Seth is!"

"I never said I doubted you. I said that you must leave this accusation alone. Have you mentioned it to your father?"

It was late, long after the evening meal. The girl was beginning to tire, for the prophet's murder touched her deeply. For all her bravado, Lillas was a true innocent, having never witnessed death before.

Charis held her breath, knowing the importance of the girl's reply. To Charis alone the Aeson confessed his opinions and judgments. She knew he thought his nephew's behavior despicable; so far he'd been able to hide his repulsion from everyone but her. If Lillas made her charge public, the resulting split among the family would upset the fragile balance of their world and put Lillas in danger.

Surely, surely, Charis prayed, her daughter had not been so rash as to openly accuse Seth of the prophet's murder! She harbored no doubt that Seth initiated the killing, just as she was convinced that the archer, having fulfilled his duty, lay dead or dying, thrown into a side street with the rest of the city's trash. Though she might hate Seth and his vicious mother, she never underestimated their capacity for cruelty. For Charis understood, as few did, that although the father of her child might bear the title, the power of the Aeson rested not in a single man, but in a group of tightly-woven and highly inbred families. The women of these families might be barred from holding the actual title of Aeson, but Charis had seen first-hand the power they wielded, none more dangerous than Scarphe, the current Aeson's elder sister. The Aeson came to power through an intricate plot of bargains and treacheries that even now, thirty years later, he refused to discuss with Charis.

Lillas didn't know that her birth rocked the family to its foundations. Had her child been a son, Charis was certain he would never have lived past infancy. Charis' announcement of her pregnancy was greeted with cold-hearted disbelief, the bloodied cloths of her first joining combined with her careful observances that she never allowed herself to be alone with any man other than the Aeson, eventually persuaded them of the child's rightful parentage.

In time, she came to understand the Seventeenth Mother's insistence that she select her foodstuff from the palace kitchens and prepare and eat her meals in private. Hiding the reason for her actions with the excuse of a delicate digestion, she selected her food and drink from the common stores. In the days directly following Lillas' birth, when the Aeson was so deliriously happy with her and the child that he could not bear to leave her chambers for a moment, she was finally forced to eat food prepared by other hands. That there was no second child was proof of what had been done to every woman who had ever lain with the Aeson. Charis' menses returned in time, long after she weaned Lillas, but were never regular again, coming and going without warning, marked sometimes by light spotting, sometimes by a heavy flow. Someone was determined that the Aeson not sire a son. It took little insight to identify that person as Scarphe, the mother of Seth.

That there had never been an attempt on Lillas' life puzzled Charis not a whit. She saw Scarphe's eyes latch onto her daughter in the first few months after her birth, watching her beneath lowered eyelids, hatching her plots. A simpler mind might have killed the unwanted offspring; Scarphe's plan was a thousand times more subtle. Let the girl grow, her eyes proclaimed as they followed the infant's progress, and let her be joined to Seth. Whether she be declared free-born by her doting father matters not. Once my brother is dead, I will rule through my son. If the girl is biddable, we will control her and gain support through a dynastic marriage. If not . . . well, the mother remains a slave, and though she and her daughter are well-known in Agave, there are other dealers . . . other towns . . . .

This was the burden of horror carried daily in Charis' heart. As Lillas replied, relief flooded her.

"Not yet. I thought I'd speak with you first, then go to him in the morning."

"Considering our earlier disagreement, I'm surprised you're speaking to me at all."

"I . . . I thought you might want to make up our quarrel. Anyway, father's busy with protests from some of the prophet's followers and wouldn't appreciate being disturbed."

Despite her upbringing in a place of secrecy and deceit, Lillas' lies lacked grace or fluidity. Her falsehoods might be brilliantly devised; to her mother's practiced eyes, her execution left much to be desired.

"Come, Lillas. Sit here beside me."

The girl plopped down on the bed, crossing her legs and resting her chin on her hands. At her age, Charis had been schooled in grace and moved as lithely as a dancer. All knees and elbows, Lillas was better suited to running than walking, and never wore skirts unless her father demanded it.

Gathered silk pants suited her best, drawing attention to her slim waist and long legs. She was playing with toes that peeked out of her bejeweled sandals, tracing each one with her index finger, a game she played from childhood and one that never failed to bring a smile to her mother's lips. Hardening herself against such feelings, Charis went to work.

"Daughter, tell me truly why you came. You know as well as I do that your father would interrupt any meeting, no matter how important, at the simple mention of your need for him. What keeps you from accusing your cousin?"

The forefinger joined its companions, forming a fist. The girl spoke without raising her eyes.

"I'm . . . afraid of Seth."

"As well you should be."

Surprised by Charis' response, Lillas looked up. Taking advantage of her surprise, Charis pushed on. If Lillas was to choose, let her chose as Charis had chosen, with perfect freedom to say no.

"Why do you fear him?"

Frowning, her color rising, Lillas chewed her lip.

"I'm not sure. No matter how badly I treat him, he never retaliates, never speaks a word against me. But . . . but he has a way of looking at me sometimes, as if he . . . as if he was promising himself a future reward for being civil."

"What do you think that future reward might be?"

"I don't know."

Shrugging, Lillas turned away. Charis caught her by the shoulders and turned her around, willing her to look up. Sullenly, her daughter obeyed.

"You know, Lillas. You've always known. It's time to say it aloud. What is to be Seth's reward?"

"Marriage to the Aeson's daughter?"

"Yes, Lillas, yes! And once he has you, every jibe, insult, and accusation will be held against you and used to punish you every day of your life. That's the reason you fear him and the reason you must remain mute. Up to now, your youth has protected you from serious harm. Soon there will be no such excuse."

The girl freed herself with a sudden jerk and bounded to her feet, her hair swinging around her shoulders, her eyes aflame.

"Father will never make me marry him! He loves me more than anyone! More than he loves you!"

The spiteful nature of Lillas' words covered her own hurt, but still they stung. Charis had no time for self-pity. In the fraction of a moment that the prophet's gaze met hers she had finally received permission to set in motion the final phase of her mission. The years had not dimmed the memories of those long sessions in the tower chamber with the Seventeenth Mother. She must guide without seeming to do so, for though Lillas might be part of a larger plan, she was not a pawn to be manipulated or sacrificed. She must come to them willingly, actively, or not at all.

"If that is so, do you think he'll allow himself to leave this earth without his daughter being properly cared for? Do you think he'll run the risk that you, his darling child, might lose her free-born status the day after his death? Remember, he's the only thing that stands between you and the shackles on the block."

Stupefied by her mother's harshness, Lillas' mouth worked, although no sounds emerged.

"Tell me, Lillas! Tell me how your father can prevent this marriage! Will another prince come calling for the Aeson's daughter? Even if he does, can you imagine how long he will live? Is there another man with whom you would mate? Is there, anywhere in this entire palace, a man who would long survive marriage with Lillas, the favorite child of Agave?"

"Mother, what are you saying?"

The look of growing horror on her daughter's face proved that she had never extended the argument this far. She knew instinctively that Seth wanted her; she had never thought to explore the extent of his desire.

"I'm saying what you know to be true. Seth wants you; thus, your choices are limited. If you want to remain free-born, a right only a parent or a spouse can extend to the offspring of a slave, you must marry a free-born man before your father's death. If you marry in Imarus, your mate must be Seth and no other."

Lillas stood as if carved from the same pink marble of the palace. Quarried by the wretched slaves who lived and died in the pits that pocked the surface of Agave's southern provinces, the satiny sheen of the cold stone was oftentimes stained by their blood when it finally reached the buyer. Lillas lived her life among slaves whose lives depended on granting her every wish. Now her mother told her a truth so horrible that for a moment she couldn't grasp it. Gradually, she started to breathe again.

"There's another way, mother. There must be."

She's desperate now, thought Charis. Yet I must be as cruel with this choice as I was with the other. I must not let her run blindly into yet another trap.

"What other way do you see?"

"I . . . I could leave here . . ."

"Let's suppose you could leave Imarus without your father's permission or knowledge. How long do you think it would take him to find you? You boasted to me of his love for you. Is your love for him such that you could disappear without a trace, knowing that you must never see him or communicate with him again? For if you do, if you weaken even once, every power he commands will track you to the ends of the earth."

Lillas' face spoke her misery. Her love for her father was the sole evidence of the tender nature hidden beneath her restless spirit and easy arrogance.

Charis watched her weigh her choice, trying to find the fulcrum point on which to balance her freedom, her love for her father, and her hatred of Seth. Charis' heart told her it was too difficult a choice for one so young, yet there was little time to spare.

"Yes, mother. I can do what must be done."

So many times Charis had rocked Lillas to sleep, watching her face soften under the sweet influence of childish dreams, and wondered about the woman she would become. Her ways might still be those of an over-indulged child, but the slim girl who stood before her was moving slowly toward womanhood. Charis took her into her arms and together they sank onto the ottoman, staring at the reflection of mother and child surrounded by the glowing orbs of the candles. Charis spoke to the reflection, resting her pale cheek against the tawny one of her daughter.

"Listen, child. Don't tell me when or where you're going. I must be able to tell your father everything that transpired here without self-reproach. Even as you must leave him, I must stay and care for the part of his love that remains."

Lillas blinked assent, her tears welling up against her will.

"Mother, will you tell me one thing before I go?"

"What is it, little one?"

"Why do you wear the collar?"

Charis smoothed the tangled hair.

"To remind him of his failure. One day you, too, will love . . . no, don't shake your head or mutter protestations. One day you will love. When you do, you'll understand why I can't forgive him."

"Forgive him for not freeing you? Surely he's afraid you might leave him."

Charis sighed.

"I can forgive him for being afraid. Everyone has fears, myself included. What I cannot forgive is his refusal to overcome those fears. Until he does, I cannot give him the greatest gift I am capable of giving."

"What is that, mother?"

"The love of a woman instead of the purchased affection of a slave; such love as he has never known."

Wrapping her arms tightly around her mother's waist, Lillas settled into her lap, burying her head between Charis' breasts. Ever so softly, she whispered her confession, her voice muffled against the silk of Charis' gown.

"I'm sorry for what I said this morning."

"Love often says hurtful things. True love forgives."

"I always seem to say the wrong thing."

Even as she answered, Charis sensed that this would be the most difficult lesson for her headstrong child to learn.

"One day you'll feel the pain of your words in your own heart. Then you'll know the awful power of words spoken in haste."

Again, Lillas spoke, her breath warm against the breasts that had nursed her:

"Mother, I'm afraid."

"I, too, am afraid. Afraid for what you will face outside the palace walls. Afraid for your father when he finds you gone. Afraid for my life without you. But, Lillas . . ," two liquid pools of indigo blue lifted to regard her, ". . . I tell you what you know inside yourself. I believe in you, in your strength and courage, and the loving heart you keep hidden so well. I also believe that what you seek, you will find."

As Charis held her daughter, she found solace in the prophet's words. It had come so unexpectedly, this call from the south, yet she did what she had agreed to do, preparing her daughter for what lay ahead. Now she must wait, praying that the vision of the woman in black was true, and that Lillas would somehow find her way to the one who had named her.

BRIGHT STARLIGHT CAST weird shadows through the trees, spilling their patterns over the marble hallways, muting their daytime splendor and rendering their well-known pathways slightly menacing. Before Lillas left her chamber, she removed her sandals, a childhood trick that stood her in good stead when she sought to avoid the prying ears and eyes of the court. The marble was refreshingly cool against the soles of her feet, for the late summer night seemed no cooler than the day. She was wet all over, her hair plastered to the back of her neck. I wish I had time to bathe before I go, she thought.

Taking the steps two at a time, she ran down them as quickly as she could, enjoying the fact that her heart was racing, feeling the blood pumping into her arms and legs. She was delighted with her body's response to her ever-increasing demands. Every day she ran, rode, and hunted, going barefoot as often as she dared, trying to toughen her feet. These midnight runs around the inside of the palace walls were doubly treasured since they were the only time she was free from observation.

Secrecy had become Lillas' new religion.

In the first few days after the prophet's death she'd become morose over her decision, fretting over her mother's logic, trying to find another way out of the trap. Reconciling herself at last to the only choice left to her, she decided to approach her escape as a game and made her plans accordingly. She was alone in the universe, the only one who knew that her smiles and considerate behavior around Seth and his spiteful mother were meant to gull them, the only one who knew that she was saying goodbye even as she overheard comments about her new-found maturity. Her mother was a master of dissembling, causing Lillas to remind herself sometimes that the conversation in her chambers had ever occurred. Never betraying a single change of feeling, Charis continued to nag Lillas for her poor grooming and lack of grace, dismissing her from her presence yesterday when Lillas used a word too filthy even for Charis' open-mindedness. Far from being distressed by her mother's seeming indifference, Lillas was lost in admiration. This was the mother she had never appreciated—dignified, resolute, unbreakable. And then there was the reassurance that these same qualities would soothe the rapidly-approaching heartbreak of her father.

Try as she might to retain her pleasure in the game, it was almost impossible to play it with him. As a result, she was forced to avoid his company. Worst of all, he was beginning to sense the change in her. Day after day he suggested an activity for them to share, something she used to plan her life around. Now she was increasingly capricious; refusing one offer to accept another. She knew she walked a dangerous path but she wanted to spare him, and hoped that memories of her thoughtless behavior might soften the blow of her departure, a departure that was almost upon her.

She slowed from a run to a dog-trot, walking the last stretch that led to her apartments. Her heart gave a surge as she saw the candles' glow through the sheers of fabric that covered the floor-to-ceiling windows of her sleeping chamber. Phoron must have lit them before he retired, old watchdog that he was, always careful of her safety.

She wondered sometimes how she'd managed before Phoron's arrival. Since childhood she'd had nurses and slaves aplenty and despised most of them as half-wits and grovelers. When her father informed her that he'd purchased a bondsman for her, she'd resisted with every argument at her disposal. For once, he'd overruled her, stating unequivocally that this man was not just another slave, but a schooled herbalist, and thus could serve as tutor and healer. This made her hate him all the more, for she was never ill and had successfully outmaneuvered every tutor ever assigned to try to make her memorize useless facts and old dead ideas. From the first, Phoron made it clear that he had other things to occupy his time that were more interesting than trying to force knowledge into an empty head. Miffed by his attitude, she outlined a few necessary duties and left him strictly alone.

As time passed, he carved a niche into her life. Now, almost three years later, she'd come to depend on him for almost everything. Phoron selected her body slaves, planned her menus, saw to all her needs, and managed every household detail, leaving her apartments clean, well-cared for, and free of the gossip, ill-will, and rancor that seemed to plague so many other apartments in the palace. It was Phoron who convinced her father that night guards were necessary both at the entrance of her chambers and to patrol the surrounding grounds. When a third cousin was kidnapped from within the palace walls, her fourth finger sent to her family along with a ransom demand, Lillas had been grateful for Phoron's forethought and her father well-pleased with his purchase. The result was the reduction of Phoron's bond from seven to five years.

Yet none of these things forged a link of mutual regard between them. That came in the first year of Phoron's arrival. She tested his will, he tested her compassion, and once satisfied with the result, they settled down to a fast friendship.

THEIR FIRST SPARRING match was brief, but brutal. Returning from a hunt, she'd been in a foul mood, her temper shortened by a fractious hawk that wouldn't rise to the lure. Stripping off her sweat-soaked garments, she asked, called, then screamed for Phoron, the other servants crouched and shivering face-down on the floor in the face of her rage. Finally, the bravest of the group confessed that Phoron could be found in the palace gardens, at which time Lillas exploded. Grabbing the first piece of clothing that came to hand, she stalked to the gardens that backed up to her apartments, finding him digging in the dirt. Without giving him time to acknowledge her presence, his arms still elbow-deep in sandy soil, she attacked.

"When I call for you, no matter what you are doing, you are to attend me immediately!"

He assessed her from head to toe, raising a dirty forefinger to scratch his nose.

"Is it your custom to leave your apartments in such a state?"

Looking down, she realized that her bathing robe barely met in the front and was almost transparent in the bright afternoon light. Flustered, she pulled it shut, becoming even more incensed when he chuckled and went back to digging.

"Don't tell me you didn't hear me! My windows open onto the gardens and I was screaming as loudly as I could."

"I heard you. I'm sure the entire palace heard you."

Incredulous that a direct order had been purposefully disobeyed, her mouth hung agape. With a self-satisfied smirk, he moved further down the row.

"Why didn't you come when I called for you?"

This time he didn't even bother looking at her.

"Because I'm doing something more important than tending to your whims."

"Digging in the dirt is more important than your duties to the Aeson's daughter? Those are dangerous words from a newly-purchased slave. I don't think my father will appreciate them."

Ever so slowly, Phoron leaned back on his haunches, brushing away some gnats that sought the moisture of his sweat. He was a medium-sized man, slightly overweight, with a pear-shaped body and a fringe of dark hair around a bald dome. She'd thought he was about to rise and follow her into her chambers until she saw his tightly-pursed lips. Black eyes snapping in anger, he let fly a scathing assault.

"Aren't you old enough to fight your battles on your own? Or must you hide behind your indulgent father, who's probably never seen the bad-tempered shrew who faces me now, angry for no other reason than her own spite? And to answer your question, yes, digging in the dirt, planting herbs that might save a life, is certainly more important than heeding your selfish commands."

Lillas couldn't breathe. No one, free-born or slave, had ever spoken to her so harshly, but the real surprise was that this servant, this non-entity, had the power to wound her. Burying the hurt, she moved quickly to retaliate.

"What makes you think I'd deign to fight a battle with you, a man who may be twice my age, but obviously doesn't have the sense necessary to remain a free man. What made you sell yourself into seven years of bondage, Phoron? What, no quick answer? Let me guess: you gambled away your profits? Or killed one patient too many with a lethal dose and had to pay a fat fine to a grieving family?"

For a moment she was afraid she'd gone too far, for he rose to his feet and took a few steps toward her, his fists clenched.

"What would a chit like you know of poverty, or grief, or anything else, for that matter?"

Unclenching his fists, he considered her for a moment, and then stooped down to pick up a spade and a clay jar. When he straightened, he seemed cleansed of anger.

"What do you require of me, princess?"

His quick adjustment threw her off balance, and in that moment, she knew he'd won, for she'd wanted nothing from him other than his attention, and she couldn't think quickly enough to concoct a lie. A rush of color suffused her. He raised an eyebrow, his point proved, and headed toward her apartments.

As Lillas moved to follow him, she stumbled over something lying in the dirt. With a quick curse, she regained her balance, discovering as she did so the cause of her near upset. In a woven basket she had kicked to its side lay tiny clay pots, each with a fragile shoot pushing up from dark soil. Scattered on the sandy soil were paper packets marked by lettering. Seeing the evidence of his work with her own eyes, her conscience stabbed her, its pangs making her angry again. Why should she feel guilty? And why was she letting him have the last word?

"Phoron, come here!"

Stopping in mid-stride, he turned, a trifle reluctantly, she decided, and walked back to her. Indicating the basket, she put her hands on her hips.

"I don't remember seeing an accounting for this expenditure in the household books. Did you steal them?"

His nostrils flared, but his temper held.

"The plants were a gift from the garden of an apothecary. I bought the seeds."

With that, he knelt down and righted the basket, stacking the seed packets into a neat pile.

"How did you pay for them?"

"Perhaps you're unaware of the fact that I'm often called upon to treat the slaves who live here. Their masters pay me out of gratitude."

Curiosity got the better of her and she found herself kneeling beside him, examining the plants, for all of them were unknown to her. Perhaps some interest on her part would bring him around. After all, open dissension would make life in her household distinctly uncomfortable and such a ploy had served her many times in the past.

"What's this one?"

"Coltsfoot, which cures a cough."

"And this?"

"Foxglove, for the heart."

"How do you prepare them?"

A half-smile crossed his lips, turning almost immediately into a mocking grin.

"Have you five years to devote to learning the answer? That is the price to be paid for the herbalist's art. Forgive me if I doubt your dedication to such a task."

Displeased that her efforts at peacemaking had been so completely rebuffed, Lillas rose.

"Finish you work here, bondsman. Perhaps we were both at fault in this matter."

Expecting him to offer his apology in return, she waited in vain.

"As you wish, lady."

It was not until several hours later that she realized how completely he'd controlled the situation. In a single encounter she had been informed in no uncertain terms that he would not be bullied, that there were higher priorities than her wishes, and that he could see through her attempts to manipulate him. Added to this was the fact that he achieved his goal by continuing to work in the garden, and never retracted his insults. There could be no misapprehensions on her part; Phoron was the victor of the first match.

They settled into an uneasy peace; Phoron cool, efficient, and obedient as long as she made no unreasonable demands; Lillas countering his behavior with casual disregard. A short time later, in the dead moons of winter, the final battle was fought.

LILLAS WAS AN early-riser, but that morning she was awakened long before her usual time by odd, repeated sounds that finally pulled her out of sleep and into consciousness. Although several things could have explained the sounds, her first thought was the shutters. Built with high ceilings and large windows, the palace was designed to insure coolness during even the hottest days of summer. During the winter, the windows were covered by wooden shutters that banged if they were not latched properly. Lying among the warm bedclothes, it was tempting to call for her body servant, who slept with the other slaves on pallets in an adjoining room. Sighing, she crawled out into the frigid night air and scampered across the room, cursing the marble floors that quickly turned her bare feet to ice.

Reaching the nearest window, she heard the sounds again. Now fully awake, she decided there was something human about them. With a grunt of pure disgust, she belted a quilted robe around her waist, shoved her feet into fur-lined slippers, and padded out of her chamber and into the adjoining room, sure that one of the slaves was having a nightmare. Not pausing to light the candle at her bedside, she pulled aside the heavy drape covering the doorway, peering through the gloom at the sleeping forms huddled together for warmth. A moving light caught her eye, a figure moving out of the room, heading for the storage rooms and pantry that lay to the rear of her apartments. Deciding that someone else had been awakened by the noise, she picked her way carefully over and around the slumbering bodies, following the candle into the hallway.

The sounds were louder now, and more distinguishable: a repeated series of words punctuated by moans. The light disappeared. She stood uncertain as how to proceed until she heard Phoron's voice emanating from a small storage room at the back of the pantry where her meals were prepared and which served as a refractory for the slaves. Her slippers made no sound as she edged nearer the doorway, listening through the rough cloth covering the opening.

"Hush! You must be quiet. You're safe now, do you understand? Safe. Drink this. It will help you sleep."

A deep sigh was followed by a strangled cough and another moan.

"Breathe deeply and push away all other thoughts. Let the potion work and soon you'll sleep."

Phoron had never sounded so tender. He spoke softly but firmly, repeating the same message with slight variations, the hypnotic rhythm of the words making Lillas' eyelids increasingly heavy. A slight rustle of movement brought her to attention and the fabric was pushed aside.

"How can I assist you, princess?"

His tone was deceptively mild. Unwilling to face his angry eyes, she looked down to the tray held between his hands. A squat candle sat in a pottery bowl. By its light she could identify a tin cup, a small glass bottle, a porcelain jar, a large basin filled with some unidentifiable liquid, and a rag.

"I was awakened by a peculiar sound. I came to investigate."

After pulling the curtain securely shut behind him, Phoron brushed past her to place the tray on the wooden block that served as a counter.

"It's nothing to be concerned about. A slave is ill;" he shrugged, "I treat him."

Pulling out the slop jar from beneath another table, he poured the contents of the basin into it, then rinsed the basin with fresh water from a jug.

"Which slave?"

She thought he hesitated for a moment, but perhaps she was mistaken, for he continued swirling the fresh water around the edges of the basin until that, too, was poured into the slop jar.

"No one of enough consequence to merit your attention."

The insult stung. She might have departed then and there if she hadn't spied the rag. He must have moved it closer to the candle when he picked up the basin, for she could see it clearly now, stained the rusty color of blood. Watching her make her discovery, Phoron's expression became inscrutable.

"It's a serious injury?"

A grudging nod was her answer. Why was he being so closed-mouthed? She might not be the most concerned of owners, but she had never harmed a slave and was always careful that they be well-fed and treated for any illness. Irritated by his secrecy, she headed for the cloth-draped door.

"Don't do it, princess. It's for your protection as well as for the one inside."

She could hear the honesty as well as the intensity of his warning. Returning to the kitchen, she pulled up a stool to the wooden block and settled herself on it.

"Who does the slave belong to, Phoron? Is he a runaway?"

"I'd never bring such danger into your household. He was purchased today in Agave."

What followed seemed extremely difficult for Phoron to say, the first and only time Lillas ever saw him at a loss for words.

"I bought him."

Her indrawn breath spurred him on.

"I was purchasing supplies in Agave when I saw him. I couldn't leave him as he was. You know I have a few coins, and the price was low because of his condition. Since he couldn't walk, I hired a cart and smuggled him in through the garden. I know he shouldn't be here, but there was nowhere else, and the other slaves promised to say nothing." A rueful smile crossed his face. "You need never have known, save the cold woke him."

Lillas felt the elation of victory. She had him at last. Even though the slave might be legally purchased, it was a crime to bring an unregistered slave into Imarus, and an act of theft to use her food, medicines, and supplies to house him. No longer need she put up with Phoron's insults and unsolicited comments on her behavior. With a single word to a palace guard, both Phoron and the slave would be sent to the quarries, the worst possible fate for any slave. Just then, she noticed the rag clenched in Phoron's fist.

"How badly is he hurt?"

"He was flayed. From his shoulders to his hips he's nothing but raw flesh. He can't bear the touch of a blanket."

For once, this self-assured man sounded helpless, a thought which gave her no pleasure.

"I've stuffed the window and covered his lower body, but still he shivers. If I can't get him warm, I don't know how much longer . . .," he continued with a bitter smile, ". . . how much longer I'll be a slave owner."

"What did he do to deserve such punishment?"

Phoron's gaze pierced her soul.

"Does it matter?"

She answered him as she was wont to do, not with words, but with actions. Pushing away the stool, she reached for a torch from a sconce on the wall and lit it with the candle. Handing it to Phoron, she turned next to the huge hearth and considered the wood box. She actually began to reach for a log before she remembered that she'd never laid a fire in her life.

"I'll wake Mia and tell her we need a fire and something warm to drink. Then we'll make a pallet and move him here in front of the fire." She gave a crow of triumph. "Maybe we could heat some stones, wrap them in cloth and place them around him! Would that help, Phoron?"

He stared at her open-mouthed, his look of astonishment rapidly transformed to one of admiration. The novelty of that expression gave her an unexpected glow of happiness. Her parents loved her, but she had never done anything to garner their respect. With a second flash of inspiration, she held out her palm to Phoron.

"Give me the bill of sale."

Digging in the pocket of his robe, he retrieved a folded piece of parchment.

"I'll have my father's secretary make the transfer tomorrow." She couldn't resist a dig at Phoron's expense. "What's your asking price?"

Chuckling, he shot back a quick rejoinder.

"Two hours each day, without interruption, to tend my garden."

"Done, Phoron."

She extended her hand. He took it firmly in his own.
"Done, Lillas."

WITH A STIFF nod, the night guard opened the door and ushered her inside.
Still barefoot, she tiptoed across the darkened foyer and into her chambers.
By now the servants were accustomed to her nightly runs; even so, she could
take no chance of waking them. Everything lay in wait for her nightly
toilette—sandalwood-scented steam rose from the bath, drying cloths were
in readiness, and the bedclothes had been pulled back. A gown of pale yellow
silk lay draped over an ottoman, jeweled sandals rested nearby. Lillas engraved
the picture on her mind, for this was what they would find when they woke
to find her gone. No sign of a struggle, no ransom demands, just a cool bath
and an empty bed. When her eyes filled, she blinked away her silliness. This
was no time for childishness; dawn would break in seven hours. She must
be far from the palace before her unexplained absence caused chaos in the
miles surrounding Imarus.

Kneeling beside the enormous bed with its silken drapes, she extended
a hand beneath the frame, finding the dirt-stained bundle she'd retrieved
from its hiding place in the garden this afternoon. Pulling it out from beneath
the bed, she untied the fastenings and removed a pair of rough-textured
breeches, a large, ill-made blouse, a leather jerkin, belt, and a knitted cap.
She'd found the clothing wadded in a ball and buried in the back of a little-used
storage room, probably the cast-off clothing of a newly purchased slave.
Packets of cheese, dried meat, and bread had been pilfered when Mia wasn't
looking. Proper footgear was her main concern (for she herself owned only
sandals and kidskin riding boots unfit for desert travel), until she'd remembered
the thick-soled boots Phoron kept with his gardening supplies. Heavy-set
as he was, he was no taller than Lillas and his feet were very nearly her size.
Hers were much narrower, but with several pairs of stockings, his boots
would serve until she could reach a market and purchase a pair of her own.
The thought of stealing from him tickled her. Phoron would appreciate the
joke of Lady Lillas running away in her bondsman's boots.

Stripping off her clothes, she considered her silken undergarments. Not
only had she never thought of procuring anything to wear underneath the
scratchy trousers and blouse, she had no idea what was customarily worn
under such clothing. Troubled, she ran her fingers over the smooth, satiny
finish of her camisole. Interrupted by the sound of Phoron's heavy tread,
she flipped the bedclothes over the contents of the pack, shoved the boots
under the bed, and faced the doorway with what she hoped was a cool,
self-contained smile.

There was no answering smile on his face. He hadn't donned his sleeping garments, proof that he hadn't retired at his usual time. Too late, she remembered her state of undress. Still, modesty in front of servants had never been a concern of hers, and after all, she should by rights be preparing for her bath. Some problem must have arisen during her absence for him to await her return.

"What is it, Phoron?"

"I see you're ready to leave."

Nothing he said could have so quickly punctured her confidence. Now he would ruin everything. Dismay was quickly replaced with resolve that nothing and no one would sway her from her plan. She would go tonight, must go tonight, for she couldn't face another day of lies and subterfuge.

"Nothing you do or say will make me change my mind. And if you call the guards, I'll . . . I'll . . . "

Unable to think of a dire enough threat, she sputtered to a halt.

"I shan't try to stop you," he said. "I came to say goodbye."

Moving aside the silken sleeping robe, he lowered himself onto the ottoman, which wheezed a complaint at his weight. He seemed to gather his thoughts for a moment, his hands clasped together between his knees, before regarding her with a troubled frown.

"Surely you're not going to wear those," he gestured toward her undergarments, "that is, if you hope to pass as a man."

Frowning back at him, she decided to ask for his help. He'd made it clear he wouldn't try to stop her.

"I don't know what to do," she confessed, hating herself for whining but whining all the same. "That scratchy cloth will rub me raw and I've so many miles to walk. . . ."

"Take these." Reaching into an inside pocket of his outer robe, he produced several lengths of cotton fabric. When she made no move to take them, he shook his head in mock disgust, rolling his eyes heavenward, and heaved a sigh.

"You've no more sense than a turkey in a rainstorm! First, turn your back and take off your camisole." She moved quickly to obey, taking hold of the end of the strip of cloth he proffered. "Now, hold this over your breasts while I wrap."

"That's too tight! I can hardly breathe!"

"Better not to breathe than to be raped."

Issuing no more complaints, she did as she was told. Smiling and nodding, pleased with their progress, he waved the other piece of cloth under her nose.

"Time to learn how to wrap a loincloth."

Turning up her nose, she made a face at him. He was not amused.

"This is no time to be stubborn. If the disguise is to work, you've got to dress like a man and act like one as well. With your build, you should pass easily for a boy. As a boy, especially a pretty boy, no one will think it odd if you relieve yourself in private. The purpose of the loincloth is to make the breeches fit correctly."

Swallowing hard, she untied the drawstring of her briefs. Patiently, he showed her how to wrap the cloth around her hips and between her legs and tie it at her waist. Not satisfied with her first effort, he made her tie and untie it several times, offering suggestions as she worked.

"Better. Now put on the rest of it."

Flying to the bed, she retrieved the rest of the clothes. This time he showed her how to tuck the shirt in properly and adjust the collar over the jerkin. Stockings followed. Grunting, he retrieved his boots from underneath the bed, his lips pursed in feigned disapproval. Laughing, she pulled them on, fastened the belt, pulled the cap over her hair, stuffing the escaping tendrils inside, and turned for his approval.

Her hopes were quickly dashed by his woeful expression.

"What's wrong now?"

"Only that you look like a princess dressed like a beggar."

"Impossible!"

Her protest was barely out of her mouth before she ran to the glass on her dressing table, realizing that his assessment was depressingly accurate. The drab browns and olives of the fabric made her skin ivory-colored and smooth by means of contrast; the knitted cap did nothing to hide her hair, its weight stretching the cap down around her shoulders. Phoron's reflection appeared beside hers.

"Take off the jerkin and shirt and we'll do something about that skin of yours."

From another pocket appeared a rag and a small bottle. When he pulled the cork, an acrid scent escaped, making Lillas' sensitive nose twitch until she sneezed.

"It's a walnut stain that won't wash off in rain or when fording a stream. Rub it on your arms while I do your face and neck."

Slowly she was transformed. Once the dye was applied to her face, the only feature that seemed linked to her former self were her eyes, enormous blue pools of wonder as she assessed the stranger in the glass. One more thing was necessary and there was no need for Phoron to tell her what it was. Jerking the cap off, she began braiding the sun-bleached tangles into a single plait. The cold metal of the scissors against the back of her neck made her shiver. Phoron pressed the severed braid into her hand. She stood for a moment, regarding the last trace of her femininity, when Phoron spoke, his voice somewhat hoarse. If she hadn't known better, she would have thought he shared her sense of loss.

"Put it in your pack. If someone questions you, tell them it was your mother's. Even the roughest man remembers what it is to love a mother."

She'd been so busy with the pressing need of the disguise that she'd forgotten to ask him how he'd seen through her plans so completely. Her question was on her lips when her pack was shoved into her arms. Grabbing it, she held it close against her chest, feeling her heart pounding an endless repetition of the same phrase, "no more time," "no more time," "no more time."

"Don't worry. No one suspects. I found the pack by pure chance. When I came in to turn down the bedclothes, I noticed a trail of dirt disappearing under the bed. It didn't take long to figure out what you were planning."

Searching his face, she knew he wouldn't betray her.

"I left a note for my father. I won't tell you where it is. One of the slaves should find it later in the day. My hope is that until it's found, he'll think I'm playing some kind of prank, and so won't search much beyond Imarus. In the note, I ask him to give your bond to my mother. Since it's my only request, I think he'll grant it."

His eyes spoke his gratitude.

"You've water enough?"

She nodded, adding, "And I know where the wells are."

"What route do you take?"

"A hunting trail I've used many times before: Due east across the desert until I reach the scrublands."

When he nodded, but didn't ask about her final destination, she was glad. Her greatest fear was that Phoron might suffer because of what she did tonight.

"Listen, Lillas. The world is a dangerous place. Promise me you'll use this if the need should arise."

The handle of a knife jutted out of a leather sheath. He shoved it into the waistband of the breeches, taking care that it was hidden. Two hands gripped her shoulders; sad brown eyes spoke of the pain of parting. In that moment, she realized she was leaving the only friend she'd ever known.

Turning swiftly, refusing a sudden assault of tears, she slung the pack over her back, striding resolutely out of a world that had betrayed all her hopes. Somewhere there must be a place that offered more than slavery or Seth, and she, Lillas of Agave, was determined to find it.

SNUFFING OUT THE candles, Phoron moved quickly to the windows overlooking the garden, pulling aside the curtains to watch her slim, boyish figure stop at the corner of the palace wall, look right and left for the guard, run lightly across the dew-heavy grass, and scale the garden wall. She paused briefly at the top, looking back over her shoulder, before dropping out of sight.

Reluctantly, he left the window and checked the room, returning the bottle and cloth to his pocket, replacing the scissors to their accustomed position on the marble table. With her frightened face so clearly etched in his mind, it was difficult to attend to such mundane affairs, but the discipline of routine took over and he smoothed the bedclothes and carefully rearranged her gown on the ottoman.

The next few days would be a nightmare for the entire household. Every slave would be questioned and re-questioned; his interrogation would be the worst. Once the note was found, things would settle down, and he blessed her silently for easing his way. It took much longer than he thought to pierce her prickly exterior, for she had practiced the art of self-deception since childhood, a skill necessary to survive in this den of foxes. Once he found the compassionate heart beneath the insolent facade, she unfolded like an exotic flower under the care of a master gardener. He could say, with all honesty, that he had never known anyone like her. Quick-tempered, proud and judgmental, yet at the same time honorable and absolutely loyal to those she loved, she was a creature of violence and delight. "What will they make of her?" he wondered, before putting that thought carefully aside.

The open window lured him back again. As high-flying clouds sailed swiftly past indifferent stars, he pictured her in his mind, her long legs flying over hard sand. Security was tight on the road linking Imarus and Agave, a road Phoron traveled several days a week with a stamped pass inspected at guard posts along the way. Built far enough away from the city so its aristocratic inhabitants might survive a slave rebellion or an insurrection by Agave's citizenry, Imarus existed as a series of elaborate marble palaces surrounded by sandstone walls and protected by the Imarus Guard. As long as Lillas avoided the primary road and traveled by night, she should be relatively safe. Not until she reached the scrublands would she turn south toward the valley of the castle, south to the place the prophet promised would receive her. Phoron was unsurprised that Lukash had willingly sacrificed himself in the marketplace. He had done much the same thing himself, saying yes (despite a plethora of doubts) to the Eighteenth Mother's request that he infiltrate Imarus as a bondsman to a princess.

Closing his eyes, Phoron sent his thoughts searching out over those long miles to the south. A mind met his, the impatience of her thoughts nearly overpowering him. For three long years she had planned this night.

Without fanfare, Phoron announced: *"Make way for Lady Lillas."*

To which the Eighteenth Mother replied: *"We await the flame of Agave."*

Chapter 6

Rendezvous

CASTING HIS GAZE far to the west, squinting against shimmering waves of heat rising from sun-baked sand, the old man could just make out a moving shadow on the horizon. Judging the angle of the sun's rays, he figured the distance quickly, humming to himself at the welcome thought of guests for supper. A good meal was called for, and luckily, he'd snared a coney only that morning. Humming into his beard, he hobbled over to the cooking fire and began to spit the rabbit, first rubbing it with wild garlic, sage, and a precious pinch of salt. The salt was an afterthought, for he hoarded his spices, but the rules of hospitality demand that the wayfarer receive the best one can offer, and besides, he reasoned with himself, "What's life without a little salt?"

The rabbit skewered and hung over the fire, he trudged down to the stream with a tin bucket, scavenging the area for last minute additions to the meal. Wild onions were abundant, so he pulled a handful and thrust them into the huge pockets on his oft-patched leather vest. An overturned log near the stream yielded several edible mushrooms, and they, too, were consigned to his pockets. These were the scrublands just east of a long expanse of desert, and although they were fit only for the hardy, the stream offered life to all of nature's creatures. He'd settled here a few weeks ago and in that time he'd seen whitetail deer, a fox, pheasants, grouse, a variety of ground squirrels, rabbits, and mice. One particular mouse with a sharp nose for food and a friendly, if not very talkative, disposition became his main source of company. Human conversation would be a pleasant diversion.

A spring some miles to the north was close enough to ensure that the water was still cold by the time it reached his campsite. The bucket filled, he placed it on the bank, and rolling up the sleeves of his tattered blouse, wet his face and hands, sluicing water through his beard, and after a moment of sober consideration, scrubbed his ears. Shaking the droplets of water off with a few shakes of his head, he climbed back up to the campsite, settling onto a conveniently placed rock that allowed him to lean his back against the thin trunk of a cedar struggling to grow above the creosote bushes surrounding the small rise.

The shadow was more distinct now, moving steadily, if not swiftly, east. Afoot, he thought, which makes for thirsty work. Squint as he might, it was still impossible to make out how many would be dining this evening, but the rabbit was good-sized, and he still had a few dried figs, soft and mold-free, to serve as dessert. To pass the time, he decided to do something useful and, taking up his knife and a likely piece of wood, began to carve.

He sang a little ditty to himself, the notes true even if his voice was scratchy from disuse. The words were nonsensical, scraps of familiar phrases bound together in a simple melody that soon had his foot tapping and his knife flashing as the shavings flew over his breeches. In time, when his composition was complete, his voice grew more robust, and soon he was singing full-voiced:

> Tula-ma-rula, Tula-mu-lay,
> Cossets and mossets and fields of hay.
> Winsome and twosome, hide where you will,
> The cock's in the rafters, the lark's in the rill.
> Tula-ma-rula, Tula-mu-lay,
> Happy is he who is done for the day.

A voice over his shoulder continued the song:

> Tula-ma-rula, Tula-mu-lay,
> Say only the word and I promise to stay.

Lost in his song and his whittling, he'd been oblivious both to the passage of time and the stranger's approach. With a start that nearly upset him from his narrow perch, he turned to the singer, finding a young boy dressed in ragged dusty garments, his head covered by an ill-fitting knitted cap. The boy's smile faded, a wary look coming over him as his hands fiddled with his belt. Although no weapon was visible, there was something dangerous about those twitching fingers. Mastering his surprise, he was quick to greet his visitor, being careful to make no sudden move.

"Well met, stranger! And thank ye for the song!"

The boy's hands dropped from his belt. There was no spoken answer to his greeting, just the careful nodding of a head. Taking his guest's silence for shyness, the most likely course seemed to be to put him at ease.

"I'm called Timon, stranger. Who might ye be?"

"I'm Skat."

"Skat, is it now? And how does a strip of a lad like yerself come to be wanderin' the desert alone?"

The boy was comely and middling tall, though to Timon's mind a trifle thin in the shanks. Tanned by the desert sun, his bright blue eyes were in startling contrast to his brown-baked skin. At his question, those eyes narrowed and a slight frown creased his brow.

"I was part of a caravan until two days ago, but I . . . I thought it better to travel on alone."

Although the boy moved quickly to hide the slip of his tongue, Timon caught the lie in his eyes. He was concealing something, but Timon decided not to pursue it. Strangers must needs be wary of one another; such was the way of the world.

"Well, it's glad I am ye've come! There's a fat coney beggin' to be eaten, and it's a rare feast we'll be havin', that's for sure! Ye're welcome to pass the night, Skat, and I thank ye for the company. Two's always better than one in the wild lands."

At the mention of food, the boy licked his lips.

"My thanks, Timon, for your offer. My pack's light and I haven't had a hot meal in days."

"Then why are we standin' here? Wash up in the stream down the bank there, and I'll have everythin' ready afore ye can trim wool from a ewe!"

The last phrase was called out to the youth's disappearing back. Timon shook his head, muttering into his beard as he rose and hobbled to the fire.

"A lad alone in the wild lands! There's a story here, Timon, or ye've never cut hay as a cropper."

THE LAST BITE eaten, for the boy ate enough for three, Timon stoked the fire and settled down on his bedding. With a quick glance at his guest, who sat a little bit removed from him, hugging his knees with his forearms, Timon reached into a pocket and pulled out a thin clay pipe and a folded leather pouch of pipe weed. He'd been hoarding his tobacco and so hadn't had a good smoke in days, but a companion made the night seem festive, and there was nothing like a good smoke after a hearty meal.

Packing the pipe, he lit it, and soon a ribbon of smoke rose in a lazy spiral above his head. The boy removed his boots and was tracing his toes through the thick stockings, one of which had a large rent in the heel. His presence was companionable enough, but Timon wasn't satisfied. He'd had silence enough in the past weeks.

"There's a price to be paid for the dinner, lad. I've fed ye well. Ye owe me a story."

Startled, the boy looked up.

"I know no stories, old man."

Timon puffed for a moment, continuing in a more persuasive vein.

"Then tell me how ye come to be here. Yer halfway between nothing and nowhere, and its little company I get in such a place. It serves my needs, mind ye, but it's no place for the young." The boy's head drooped, his hands clenching his feet. "Come, lad! If it's a secret ye're hidin', Timon's not one for gossip, and sure, who'd I tell if I was?"

A half-strangled laugh was the boy's response. Raising his head and lowering his knees, he sat cross-legged on his blanket.

"Fair is fair. I'll give you my story for the meal, but I warn you, I'm not sure of the ending."

The boy threw his head back, looking up at the stars. The air was clear with a two-horned moon, and the fire seemed to rise high into the night sky, its flames reaching out like fingers yearning to touch its far-away friends gleaming coldly in the vast distances above.

"I . . . lost . . . my parents not long ago and decided to travel east across the desert. At first, I traveled alone. The third day I met a caravan and asked if I might join them."

When Timon nodded, the boy seemed to hesitate, looking askance at him as if doubtful of his understanding.

"At first it was fine, good, in fact, for they were generous with their water. But then . . . then one of them started . . . started to bother me. When I tried to avoid him, he . . . he . . . "

The boy brushed the back of his hand across his eyes. Timon interrupted.

"Say no more, laddie. You're a pretty one and men sometimes have feelings for other men. Some say it's wrong, but who's to say? Seems to me 'tis only wrong if t'other is na so inclined."

The boy nodded tiredly and Timon's voice lowered.

"Did he hurt ye, Skat?"

In a voice so faint Timon struggled to hear it, the boy whispered, "No."

"What did ye do, laddie?"

"Hit him on the head with a cooking pot."

At the description of such a violent act coupled with the meekness of the speaker, Timon chortled in delight.

"Did ye now? Here I'm thinkin' he's the one to blame when it's him I should be pityin'."

Roused by the old man's laughter, the boy was quickly on the defensive.

"He gave me no choice! It was either the cooking pot or my knife, and I, uh, I've never used a knife on a man before."

"It's my hope ye'll never have cause to do so. A sore head trumps a slit throat."

A few more puffs of smoke rose toward the heavens.

"And then what did ye do?"

"I grabbed my pack and ran. I don't know if he followed since I never looked back. I walked two days and a night and then I saw the smoke from your fire. I've never been so happy as when I heard your song."

"Aye, a song warms the heart as no words can."

The boy said nothing. Timon took his own suggestion and hummed to himself for awhile, enjoying the night. When a cicada began its whir, the boy jumped, emitting a surprised yelp. Timon shook his head in disbelief.

"The next thing ye'll be tellin' me is ye've never passed a night in the wilderness afore! It's only a cicada, lad, rubbin' its wings together before it mates and dies."

"I've been on the desert so long; I'm not used to the voices of the night. The desert is so quiet, just the sound of wind and sand."

"Well, Skat, if you're headin' south across the scrublands, there'll likely be more sounds than ye can count. Tree frogs, owls, and wolves all talk in the night."

The boy's eyes were round with fear.

"Wolves?"

"Aye, they hunt at night. Build a good fire and they'll not bother ye."

Gathering his blanket up around his shoulders, the boy settled down on the ground, pillowing his head on his arms.

"One thing ye've not told me, lad, although if it's a secret, ye need not satisfy the curiosity of an old hermit like me. Have ye any particular destination in mind?"

His voice dreamy and heavy with ensuing sleep, the boy replied:

"A place that comes to me in my dreams."

"Has it a name?"

His question hung unanswered in the night air. Soon he realized there would be none. The boy breathed the regular rhythms of sleep, his body curled in a tight ball. Timon rose quietly and banked the fire. Wrapped in his blanket, he hobbled away to settle himself on a rock overlooking the western desert.

"I'VE FOUND HER, or more accurately, she's found me."

The relief that flooded the mind he touched was profound. The patrol tracking the caravan discovered her absence at dawn two days ago. The Eighteenth Mother was frantic with worry, almost in despair, he thought, although she never revealed any details as to the girl's importance. But then, he'd had long years of experience with women who wore the black robes and was used to being told as little as was possible. Questions flew at him now and he struggled to answer as clearly as he could.

"How does she fare, Timon? Is she unharmed?"

"She sleeps now, well-fed and dreaming of Lukash's prophecy."

"Ah!"

That single syllable conveyed joy, hope, and renewed dedication.

"You needn't worry about this one, Mother. She's tired and lonely, but she's got a head on her shoulders and she's certainly able to defend herself."

Something of his wry tone must have communicated itself to her, for her next question contained an element of teasing.

"What role do you play this time? I've seen you perform, but always onstage with appropriate props and make-up."

Timon scratched his beard. It was a pleasant change to rely on nothing but his natural talents, although he'd chosen his costume with care, building his character from an amalgamation of many he'd played in his career.

"I'm Timon the hermit; short of breath, endowed with the gift of gab. I thought an elderly eccentric would do the trick, and so it has."

"Can you convince her to stay with you a few days and rest? She has twelve more days on the road, although an escort will pick her up soon after she leaves you. She must not lose heart."

"I've already planted a warning in her ear. I'll strike a bargain with her tomorrow that if she'll stay and keep me company, I'll teach her some skills of woodcraft, a safe route south, and help her refill her pack. I think she'll agree."

No individual words were used to express her gratitude; they came in a surge of heartfelt thanks.

"One question, if I may, Mother. If it's so important that she go to Pelion, why didn't a patrol simply pick her up outside Agave and bring her to you?"

The answer, when it came, was slow and deliberate.

"It's not enough that she be brought here. She must want to come. Her journey will help test her dedication to the task. I risk much with this decision, yet Lillas must find her own way. She values those things most which are difficult to achieve. If the path is too easy, she might spurn what lies at its end."

Even over the long miles between his lonely outpost and the valley of the castle, he could sense her determination.

"My thanks, Timon, for sharing the gift of your talent."

She was gone, leaving him suddenly and painfully alone. To share her thoughts, at any time and under any circumstances, brought true beauty to the soul, for she shared with each one who touched her mind a sense of something bigger, a view of the future, he guessed, although he was not one for speculations of that sort. Timon never mated, yet each time he touched and was touched by one who wore the black robes, he realized what he had missed, a realization that both inspired and saddened him. As an apprentice to the Guild of Players, a Master Teacher once told him that an actor played best when he connected certain parts of his character with the empty places inside him, for in that way the vulnerability and truth of the character would best be conveyed to an audience. It was easy to create this Timon for the boy Skat—he played the role of the father he would never be.

THE DAYS PASSED quickly as the old hermit taught Lillas the tricks of survival. Even though he was often testy with her, she came to understand that it was her ignorance that irked him. And she had never felt as ignorant, as completely at a loss. She'd hunted for years with her father and considered herself a good archer and an excellent falconer, but the stakes were different here: hunger or a full belly. No slaves beat the quarry toward her hunting party and no highly-trained hawk perched on her glove. Instead, she crawled on her belly to stalk the game, testing the wind repeatedly so her scent remained upwind of her quarry. Filthy and sore, she often returned with nothing more to show for her efforts than a new set of bruises on her aching knees and elbows.

Yet Timon took all her defeats in stride, patiently teaching her the most basic of lessons: how to use a flint, how to start a fire with green wood, the basics of cooking, camp maintenance, and how to dig out a splinter or treat a blister. She had always been a rebellious student, for she saw no reason to learn; now she was hungry for everything he could teach her. Never again need she find herself in the position of being beholden to anyone for anything. Timon's lessons were the price of her independence, and though she paid dearly for them with skinned knees and burnt fingers, nothing she had ever done matched her feeling of pride when she placed in front of him a meal hunted, gathered, cooked and served by her two hands.

Only one time did she displease him and, afterward, was unable to cajole him out of his black mood. They were gleaning the last of the summer's harvest one morning, moving with bent backs over the eastern bank of the stream, searching for anything edible among the thickets and brush. He'd just pointed out an empty pheasant nest, when without warning he forced her down onto the ground beneath a thorn bush and placed a horny hand over her mouth. He fell on her so hard the breath was knocked out of her. As she came up out of blackness, he whispered inches from her ear:

"Not a sound, laddie, if ye value yer skin."

Too stunned to move, she lay frozen underneath him, feeling his harsh breath against her cheek, smelling the raw onions he insisted on chewing after every meal, convinced they helped his digestion. She was tempted to ask him from whom or what they hid, but before she could form the words a threatening growl rumbled deep in his throat. As her heartbeat returned to normal, she closed her eyes, trying to concentrate on the sounds around her, identifying the swift flow of the stream and the buzz of insects swarming near its banks. Not until then did she realize that no birds sang. All was ominously still to the point that she almost screamed when a rough voice spoke up only a few feet from where they lay.

"Let them drink here. There'll be no more water until we reach the first well and that's ten miles into the desert."

The bushes crackled as someone passed through them, a large booted foot stepping within inches of her head. Holding her breath, she waited for them to be discovered, feeling Timon's entire body tense, his arm moving slowly across her back as he reached for the knife slung at his belt. Regardless of who it was that threatened them, he was primed to attack and to kill, something that frightened her far more than the sight of the boot or the harsh manner of the speaker.

From the northeastern edge of the bank came the tramping of many feet combined with the clanking of metal. The speaker, off to their left now, sounded bored and dispassionate.

"Drink quickly. Not a word or you'll feel the lash."

Water splashed. Occasional sighs of relief mingled with the sound of water being slurped from hand to mouth.

"No more or your bellies will cramp. Move out!"

A whip cracked and feet splashed obediently across the stream and up onto the western bank. As the sound of their footsteps receded and finally passed away, a single jay sent out the all clear. A few more heartbeats and the sounds of the scrublands continued undisturbed.

Timon rolled off her with a grunt and rose cautiously to his knees, keeping a warning hand on her shoulder. Satisfied of their safety, he leaned back on his haunches and began picking burrs and foxtails out of his beard. Lillas picked herself carefully out of the thorn bush, noting that her palms were scratched and bleeding, although she'd been unaware of their sting until this minute. Sucking on them to clean away the blood, she asked:

"Who were they, Timon?"

He shot her a look of pure disbelief, his thick grey eyebrows disappearing into a mat of tousled hair that strongly resembled the pheasant's abandoned nest.

"Who do ye ken they were, laddie? Ye heard the chains and the snap of the whip. Who do ye ken travels toward the desert and the god-forsaken city that lies beyond?"

"If you're referring to Agave," she replied pertly, "I don't see why it was necessary to nearly knock the life out of me. They may have been slavers but we are free-born and so have nothing to fear."

Gnarled hands stopped grooming his beard. He considered her for a long moment, squinting his eyes into slits and pursing his lips.

"It seems I must beg yer pardon, Skat. Dolt that I am, I'd no idea ye were so worldly wise in the ways of slavery! Humor me if ye will, laddie, and tell me who ye ken those slaves to be?"

Lillas answered without really having to think. Her father explained all of this to her years ago.

"The slave population is made up of equal measures of ne'er-do-wells, criminals, and those who, for some reason or another, must sell themselves into bondage in order to pay creditors. Slavery is highly regulated in Agave. Few slaves, if any, receive less than humane treatment."

"Ah!" Pausing, he fingered the knife in his sheath. "Is it humane treatment, do ye ken, to cut out tongues if a noble needs a mute, or to castrate if a eunuch must be had? What ken ye of women forced to breed children for profit? Or girls of twelve, stripped and examined to certify their virginity, then sold into brothels?"

Lillas sat mute and uncomfortable, but Timon was only beginning.

"Would ye believe me, Skat, if I told ye that if we'd been discovered, a young boy would have joined the line while an old man would have breathed his last? Ye're free-born, ye tell me, with shinin' eyes and a juttin' chin, but how could ye prove it? After five days in chains, the sun beatin' down, your thirst so great ye'd sell yer mother for a drink, yer back achin' from the kiss of the slaver's lash, do ye ken ye'd be able to convince anyone ye were born proud and free?"

Such a thing was impossible. Her father ruled Agave and would never allow the cruelties Timon described. How dare this old hermit try to frighten her? He really must be put in his place, once and for all. With a wave of her hand, she dismissed him as the garrulous fool he was.

"You can't know that! Maybe a few slavers are unprincipled or unnecessarily cruel, but all this sounds like so much gossip."

The old man's tongue could have etched glass.

"Gossip, ye say? Look here, laddie, and tell me I know nothin' of what I speak!"

Sticking out his feet in front of him, he unwound the strips of cloth wrapped around the bottom of his breeches, rolling the ragged hem up to his knees. Next, the sleeves of his blouse were pushed up to his elbows. Burly forearms and muscular calves roped with knotted blue veins were covered with curly grey hairs, except for wide bands of pale scar tissue circling both ankles and both wrists. Her stomach lurching, Lillas looked away.

Miserable and out of sorts, she tried to order her thoughts. Was this why Timon lived as he did, far from village or town, alone in this isolated place? He'd been ready to kill to protect her, testimony of his hatred of the slavers and his regard for her. Still, she couldn't dismiss everything she'd been taught because of one man's experience, wretched though it might be.

"Come, lad. We've work to do. It's time yer off."

She placed a hand on his shoulder in an attempt to placate him.

"Tell me, Timon, how did you escape?"

He shook her hand off roughly, peering down at her with a twisted smile and something like pity in his heavy-lidded eyes.

"Ye haven't heard a word, have ye? Do ye ken such memories ever fade? Ye can never escape. For forty years, I've lived free. Yet each dawn finds me still in chains."

With that, he hobbled up the bank, leaving her without a backward glance.

TIMON WATCHED HER departure the next morning without regret. She was fit and rested, her pack full, the detailed map he'd traced for her committed to memory. His duty done, now she passed on to another's care.

Then why this empty place inside him? Was it the knowledge that they'd hardly spoken since yesterday morning when the slavers caught him unaware, his fear for himself nothing in comparison to the clearly-drawn picture in his mind of what the girl would face in the hands of those brutes with their whips? Was it guilt for his lapse in security? There was always the chance of danger in the scrublands, although he'd been assured that no raiders were within twenty miles of them. Or was it the fact that he'd laid his heart open to her, showing her scars no one was ever allowed to see, and watched her dismiss his experience with a wave of her hand?

His first reaction was disbelief. How could someone raised within five miles of that accursed city be so naive, so completely ignorant of the horrors through which he'd passed? As he'd rolled down his sleeves and re-wrapped his leggings, cursing the fact that for forty years he'd felt it necessary to hide his scars, he'd disobeyed the Eighteenth Mother and reached out to touch her thoughts, finding, in that tumult of doubt and denial, something which disturbed him far more than her refusal to believe.

She didn't believe because it was simply unbelievable. What he suggested was too threatening to her equanimity. He saw her picture of slavery—attractive, highly-skilled people who valued their positions and worked hard to insure their continuance in such a place of luxury. She'd been to the markets, but always with an entourage that announced her presence long before she arrived, every care taken to prevent her from seeing the unpleasant sights lurking on the fringes and down the alleyways of Agave. A recent incident challenged her shielded existence; a male slave with a lacerated back being nursed somewhere in her living quarters, although he'd sensed her smugness at the thought that she was responsible for his medical treatment and eventual acceptance into her household. Her mother's position reinforced her views;

she saw a woman adored, pampered, groomed and perfumed to perfection, the single factor marring her sense of well-being the silver slave ring circling her mother's throat.

As he watched her march confidently over the rise, her knitted cap set at a jaunty angle, he decided the Eighteenth Mother had judged her correctly, just as she had judged his worth in being the first contact. His task was to ease her along the path, teaching her the skills necessary to survive the rigors of the trail and in time, the discipline of the Maze. There had also been his sensitivity to this particular mission. Twenty-one years ago another woman in black selected him for his acting skills combined with his first-hand knowledge of Agave. There, he had played the role of slaver, fawning over the buyers, lusting after the women in his charge, playing his role with furious, unstoppable abandon, inspired by the intensity of this theatre of the real. Having sold the mother into slavery, he jumped at the chance to deliver her daughter to Pelion. No one warned him that while playing Timon the hermit, he might find himself reliving the role of Timon the slave.

As he had done so many times before, he buried the past as deeply as he could, shutting the door against its power to possess him. Calling on the discipline of a lifetime, he considered his next impersonation, the leading role in one of the most popular dramas of the repertoire. These past weeks he'd studied the part, finding the wilderness an apt place to consider the wilderness of his character's soul. The last few lines came to him out of the well of his memory.

He declaimed them toward Agave; the hated site of his talent's genesis, the source of his understanding of all things tragic and pathetic, the dark muse from which his creativity sprang:

> Now do I applaud what I have acted.
> *Nunc iners cadat manus.*
> Now to express the rupture of my part,
> First take my tongue, and afterward my heart.

Chapter 7

Inquest

It WAS ONLY the second time in her life Lillas had been truly alone and the first time she was neither frightened nor lonely. In fact, the last three days found her exhilarated, much happier than she'd felt since witnessing the death of the prophet. She made good time, for the weather was dry and cool, just right for walking along the trail Timon traced in the dirt, her eyes darting constantly about her to look for the signs he drilled into her. As she found each landmark—a lightning-struck oak, an outcropping of rock, a huge copper beech—her spirits soared and her confidence grew, for each sighting brought her closer to her destination.

Her nights retained the charm of her days. If wolves skulked under the cover of darkness, their night-songs were never sung for her, and the crickets provided a monotonously droning chorus that lulled her to sleep each night. A small, almost smokeless fire was all she allowed herself, for thanks to the old hermit, her pack was full of provisions and there was no necessity to hunt or cook her meals. The dust cleansed from her face and hands in a nearby stream, her thirst quenched and her belly full, she would lay face-up on the rough blanket, her arms under her head, and lose herself in the stars.

She was not given to self-reflection, for she shied away from difficulties of the spirit just as she hurried toward challenges of the body. Still, the quiet hours after the sun's descent seemed ripe for contemplation, and her thoughts turned from the wilderness of the landscape to the unknown territories inside her: alien, unexplored, and intimidating for one who visited there so rarely. On a whim, she decided she'd try to work out her reasons for her headlong rush toward the south. After all, sooner or later she would reach this place. Surely it would be prudent to have some sort of plan upon arrival. The resultant impasse was annoying to a degree: each time she tried to explore her situation, the more elusive it became. Yet at the same time her efforts ended in frustration, her desire for the prophet's promise grew more and more forceful. "Enlightenment", "gift beyond price"; under close scrutiny they were simply words, amorphous, without context or meaning, and it was tempting to let Seth's disdain become hers. At such moments, the prophet's voice would echo inside her, and then she would be back where she started, hungry for some kind of food she'd never tasted, craving its taste on her tongue, sure that nothing else would content her. Baffled, she finally gave it up as fruitless. Come what may, she must satisfy her longings. Each morning found her bright-eyed, refreshed, and resolute in her quest.

This morning was chilly and overcast; a thin coating of frost tinted the grass and bushes a delicate silvery-green. Embers from her campfire yielded the necessary spark and soon she coaxed them into a merry blaze with which to cook her porridge (the grain begged from Timon's reserves) and warm a cup of herbal tea. Grimy and smelly as she was, the thin layer of ice along the banks of the stream made the thought of immersing herself decidedly unappealing, so she made do with a quick dousing of her face and neck. Sputtering with the cold, her teeth chattering like dice shaken in a cup, she dried her face on the hem of her blouse, pulled the cap firmly down around her ears, stuffed her dagger under her belt and, throwing the pack over her shoulder, headed toward the pale orange-blue horizon.

According to the angle of the sun, she'd walked for several hours, stopping once to marvel at a waterfall, the first she'd ever seen. Desert-born and accustomed to deep wells or slave-constructed reservoirs, she was stunned at the thought of so much water pouring unchecked down a steep hill, dissolving into foam and mist as it hit the surface of the ever-widening stream flowing south. There were more trees now, their leaves littering the trail and crackling underfoot with each step. Sheer delight overcame her, for she was a stranger to autumn's bounty, and suddenly she was running, kicking up the leaves as she passed, the pack bouncing companionably against her back.

The shrill whinny of a horse caught her in mid-flight. Instantly, she dropped to the ground on all fours, scuttling desperately toward a stand of juniper bushes, hoping her clothes blended with the leaves carpeting the forest floor. Huddled under the prickly fingers of the evergreens, she resisted the impulse to close her eyes against what might come down the trail to catch her. You brought this on yourself, my girl, she thought, and now you must pay the consequences. The smell of resin and pine sap filled her nostrils, her eyes watered, and she fought the urge to sneeze. By the time her nose was under control, there was still no sound of pursuit. Motionless, she counted to a hundred, then counted again, remembering Timon's cautious behavior long after the slaver's band passed them by. A linnet broke into song in the branches directly overhead. In the exact moment she knew she was safe, a stern voice demanded:

"Stand up slowly, your hands in plain sight."

Nothing had announced his approach behind her, not a footfall or even a breath. No one should be able to move that quietly, she thought angrily, and in the next moment she made her decision. Her head bowed to signal her submission, she stood slowly, keeping her knees bent and her center of gravity low. Then, just as she felt him reach forward to grab her, she feinted right and took off to her left at a dead run, hearing him crash into the juniper bush with a grunted curse.

She'd always been fleet of foot, winning races with her cousins so often they finally stopped responding to her dares. Those races were run over flat ground; now she had to negotiate around trees and bushes, unable to see the ground under her feet because of the leaves, praying no roots tripped her, for he was close on her trail. Even though she was frightened, her head was clear and her legs and arms pumped obediently as she asked herself for another burst of speed, hearing the sounds of pursuit gradually fade away. She nearly laughed aloud in triumph, when off to her right she caught the blurred shape of a figure in motion and two arms wrapped themselves around her knees. Attacked so quickly she didn't have time to throw out her arms, she fell flat on her face, her breath leaving her lungs even as her nose and mouth filled with the rich humus of dead leaves. An enormous sneeze cleared her nasal passages. From behind her she heard a highly creative string of profanities delivered through pants and gasps for air.

"By the broad backside of a rum-drunk whore, what devil stuck his rod up your arse? You were off like a rabbit heading for a breeding spree! By all the gods, boy, what were you thinking?"

Her captor regained his breath. When she began to struggle, his arms locked around her legs like metal pincers.

"Stop wiggling, or you'll feel my hand on your backside."

With that threat, he flipped her over on her back and knelt astride her, a deep frown furrowing his brow and pulling the corners of his mouth down into deep folds that ran along each side of his nose. She'd never seen a free-lance slaver before. Unfortunately, he was everything she expected. Swarthy, dark-haired and stone-faced, his round head rising above a bullish neck and powerful shoulders, his bulging muscles gave the impression that he could break every bone in her body without breaking a sweat. He hadn't relaxed his grip, although he'd shifted it to her upper arms. Held fast by shoulders and waist, she stared up at him with what she hoped was a look of unadulterated hatred.

"I'll never stop trying to escape!"

His eyes widened. Before he could reply, the sound of running feet brought his head up and around. Another man's face appeared behind her captor's shoulder, his hair plastered to his forehead and his breath coming in ragged gasps. He was dressed exactly like the man who held her, from the bronze clasp at the neck of his knee-length brown cloak, to the tips of his calf-high leather boots.

"So you got him, hey, Hume?"

"No thanks to you, Spence. Maybe you'd better make use of the track on your next leave. Either that or lose a few pounds."

Both men pulled her roughly to her feet, the newcomer shooting her captor a sheepish grin.

"Sorry, Hume. He used the oldest trick in the manual, and still I fell for it."

When Hume growled and shook his head, Lillas caught herself thinking he wasn't angry so much as annoyed. There was little time to pursue that thought before the rattle of bridle rings announced another presence, this time a brown-garbed man on horseback. Lillas felt her courage ebbing. There was a chance of escape from two men on foot. Those chances were slipping away with each arrival of the slaver's band. A hand on her shoulder pushed her forward. Stepping out on her right foot, her knee buckled under her, a sharp pain coursing up her thigh and down her shin, making her bite her lips to prevent the high, girlish scream that would betray her.

A sharp expletive broke from Hume's mouth and she found herself being lowered to the ground.

"Rafe, head back to camp and bring Didion."

The horse moved off at a quick trot. Hume knelt at her side, his frown even more forbidding and his voice harsh.

"How bad is it, boy?"

She almost whimpered in fear and pain before remembering who and what she was. "I am Lillas of Agave," she told herself, "and no one has ever made me cry." She stared up into that black thundercloud of a face, sure that this man would never burden himself with an injured slave. She had doubted Timon, but judging from the slaver's treatment of her so far, she'd never survive what the old hermit described. There might be no escape, but perhaps there was still a chance for self-respect.

"You've no time for a cripple. Kill me quickly and be done."

Not a muscle in the slaver's face moved, as if he was asked daily for death by young boys found wandering in the woods. At last he spoke, quietly and distinctly, each word delivered as if it were a gift.

"I'm not a slaver, boy, and I don't harm cripples. A healer will be here in a moment. Lie still until then."

With that he turned his back on her. She sank back into the leaves, her knee throbbing, her eyes finding patches of blue sky through the empty branches of the trees. She might be trapped, but she was no slave, and at that joyous thought, she did something so remarkable, so completely out of character that no one, not even Lillas herself, would have thought it possible. Her lips upturned in a smile of pure relief, Lillas fainted.

*   *   *

"WELL, HEALER?"

"She twisted her knee. I made her soak it the stream and gave her something for the pain. It's swollen, but not so badly that she can't ride."

The healer crouched near the fire, extending his hands to the warming blaze. The afternoon turned colder, a quick snap to remind them that autumn would soon slide into winter.

"How are her spirits?"

Didion's laugh brought a slight lessening of the tension between Hume's shoulders.

"How *were* her spirits, you mean. She's fast asleep now, curled up in a ball as far away from the others as she can possibly get."

"How were they, then?" was Hume's gruff rejoinder.

The healer reached for the kettle that hung over the fire, poured steaming liquid into a tin cup, and dropped onto the ground with a tired sigh.

"She's nearly done me in. She fought like a bobcat when I tried to get her breeches off, hissing at me the entire time with some of the worst profanity I've ever heard," Didion took a sip from his cup before adding, "present company included."

If he'd hoped for a reaction to his jest, he was disappointed. Hume didn't budge. Didion made yet another attempt to breach the wall of non-characteristic silence that hung over his commander since capturing the boy Skat.

"Hume, stop blaming yourself! You don't even know if you caused the sprain. You tackled her, yes, but according to Spence she was running full-out over rugged ground."

"She thought I was a slaver. Not only did I hurt her, I scared her nearly to death."

Didion recalled that Hume's daughter of fourteen had just offered her second gift. The boy Skat looked not a day over fifteen in those ill-fitting clothes and that ridiculous cap. Didion gazed tiredly into the blue-hazed dusk. This patient was in considerably worse shape than the one he'd just left.

"How can you know what she was thinking? Besides, no serious harm was done or she wouldn't have been able to make my life so miserable."

Nothing was forthcoming from Hume. Didion placed a tentative palm on his muscled shoulder, feeling the tension that held it rock-hard beneath his hand. At his touch, Hume flinched, then heaved a sigh. Sensing that he had been invited inside, Didion closed his eyes, stepping over the chasm which separated them until he found himself looking out of Hume's eyes, staring down at a girl who begged him for death, her chin trembling although her face remained serene and composed. Underneath the fear, her courage and proud disdain for the man who threatened her rose up to sustain her. Now Didion knew how to proceed.

"You know we're more than escorts. This is part of Preparation for all ernani, to find their way to Pelion despite the rigors and dangers of the path. You frightened her, yes, but how do you know that isn't part of our mission? In her mind, she faced slavery and chose death. Who are we to judge that lesson won't stand her in good stead in the future?"

The image of those haunting, fearful eyes swirled and dissolved as he spoke. Didion replaced them with a picture of the shabbily-dressed boy curled up on his side, his dirty face relaxed into a sweet smile of peaceful slumber.

"She rests now, Hume, and so must you. According to your orders, we must be off shortly after dawn."

Didion broke the connection, but not before he felt Hume's shoulders slump in sudden fatigue. As Didion removed his hand, Hume spoke up, his face illuminated by the fire's blaze, for the evening was over and night had begun.

"My thanks, healer."

"Anytime."

Didion couldn't resist a final test of his patient's recovery.

"By the way, I saw your mate at the northern gate the day we left. She said you've agreed to leave off swearing altogether. Something about such language not being appropriate for a newly-promoted officer . . . ?"

Didion ducked as a tin cup whizzed by his ear. The curse that accompanied it was so disgustingly foul that Didion nearly choked with laugher.

Hume was cursing again; all was right with the world.

SEATED AROUND A wooden table, its well-polished surface scarred by dents and scratches and lit by an enormous chandelier suspended from the rafters by an iron chain, the Eighteenth Mother's Council regarded Hesione. Each member was a specialist; some selected by her, others members of her predecessor's Council retained by her for reasons of continuity as well as their wealth of experience. In the six years of her reign they became more than colleagues; they became friends. As friends, she greeted them, and began the meeting.

"Two items head our agenda this evening. Prax, you should begin, I think. How fares the boy, Skat?"

Once Prax had been Hesione's most daunting opponent; since the day he saw her power revealed, he became her most ardent supporter. Some are men of faith; some are convinced only by the testimony of their eyes.

That Prax required proof of her call was not her concern. Having witnessed her power firsthand, he was a vassal for life.

As much as she valued his loyalty, she had come to rely on his judgment. Close-mouthed and crafty, pragmatic and opinionated, he best understood the forces at play outside their thickly-walled city, and could convey them with devastating clarity to the more sheltered members of the Council. With Prax as its Commander, the Legion functioned like a well-oiled clock, each part fitting precisely with the other, measuring out the exact passage of time necessary to reach his goals. With the exception of Lukash's role, which was exclusively the province of Hesione, the entire expedition to escort Lillas from Imarus to Pelion was devised and executed by Prax. That the plan was close to fruition put him in the best of moods. His gestures expansive, his bald head shining like the great dome of Guild Hall, he leaned back in his chair and began.

"Hume contacted me at dusk to inform us that Skat's knee is nearly sound. They've five, maybe six more days to travel, and a good thing too, since the nights grow chilly. There was a film of frost over everything this morning, including, it seems, the boy Skat."

A wave of laughter broke over the table at Prax's drawled delivery of the boy's name. It was Kazur, Head Scribe and an accomplished historian in his own right, who informed them of the derivation of Lillas' pseudonym. Having made Agave his field of expertise, studying its politics, economics, and culture, he supplied them with several references to Skat, a folklore figure celebrated for his thieving ways, a famous scoundrel of considerable charm.

"It seems Skat is unwilling to warm himself by lying close to the other ernani. Hume, who woke him this morning with a boot in his rump, reported Skat's nose was nearly as blue as his eyes."

Chryse spoke up, ignoring the laughter around her, her braid-crowned head shaking in gentle approbation.

"You laugh, Prax, but Timon told us she'd been approached by a man on the first leg of her journey. Certainly she's wary and we mustn't judge her so severely. From all accounts she hides her gender well. Who among us has ever attempted such a thing?" When several pairs of eyes dropped their gaze to the table-top, she continued serenely, "We should be grateful that she's able to protect herself."

Her defense of the girl rang true, causing Prax to nod his head apologetically. With the gracious ways of her calling, the Mistress of Joining forgave him with a smile and a feather-light pat on his sleeve. That Chryse could so neatly handle any situation, never raising her voice or indulging in sarcasm or anger, was a continuing source of enjoyment for Hesione. Her elegant, decorous manner marked every duty she performed within the Maze. Male and female ernani alike chose her as their favorite confessor, bringing her their problems and heartaches on a regular basis.

Chryse's most pressing duty at the moment was forming the next class for Preparation. Hesione sensed her anxiety. Chryse needed more information about the group of ernani under Hume's care and she needed it quickly.

"Can you tell us anything more of Hume's party, Prax? I must post the list of women in a few days and the male interviews are nearing completion."

Rubbing the side of his prominent nose, Prax considered the question.

"There are four males besides Skat: Two from the colony at Lapith, one from the Sarujian Mountains, and another who is something of a mystery. He's a long-hair, so Hume assumed he was part of the Lapithian party, but it seems they'll have nothing to do with him. Hume says he speaks our language with difficulty and keeps to himself. As a matter of fact," he paused and frowned, trying to recapture the impressions fed to him over so long a distance, "Hume indicated that this long-hair is the only one Skat will have anything to do with."

Hesione felt a surge of concern from the Mistress of Joining that matched her own. This was Chryse's primary worry since the conception of Prax's plan, which necessitated Lillas meeting male ernani before entry into the Maze. Chryse voiced her distress before Hesione could speak.

"Prax, this cannot be allowed! You must contact Hume immediately and tell him to keep them apart! What if she begins to bond with him, or he to her? Such an event could ruin both their chances for achieving Transformation!"

A thoughtful voice spoke up from Hesione's left, its flat vowels and slight nasality decidedly different from the other speakers. Kazur of Endlin was the most recent addition to the Eighteenth Mother's Council. Like Prax, he was a transformed adept; he was also the only member of the Council not born-of-the-city. He spoke rarely as of yet, perhaps the result of the newness of his position.

"Are we sure of this stranger's gender? We've been fooled in such a manner before, have we not? Perhaps the girl senses something we've overlooked."

The looks of chagrin on the faces of Prax and Chryse announced their dismay at such a prospect. Before anyone could react, Hesione redirected the discussion.

"I see an even greater possibility here than the one Kazur suggests. Let us say he is correct. The entire city knows we're looking for three male candidates, since to date only three women have passed through the northern gate. We know there will be a fourth; that there might be a fifth gives us more leeway when it comes to the upcoming Trial."

Ranier was first to pick up Hesione's train of thought. He sat, as always, next to his mate, their clasped hands evidence of their linked minds. Although

Ranier was the one who spoke, no one would ever know if the ideas expressed came first from him or Nadia. The High Healers of Pelion, they were born adepts and served the Seventeenth Mother before Hesione's ascension.

"Five male candidates from Pelion? A first, Mother. And good news indeed!"

Hesione sighed and leaned back in her chair. Every autumn without fail she brooded over the Trial and the circus that resulted from its inclusion into the process of selection. Her predecessor did her best, of that there could be little doubt, but the Seventeenth Mother's attempts to control the situation were futile; nothing could prevent the citizens of Pelion from turning a serious matter into a contest of popularity, athleticism, and beauty. The careful statistics kept on all matters concerning Transformation revealed an alarming tendency dating from its inception: one out of every five male candidates chosen by the Trial failed to complete the steps necessary for Transformation. This percentage contrasted with a perfect record in the years preceding the Trial. Not only had the selection process become needlessly demeaning, it kept many worthy candidates from competing, for unless a man was a gifted athlete, gregarious, and physically attractive, he had almost no chance of winning a high place on the list. Male candidates from Pelion who passed the screening interview and a physical examination were allowed to compete on the day of the Trial. At the Trial's conclusion, all were ranked by a city-wide vote. With the continuing shortage of female ernani, only the first few names (and thus the favorites of the masses) ever actually entered the Maze.

Twisting the silver band on her finger, Hesione focused on the problem at hand.

"What if we delay the approach of Hume's party? Although the stranger from Lapith may be a woman, there is an equal possibility that he is a man. The Trial must continue on schedule, but if we delay news of the arrival of a fourth or even a fifth female ernani, might the competition for the fourth and fifth positions be lessened somewhat?"

Prax regarded her with a twinkle in his eye.

"You're saying we might be able to slip in a cuckoo's chick. Someone the populace might rank as high as fourth or fifth as long as they think only the top three are headed for the Maze. You're a cagey one, aren't you?"

"If you say so, Commander," she replied coolly before turning to the others. "There is no guarantee that the fourth or even the fifth candidate selected will be the best choice for joining with Lillas. My question is a simple one: Should we hide the presence of additional female ernani from the populace before the Trial of Selection?"

She regarded each member in turn.

"Guide me in this, friends. When you reach your decision, offer it to me silently."

Cleansing her mind, she waited for their responses. With so much at stake it was tempting to be ruled by her instincts, all of which told her that this Trial would be like no other, for out of it must come a mate for the one on whom so much rested. For if Hesione's mission was successful, the necessity of the Trial might disappear forever.

Prax voted quickly for her plan, as she knew he would. Understandably, Kazur believed whole-heartedly in selection by the Mistress of Joining, for in that way he had found the mate of his heart in the last class begun before the Trial was adopted. His vote to delay was immediately seconded by Chryse, whose dislike of the Trial was second only to Hesione's. Ranier and Nadia's decision remained. Although the majority ruled all Council policies, Hesione waited with some trepidation for their opinions. While the others had given her the ability to pursue her plan regardless of the healers' vote, a unanimous decision was always preferable.

The touch of Nadia's mind was as light as her healing hands.

"Too much hinges on this Trial. Let it be as you see fit, Mother. We judge that the first priority must be a mate for Lillas. If bending the rule might help achieve such an outcome, it is always better to bend than to break."

The tension around the table dissolved as Hesione smiled.

"We are in agreement. Prax, you will contact Hume immediately, since your presence is not necessary for the next item of discussion. He is to delay the party's arrival until two days after the Trial. In addition, ask him to consider the question of the unknown ernani's gender and pass on Chryse's request that Skat be prevented from unsupervised contact with any of the male ernani." She tried to swallow her growing amusement, although it flavored her next words despite her efforts. "Given what we know of Lillas, I don't envy Hume his task. Make it clear that anything he devises will meet with our approval."

Grinning as he rose from the table, Prax fired a parting shot.

"My officers are trained to improvise. If Hume isn't devious enough to think of something, I've a few ideas of my own."

As the door swung shut behind him, Hesione smoothed the folds of her gown, preparing herself for her next task. This discussion would be crucial to the events of the next few days. She must find a way to bring the others around to her way of thinking.

"I know it's early for this discussion and perhaps you think me over-anxious, but each of you senses the importance of this Trial." She chose to conduct this meeting without inner speech. Even so, she could sense their growing apprehension. "I have not said it openly, perhaps because of cowardice or the fear of disappointment if I am in error, but tonight I announce that I am convinced that Lillas and her mate are integrally related to the next step the city must take."

"You were required to read the prophecy under discussion at the time of your appointment and thus you know of what I speak, although my duties demand that I, and I alone, study and interpret the promise of the new age handed down to us at the time of Transformation. This is not something I am prepared to discuss since it is still unformed in my mind."

"What I propose may seem an improbable task, and in some ways nearly impossible, for we must begin the search for a man within our walls who provides a harmonious balance to a woman we have never met."

"Hopeless as this task may seem, we do have certain tools—the descriptions of Lillas forwarded by Phoron and Timon, Kazur's work on the nature of Imarus and the life she has lived, and of course, the information related by Lukash."

It was difficult to speak his name out loud. Intuition told her the exact moment of his death. She had cradled his book in her arms, mourning the first person she had knowingly sent to his death, wondering how many others might be sacrificed, agonizing over the price of the war she'd sworn to win.

"We have yet another tool, one not based on fact or observation, and one which we too often underestimate. I want Chryse and Ranier to connect themselves directly to their memories—to your instinctual reactions to the men you've interviewed and examined so far. For we must believe, my friends, that if Lillas is the one named, then her mate-to-be resides with us and has already applied for a place in the Trial."

The darkness that lay outside the reach of the candles seemed less forbidding as she reached the end of her speech. It reminded Hesione of those quiet moments upon awakening in the winter's black dawn, moments passed in total darkness which nevertheless held the promise of light. Judging from her listeners' reaction, they, too, responded to her mood, for each one seemed lost in thought, unwilling to break the silence of the tower chamber.

"There is one."

Her voice full of dreamy reflection, Chryse spoke barely above a whisper. Rousing as if from a dream, she struggled to describe something intangible.

"He's driven, yet seemingly passive; unsure of himself, yet confident in what he desires. There is a duality to him. Could this be the quality we seek?"

"What balance is possible between them, Chryse?"

A gossamer thought wafted through their minds.

"Her fire melts his ice. His ambitions counter her lack of purpose. She is inspiration, brief and violent; he is endurance, patient and eternal."

Chryse broke the spell with a sad smile.

"It will not be an easy mating."

"Would Lillas be an easy mate for anyone?" Hesione countered.

Wordlessly, Chryse shook her head.
"Tell us more . . ."

A SHARP RAP announced the presence of the next candidate. Ranier pushed
away an unfinished report and readied himself for the next interview. In the
past ten days he'd examined nearly a hundred men and they were starting
to merge into one long line of naked bodies and frowning faces. Chryse
interviewed the same number, but she sat with Tubal, the current President
of the Guild Assembly, and thus had only half the paperwork Ranier was
expected to complete. Five more names remained on the master list. For that
he was truly and tiredly grateful, until he remembered that tomorrow would
begin a new round of battles as he and Chryse joined forces to eliminate the
worst, fight for the best, and settle for the ones Tubal was bound to support.
Sometimes it all seemed so trivial that he was tempted to resign and take up
teaching again in the House of Healing. To be sure, there was bureaucracy
aplenty in the realms of the academe, but at least he'd be able to make his
decisions along independent lines. He'd worked with Tubal for the last four
years and thought him the worst Guild President in the history of Pelion.
The man was an insensitive lout and a bully to boot. He'd said so that morning
when he woke beside Nadia. She'd smiled, as she always did, and pulled
his chest hairs.

"You've said that every fall for the past sixteen years. Be content. This is
Tubal's last year in office. Soon you'll have a completely new president to
despise."

"Perhaps it's time we let others take our place. Didion and Lara are
qualified. Sometimes all I want to do is sit in the atrium with you . . ."

She kissed the tip of his nose to make him stop.

". . . and you would be happy for six moons at the most, at which time
you'd start fretting about the Maze, making my life a misery, and then what
should we do? Do you truly think you can give up the sight of the
newly-transformed, knowing that we've helped bring them the closeness
we share, knowing that they're no longer trapped by their body's isolation?"

He rolled over on top of her, resting his weight on his forearms, looking
down at her dear, careworn face, sensing the untouched loveliness of the
mind he'd first met three decades ago and sworn never to relinquish. She
was so much a part of him that he often found himself unable to think of
himself as Ranier. He was Ranier/Nadia, and something of him had passed
into her as well. His desire fueled by her understanding, they joined together

as only adept mates could, greeting the morning as they celebrated their love with two bodies and one mind.

A POLITELY CLEARED throat announced that Ranier was no longer alone. The candidate proffered him a thick sheaf of documents.

"I don't envy you the task of reading this. I gathered everything in less than a week."

Ranier had the unsettling feeling that he was being read, so shrewdly had the man guessed his thoughts. Reaching out with a single inquiring thought, he felt the unawareness of the non-adept mind. Hiding his relief by accepting the file, Ranier was careful to keep his voice abrupt and his manner curt.

"You shouldn't envy me . . . Reddin, is it?" The name at the top of the first page was written in a neat, angular hand. "Sit for a moment while I look these over." He skimmed the documents rapidly, noting points of reference for further discussion.

Twenty-nine, third child of adept parents, normal childhood diseases. Excellent student, especially high marks in the sciences, entered the House of Healing at twenty-three as a non-adept apprentice. His interest sparked by this last entry, Ranier began to read more slowly, recognizing the signatures of many colleagues and former pupils. Having completed all his studies in a record three years (normal completion time was four with the fifth year reserved for adept students), he achieved marks of distinction in anatomy and biology. For the past three years he'd worked in the wards and from all reports was efficient, if a trifle cold. This last comment was supplied by Ranier's assistant, Lara, her opinion one Ranier valued. Glancing up, he noticed Reddin was watching him intently. When Ranier caught his gaze, he looked away.

Having reached the end of the file, Ranier went back to the beginning, trying to read not only what was written, but what had been left out. This was the first time Reddin applied to compete in the Trial and his papers arrived at the Guild Hall on the last day of the strictly enforced deadline. What had sparked this last minute decision?

"Would you prefer the physical examination first or last?"

"First, if you please."

No trouble making decisions, thought Ranier. Cool, crisp, and totally self-possessed, Reddin rose and started to disrobe, folding his clothes neatly and hanging them off the arm of the chair he had so recently occupied. Watching the body emerging from the somewhat somber clothes, Ranier's attention was broken by a quiet question.

"Should I remove my loincloth?"

Rising to his feet, Ranier moved around the desk toward the examination table.

"That's not necessary to begin. Lie on your stomach and breathe regularly."

Bending over the basin and pitcher kept just to the right of the examination table, Ranier soaped and rinsed his hands and dried them thoroughly on a clean cloth. Out of years of habit, he rubbed his hands together to warm them before beginning. His examinations rarely revealed any serious physical problems. In sixteen years he'd removed half a dozen applicants from the list for such things as chronic asthma and arrhythmia. The Seventeenth Mother's directions to him at the time of the First Trial came back to him:

"Center your impressions on the way they respond to the touch of a stranger's hand, to an invasion of their privacy, to tones of command."

As his hands warmed, he studied the body on the table, a man of middling height, lean and finely-boned with skin the color of soil freshly tilled for planting. He'd tied his hair in a club at the back of his neck and it shone black with reddish highlights in the afternoon light flooding the chamber. Ranier started at his shoulders, running his hands down the straight spine recessed in a cleft of muscles, feeling the tension that was normal in any new patient. Moving away from his ribs and down his flanks, a bruise was evident on his right buttock. Ranier considered questioning him, but decided to bring it up later. He moved down the back of his legs, kneading the flesh. When he reached the back of the right thigh, he felt, rather than saw, the man's wince.

"You've had a fall, and a bad one at that."

The man lifted his upper body onto his elbows and turned his head back over his shoulder, frowning at the right side of his body.

"I've been working with a trainer who sometimes asks me to do more than I'm able."

A brusque nod indicated Ranier's understanding. Reddin wasn't the first man to be bruised and sore. The Trial events were long and short distance running, wrestling, archery, javelins, rope climbing, hurdles and the long jump. Eight events, yet in the past few years it was becoming increasingly important to the crowds that candidates win one event rather than placing highly in all eight. Some men went so far as to hire experts to coach them in a single event, sometimes devoting an entire year to something that was devised to encourage well-rounded individuals rather than muscle-bound specialists who could throw a javelin to the far end of the arena but couldn't jump a hurdle if their lives depended on it.

"Turn over onto your back and loosen your loincloth."

Ranier worked more slowly now, checking pulse and heartbeat. The man had relaxed a bit, his muscles becoming smoother and less resistant to the healer's touch. Ranier soon discovered there wasn't a pound of extra flesh on his lean frame. He put up no resistance to Ranier's prodding and probing, lying quietly with his eyes focused somewhere on the ceiling, nor did he flinch as the loincloth was removed, or jerk or pull away as Ranier examined his genitals.

"Sit up and hang your legs over the edge of the table."

Ranier thumped his chest and back, listened to his lungs, tested reflexes, and peered up his nose, into his ears, and down his throat. Satisfied, he gestured to the man's clothes, washed his hands, and returned to his desk, sifting through the papers once more as he waited. The man neither hurried nor dawdled, but dressed methodically and resumed his place in the wooden armchair.

Ranier was usually more attuned to bodies than faces, yet this one drew his attention, perhaps because it was as finely sculptured as his body. Prominent cheekbones and a strongly-defined nose contrasted with large dark eyes below thick eyebrows. His teeth were evenly-matched and shone brilliantly white against his copper-colored skin. He was smiling now, obviously relieved that the examination was over.

"A few questions, Reddin, and you can be on your way."

Ranier was struck again by his composure. Even the most confident applicants didn't appreciate being stripped and handled by a total stranger, yet this fellow was unperturbed to the point of nonchalance. Perhaps it was necessary to dig a trifle deeper.

"Your documents tell me that your parents are adept. Are your older brother and sister gifted as well?"

"Yes."

Ranier touched his mind lightly as he asked the question; the eruption of envy it engendered took him completely by surprise. The man's eyes narrowed slightly, but there was no other outward sign to indicate how thoroughly Ranier's query had unsettled him. His control is impressive, the healer mused. I wonder how far he can be pushed.

"Are you content with your work in the House of Healing?"

Again, a surge of bitterness rose up to meet his inquiry. This time Reddin's jaw clenched, the muscles underneath the skin twitching as he ground his teeth.

"I'm as content as I can be considering the fact that I can go no further with my studies."

No wonder he was bitter. Reddin possessed all the requisites of a Master Healer: intelligence, expertise in anatomy and biological functions, ambition, and love for his craft. A single thing was missing, and for that reason he could never rise to the ranks of surgeon, diagnostician, or teacher. Many non-adepts were valued practitioners, researchers, and herbalists, but the first healers of Pelion were adept. Even after five hundred years, certain doors were closed to those without the gift.

"Are you a virgin?"

Reddin's lips quivered in an attempt to suppress a smile.

"Not for many years."

"And you have no objection to the requirement that you join with an ernani?"

As emotions washed over Reddin, Ranier tried to select the most pertinent ones. There was a certain amount of distaste, not toward the idea of joining, but at the idea of living with a barbarian. It was not an uncommon reaction for a native born citizen—ernani still did not frequent many circles of society and doubtless Reddin had never come into close contact with one. Floating over and around this concern was something that Ranier understood more clearly—this man had a better idea than most as to what this joining would entail. The prospect of prolonged intimacy with any woman, let alone an unwashed savage from outside city walls, troubled him.

"I've no objection or I wouldn't have decided to compete."

"One last question, Reddin."

"Of course."

"What's your strongest event?"

There wasn't the slightest hint of humor in Reddin's reply.

"I'm fast and agile, but I started training too late to gain much strength or stamina. My trainer tells me I've a chance at the ropes, and a better one at the short run, especially if the track is wet enough to slow down the heavy-footed ones."

"Then I suppose you must hope for rain."

All traces of Reddin's former composure melted away. Dark eyes intent and full of fervor, he spoke from his heart.

"This is the only thing I've ever wanted. It's taken me twenty-nine years to admit it to myself and now I'm nearly too old to compete. All I need is a little luck," he admitted, "although I've never really believed in luck."

When, with a respectful nod, Reddin took his leave, Ranier leaned back in his chair to peruse the ceiling. Chryse was on target. Even without her guidance, Ranier flattered himself he would have picked this one out of the crowd. Driven, intense, immensely strong-willed, there was a cold hard center inside him begging for attention.

Ranier sighed. It would be an uphill fight to keep him in the running. By law only twenty-four men could compete in the Trial and Tubal never favored scholars or healers. The Guild wanted adept inventors and craftsmen, not a healer who'd completed his studies and was already making a useful contribution to society. This was why the Eighteenth Mother was so adamant that they start looking now, rather than waiting until the day of the Trial. It was up to Chryse and Ranier to ensure a place for Reddin, who, like Ranier, didn't believe in luck. Ranier's sigh was deeper and louder than the previous one.

Suddenly, Ranier announced to no one in particular:

"Three days of solid downpour would be best, but one heavy shower on the morning of the Trial might suffice."

A knock on the door brought him back to earth. Pushing aside the growing stack of papers, Ranier welcomed the next applicant.

Chapter 8

The Trial

REDDIN LOOKED UP with a frown, his pen poised over a thought he was unable to complete because of the mournful scratch of a tree branch against the panes of glass in the window over his desk. At one time, such glass would have been a costly luxury, used solely in the Sanctum and the Greater and Lesser Libraries and other places where light was necessary, either for the tasks of scholarship, or in the former case, an architectural reminder of the path toward enlightenment. More recently, the Glassworks began offering windows to residences and shops at a more reasonable rate. Elan, Reddin's father and a devotee of anything innovative, was one of the first citizens to have windows installed in his home. As a boy, Reddin found the thick, leaded panes an endless source of imaginative speculation. The glass was not quite clear, having a yellowish cast that dyed everything seen through it in a weird, unearthly light. To that quality was added the irregular surface's tendency to distort. Standing perfectly still, his nose pressed wetly up against the cold, hard surface of the panes, Reddin would play at being in another world, one where foreshortened human figures moved jerkily to and fro on the crooked street underneath yellow wizened trees with boxy clumps of irregular leaves.

This day was overcast, dull and dreary, and unseasonably cold. The leaves of the tree outside his attic window were memories scattered on the pavement below. There was no fire in the grate, for he arrived home late from the House of Healing and immediately set to work on his journal. He'd considered lighting one and then discarded the idea. The evening meal would soon be served below and there was no need to waste firewood. Instead, he leaned back on the chair's legs and reached over for the foot of his bed, pulling a heavy quilt toward him and wrapping it around his back and shoulders. Picking up his pen, he reviewed what he had written and actually placed the nib on paper when someone scratched at his door.

"May I disturb you?"

At his word of welcome, the door was pushed open and Pasiphae stepped into the room, taking in his quilt-wrapped body with raised eyebrows and a slight smile.

"Don't be a miser, son. Sometimes you forget you have a salary now and needn't play the role of impoverished student."

With her usual wisdom she hit at the root of his problem. He'd been forced to live at home much longer than he'd planned. Once accepted into the House of Healing, his studies allowed no time for other work, and even though his parents took immense pride in his abilities, never complaining about the cost of rent, fuel, and provisions, he felt guilty. Now that he was able to make a sizable contribution to the housekeeping budget there was no reason for him to sit shivering in the attic.

Before he could make his way across the room to the fireplace, she pulled her other hand from behind her back. Seeing that she held a folded document with an official-looking seal firmly implanted in red wax, Reddin looked up into his mother's face.

He was her last child, born late in her fourth decade and now she was fast approaching her seventh. The frost that covered her dark hair revealed her maturity, although her unlined face seemed ageless. He inherited her size and coloring, while his elder brother and sister, with their lighter skin and larger bones took after his father's people. Pasiphae could trace her line back to the first wave of immigrants to arrive in Pelion after the Eighth Mother opened the city to non-adepts. Reddin's study of genetics included Surnan's theories on inheriting adeptness, and though they had finally been disproved in the most controversial medical experiment in Pelion's history, Pasiphae was proof that the great scientist's dream could sometimes come to fruition. After intervening generations of mixed bloodlines, her grandparents and parents were born adept, as was Pasiphae. Her mating with Elan, another born adept, resulted in two children with like gifts. Only Reddin, her last-born son, had been passed over, a joke Reddin always thought Surnan alone could appreciate for its cruel ironies, for it was Reddin's ilk, the throwbacks from past generations, the atavistic flaws that behaved according to no scientific rules, that crushed Surnan's hopes as surely as they had crushed Reddin's.

"I thought you should read it in the privacy of your own room."

When he didn't reach for it, but stood stony-faced and unapproachable, she laid it on top of his open journal and turned to go.

"Don't leave, mother."

Betraying neither surprise at his request nor her own inner thoughts, she moved to a chair that stood by the empty grate, and sat, leaning back into the padded leather upholstery.

"Is it truly so important, Reddin? You love your work and you're highly respected in the ward. No one will think less of you if you're passed over . . ."

He cut her off impatiently.

"You of all people should know why it's important."

He hadn't meant to sound so accusatory; nevertheless, she closed her eyes for a moment before opening them slowly to meet his anger.

"I should never have done it, Reddin. I knew better, but let my love for you persuade me to break the rules I've obeyed for a lifetime. It was wrong, and the thought that I'm the cause of this obsession of yours is . . .," her eyes darkened with misery, ". . . unbearable."

Reddin swallowed hard. It wasn't her fault and he'd been childishly dishonest to suggest that it was. The only reason she'd capitulated was because he'd used every ploy, every argument, every means at his disposal to nag, chide, and bully her into showing him what he'd always longed to experience.

"Don't blame yourself, mother. You know it was the session that started me on this path . . ."

"The session . . ." she murmured as both of them retreated into their own thoughts.

ATTUNEMENT. The ability of a healer to enter a patient's mind and diagnose the source of pain or sickness. To put a restless patient to sleep or prepare another for painless surgery by helping them enter a state of unconsciousness. To work with mental disorders — anxiety, depression, melancholia — healing from the inside. To be able to enter a dead woman's mind and bring her back to life.

This was the session Reddin observed, a completely unprofessional eavesdropping that, had it been discovered, would have barred him forever from the House of Healing. The woman had been on his ward for several days, the surgery demanded for her head injury so involved that her adept healer, exhausted after twenty-four hours of unbroken contact, had fallen asleep during the procedure, waking to find that although the surgeon had successfully completed the operation, the women existed in a comatose state, floating in the darkness. Reddin knew her to be all but dead, her pupils unresponsive, her reflexes null, the single sign of life the barely distinguishable pulse of blood moving through a vein in her neck. When he saw her healer pull the screens around her bed, he took his future into his hands, deciding to watch what was by established tradition the most private and holy moment between an adept healer and a patient.

It looked like sleep: simple, natural, undramatic. The healer positioned himself on a low stool at the head of the bed, placing his arms and hands over her shoulders and upper arms, and leaning over her, lowered his head until it rested beside hers on the pillow. Closing his eyes, his face gradually became as blank as hers. Finally, after hours of rapt observation, Reddin saw something miraculous. At first it was no more than a twitch of facial movement on the patient's part, a movement so quickly executed that at first he doubted his eyes. Gradually, other movements occurred, the forefinger of her left hand raised and lowered, her mouth opened and shut. Once he began to accept these signs of returning consciousness, he'd turned his attention to the healer. His face was still unreadable, the muscles of the jaw slack, his tongue lolling out of his mouth, a face devoid of intelligence and verging on the grotesque, until Reddin began to notice that each movement made by the women was precisely matched by the healer. That recognition was the turning point for Reddin, the living, incontrovertible truth that the healer was not a self-assured puppeteer manipulating his patient (the commonly-held view of Reddin and most of his fellow non-adept practitioners, who used to roll their eyes at the "mystery" surrounding adept healing), but had actually entered her physical and mental state, putting himself in a position of jeopardy, risking his own life.

Chastened, sickened at the thought of his jokes and jibes made at others' expense, Reddin stole away from the House of Healing and climbed up the attic stairs hoping to find sanctuary from the vision that would not leave his mind. There was no sanctuary, only a purgatory of shame, a limbo of purposelessness—for how could he ever be content with his former tasks when he would always be denied access to the true healing experience; and finally, a hell he wrought for himself out of envy, bitterness, and furtive, soul-destroying anger. He sulked for days, refusing food and conversation, the constant taps on his door by father, mother, and both siblings driving him deeper into depression, for the only thing he wanted, the only thing forever denied to him, was experienced daily by every member of his family. Finally, he could bear it no longer.

Pasiphae was his goal, his quiet, self-effacing mother who loved him as all elderly women love their youngest child—uncritically and without reservation, as if that young soul was a link to their own youth, now long-departed. And finally, on one long afternoon of tears, accusations, excuses, and demands, he caused her to break an oath to a code of ethics written by the Eighth Mother, the very one responsible for Pasiphae's family's entrance into Pelion.

"YOU'VE DONE IT before, or so you've admitted! Why can't you do it again, especially if I give you permission? That's allowed between a healer and a non-adept patient! What's so different in this situation?"

"You twist my words, son. Your father and I entered your thoughts as we did all our children, at the correct age and under the strict guidelines of the oath we took. We never entered your mind again, nor has your brother or your sister. We made them understand. I thought you understood as well."

"But I don't understand, mother! That's why I want you to try!"

He thought his fury would force her into action, but she sat unmoved. Despairing, he'd knelt at her feet, wanting desperately for her to touch him, to stroke away the bitterness that made him cruel. Her hands remained clasped in her lap.

"Will you tell me the truth, mother?"

"I always have, son. I shan't begin lying today."

"When you and father tried to contact me, what was it like?"

"It was . . . ," her voice thickened, and he could hear her reluctance to continue, " . . . difficult to accept the fact that we had a child cut off from the gift."

"What was my mind like? How is it different from when you touch Orrin, for instance?"

She regarded him for a moment, then folded her hands together, the fingers entwined, a gesture that had always been the signal of a favorite story told and retold to a young son who sat cross-legged at her feet.

"It's not as simple to describe as you may think. When I touch Orrin's mind, I pass through a kind of darkness and enter a place of light where his consciousness lives. Once there, words aren't necessary, for our language is composed of images and emotions. It's not as easy as you may think, for nothing can be hidden," she corrected herself, "or at least, if Orrin chose to hide something from me, I would perceive that barrier and not attempt to cross it."

"And when you touched me?" Reddin urged.

"We traveled the same path, over darkness and into light, but there was no greeting from the other side. You were unaware of our presence—a mind without shadows, inquisitive and restless."

"Please, mother, please do this for me. If you don't, I think I shall go mad . . ."

There was no fury left in him; only misery.

"What will be gained, my son?"

"Perhaps nothing. Perhaps everything."

"There's no hope that you've changed in some way."

"You've told me there's always hope."

This was the appeal that won her; not rationality, fury, intimidation or cruelty. She closed her eyes and placed her hands on Reddin's shoulders.

"Breathe regularly, my son, and think of something that brings you happiness."

Trying to do as he was told, he thought of the Sanctum and the offering of his hair that had taken place at the age of five. Twenty-four years later, he could still remember the scent of the incense and oils as they first touched his nostrils. White stone, brass fixtures without decoration of any sort, columns so high that he almost fell over backward in his attempt to see where they ended. A woman dressed entirely in black, a color he had never seen anyone wear, her cheeks like ripe apples, with a glow in her eyes that made him forget his fear of the pedestal that he climbed alone, his father and mother standing close by on the Sanctum floor, united in their demand that he perform this act all by himself.

The memory grew in clarity as he recalled the woman in black's easy manner, the way she spoke without a trace of pomp or splendor that one might have expected in such a hushed place.

"What gift do you offer, child-of-Pelion?"

Reddin could hear his voice echoing in the high vaults of the ceiling, a shrill treble responding with the memorized text.

"I give my hair."

"Do you give this gift of your own free will?"

Her eyes shone down on him as she nodded her encouragement.

"I do."

The silver knife cut smoothly through the locks gathered at the back of his neck. As she consigned them to the flames that burned on the altar, her voice rose in a loud shout of thanksgiving:

"Reddin gives his first gift!"

He knew there were no more lines to be spoken, for his mother had coached him carefully, but suddenly it occurred to him that he should be given a present in return. After all, his mother taught him that when one received a gift, a gift must be returned to the giver. This was the principle of giving on which Pelion was founded.

"What gift will you give me?" he demanded of her.

The apple-cheeked woman grew thoughtful, as if she was considering his question carefully. He liked her from the first; now that he saw she was really listening to him (as few adults did), he liked her even more.

"What gift do you require, Reddin?"

She didn't seem to be in a hurry, as almost all adults were, so he thought about it for a long time. He'd always wanted a dog, but somehow it didn't seem a proper request. Nothing else important came to mind, so he decided it might be better to think about it.

"I'm not sure. If I think of something later, can I ask then?"

She looked funny for a moment, the way his mother looked when she remembered something she'd forgotten.

"Of course, child. Ask when you discover what you truly desire."

In all these years, he'd never remembered it so clearly. The smells, the sights, the exact words and thoughts . . . and then he saw his mother's face, ashen under her dark skin, her eyes full of fear. Her hands jerked away from his shoulders as though they'd been burned.

"What happened, mother?"

"I don't know."

She stood abruptly and began to pace the narrow confines of the attic room, rubbing her hands together like she was cleansing them under a stream of water. He watched her helplessly, not understanding anything, either the nature of his vision or her agitated state.

"That was unlike anything I've ever experienced and something that should never have happened."

Unless she told him what had transpired, he knew only that he'd remembered something he'd forgotten, although even now he felt he could relive it without any effort whatsoever.

"Tell me, mother."

She wheeled to face him, her robes swirling around her ankles in her haste to confront him.

"I told you to find a place of inner happiness. When I entered your thoughts, you were in the Sanctum, as completely unaware of me as you were as a child. I was ready to leave, content that I had done as you asked and that finally you would be satisfied, when I found I couldn't leave! I was trapped, something that's never happened to me before—not with anyone, not my parents, your father, the Seventeenth Mother, Orrin, Cynthia, not anyone!"

Recognizing the symptoms of near-hysteria, Reddin helped her into the leather chair. Running to his desk to retrieve a cup of water, he lifted it to her lips. She drank thirstily, her eyes never ceasing their rapid blinking, and eventually quieted.

"Forgive me, my son. I can only blame myself. I broke my oath and I was punished."

"Is that what it seemed to you, a punishment?"

Her reduction of one of the most liberating moments he had ever experienced into some kind of retributive act hurt him deeply.

"What else could it be?" was her helpless question.

"I think it was a sign," was his curt response.

If anything, Pasiphae's distress increased.

"No, Reddin! It was only a memory, chosen by you and enhanced by my presence. One can't become adept simply by wishing for it! You know better!"

Her condescension hurt even more than her dismissal of what he'd just experienced. Struggle as he might, he couldn't keep the resentment out of his voice.

"You take your gift too much for granted. It's no wonder you've forgotten there's a different path for those like me."

In that moment he decided on a course of action he would have dismissed as ridiculous a few short days ago. His mother was staring at him as if he had, indeed, gone mad.

"I will compete in the Trial."

SHRUGGING OFF THE quilt from his shoulders, Reddin walked to the desk, broke the seal with the end of his penknife, and unfolded the letter.

> Reddin, third child of Pasiphae and Elan, you are accepted into The Trial of Selection to be held on the last day of the tenth moon. May the citizens of Pelion find you worthy.
>
> Tubal, President of the Guild Assembly

It took several readings to seem real. For three days he'd imagined these exact words. Now they were before him, the handwriting puerile, the pristine surface of the thick paper marred by several blots, as if the writer wrote infrequently and carelessly when he was finally forced to put pen to paper.

Twenty-four candidates vying for three female ernani. Today his chances narrowed to one in eight. Through interviews and examinations he'd stifled any reservations, intent on presenting his examiners with a calm, confident demeanor. Now that the incredible had occurred, all his doubts resurfaced.

He'd attended the Trial every year of his life, as did everyone in Pelion. As a child it seemed a festival, the entire city gathered together to celebrate a day of thanksgiving. Shops, schools and libraries closed their doors, everyone dressed in their finest clothes, and an enormous procession of citizens wended their way through the broad city streets to the northern gate and on to the Legion cavalry grounds east of the city. All but the most severely ill patients from the House of Healing were transported by stretcher and cart, the elderly were carried, the young danced their way to the music of fiddles and fifes; and everyone witnessed the events that would yield a clear choice as to the people's preference.

In a matter of days, he would be a part of that great celebration, expected to parade his half-naked body in front of thousands of people, forced to compete in physical trials for which he had little love and no talent, hoping that somehow he could make himself attractive and likeable enough so that when the events were over and the ballots cast, a majority of adult citizens would choose him over twenty-three like contestants.

Crumpling the paper in his hands, he stared out the window.

"I'm sorry, my son. I know how much this meant to you."

His laugh was aimed at no one in particular. He continued to watch the bare branches cast about wildly by the wind.

"You misunderstand, mother. I may compete if I choose."

He didn't need to see her face to know she was mystified by his reaction.

"Then you must compete! If they selected you, they must believe you have the ability to succeed."

His smile was crooked as he turned to her.

"Look at me, and try not to be my mother for the moment. I'm twenty-nine; most of the candidates are younger. I'm neither tall, handsome, or covered with bulging muscles, I'd never thrown a javelin or bent a bow until recently, and the only event I've a chance of winning is the short-distance run. In addition, I'm not much given to smiling, easy phrase-making, or flirting with women I don't know. You know the type of men who win. Now in all honesty, mother, do you truly think I have a chance?"

Reddin had once seen a bantam rooster fluff his feathers to the point that he grew twice his normal size and emit a crow so impossibly loud that several people in the marketplace, himself included, had actually jumped in alarm. So his mother rose to her feet, her hands on her hips, her voice shrill with disbelief.

"Do you mean to tell me that you've turned this entire household topsy-turvy for the past three moons, sulking, moody, dragging in here late at night, your body so sore that your father and I can hear you groan with every step you take up these rickety stairs, and that once you've taken the first step toward what you told me was the one thing in this world you wanted, that you are seriously considering not competing?!"

He opened his mouth to respond but she was not through with him.

"As to your looks, your behavior, and your abilities; you're right—I'm your mother, and to me you are the most beautiful of men. Don't you dare shrug off my compliment in that infuriating way of yours! The important point is that Orrin can help you."

"Orrin?!"

This was becoming not only embarrassing, but painful. Orrin was twelve years his senior and at forty-one was one of the most perfect specimens of masculinity Reddin had ever met. Tall and big-boned, he moved with a grace and fluidity rarely found in so large a man. A natural athlete, he excelled at everything he put his hand to. After nearly twenty years in the House of Hetaeras, he rose to the level of Master a few years ago. They had never been close, whether because of the difference in age or the question of adeptness, Reddin wasn't quite sure. He only knew that he felt uncouth and unlovable around Orrin's perfect manners and winning ways. True, it was Orrin who recommended a trainer for him. Reddin had even seen him in the gymnasium when he worked there late into the night, covered in sweat and cursing in pure frustration. On these occasions, his brother raised a hand in greeting and went about his own affairs.

Pasiphae may have slowed, but she didn't falter.

"Have you never asked your brother what he does, Reddin? Or do you think that because he's not the scholar you are, he has no talents?"

The image of the bantam rooster came to mind again and was transposed into a clucking hen as he watched her bridle at the thought that anyone might question the talents of one of her brood.

"For your information, your elder brother is an expert in instilling confidence. Not just confidence in joining, as most people seem to think, but in his client's perceptions of themselves."

She finally had to stop for breath. For that reason alone he was able to interrupt her.

"Only two days remain until the Trial . . ."

"In two days Orrin can help you in ways you cannot help yourself. As to the events, you must do your best."

Her enthusiasm was contagious and her beliefs were fast becoming his.

"Do you think he'd mind me asking?"

Throwing her hands into the air, she addressed the attic rafters with something akin to despair.

"Mind you asking?! Sometimes I think you're blind to everyone who cares about you! Orrin's monitored your progress every night for three moons, telling us how hard you've been working, advising the trainer before every session. He's wanted to help since the day you announced your intention to compete. It also might interest you to know that unlike your father, your mother, and your sister, he's the only one who thinks this is a good idea!"

"You've made your point, mother."

"Orrin wasn't my point at all."

He wandered back to the window and examined the crumpled piece of paper lying on his desk. Tree branches scratched at the window, a sudden gust of wind throwing an avalanche of raindrops splattering against the glass. Reddin shook his head to clear it. The leaden skies finally opened and released their contents over the valley of the castle. The staccato beat of rain on the attic roof was a fanfare inviting him to action.

"I'll do my best."

She moved slightly behind him, resting her head lightly against his shoulder. Her touches had been rare when he was growing up and were all the more precious to him now that he understood the reason behind her reticence. Difficult as it must have been, she restrained herself so she wouldn't be tempted to invade the privacy of his thoughts. How sad for both of them, this division of gifts for which he'd blamed her for so long. He could see their reflection clearly in the panes of glass, mother and son watching the wind-tossed branches as a rainy night fell on Pelion.

THE ONLY THING that enabled Reddin to maintain the studied air of neutrality he assumed the moment he ascended the reviewing stand was the thought that everything would be over in a few hours. Mentally he ticked off the time; a few minutes more on this platform, so many for this or that event, so many until the ballots would be cast, counted, and the decision made. Had he thought of anything else, his surroundings would have overwhelmed him. The thought of being drowned in this sea of humanity, losing himself to the crowds' appetites, was something he was determined to avoid.

Here he stood, a man fully-grown who prided himself on his reserved manner and intellectual abilities, enduring strangers ogling his half-naked body. The fact that many of them were doing just that was not encouraging—in fact it caused him to retreat deeper into himself, trying to hold on to his purpose here. When comments drifted up to him, he struggled gamely not to hear them, choosing instead to concentrate his attention on the trial grounds in front of him or the food booths that lay beyond the running track in an open meadow to the north.

The other factor that threatened his equanimity (besides the seemingly endless stream of onlookers who were passing by the line to take their first look at the candidates) was the fact that he was slowly turning into a block of ice. The rain stopped in the middle of the night after two days of solid downpour, leaving the air damp and decidedly cold. Over Reddin's strenuous objections, Orrin insisted on a thick application of oil, assuring him that it would highlight what muscles he possessed and pointing out (with a knowing smile that fast became a source of major irritation to his younger brother) that Reddin's skin would darken considerably, thus contrasting all the more with the lighter-skinned contestants. The oil seemed to be having the desired effect but was lowering his skin temperature at an alarming rate. His teeth chattered so loudly he was surprised the noise drew no comments from the spectators.

That his brother had been proved right in almost every way was small comfort, although Reddin had grudgingly approved the changes he'd put into effect. That Orrin had discriminating tastes was undeniable, although the steps to achieving his notion of perfection were embarrassing to a degree.

The first thing under attack had been the club of hair Reddin customarily wore knotted and tied at the back of his neck. When Orrin suggested it be cut, Reddin assumed he meant that it be cropped close to his head in the current fashion and agreed without a fuss. The length of his hair had nothing to do with vanity—it was a holdover from student days when he'd hated the thought of asking his parents for money to be wasted on the luxury of barbers. Only later did he come to understand that Orrin had no intention of making him look ordinary. If everyone else had cropped hair, then Reddin's would be worn long and unbound, cut evenly to meet his shoulders and falling from a center part. When Reddin complained that it would be continually in his face, Orrin produced a white length of cloth to be tied around his forehead during the events, silencing him with a knowing grin that put Reddin's teeth on edge.

Then there had been the matter of the loincloth. Since it was the only thing he'd be wearing on a day in late autumn, Reddin chose a soft woolen fabric of serviceable grey, judging that warmth, comfort, and a dark color that would not show dirt made it the perfect choice. Orrin's preference for pure white cotton seemed nothing short of insane considering that he'd be streaked with dirt and sweat by the end of the first event. After a heated disagreement, Reddin put it on and regarded himself in the glass.

A stranger looked back at him, someone whose perfectly straight black hair, burnished skin, and dark eyes existed in stark contrast to the white fabric circling his hips and forehead. His face must have reflected his shock, for Orrin smiled, almost tenderly, and spoke to him as the older brother Reddin never really knew.

"There are two ways to go about this Trial. You can compare yourself to everyone else, try to look and behave like everyone else, and hope you'll appeal to the crowd's idea of what a man should be. Or you can take advantage of your uniqueness and impress upon them that some men are neither athletes nor exhibitionists, yet remain worthy of consideration. I've prepared you to look different from anyone else—and yes, your loincloth will soon be covered in dirt and sweat. But why hide the fact that you're going to be exerting an enormous effort on the trial grounds? Let the others cater to the crowd. Show them instead that you will persevere no matter the cost."

A quick laugh punctuated Orrin's seriousness.

"A smile now and again wouldn't be out of place, mind you, but don't let them turn you into something you're not."

Moved, yet unable to respond to such unexpected concern with anything besides gruffness, Reddin could only reply, "I never thought I'd be appealing to their pity."

"Not pity, but their understanding that there are many different things that go into the formation of a man, and not the least of these are self-respect and the courage to be different."

His mother was right—Orrin helped him in ways he couldn't help himself, giving him confidence in his appearance as well as a methodology by which he could attempt something absolutely alien to his nature. Orrin's advice became his manifesto: somehow he must not lose himself to the crowd. Pelion must choose Reddin rather than some figment of Reddin that denied his essence.

The muted tones of a gong struck three times signaled the end of the viewing of the candidates. By craning his neck over his right shoulder he could see members of the Guild Assembly, the Council of Pelion and the Eighteenth Mother take their places behind a long table set in the middle of the viewing area on the southern side of the track. Some of the citizenry brought stools, some sat on the ground, while others milled about in a constant state of restlessness—ten thousand people gathered to watch the efforts of two dozen men.

The trial grounds themselves were laid out in an oval ring that constituted the track on which the short distance race and the hurdles would be run. In the center were the vertical posts that held the climbing ropes, a wrestling ring, and a pit of sand for the long jump. After these events were finished, pieces of equipment would be removed and replaced for the archery and javelin events, the contestants aiming toward targets set at the cleared area on the far northern edge of the track. The long distance run was the only event that didn't take place in full view of the crowd, wending its way through the hills east of Pelion, a ten-mile course through woods and over streams, the final test of endurance that signaled the end of the Trial.

Reddin's trainer had competed in the Trials for three years, although he'd never won a place high enough on the list to enter the Maze. He reviewed the strategies for the day early that morning as Reddin stripped and oiled himself in the large tent set aside for the participants and their noisy entourages of family, friends and last-minute well-wishers. Having forbidden his family to accompany him past the tent flaps manned by solemn-faced Legionnaires, Reddin's last contact with the outside world was his trainer. Reddin appreciated his frankness, even though his predictions were not encouraging.

"You're fortunate that your two best events come first. Remember there will be two heats before the final race, so don't expend so much energy in the heats that you won't have anything left for the one that counts. Try to finish with the top three runners each time. With all this rain, the track will be slow, and you'll have a better chance than the heavier men. As to the ropes, you're nimble but some of your competitors have much more upper body strength."

The next set of instructions was even more discouraging.

"The first thing you should do is study your wrestling partner. They'll pair you with someone as close to your weight as possible, and since they award points for aggression as well as actual pins, it's best to rely on offense rather than defense. As to the long jump, archery, and the javelin," he'd scratched his chin, "well, it's best not to worry. Concentrate on conserving your energy and resting between bouts."

"You're not a bad hurdler, Reddin, if you get the timing right from the outset. If you're rested, you might have a chance to place. As to the long distance run, well . . ."

Reddin prepared for the worst. To his surprise, the trainer winked at him.

"Strange things happen out in those hills. There's no doubt it's the worst event—everyone's tired, nearly everyone's discouraged, and by that time you'll be running on sheer nerve. The thing to remember is that you must finish. If you don't, you'll automatically be dropped from the list no matter how well you do in the other events."

His last comment was shrewdly speculative, as if he was privy to a secret.

"It's my opinion that the old Mother, the Seventeenth, thought the most important event was the long distance run. She was downright canny when she insisted on the rule about finishing. I've run it three times myself and coached some twenty men in the last ten years. Each and every one of them swears that the long run was the true Trial. I've seen frontrunners up to that point, some of them winners of three or even four events, unable to finish. I've also seen men who didn't seem to have a chance, win it to their own, and everyone else's, surprise."

"It's the loneliness out there that will either finish you or bring you home. Somehow she knew that, she, who'd never run a step in her life. She was a cripple, you know, but a woman of keen perceptions. Yes, keen perceptions . . ."

The crowd around the reviewing stand began to disperse as the candidates moved down the stairs and onto the playing field. A Legionnaire marched up to Reddin, a hearty fellow with a square jaw and keen eyes.

"I'm called Flavius and I'll be your escort through the Trial. You're in the first heat of the short run, so we must hurry. If you need anything—water, blankets, resin or the like, let me know."

The pit of Reddin's stomach dropped to the nether regions as Flavius clapped him on his shoulders.

"You'll soon be warm enough. The weather's clearing and the wind is dying down."

In the face of such good-natured optimism, Reddin muttered, "I'll need more than fine weather."

The Legionnaire must have heard him, for the smile left his face and he continued in a more serious vein.

"You must put everything aside now. Nothing is important except what must be accomplished here and now. Come."

Following Flavius' straight, soldierly back as he descended the platform and cleared a path through the masses of spectators, Reddin tried to clear his mind of the noise of the crowd and the ever-present cold, pushing away doubts and resentments until there was nothing left but the task. A trumpet rang three shrill blasts, and the Twenty-Sixth Trial of Selection began.

HESIONE PREPARED HERSELF for this day as she did for no other. Methodically stripping herself of all preconceived notions and prejudices from past experiences, she read and re-read the Seventeenth Mother's notes on the Trial, notes she committed to memory six years ago. Scribbled on the leaves of a leather-bound book, the notes were copious and detailed to a fault. She-Who-Was-Meliope left nothing to chance. With a far-reaching gaze and a remarkable understanding of the people of Pelion, she outlined a process for selection she hoped would try not just the men seeking Preparation, but the citizenry itself. While the document outlined order and procedures, the mood behind its legalistic jargon revealed her bleak outlook. There was no joy in her creation; she knew, somehow, what would result.

As Hesione assumed her place at the table littered with the profiles, documentation, letters and assorted forms and reports of the candidates submitted to the Guild Assembly, she acknowledged the formal greetings of the others with a smile and nod and immediately began to assess the twenty-four candidates on the reviewing stand. One of the conditions necessary for the populace's acceptance of her predecessor's plan was that the Mother of Pelion be completely removed from the selection process. She-Who-Was-Meliope was shrewd enough to accept this demand, gaining from her concession the inclusion of the Mistress of Joining and the male High Healer in the first process of elimination. Thus, Hesione might be prevented from first-hand knowledge, but was privy to everything gleaned from the perceptions and observations of the members of her Council.

She identified Reddin immediately, standing aloof from the passing crowd, exuding an exterior reserve not present in the others, many of whom actively encouraged passersby to speak or linger, often bending down to grasp a proffered hand or pinch an admiring cheek. Here was the iron-clad control that Ranier witnessed and Chryse identified by intuition. There was no apology in his stance, no resentment of the crowds, merely a quiet contemplation of the raucous festival surrounding him. His appearance, too, accentuated his difference from the others. Slight and sinewy, clothed in immaculate white that made his darkness a vivid and compelling force, the others seemed either brash or lackluster in comparison. That the crowd was responding to him was clear, for Hesione noted that they tended to lower their voices as they passed him, as if they feared to disrupt his patient watch.

The review over, twenty-four Legionnaires hand-picked by Prax and Strato, the Head Trainer of the Maze, were herding their charges to their first event. Before the revisions penned by the Sixteenth Mother, these men were guards armed with cudgels and clinking key-rings as they escorted the manacled ernani from place to place within the Maze. With the arrival of volunteer ernani, their roles evolved from guards to monitors, present to insure order and adherence to rules and regulations. It was not uncommon for newly-transformed adepts within the Maze to choose duty as monitors, a custom Hesione heartily approved. Prax began his distinguished career in this way and such was the case of Flavius, whose own Trial was not so long ago that he had forgotten the challenges now faced by his charge.

Tubal, seated immediately to her right, gestured impatiently for her to undertake her sole duty for the day. As she rose to her feet, the crowd hushed, and she recited the appropriate words, hoping the one with whom her hopes resided would hear within its words the cadences of blessing.

HIS CHEST HEAVING, his legs aching in one fiery band of pain that ran from the top of his buttocks to the back of his ankles, Reddin barely felt the blanket Flavius wrapped around him, so intent was he on trying to pump air back into his spent lungs. The Legionnaire had proved invaluable; even now he was walking his charge around the space cleared for waiting competitors, half-supporting him against his solid frame while Reddin recovered from the final race over the hurdles. Once his breathing began to return to normal, he wiped away the stinging sweat from his eyes with the corner of the blanket, offering what he hoped was a careless smile to his escort.

"Tell me, Flavius. How did I finish?"

The Legionnaire's arm tightened around his shoulders, communicating his commiseration better than any words could have done.

"Third. The wiry fellow second; the long-legged one in the dark-blue loincloth was first."

Strange that we have no names among us, Reddin thought. There was a logic to the anonymity of competition — to learn their names would make them persons in their own right rather than ones to be defeated, although in his case it was not a question of defeating so much as being defeated. Prepared for disappointment by his trainer's honesty and fully aware of his inadequacies, it was still difficult to accept his performance of near-misses and solid losses. Second in the short race, third in the ropes, the other events were so far beyond his abilities that he didn't even bother to ask Flavius his placement. The only badge of merit he could claim was his continued participation. Once he lost the only event he'd ever dreamed of winning, he settled down to making the best of it. Not for him the roars and applause of the crowds as the winner of each event stepped forward to receive the President's personal congratulations.

The crowd was cheering now for the winner of the javelin throw. Picturing his total ineptitude in that event, Reddin could no longer contain his mirth at his plight. Pushing wet hair out of his eyes and retying the headband, he jerked his thumb toward the ceremony in progress.

"Come on, Flavius. I can take it. Was I last, or next to last?"

When the Legionnaire hesitated, a surge of color causing his naturally florid features to glow an even brighter red, Reddin laughed all the harder. It was good to laugh—something he hadn't done in such a long time he'd forgotten how restorative it could be. Everything else receded except the picture of him throwing a stick through the air and actually being judged on his ability to do so.

The cheers of the appreciative crowd faded as the ceremony at the table ended and the agonized scream of a man rose and hovered over the suddenly hushed grounds. In a single instant Reddin located the source—the wrestling ring where the final match of the heavy-weight group was in progress. In the next, he dropped the blanket and was off across the wet grass, Flavius' wide-eyed look of astonishment a memory left far behind as he ran toward the source of another scream, this one more agonized than the first.

Shoving his way through the group gathered around the downed man writhing on the ground, Reddin saw his mouth open to scream yet again and his left fist pound the ground as if he hoped he could force the earth to open and sink into it. Choosing to concentrate of the source of the man's pain rather than the pain itself (which seemed to be the helpless reaction of the others) Reddin's attention went quickly to the motionless right arm, hanging at an unnatural angle from a shoulder that had been dislocated in the midst of the bout. There were healers in the area of competition, for he had seen their leaf-green robes on the fringes of the grounds, but none were as close as he was to the injured man. Not only was this an injury he'd treated before, it was a relatively simple procedure and would relieve the man's agony almost immediately. Kneeling, he placed a hand on either side of the wrestler's head, forcing him to concentrate on something besides the pain.

"I'm going to put your shoulder back in its socket. It will hurt, but quickly be over."

He rubbed his hands on his loincloth, trying to clean off the oil, sweat, and grime covering them. Turning the wrestler's head over his uninjured shoulder so he was prevented from anticipating Reddin's next move, Reddin adjusted his position, grasped the arm firmly, and exerting pressure that brought another, higher-pitched scream out of the wrestler's throat, eased

the joint back into the socket. The man's panting chest was the only thing
that moved for a moment, and then he pulled himself up into a sitting position,
rubbing the sore shoulder with his left hand, while he tentatively flexed his
right. Green robes flashed in front of Reddin's eyes and Ranier, High Healer
of Pelion, the man who examined him for admission to the Trial, crouched
by his side. Running his hands briefly over the wrestler's shoulder, he turned
to Reddin with an unreadable expression.

"Return to your escort. You must conserve your energy for the long
distance run."

Without waiting to see if his command was obeyed, the High Healer
turned back to the injured man. Reddin backed away in confusion. He hadn't
expected praise, but the healer's cool dismissal surprised him. Surely he'd
performed correctly and in accordance to his oath. If he'd waited for another
healer, the man's agony would have been prolonged. Unsure how to proceed,
worried that the man's injury might demand further care, Reddin heard the
High Healer speak again, this time with quiet approval.

"There's nothing more you can accomplish here, Reddin. Concentrate
on the Trial. I give you my word that I'll attend him."

Relieved, Reddin backed away from the ring. A firm grip on his bare
shoulder turned him around and Flavius was there. As they cleared the
crowd of contestants and escorts gathered around the ring and set off across
the center of the track, a smattering of applause made Reddin lift his head.
The applause grew stronger, several voices calling out something he couldn't
distinguish. Perplexed at their behavior, for no one stood in front of the
President's table, it was Flavius who relieved his ignorance.

"They're cheering for you. They saw what you did. Now they show their
appreciation."

Orrin advised him that a smile at the crowd would not be out of place.
Up to this moment he'd found no reason to smile. In the face of the crowd's
approbation, not even his own natural reserve could prevent the wide grin
that split his face at the thought that finally his talents had been seen and
judged worthy. As he neared the starting line of the long distance race, his
spirits rose, buoying up his tired body, putting a spring in his step and
purpose in his stride. One more event, and even if he had to crawl on his
hands and knees across the finish line, he knew he would do just that. No
matter if his final standing was fourteenth or twenty-fourth, no matter if he
was attired in a dirt-stained rag, his sweat-drenched hair matted flat against
his head—Reddin had made the Trial his own.

IT SEEMED AS if they had been summoned to the reviewing stand an age
ago. Reddin was unconscious from the moment he crossed the finish line

and sagged into Flavius' waiting arms. Now, almost three hours after the last candidate finished the race, he was groggy and barely able to stand. Flavius stood directly behind him, as did all the escorts, their upright figures in complete contrast to the exhausted men who struggled to assume their former poses as they waited for the tabulation of the ballots.

Reddin closed his eyes for a moment and would have fallen asleep again if he hadn't felt two firm hands grasp his upper arms from behind and shake him awake. A complete stranger to him this morning, over the course of the day Reddin felt closer to this Legionnaire than he did to many of his childhood friends. Flavius must have picked him up and carried him to the tent at the conclusion of the long distance run, for Reddin couldn't remember anything except the relief of finally being able to lie down. Regular strokes of a rough cloth wiped away the sweat and oil, leaving him dry and warm for the first time since morning light.

It was also Flavius who woke him with a steaming mug of salty broth and the welcome news that Reddin had finished seventh in the long run. Two other candidates, one of them the winner of the javelin event, didn't finish the final race. The man whose shoulder was injured chose not to participate in the final event, bringing the total to twenty-one. Flavius conveyed this last bit of information to a slowly-reviving Reddin with a serious demeanor and a decided gleam of enjoyment in his eyes. Besides Reddin, twenty exhausted men remained. Even Dysponteus, the long-legged hero of the afternoon who'd won two events, the short run and the hurdles, listed slightly to the right, rubbing his thigh as if it pained him.

Reddin was swaying again, wanting nothing more than to sleep forever. His legs felt as if they were no longer connected to his torso while muscle spasms sent regular tremors through his shoulders, back, and arms. Again, Flavius held him upright, whispering a warning close to his ear.

"The President's ready to announce the standings. Wake up, now, or I'll let you fall on your arse!"

Obeying his well-meaning threat, Reddin shook his head to clear it, blinking his heavy eyelids a few times to bring the world back into focus. Tubal mounted the reviewing stand and stood facing the enormous crowd, which grew silent at his approach. His sense of self-importance was matched only by the size of his belly as he cleared his throat, quite needlessly since the entire grounds were hushed with expectation, and began to read off the names. Tradition demanded that they be read in reverse order, a tradition that suited Reddin perfectly, since once his name was read, he could limp off the reviewing stand, locate his family, and stumble home.

The names were reeled off one after another—some greeted by angry shouts and demands for recounts by disgruntled supporters (who were largely ignored since there was no one to blame: every adult citizen voted and the votes were tabulated by a group randomly selected by numbers at the top of each ballot); others by cries and tears as they surrounded their friend or relative and helped him off the stand. Inexorably, the President continued reading, pausing until the named one stepped off or was carried off the stand before he announced the next name and ranking.

The President's droning had a hypnotic effect and Reddin was nodding again, until one particularly shrill-voiced woman began to harangue everyone who had over-looked the qualities of her son, Reddin roused to look around him, realizing only eight men remained on the platform. Without turning his head, he spoke through lips that barely moved.

"This is impossible! Flavius, did I miss my name?"

"You did not. I've been listening carefully since I noticed you were sleeping."

The groans of disappointment were louder and more profound as Tubal read on. At last, Reddin heard his name.

"Reddin, child of Pasiphae and Elan. Fifth."

There might have been an outcry or applause of some kind, yet if there was, it flew over him like a flock of winging birds, passing so far above his head that he sensed their shadow without noting their number or direction. He felt a brief pang of regret that he would not enter the Maze, then dismissed it at the sight of his brother standing below him, his arms outstretched and welcoming; his father, too, reaching up for him, as were many friends and even greater numbers of strangers. Reddin turned to Flavius and extended his arm, to be encased in a fierce bear-hug that left him limp and shaking. Breaking the embrace as quickly as he had initiated it, Flavius lowered Reddin off the platform and into the waiting arms of his family.

Amidst the resulting confusion, two things broke through Reddin's exhaustion: his mother's radiance, and as they passed the reviewing stand, an odd expression on the Eighteenth Mother's face. Reddin noticed her several times that day as he crossed and re-crossed the trial grounds, watching her as she sat motionless behind the table with the other important personages, her face smooth, tranquil, and slightly distant from the festive mania of her people.

As Orrin lifted him into the hired cart and Reddin sank down into the cushions, it occurred to him what had been disquieting about the woman in black. Her strangely colored eyes looked directly at him, the expression in them containing none of their former neutrality. As the monotonous motion of the cart increased his drowsiness, his last thought before sleep claimed him was that as incredible as it might seem, his efforts today had received the personal benediction of the Eighteenth Mother of Pelion.

Chapter 9

Keeper of the Flame

AN ENORMOUS ORB floated majestically above the stone battlements of the sleeping city, its turreted towers reaching out like greedy hands for a golden coin held just beyond their grasp. The patterns of the stars were indistinct, their brightness dimmed by the moon's domination of the night sky. Her father called its crimson coloration a "hunter's moon," but as a child creating fancies of her own, Lillas' imagination spun a private explanation for its altered hue. Lillas' moon proclaimed its authority at the moment of the diminishing warmth of the dying sun; no longer limited to a wardrobe of silver, white, and palest blue, the moon garbed itself in the colors of the sun, proving its ascendancy at the onset of these, the frigid moons of winter.

"Awake are you, Skat?"

Halys lay roughly a body's length beyond Lillas, his lean leather-clad body stretched flat on his stomach under the striped blanket, his head turned slightly toward her on the flat saddle that served as his pillow. The others slept soundly, joining in a medley of snores, grunts, and mumbled words. Men sleep noisily, mused Lillas, as if they argue even in their dreams. She had thought everyone asleep until Halys interrupted her contemplation of the moon with a whisper so low that, had she been sleeping, it would not have disturbed her rest.

Such thoughtfulness seemed an inbred trait of this shy man from the north. The other sojourners in the caravan, Jarod and Stym, twin giants from Lapith, and Altug, the hawk-nosed cynic from the Sarujian Mountains, treated her as grown men are apt to regard a half-grown boy—as a decided nuisance and a constant irritant. Only Halys made a place for the boy Skat around the evening fire, his eyes cast down and away from the firelight as his thin fingers played restlessly with the rawhide laces of his tunic. Like Lillas, Halys studiously avoided the other travelers, guarding his privacy like a precious commodity. Quick to understand the advantage offered her by his behavior, Lillas was thankful that his habits made hers less noticeable.

For the first few days after joining the caravan, Lillas played the invalid at every opportunity and became accustomed to having her meals prepared and the camp maintenance handled by Hume's men. Then, seven days ago, her life of luxury came to an abrupt end. Awakened by the sound of departing hoof beats, the travelers were informed by Hume, the foul-mouthed leader of the caravan, that half his party was called away on pressing business and that they must earn their keep. From that day forward, she'd been forced to work and work hard, rotating duties with the others and supervised by Spence, a blunt fellow who kept an eagle-eye on her at all times and seemed to find fault with everything she put her hand to. Gathering firewood, laying and banking fires, preparing food, drawing water from the streams, all these tasks she tackled with good will if not any particular skill. When it came to the drudgery of digging holes for the privy and the even more hateful task of filling those holes every morning, she balked. Her nose had always been sensitive and the smell of excrement on an empty stomach brought her to the brink of nausea whenever her turn came round. Always resourceful in finding ways to avoid anything she didn't find to her liking, Lillas' request to switch assignments was met with an icy stare. When she retaliated with a fit of sulks and pouting, a bucket of ice-cold water was thrown on her by a less-than-impressed Spence, a round of hearty guffaws erupting from the twins and the mustachioed mountaineer. Enraged at their laughter and the fact that her ploy hadn't worked, she shoveled dirt into the holes with a vengeance, swearing revenge under her breath, which set them off into yet another laughing fit.

Besides slowing down the pace of the journey, the change in routine allowed her no time to herself and prevented her from any but the most cursory exchanges with Halys. That he was still awake and in need of companionship fit her own needs exactly. Tomorrow morning they would reach the city and whatever lay within those sheer forbidding walls.

"Yes, Halys, I'm awake."

He rolled over on his side and pulled a long strand of hair out of his face. He was clean-shaven, as were Jarod and Stym, which made Lillas less self-conscious of her smooth face, for no one challenged a Lapithian male's masculinity.

"I ask myself, `Halys, what waits tomorrow?'"

Unlike the twins, Halys spoke with a strong accent and an unusual ordering of words, causing Lillas to guess that he'd learned from a book rather than conversing with a native speaker. She'd grown accustomed to Halys' odd syntax with the result that it no longer interfered with their ability to communicate.

"It's the same for me. I don't know what I expected, but when Hume pointed out the city this afternoon, I . . . I was unprepared."

"Large it is, with many peoples. More peoples than stars, I'm thinking."

He sounded forlorn, this long-limbed quiet man who sat a horse with such easy mastery that Lillas aped him as she followed his horse's rump down the trail. That Halys, too, feared the unknown was reassuring.

"Don't worry, Halys. We've come this far, what's another few miles, more or less? Once inside, we'll still know one another."

Halys blinked once, twice, before he rolled over on his back.

"One friend among so many peoples. To be lost, I think, might happen."

Lillas refused to be affected by his melancholy. Instead, she tried to humor him out of his despondency.

"What makes you think you can lose me, Halys? Unless, of course, you'd rather not have a boy hanging about. The others don't like me. I thought you did."

A troubled sigh followed.

"Divided are the men and women. Of boys, I know little."

"Divided how?" Lillas asked sharply. This was the first she'd heard of such a notion. The thought of being separated from her only friend disturbed her.

"Divided first and mated last."

"Mated?!"

Her voice threatened to rise to a screech, a firm hand placed over her mouth and a warning shake of Halys' head reminding her that they must not wake the others. Once she nodded to indicate her compliance, the hand was removed and Lillas was soon engaged in her own calculations. This bit of information turned her plan head over tail. She'd come all this way to insure her ability to live free; now Halys' comment put her into yet another trap. As her thoughts raced, Halys spoke again.

"Too young are you to mate, Skat. A beardless boy of high voice . . ."

"You've no beard, Halys," Lillas retorted sharply.

"My peoples have little hair on the face. Jarod and Stym the same."

He hadn't taken offense as Lillas had half-intended. His reference to the twins piqued Lillas' curiosity. She'd never understood why Halys, who dressed and rode exactly like Jarod and Stym, was treated by them with disdain.

"Why don't Jarod and Stym talk to you, Halys?

"They from Ariod's lake come; I from more eastern lands. We make raids on each other—steal horses and women. Such is life on the plains and these grudges they bring with them." He paused, searching for the right words. "The tribe from Ariod's lake, they become. . ." a frown of concentration announced his efforts to convey something of great import, ". . . stronger than we. They have the gift long time. We must have it now, or soon we will be no more." His hand drifted down to his side, silent testimony to the future of his people.

"What is the gift, Halys?"

This was the question Lillas longed to ask but had never found an opportunity to voice. With breath held tightly, she waited for enlightenment.

"I know not, but with this gift comes ease and peace, knowledge and good things for the tribe. They have much and we too little." His voice hardened and Lillas could hear his determination. "For this I leave my peoples. I come for my tribe."

His selflessness gave Lillas a twinge of shame. Her desires were purely personal and based on curiosity rather than real need. Still, this information about mating needed more investigation.

"And you're willing to mate with a woman you've never met in order to bring this gift back to your people?"

The silence which greeted this question stretched to the point that Lillas feared Halys might have fallen asleep. When he spoke at last, his voice was no louder than a sigh.

"I will mate, yes."

With that, he rolled over, his back announcing his intention to sleep.

Lillas' eyes found the moon again; sleep was more elusive. Over and over again she heard Halys' quiet declaration of his intent to do whatever was necessary to achieve the gift. Were Lillas' desires so strong? Was this mating truly a requirement, or might there be some way to avoid it? Her eyes heavy-lidded, she grasped onto the thought she would carry with her into the city. I am not bound as Halys is bound. If this gift suits me I will persevere. If not, I will journey on.

In true Lillas-fashion, she didn't allow herself to dwell on the fact that no other destination came to mind.

USUALLY A PLACE of profound silence and measured footsteps, the Sanctum was invaded by noise, bustle, and seeming chaos. The unannounced arrival of five ernani at the northern gates placed an even greater burden on the caretakers of the Maze. Teachers, healers, and monitors sped haphazardly from entry to narthex, from narthex to altar, and from altar to the bronze portals of the Maze. The babble of strange tongues and unfamiliar dialects could be heard echoing in the glassed corridor. More than once Chryse sailed by like a ship rigged with saffron sails, ushering the candidates from Pelion toward the entrance to another world, one from which they would not emerge until spring. Families littered the antechambers like abandoned lovers as they watched their son or daughter, sister or brother, being escorted to the bronze doors and heard a resounding boom as they were closed to outsiders by the brown-clad members of the Legion.

If Hesione had not been so tired, she might have laughed. Not for her the awe-struck atmosphere that typically marked the place where Pelion's citizenry offered up their gifts. Hesione preferred the Sanctum as it was today, full of the clamor and commotion of humanity actively engaged in the pursuit of a plan. Far from being upset by the frenzy surrounding her, she reveled in the diversity represented by the ernani of this class. To be sure, there were the habitual representatives of the nearby communities to the southeast—Cottyo, Cinthea, and Cyme, as well as the yearly contingent from Ariod's Lake. Since Kazur's arrival two decades ago, representatives from far-off Endlin were occasional participants. This year brought several ernani from places hitherto either unexplored or unknown by anyone other than the Chartists or the far-flung Searchers of Souls.

A certain Keret by name, with blue-black skin stretched tightly over a frame that dwarfed even the tall men of Lapith, came from The Flowering Lands, a place far beyond the southern borders of Pelion, a place so distant that it was nothing but a roughed-in scrawl on a ancient map. How he found his way to the valley of the castle would remain unanswered until he could be schooled in their tongue. At the altar he made himself understood in a kind of gestural language, Hesione welcoming him without a qualm, finding within him vast curiosity and a rich vein of resourcefulness.

Others, too, came from afar. A placid moon-faced woman of middle age, who called herself Fenja, identified her home as an island beyond the Eastern Shore. A fierce-looking fellow named Altug, wearing a top-knot and a trailing black mustache, waved his hand vaguely toward the northeast at her questions as to his homeland, grinning when Hesione confided to him that she had always longed to see the mountains. Everyone had been interviewed and undergone the Ceremony of Blessing with the exception of a blue-eyed ragamuffin who was cooling his heels on a bench outside the narthex. The sole representative of the western lands, the boy Skat had been purposefully delayed until Hesione could free herself from the others and devote herself solely to the one she had lured here. Now it was time to discover if this child of Charis was a likely candidate for Preparation, for Hesione could take her no further along the Path. Lillas must come of her own free will, or not at all.

Summoning Flavius with a single thought, Hesione leaned back in her chair, forcing herself into a state of calm that was pure pretense. The door flew open with a bang. Momentarily nonplussed at such a display of temper from the normally good-natured monitor, Hesione fought to prevent her lips from curving upward at the sight of the whirlwind confronting her with legs widespread, two nut-brown fists clenched on narrow hips. A woefully misshapen knitted cap circled a tanned face whose bright blue eyes regarded her with outraged pride.

"Why have I been kept waiting so long? All the others left hours ago! I've had nothing to do but count tiles and be stared at. I demand to see whoever is in charge!"

Flavius appeared over the urchin's shoulder, raising his eyebrows at Hesione with a helpless shrug. Dismissing Flavius with a nod, Hesione flicked a non-existent piece of dust from her robes before meeting these furious accusations with icy calm.

"You were left until last because I have serious doubts as to the merits of your application. My first duty is to interview those who meet our qualifications."

The boy met her calm with easy arrogance.

"And who are you?"

"I am the Eighteenth Mother of Pelion, Legislator of the Maze and Keeper of the Flame." Hesione paused for effect before asking mildly, "Who are you?"

Everything in the boy wanted to reveal his own list of titles. Somehow he maintained his self-control despite his urge to squelch this overbearing woman in black.

"I'm called Skat."

Picking up the pen that rested across a thin piece of parchment before her on the small table, Hesione wrote a single word at the top of the page.

"Well, Skat, as I mentioned before, you do not appear to be qualified for entry into the Maze." When the boy made to interrupt, Hesione overrode him. "However, I will offer you the courtesy of an interview if you will do me the kindness of seating yourself, removing your headgear, and answering my questions."

After weighing Hesione's request for a moment, the boy accepted her stipulations, pulled off the cap with obvious reluctance, and sat cross-legged in the armless chair. The hair under the cap was a clumped mass of dirty tangles, causing Hesione to wonder at this spoiled princess of Agave. How many could play a role so foreign to them with such bravery and skill? Her talents were wasted in that citadel of luxury built on the backs of an enslaved population. What might she become with discipline mixed with equal parts of compassion?

"What is your age, Skat?"

"Twenty summers."

Raising her eyebrows to signal her disbelief, Hesione let her eyes play over the boy, watching as he squirmed under her gaze.

"I find that difficult to believe. If you have, indeed, seen twenty summers, then you must have a problem our healers might solve."

"I'm as healthy as the next fellow," the boy complained.

Hesione continued undeterred.

"You show no signs of the fully mature male and for that reason I must deny you entry. If you are willing to undergo treatment, perhaps a place may be found for you at some later date."

Hesione lowered the pen. A dirty hand reached out to grasp the edge of the table.

"I . . . I'm not a boy."

Leaning forward in her chair, Hesione let a welcoming smile replace her formerly stern demeanor.

"Then let us begin again. How are you called, stranger-to-the-city?"

"I am Lillas of . . . of the West."

The girl chose instinctively to maintain her anonymity. After an instant of reflection, Hesione concurred with her decision. This had been a point of debate with the Council, Kazur adamant that even among the triple-layered walls of the Maze, her identity remain concealed. Lady Lillas, daughter of the Aeson, must be lost to Agave.

The ritual commenced.

"What do you seek, Lillas of the West?"

As she had seen happen many times before, the proscribed words brought a change to the one she addressed. The girl straightened in the chair, placed her feet flat on the floor, and her face grew serious. For the first time since she burst through the door, she looked her age and her gender.

"I seek the gift promised by the prophet." When Lillas began reciting from memory, Hesione heard the cadences of Lukash's voice. "For freedom, for knowledge, for a gift of worth freely given."

"The gift you seek is not given lightly. Each part of you—body, mind, and soul—will be tested and judged as you make your way on the Path of Preparation. Much will be demanded of you, Lillas of the West. Are you prepared to meet our challenge?"

Hesione had no need of inner sight to see the girl's indecision. She was troubled, deeply troubled, and in ways unconnected with her flight from Agave.

"I was told a woman must mate with a man. Did my friend speak truly?"

Unsure as to exactly what difficulty was being discussed, Hesione proceeded with care.

"It is true that the gift cannot be offered to you alone. You will live with women for a time, and then be joined to a man born-of-the-city." Hesione foresaw her next question and answered it before she could speak. "The choice of the one selected to join with you is not yours. However, after a proscribed length of time, you may reject him just as he will be free to reject you."

The girl sat silent, her eyes blank and unseeing, lost in some private memory. Worried, but unable to discern the source of the girl's distress, Hesione continued, hoping that something might spark a reaction.

"All this will happen slowly, Lillas, with many people within the Maze offering you guidance and counsel. We hold classes to ease the difficulties of joining . . ."

Her last statement produced the desired effect, for the girl cut her off rudely.

"I need no classes in joining. I am not a child."

This last remark was delivered with a sneer, as if Hesione had attacked her womanhood in some way. Choosing to ignore her outburst, Hesione continued the ritual.

"You must pledge your intent to live and work according to our rules for the next five moons. You enter Preparation as you came into the world, naked and alone."

When Lillas didn't flinch, Hesione slowed her delivery so that every word would grind its way into the hard-headed woman seated across from her.

"If you choose to leave the Maze, you may never enter again. There is only one chance for obtaining the gift, and that chance lies within these walls."

There was nothing to be done but wait for Lillas' response. Hesione offered her no promises nor smoothed her way. In three years of study, reflections, and dreams, this had always been the missing moment, eluding all her powers of divination. All the signs seemed to point to this girl-child of the west, but individuals rarely behave as prophecies predict, for prophecies tend toward the non-specific, speaking through a language of innuendo and veiled meaning. Hesione's studies of literature proved that throughout written history, the human element retained an immense propensity for reversal, denial, and surprise. It was Hesione's opinion that humanity was best defined by its tendency toward contradiction, and she had never met anyone quite so contradictory as the girl who sat before her. Long after this moment passed, Hesione would never be able to remember if they sat together in silence for minutes or hours.

"I accept your requirements."

Hesione had sensed homesickness, loneliness, fear, and doubts from the pilgrims to Pelion; never had she felt such sadness. The hellion who bounded into the chamber had become a slender girl of middling height who seemed to sag under the weight of the promise just made. Now Hesione could speak to Lillas as she had longed to speak, not to the tempestuous child, but to a tired, lonely woman who had no friends, no family, and no home.

"You are accepted into Preparation. You will come with me now to the Sanctum, and on the pedestal, you will receive the gifts."

The girl rose and bent to lift the pack she had thrown on the floor as she entered.

"The pack remains here. You can take nothing with you where we go."

Blue eyes floated in unshed tears. Reaching into her pack, she removed something and held it tight in her right hand, cradling it against her flattened breasts. As her chin came up, her tears remained unshed.

"I will not go unless I can take this with me."

"What is it, Lillas?"

Her hand thrust out and her fist opened. A thick braid of light brown hair rolled into a tidy ball lay in her palm. Hesione blessed Phoron for his foresight. Here was Lillas' first gift, offered a moon ago to be accepted today.

"It shall not be taken from you without your consent."

The girl flashed a look of silent thanks. Hesione offered a balm to her troubled soul.

"We must finish the ceremony with all speed, for a friend awaits you within the Maze. It's my belief you'll find a bed for yourself beside hers."

Mystified, the girl murmured, "You must be mistaken. I have no friend in this city."

"Sometimes I am mistaken, Lillas, but not in this. Your friend is called Halys, a woman of eastern Lapith, who received her gifts early this morning."

A burst of uninhibited laughter emanated from her dye-stained throat as Lillas took up her former pose, hands on hips, blue eyes flashing with good humor.

"Now I understand why you weren't surprised to learn I wasn't a boy! Such things must happen to you every day!"

This time Hesione didn't try to mask her smile.

"No, ernani, not every day. Certainly not every day."

HEARING FEET TAKING the attic steps two at a time, Reddin smiled to himself, guessing his visitor's identity long before an immaculately coiffed head of curls appeared around the doorjamb. It had been an interminable day, both because of his aching body (which still protested the slightest unplanned movement) and his attempts to forget that three male candidates entered the Maze this morning. At his mother's suggestion, he applied for a week's leave from the ward, planning to use his time to further his reading while he recuperated. Today not even his beloved books offered a much-needed diversion. More than once he found his mind wandering, drifting away from the subject at hand, and forced himself back to the regimen of study. Now it was late afternoon and the sky was a purplish haze through the leaded glass window. His parents would return from Guild Hall in an hour or so, and it seemed his brother had timed his visit to exactly coincide with their absence—a gesture typical of Orrin's thoughtfulness, for even more than their mother, Orrin knew what Reddin gained and lost on the day of the Trial.

"How fares the athlete of the family?"

It was a game between them, Orrin's insistence that Reddin had stripped him of his former laurels as an athlete. With an exaggerated groan, Reddin put down his pen and closed his book.

"So sore that I can barely move from bed to desk. So pitiful that mother brings my food up the stairs."

Pulling a face, Orrin shook his head reproachfully.

"She needs no excuse to baby you, brother, since you've always been her favorite."

"As you say, brother," was Reddin's smug retort.

Orrin pulled the leather chair around so it faced Reddin's desk, lowering himself into it with a contented sigh. Pulling aside his cloak, he reached to an inside pocket, removed a small glass jar, and lobbed it in a high arc toward Reddin. Catching it one-handed, Reddin grunted at the effort of moving his right shoulder. Orrin smothered a laugh.

"I see you don't exaggerate. Perhaps this will give you some relief. The trainer swears it works miracles on sore muscles."

Reddin examined the jar doubtfully.

"There's not enough here to cover everything that hurts."

Orrin laughed outright this time, throwing his head back, his rich baritone filling the room. If nothing else has been accomplished, thought Reddin, at least the Trial has brought me a brother.

"Any news about the Maze?"

There was no reason for him to be subtle with Orrin. Frowning, Orrin readjusted the folds of his robes, unable to offer hope of any last minute miracles.

"In truth, Reddin, there is news, but none that affects you, I fear. Five more ernani arrived early this morning—all male. Rumors spread quickly, as you know, but one of my apprentices walks by the northern gates on his route to work and reported that there were three Lapithians, one fellow with a curious mustache, and a boy."

When Reddin offered no response, they sat for a while in silence, each considering the unfairness of something over which they exerted no control. Moving his gaze back to the window, Reddin spoke his private thoughts aloud.

"Then it seems I will never mate. Strange, isn't it? My strongest reservation was joining with someone not-born-of-the-city, but now that it will never take place . . ."

He waited for Orrin's response, expecting comfort and numerous suggestions of prospective mates. Instead, his brother sat mute. When his refusal to speak became irksome, Reddin turned on him.

"Haven't you any words of wisdom on the subject?"

"None."

Orrin's expressionless face irked Reddin all the more.

"Perhaps now would be an appropriate time for you to tell me why you've never mated, elder brother? I'm sure you haven't lacked for opportunity."

That last dig was childish—a desire to strike back at his handsome, gregarious brother. Yet still there was no response to his baiting other than a sigh from Orrin as he spread his fingers wide and rested them on his thighs.

"There's an enormous difference between opportunities for joining and opportunities for mating. You've never given any indication that you preferred one to the other."

It was a fair observation. Reddin's experiences with joining was that of most young men: instruction at an early age in the House of Hetaeras, and by his own choice, the loss of his virginity with an experienced hetaera. After completing his first sequence of schooling he'd joined with other women, but finally, out of frustration, boredom, or simply because it was the easiest course, he found himself returning to the House of Hetaeras to satisfy his body's needs. In that place there was no need to invest in anything more substantial than shared delight, although his parents' mating was a constant reminder of a crucial element missing from his life.

"You're right, of course, Orrin. I apologize."

Leaning forward in the chair, his brother hesitated for a moment, an abashed expression making him look for all purposes like a guilty child confessing a bad deed.

"Perhaps this isn't the most opportune time to mention it, but it seems your elder brother might actually mate after all."

In the face of Reddin's open-mouthed astonishment, Orrin smiled, holding up a hand to ward off the questions he knew his declaration would engender.

"I can say only that she is a Master of my Guild. And you must give me your word that you'll say nothing to mother or father."

"Why all the secrecy?"

"We've many things to discuss between us, and we neither want nor need outside pressures influencing us. This is the most difficult decision I've ever made, for my work, by necessity, must change."

The problems facing a practicing adept hetaera who decides to mate never occurred to Reddin. It was certainly not a topic he was qualified to discuss, nor did Orrin's air of seriousness encourage him to explore the subject. Rising, he extended an arm, offering congratulations. Orrin grasped it tightly.

A rapping from below drew both their attention. After a brief pause, it resumed, more insistently than before. Orrin was the first to react.

"I'll answer it since you've convinced me of your inability to manage the stairs."

With that, he was out of the room and bounding swiftly down the steps. The door to the outside street creaked on its hinges, and Reddin could hear a man's voice raised in question, Orrin's response, and then a longer period of explanation from the unidentified voice. Orrin's feet took the steps two at a time once again, and he was standing at the door, ushering in a solemn-faced Flavius.

"Reddin, third child of Pasiphae and Elan, you are summoned to the Sanctum for your indoctrination into Preparation. We must leave immediately, for the portals close at dusk."

Coming as it did on the heels of Orrin's unexpected announcement, it took a moment for Reddin to understand what had just been said. When it finally sank in, he was not amused.

"This is a poor jest, Flavius. My brother informed me the five ernani who arrived today are all male."

A wide grin split Flavius' face, erasing its formality.

"Well, the Eighteenth Mother seems to have discovered two women among them! She's sent me off to gather in the fourth and fifth candidates. You're my last duty of the day."

So stunned he couldn't utter a word, Reddin moved like someone walking underwater, picking up the jar of salve and the book on his desk, only to have Orrin take them away from him. His brother's voice finally pierced the waters threatening to drown him.

"Reddin, you know you can't take anything with you."

His warmest cloak was wrapped around him and he felt Flavius' arm rest on his shoulders as it had two days ago. This moment was what he'd fought for; now that it was upon him, he could only mutter protests as Flavius herded him toward the door.

"I must wait for mother and father. They'll be worried if I'm not here when they return."

"I'll wait for them," promised Orrin.

"I can't leave my books! I'll need them . . ."

"Once you've settled in, the books can be sent for," Flavius assured him.

All the old doubts resurfaced and he fought his way out of the well he'd fallen into, thrusting away Flavius' arm to grab hold of his brother's tunic. Searching his brother's down-turned face, he asked for the single reassurance that might content him.

"This woman you told me of, Orrin. Is she adept?"

Orrin nodded his head.

"Is it worth it, Orrin? Is what you share with her worth the Maze?"

A stream of memories flowed over Orrin's face, a wealth of his most private feelings, among them joy, passion, and fulfillment, offered up freely, without complaint or resentment, for his younger brother's benefit. There could be no more protests on Reddin's part. Quickly embracing the brother he had just begun to know, Reddin followed Flavius down the rickety attic stairs.

* * *

MOVING QUICKLY TO the window, Orrin watched his brother's slight form move down the street beside the stalwart figure of the Legionnaire. Even from this distance, Orrin could see Reddin was favoring his right leg, silent testimony to his efforts in the Trial, efforts which humbled Orrin as he sat on the damp grass watching his brother move the heavens and the earth alone and against all odds. Craning his neck, he finally lost sight of them as they turned a corner at the end of the street. In his mind's eye, Orrin traced the route they would travel through the Plaza and on to the Sanctum and the Maze.

There was nothing to be done but wait for his parents' return. Sinking into the leather chair, he regarded the dying fire in the hearth. This had been his room before it was Reddin's, and it was basically unchanged except for the vast array of Reddin's books, tablets, loose papers and writing supplies. At the thought of the desolation that crossed Reddin's face when he realized he must leave his precious books behind, Orrin winced. At twenty-nine, Reddin was a man full-grown, yet he seemed a lost child in those last few moments, unsure of what he had nearly killed himself to make possible. His final question touched Orrin to his heart. He tried to reach Reddin in that moment, tried to set aside the barrier that rendered Reddin isolated and include him in the gift denied him by either a quirk of fate or biology.

Hunching himself deeper into the upholstery, Orrin considered what Chryse had asked of him, something which caused him to question her judgment for the first time in their relationship. Having told her of the promise made by himself and his sister when they came to understand that Reddin was different from them, he was loathe to trespass into his brother's inner thoughts, even when the Eighteenth Mother's added request gave sanction to the act. At long last he agreed to assist them, but steadfastly refused to lead the conversation toward the subject both women wanted broached. It was nothing short of eerie when Reddin began to speak in a faraway voice about the exact things Chryse wanted to know about Reddin's previous experiences with women and the relative strength of his desire to take a mate. Aware of his limitations as an actor, Orrin chose silence, refraining from comment only to have Reddin respond with even deeper, more personal revelations that nearly overwhelmed Orrin's ability to mask his reactions to the non-adept mind he was probing.

Now it was accomplished, and he need never do it again. At that thought, a rueful smile crossed his face. Far from being the last non-adept mind Orrin would touch, Reddin's was the first in a long line of prospective male candidates for Preparation Orrin would be expected to read and evaluate with ease and expertise. What he was unable to tell Reddin was that his entry into the Maze was the one and only reason Orrin and Chryse could not announce their intention to mate. If the unexpected female ernani had not entered the gates this morning, Orrin would have begun his duties with Chryse as joint Instructors of the Maze today. Those plans were now postponed for another five moons or a year, as long as it took Reddin and his ernani to be transformed, for it would be impossible for Orrin to counsel him or even to be physically present inside the Maze while Reddin walked the Path—such an action being both an unforgivable breech of hetaera etiquette and a direct violation of the Rules of Preparation.

The moment Pasiphae informed him of Reddin's intention to compete in the Trial, Orrin removed himself from every aspect of Preparation planning, with the exception of his mental and physical intimacy with Chryse. Their joining proved impossible to give up, although they did their best to build barriers around Reddin in their minds, an action which hindered their closeness, but one that they decided jointly to endure. No barriers could completely contain emotions, and he felt her interest in Reddin just as he knew she perceived his anxiety for his brother and the difficulties the Trial would pose for one unused to athletic pursuits.

A waft of thought drifted by him as he sensed his parent's greeting from the street below. Sending them proof of his presence in the attic, he felt them enter the house, looking through his mother's eyes as she lit a lamp and placed it in the front window, a habit she kept every evening of her life. "Casting out the darkness," Pasiphae called it. A proverb worked in needlepoint on a small pillow handed down from Orrin, to his sister, and finally to Reddin, read:

> If you cannot be a star in the firmament,
> Light a candle in your window.

It was time to descend now and inform them that they could not see nor talk nor receive any word of their youngest child throughout the winter, spring, and perhaps long into the summer moons. The child of their middle age had finally left the nest. Sad for them, happy for his brother, their firstborn walked down the attic steps to offer them what comfort he could.

REDDIN STOOD ON a raised pedestal of stone facing a rectangular block of white marble on which burned the Flame of Pelion. Kindled by the hand of the First Mother on the outcropping of rocks she chose as the home of her people, transferred to this altar by the hand of the Fifth Mother, it was tended now by the woman who stood before him, her back turned to him as she faced the flame of which she alone was the keeper. Around him all was darkness, for dusk had passed into evening and the sole source of light within this vast, vaulted chamber were the tongues of fire that leapt from the altar, turning the ivory surface a slight pink, as if it had been carved not from stone, but from an enormous translucent pearl found in the ocean's depths. From where he stood, the columns supporting the high ceiling were barely visible, their outlines faded away to merge with the surrounding darkness. If he had never stood here before in the light of day, he could have been persuaded that the Sanctum was an intimate place rather than an architectural wonder, for it seemed that he and the Eighteenth Mother, separated by a few paces, were alone in a tiny cubicle of space illuminated by a single flame.

On the stone table near the altar, arranged much like the four points of a compass rose, stood a goblet of gold, one of silver, a marble bowl, and a silver knife. It was this knife that cut his hair on the day he offered his first gift, and he greeted it inwardly as a friend of long acquaintance. The other gifts—the water, wine, and oil contained in the goblets and bowl—were given to him on the day of his birth.

The stiff rustle of heavy silk drew his attention. The Eighteenth Mother turned toward him, her black robes causing her white face and hands to float as if disembodied. Her face was a triangle, a broad unlined forehead narrowing to a pointed chin, a fox-like face, Reddin decided, inquisitive and with little beauty until one considered her eyes. Warm and luminous as seawater under which a pale green flame burned, they seemed to pass through his clothing and skin, resting their attention on that part of him eternally hidden from the eyes of the world. He felt no disturbance at her rapt perusal, for he was lulled by the remembrance of their expression as they rested on him at the conclusion of the Trial. His response to that measuring stare seemed to trigger a like memory in her, for a fleeting smile passed over her face, disappearing as she began to speak.

"What do you seek, son-of-the-city?"

Her voice continued the illusion of intimacy since it barely broke the silence of the Sanctum.

"I seek the greatest of gifts."

Her next question took him unaware.

"What is that gift?"

The difficulty of describing something he had never experienced made the words come slowly. Her expression never altered as she waited for his reply.

"The opening of the mind to the thoughts of others."

She nodded as if well-pleased. Reddin took a relieved breath. The next question equaled the first in difficulty.

"Why do you seek this gift?"

"I want to serve others as a healer. To ease pain and suffering. To cure injuries of the mind as well as those of the body."

Again she nodded, more thoughtfully this time.

"In the Place of Preparation, the gifts of a man are three: his beauty given with the hair of his head; his strength given with the blood of his body; his fertility given with the seed of his sex. You gave the first gift as a child; the remaining two must be offered as an adult."

She slowed her pace; this time her words held a warning.

"Yet the gifts you give are not enough, for as one born-of-the-city, your duty in the Place of Preparation is to enable your partner to offer her gifts as well. Your role is not an easy one, for you must share with her all aspects of your being. Are you willing to pledge yourself to this task?"

Reluctance was his first reaction. He wasn't perfect; he was only a man. Perhaps sensing his doubts, her countenance lost some of its severity.

"You need not preach nor persuade, Reddin. Put simply, you must act, for we are the sum not of our words, but our actions."

After a pause, she resumed speaking, her voice like the ringing of a distant silver bell.

"Do you accept this duty, son-of-the-city?"

"Aye," Reddin whispered.

"The last oath I must hear from your lips is the most sacred. Without it you may not pass through the bronze doors. Each candidate from Pelion has sworn it." Her voice hardened and her face became implacable. "To reveal it to anyone will mean your immediate removal from the Maze, without explanation, excuse, or appeal. Do you understand the terms whereby you swear?"

He nodded, and after regarding him closely, she came to the end of the ritual.

"Do you pledge that you will never reveal by word or action the nature of the gift you seek to any ernani or stranger to the city? Think well, for I ask that you surrender your life before you break this vow."

For a moment Reddin was taken aback by the simple nature of her request. Compared to the other requirements, this one seemed child's play. Posed as it was, with such dire consequences, he expected something far more difficult to perform. He had no doubt but that he could honor this oath under any circumstances.

"I pledge my silence with my life."

It was as if the warm seas that swam in her eyes glistened in the sparkling radiance of gilt-edged dawn.

"You are accepted into Preparation, Reddin of Pelion. May your gifts be offered freely, your path one of joy."

As Reddin made his way down the curved staircase and onto the Sanctum floor, he looked back over his shoulder to find her standing there still, unmoving, seemingly carved from black marble, a shadowy figure feeding the flames of Pelion, stoking the source of the city's blessing without coal, wood, or oil, her fuel the combined energies of her own small person and all those who came before.

Chapter 10

The Moon of Waiting

HER BACK SIGNIFYING her rejection of the others, Lillas perched cross-legged on one of the many window seats that lined the longest wall of the room in which she passed the greatest part of each day. On the tour they were given on their first morning in residence, the Instructor called it the Hall of Gathering. When the monitors and servants referred to it as the dayroom, the women quickly adopted the less formal and more descriptive name. Day in and day out, they studied and worked within its white plastered walls. Meals were taken in a large refractory just a few steps away from their dormitory. Except for regular sessions with the healer, their hours were measured by the changing light outside the draped windows Lillas chose as her refuge.

She'd gathered her heavy skirts in a ball in her lap to free her legs for the posture most comfortable to her with the result that her knees stuck out from beneath the cotton shift. Pressing her nose against the glass, she watched the raining world outside her prison, for a prison it was. No matter that they tried to hide the true nature of the place with talk of "adjustment" and "transition," and other such chatter to which she turned deaf ears. In twenty days she had heard more rules, been given more orders, and suffered more indignities than she thought possible. And the thing that irritated her the most was that the others—spiritless, spineless, and sluggish to the point of immovability—smiled and laughed and acted as if they would rather be no other place in the world.

They were laughing now. She could hear them over her shoulder, soprano and contralto bursts of merriment filling the high-ceilings of a chamber large enough to contain four or even five times their number. Refusing to look, she told herself it was yet another joke she didn't understand, another reference to something she'd never learned and had no interest in knowing. Like sheep, they allowed themselves to be herded from one place to another, their lives ruled by morning bells and evening trumpets. Also like sheep, they were perfectly content to huddle together in groups, their heads lowered over books, needlework, or whatever form of torture devised for that particular day. Worst of all, they never did anything but sit.

Sit, then stand and walk to the next destination, only to sit again; this time over a meal, now for a lecture or demonstration, again over studies, and finally for the evening meal. By the time the torches were removed and she found herself lying on her bed in the Hall of Women, she was wound so tightly she thought she would burst the seams of the nightgown they gave her, the bulk of its fabric confining to the point that she often found herself waking from dreams of entrapment. Nightly she laid awake, her mind racing, her body tense and restless, hating the fact that in a few short hours the bell would ring and another day of imprisonment would begin.

At first she'd honored her pledge to the woman in black and attempted to blend in with the others, memorizing the endless lists of rules and regulations, and even mustered some semblance of interest in the subjects they studied, all of which bored her to distraction. What did she need to know of cooking, sewing, weaving, knitting, or the myriad of crafts the others attacked with a vigor that left her sneering and contemptuous? It was one thing to learn how to cook when Timon was her teacher and the only way her belly would be filled was undertaking the task herself. She could find no logic in learning to use herbs to make food more palatable when she was fed three full meals a day. And what need was there to learn to design, cut patterns, and sew clothes for herself when they'd issued her three dresses and a cloak? Granted, they were woven of wool rather than the thin, breezy silks she was accustomed to and so not at all to her taste, but she felt no inclination to make others. And what possible use could she have for healing skills when part of everyday was spent with a woman healer who asked her every conceivable question about her health on the first day, and then examined her with such scrutiny that for once in her life Lillas, who'd daily stripped to her skin without a second thought to be bathed by her slaves, felt her modesty violated?

It was all pointless, a ruse to keep her from noticing that she had relinquished her freedom when the bolt of the bronze doors slid into the lock. The others might choose to bury their heads in books to escape the true nature of their situation, but Lillas was not fooled. There were guards everywhere, and though they might be called "monitors", they were guards all the same. Every corridor and doorway through which she passed reminded her that escape was impossible.

In the past few days she'd stopped feigning interest, refusing to join in the activities of the day. When a few of them tried to lure her back to the group, she simply stared at them until, their brows knitted with bewilderment, they left her alone. Only Halys refused to abandon her, sitting silently by her side through meals for which Lillas had no appetite. And it was Halys, her hair trimmed to just below her shoulders, her long-fingered hands now clean and manicured, although her left forefinger was sore from the repeated pricking of an awkwardly-held needle, who tried to break through Lillas' carefully constructed wall with a single comment:

"Hard it is, Lillas, to be what we are not."

Tempting though it was to maintain her indifference, this was Halys speaking, not some snooty resident of Pelion. Despite her worries over her own predicament, Lillas wasn't blind to the fact her fellow ernani became noticeably uneasy in the presence of the fifteen women from Pelion, who chattered knowingly of books and music and who read, wrote, and multiplied rows and columns of figures with decided ease. Five ernani made the odds four to one, a risky bet for inclusion and, in Lillas' not-so-humble opinion, a guarantee that equality among them was impossible.

Fenja, an ernani who at five and thirty was the eldest woman in the class, had been moved to tears by one of the candidates from Pelion only yesterday. Like Halys, Fenja was a newcomer to the southern language, speaking it with a limited vocabulary and a sing-song cadence which Lillas found charming. Not so the women of Pelion. When Phoebe, a red-haired woman with a sharp-edged tongue, corrected Fenja's grammar for the twentieth time that day, Fenja's moon-like face grew pale and wan, a single tear dripping down each of her full cheeks. The picture of her misery brought Lillas to the point of physically attacking Phoebe, who never knew how close she came to total destruction. Lillas was up from the window seat and half-way across the room when the Instructor took charge.

Her elegant movements those of a dancer, the Instructor glided to Fenja's side. After observing her for a moment, she turned to Phoebe, asking, "Is perfection so desirable that you would induce tears in one who doesn't measure up to your standards?"

"You asked us to help the others learn, Instructor."

Lillas gritted her teeth at Phoebe's simpering reply. The Instructor must have shared her feeling, for her manner, which had been mildly reproving, turned cold and biting.

"There is a vast difference between correction and harassment." Phoebe wilted, but the Instructor was not finished. "Soon you will share a cell with one who may have little or no knowledge of your language. Is this the tack you will take with him, Phoebe? Criticizing every word he utters?" Confronted by the Instructor's grim-faced censure, Phoebe dropped her eyes to the floor. "If you do, I predict he will stop speaking altogether, as Fenja will if you cannot offer your help with true charity."

"I apologize, Instructor."

"I need no apology," came the chilly and decidedly remote reply.

Swallowing hard, Phoebe turned to Fenja, who was desperately trying to follow the conversation of which she knew she was the subject. Observing her confusion, Phoebe spoke slowly and carefully.

"Forgive me, Fenja. I never meant to make you cry."

The woman of the Eastern Isles nodded her head, her eyes showing her understanding even if her tongue lacked the ability to answer in kind.

Thinking the affair over, Lillas resumed her place at the window when the Instructor raised her voice to carry over the twenty lifted heads spread about the dayroom.

"Soon each of you will be joined to a stranger, someone who shares none of your background or beliefs. What will be your choice? To set yourself the task of instructing him in your ways or to discover a better way of approaching the path you must walk together? Will you close your mind against his strangeness or embrace his differences, making some of them your own? Consider it carefully, for no one completes the Path unchanged."

The Instructor drifted away to a corner where a visitor was setting up a display of fabrics and threads. Twenty women sat lost in thought, considering, as did Lillas, that the price for this nameless gift was not one of currency, but of self.

WHEN ANOTHER WAVE of laughter rippled through the dayroom, Lillas hunched her shoulders. The morning dragged by, the weather adding to her gloom. Nothing was visible through the window but furry edges of thick fog. A quiet voice spoke near her shoulder.

"Those from the western lands consider rain to be something of a miracle, do they not, Lillas?"

A quick glance out of the corner of her eye confirmed that the Instructor had seated herself on the window seat. She, too, was considering the world outside the window. When Lillas made no answer, the Instructor seemed not the least disturbed.

"I remember a phrase I heard once: `It rains in my heart.' Is it so with you?"

It occurred to Lillas that to answer would be to commit herself to a conversation she had sworn to avoid. Still, there was something about this raven-haired woman, something so compelling as to be impossible to deny.

"If it rains in Agave, my . . . ," she caught herself before she blundered, ". . . the Aeson declares a holiday. Here, it only means another day like all the others."

The Instructor nodded briefly, never moving her attention away from the window.

"There is something to be said for holidays. We have them in Pelion as well. In fact, we celebrated one of them a few days before your arrival."

As long as the Instructor kept to subjects like these, Lillas felt safe. In addition, she was curious. She'd caught a brief glimpse of the city before being spirited away to the Sanctum. Pelion seemed glorious—a hundred times bigger than Imarus and bustling with activity.

"What kind of celebration was it?"

"I think it's best described as a day of thanksgiving. Most of the crops have been harvested and the fields made ready for winter. We may be a city people, but we've never lost our connection with the land that feeds us. On this day, we pass through the gates to gather on a large field to the east of the city walls." For the first time, the Instructor addressed Lillas directly. "Once there, we mill about, greeting friends and neighbors, or gather in large family groups. There are food stalls aplenty, although my parents always bring a basket full of favorite delicacies and my father opens a bottle of his finest wine."

Lillas never considered that the Instructor, or any of the people who worked in the Maze, might have family or friends. Her own loneliness caused her to believe everyone shared her condition. Somehow it pleased her to think there were people living beyond these walls, that everyone wasn't forced to live in a place where all doors were locked. As she remembered former days of freedom and festivity, some of her longing found its way into her voice.

"Is there drinking and singing and games of chance? Are there fire-eaters and sword-swallowers and dancing bears?"

The Instructor laughed and shook her head, some of the tendrils of her hair escaping her braids and floating about her face.

"I must confess we do not, although I think I would enjoy watching someone eat fire." Another laugh escaped her, and then she sobered. "I fear we have no such entertainment," she remarked with surprising bitterness, causing Lillas to wonder about the reason for such a rapid change in mood. Abruptly, the Instructor changed the subject.

"A report from your healer disturbs me, Lillas. She tells me you've lost weight since your arrival. Also, you suffer from lack of sleep. Is she correct?"

There was no use denying it. The waist of her dress was noticeably looser than it was twenty days ago.

"I . . . I've no interest in eating."

"Is the food not to your liking? Many of the ernani have tastes different from ours. Our cooks can prepare anything you desire." When Lillas shook her head, the Instructor's face softened. "Lillas, I can't help unless you tell me the source of your unhappiness. Will you force me to ask you a long list of questions until I stumble onto the real reason you sit day after day by this window?"

She wanted to confess everything to this generous, good-hearted woman who came to Fenja's defense and had never treated Lillas with anything other than friendliness and warmth. Yet at the same time Lillas looked into her pleading eyes, she heard her mother's warning that she must tell no one, that the slightest word would invite the long reach of her father's arm. The thought of her father threatened her composure, for she had thrust him out of her mind. When a thin-lipped, ginger-bearded face replaced that of her father, she sat mute and close-mouthed, reminded of the conclusion she had drawn during her interview with the woman in black—better a stranger than Seth. At least with a stranger she would receive a gift, small enough recompense for having to forgo her freedom.

Sensing the Instructor's disappointment, Lillas turned away from her, hoping she would leave.

"Let it be as you think best, ernani."

As she rose from the window seat, The Instructor seemed defeated, her shoulders drooping and her usual buoyancy of spirit noticeably absent. In the next moment, she turned back to Lillas so swiftly that the folds of her skirt lifted to reveal slender ankles, a surge of color dyeing her pale cheeks bright pink.

"Come with me, and we'll both escape the dayroom for a little while!"

Heartened by the Instructor's dancing eyes and flushed face, the idea of escape so welcome that she didn't think of protesting, Lillas took her outstretched hand without a second thought and was pulled away from the window and out of the dayroom.

They passed the only rooms Lillas had ever frequented, moving steadily downward, past windowless corridors and hallways lined with unopened doors. Her feelings of disorientation increased, for every few minutes the Instructor would change direction, turning corners at places which bore no signs, to descend a short staircase and turn in another, and even more unlikely, direction. For the first time Lillas understood the appropriateness of the title chosen for this warren of dead ends and false exits, for it was a labyrinth designed to confuse any would-be wanderer within its bowels. Without guidance, Lillas would be helpless to return from whence she came. Careful to dog her escort's steps, she discarded her original idea of committing their route to memory for future purposes of escape.

Even though the surrounding iron doors were shut tight, she knew instinctively that the rooms behind them were empty. The air was cool but stale, as if it had not been breathed for a long while. She also had the impression that they were at least partway underground, although the path was moving uphill again, her body responding to her exertions by increasing her heart rate. It seemed ages had passed since she'd felt so alive—the brisk walk causing a slight cramp in one of her calves, her anticipation for whatever lay ahead clearing her eyes of the film that previously covered them. When the Instructor came to a halt at a chest-high wooden gate guarded by two men dressed in identical brown cloaks, Lillas was sorry their journey had ended.

"Greetings, Captain. I seek entrance with an ernani from the Hall of Women."

It was clear that the man the Instructor addressed was reluctant to let them pass. Taking a sidelong glance at his cohort, he cleared his throat.

"We've not had clearance for such a visit."

"As the Instructor of the Maze and a member of the Eighteenth Mother's Council, I take full responsibility for my actions, Captain."

From anyone else's lips her reply might have seemed boastful. Coming from the Instructor, it became a pledge of accountability. With a respectful nod, the captain swung the gates open to allow them entrance.

"I fear it's not particularly inviting on such a gloomy day, but it's the only place within the Maze that opens to the sky." With a brief smile and a slight inclination of her head, she invited Lillas inside.

For a moment Lillas stood stock-still, her gaze sweeping across the oblong arena surrounded by a clay track, the center of which was covered with dull green grass turning brown with the oncoming chill of winter. A tall wooden frame held climbing ropes with a pit of sand nearby. Strewn haphazardly within the center of the track were straw targets, some of them marked by deep gashes that had not yet been repaired. Its purpose was clearly functionary since all the equipment was well-worn, although the ropes had been newly strung. Yet for all its spartan qualities, the arena suited Lillas as no other place within the Maze. Her hands itched to string a bow, to climb the ropes and consider the view from thirty feet above the ground, to lift her skirts and run the track, even if it meant dodging the puddles of standing water and streaking her spotless dress with mud. Standing poised for flight, afraid she might alarm her hostess if she sprinted away on feet tingling with anticipation, a laughing voice set her free.

"Go, ernani! Run until you can run no more!"

CHRYSE STOOD UNMINDFUL of the light drizzle, watching the long-legged girl speed swiftly over the sodden track, her hands clutching the long skirts at her sides, her short curls bouncing as she flew around the empty arena. Unfettered at last, Lillas ran like a wild thing that had just caught the scent of a hunter on the wind. Surveying her charge with narrowed eyes, Chryse bit her lips, allowing her face to assume the worried frown she'd hidden from her charge. This was the first sign of life Lillas had exhibited in days that took their toll on Chryse and everyone who came into contact with her dull, lifeless stare. Nothing and no one, not even Halys, was able to rouse her, although Chryse witnessed Lillas' leap across the dayroom to come to Fenja's rescue and had been touched that Lillas' absorption in her own plight didn't prevent her from defending one unable to defend herself. In the first few days of the waiting moon, Lillas seemed exactly as Phoron described her in journal entries forwarded to the Eighteenth Mother for the past three years. Chryse readied herself for tantrums and fits of sulking, finding herself completely bewildered by the girl's listlessness. It was Nadia who finally suggested something Chryse never considered—something so simple, so basic, that watching Lillas fly over the track, Chryse knew she had found the answer, but despaired of putting it into practice.

"Daughter of Agave," Chryse thought, shaking her head as Lillas jumped a puddle only to run headlong into an even deeper one, her skirts drenched and her legs stained in mud to her thighs, "who among us could guess that in only twenty days you will force us to change what has remained unchanged since the Novice class?"

With that thought, Chryse pulled her shawl tighter around her shoulders and walked to the center of the arena, where she could better appreciate the sight of the flame of Agave, flickering stubbornly despite the surrounding cold and damp, heedless of anything or anyone who might stay her course.

"I TELL YOU I'll not stand for it! Let her take brisk walks around the dayroom if she needs exercise! I won't have her in the arena!"

Thumping the table one last time for emphasis, Prax flung himself into his chair and crossed his arms over his chest, staring fixedly at Hesione. She felt his need to express his rage to her in private, but shook her head at him, refusing him entry into a mind that was reeling after more than two hours of hotly-contested debate. She had thought Prax angry three years ago when she insisted on riding to the gravesite. Never had she seen him like this, raging at Chryse, bellowing at Nadia, throwing his arms up in wordless appeals to Kazur, who sat with eyes downcast, fingering the golden rings hanging from his left earlobe. Ranier joined their session an hour ago, a slight bout of indigestion by a male ernani demanding his attention even at this late hour. Unlike Kazur, he listened with his head thrown back, although his face was equally impassive. Gathering her wits about her, Hesione met Prax's gaze with one of equal strength, willing him to behave. Like a sullen child, he frowned at her, shifting uncomfortably in his chair.

"Prax, since you've made your opinion on this issue well-known, we'll proceed with discussion. I remind you that Council decisions are ruled by the majority. If you are to convince us of the validity of your beliefs, we will best be persuaded by evidence rather than emotional outbursts."

Hesione thought she saw Kazur's lips curve upward for a moment and wondered briefly what he thought of Chryse's proposal. Like Prax, Kazur had passed through the Maze and knew better than anyone at the table the experience of an ernani in the first moon of Preparation. No wonder Prax was frustrated by his silence; doubtless he felt confident that Kazur would resist change as stringently as did Prax himself.

"If you have calmed yourself, I have a question for you."

Hesione had been careful to maintain her neutrality from the moment Chryse began her appeal. As a result, Prax had no clues as to her opinion. His eyes sparked with interest as he leaned forward in his chair.

"Ask away, Mother."

"What Chryse proposes will allow the morning conditioning and arms training to continue as before. The men will pursue their studies after the midday meal, after which Lillas will be allowed to enter the arena and involve herself in those activities we deem fit. It seems obvious that she should not wrestle, nor engage in any activity that might bring her into bodily contact with either an ernani or a male from Pelion. Chryse thinks she will most likely be interested in running and archery, since these were her daily pursuits in Imarus. Now," she paused, "explain how her presence will disturb the men."

At least he listened to her without interrupting, although a gathering storm darkened his face.

"First of all, and I'm surprised no one's mentioned it, the men train unclothed. That such a fact might disturb her seems to me a relevant point."

Hesione found herself fighting the impulse to smile. Lillas competing with twenty men in the arena was daunting enough; competing with twenty naked men strained even Hesione's powers of imagination. Erasing the picture, she concentrated on the question at hand.

"Why must they train in this manner?"

Before Prax could reply, Kazur broke in, his voice flat to the point of indifference.

"Most trainers prefer nudity because the limbs are free from binding or chafing. It's also possible to judge more clearly how muscle groups respond to particular activities. However," he glanced briefly around the table, "neither of these explanations are the true reason behind the custom."

Hesione was fascinated. For the first time in Council, Kazur was making a private judgment public. Something in his manner, a stiffness in the set of his jaw, indicated his allegiance did not lie with the policies of former years. He was eyeing her warily now, waiting for permission to proceed.

"Continue, if you please."

"Many of the first ernani were criminals—thieves and murderers. The trainers believed that given the opportunity, they would steal knives from the weapons room, secrete them on their persons, and either cut their guards' throats or those of their fellow ernani. Since naked bodies cannot conceal weapons, they trained unclothed."

Kazur pressed his lips into a thin line, damming up the flow of words that might rush out if he were to continue. He might have maintained his self-control but for an ill-timed grunt of approval from the Commander of the Legion. Twisting in his chair so as to more fully regard Prax, who grinned back amiably, never suspecting what he'd just unleashed, Kazur lost his temper.

"I was not a criminal, Prax, nor was a single member of my class! We came of our own accord, yet were treated as you have treated everyone since the Novice class. Some of my fellow ernani were raised with different standards of modesty; some with strong taboos against nudity, especially among members of the same sex. In Pelion you are amused by such things. I can remember the guards laughing at us the first few days, our humiliation as we were stripped and herded from place to place, treated little better than slaves, while many of us were nobles in our own right—princes, tribal chieftains, myself the son of an Equerry of Endlin!"

In the silence that greeted Kazur's outburst, Hesione regarded her companions. Chryse's eyes were wide with horror, her reaction a mirror to Hesione's. Acknowledging the fact that voluntary ernani had different backgrounds than their predecessors, the Sixteenth Mother revised the rules of Preparation in the years after Transformation. One of her first acts was the construction of the Hall of Men, an exact duplicate of the woman's quarters, thus delaying their entrance into the cells until the first night of joining. Hesione wasn't surprised that this particular aspect of Preparation had been overlooked; Hesione herself had never thought to question it, although Kazur's recitation sickened her. Prax cleared his throat.

"I never thought . . .," he began slowly, ". . . never considered . . ."

Unable to continue for a moment, he stared blankly at his hands. When he had mastered his emotions, he began again, slowly and with great difficulty, his voice softer than usual and surprisingly tender.

"My father, Phylas, was a pre-Transformation ernani. Now that I think of it, he would never have questioned such a rule. He had always been treated as a slave and was accustomed to such things. He was a modest man by nature, far more modest than my mother. I was twelve years old when he decided it was time to teach me how to wrestle. When he removed his blouse, I saw the scars covering his back for the first time. Someone had beaten him nearly to death." Prax ran his palm over his bald dome, a gesture that always signified tumult in the mind of the iron-willed Commander. "I never thought what it must have meant to him, that everyone in the arena could see the marks of the lash, the proof of his enslavement."

Hesione spoke quietly, respectful of the powerful memories that had just been re-lived by two former residents of the Maze.

"Are we in agreement that our policy concerning this issue must be amended?"

When five heads nodded, Hesione turned to Chryse.

"Now that this matter has been resolved, have you given any thought to what Lillas might wear? She cannot exercise in the clothing she's been issued . . ."

Chryse shook her head. "Her dress was consigned to the rag pile after her run. I hadn't really thought about it. I suppose I could supply her with garments the apprentice hetaeras wear in our gymnasium . . ."

Prax interrupted again. His former anger might be forgotten, but his opinions concerning Lillas remained unchanged.

"I remain unconvinced that this is necessary."

Nadia re-stated her case, her impatience with Prax bordering on irritation.

"I've told you repeatedly that her health is at stake. For twenty years she has been active, more active than most women of Pelion, including farmers and animal-breeders. Our work with her is doomed to failure if we can't reach a compromise on this point. Chryse has tried everything to no avail. We can no longer harbor notions that she will adjust to the Maze without sustained physical activity. She is tense, nervous, sleepless, has no appetite, and I predict she will not have a monthly flow during this moon. Do you realize how difficult it will be to monitor her chart if my prediction is correct? She will be joined in ten more days and we must be able to guarantee her the same freedom from pregnancy we offer all the others."

Hesione had heard enough.

"Prax, I held my tongue in order to consider all arguments in full. I understand your reticence, for it will mean change, and change is always difficult. I know we'll probably make mistakes without proper time for planning, but I want you to consider how we can best go about this, because, quite frankly, I don't see that we have any choice. Lillas has withdrawn to the point that Chryse can barely engage her in conversation. You've suggested she exercise on her own; Chryse thinks she will quickly tire of individual work. Everything we know about her indicates that she needs activity in order to thrive. Until we can restore her to health, it is the men rather than the women who must supply her with competition and the desire to succeed. We must help her abandon her window seat and enter our world."

Hesione leaned back in her chair and closed her eyes for a moment, feeling twice her age. Even if the Council approved Chryse's plan, if Prax could not be convinced the entire matter would be doomed to failure. Every monitor and trainer within the Maze was a member of the Legion. If they perceived Prax's disapproval, she had no doubt but that they would subvert the Council's decision before it could be given a fair trial. Opening her eyes, she met Prax's measuring stare without flinching.

"Two things."

She nodded curtly.

"First, for this to work there must be more than one woman or Lillas will be considered a freak."

When Chryse blurted out an objection, Prax held up his hand.

"You're wrong about this, Chryse. Remember, please, that my mate is an ernani. There are enough bad rumors about them, most of them not fit to repeat. Whoever's joined to Lillas will have enough problems without thinking she's even more peculiar than the others."

Ranier entered the discussion.

"I agree with Prax on this point. My sessions with the candidates revealed the perceptions regarding female ernani Prax just described. These men are willing to join with an ernani or they would not have been accepted into the Trial, but without notable exception, they consider them to be unwashed savages. We're already changing a major condition of Preparation—that men and women remain separated until the first night of joining. I think I must insist that Lillas not enter the arena alone."

Chryse broke in before Hesione could respond, her expression hopeful for the first time.

"Two women might be persuaded to join her. Halys frets under her heavy skirts and would happily join any venture that guaranteed her an unobstructed view of the sky. The other woman is born-of-the-city, Thaisa by name, and comes to us from a farm in the southeast. She grew up hunting in the hills and almost cried when I told her she must leave behind her quiver and bow."

Ranier leaned back in his chair, well-satisfied. Hesione almost sighed in relief until she remembered Prax and braced herself for another argument.

"And the last consideration, Commander?"

His mouth twisted into a wry grin, Prax's hazel eyes sparkled with pure devilment.

"If we're to have women in the arena, so be it. Here's my final request: can you assure me that they won't run faster, climb higher, outshoot, or otherwise best the men?"

Kazur hooted aloud, to be joined by Chryse's giggles, Ranier's deep chuckles and Nadia's soft-voiced laughter. The tower chamber vibrated with hilarity as Hesione threw back her head, adding her grateful mirth to that of the Council of Pelion.

"YOUR PARDON, REDDIN, but could you . . .?"

Stifling his irritation at yet another interruption to his work, Reddin regarded the tablet being placed on the table beside him, following the long finger that drew his attention to a series of figures in need of his attention.

"You've forgotten to reverse the numerator and denominator. Let me show you."

It was no wonder they came to him for help, Reddin thought (not without a measure of resentment), as he wrote out an example in his neat, angular script. The fifteen ernani ran the gamut from complete illiteracy to basic reading skills, many of the ones who could read a little could write nothing other than their name. None of them, with the exception of Jarod and Stym, knew anything about mathematics other than simple calculations worked on fingers and toes. Several tutors were hard at work in various corners of the Maze's library, the combined babble of explanations, questions, repetitions of the alphabet, and counting aloud making it almost impossible to concentrate on the book Reddin was gamely trying to read.

Finishing the equation, he looked up into the deeply-tanned face of the long-haired Lapithian who followed his calculations with intense concentration.

"Multiplying and dividing fractions is difficult. Don't get discouraged."

Jarod jerked his thumb toward his twin brother sitting at the far end of the table.

"Whatever we learn, it takes two of us to understand. Without Stym, I would be lost."

In twenty days, Reddin had not heard Stym utter a single word. In the training sessions and the arena he was unbeatable—a master swordsman, an impeccable marksman with a bow or a javelin, and a fine wrestler to boot. Jarod held his own, although Reddin noticed he never competed with his brother, whether because he knew he would be beaten or because of an agreement between them, Reddin couldn't be sure. His observations told him they were identical twins down to the clefts in their chins, although Jarod's affability and Stym's reserve made them an oddly-matched couple.

"Does your brother ever speak?"

Jarod stiffened, perhaps suspicious of some implied criticism. Reddin rushed to qualify his question.

"I was a healer before I came here. I wondered if there was some physical reason for his silence."

Glancing quickly at his twin, Jarod lowered his lanky frame into the empty chair beside Reddin. Reddin readied himself to hear a confession. When it came, spoken slowly and with many pauses, Reddin felt a commiseration of sorts for Jarod. Most of the ernani kept to themselves. The five candidates from Pelion, despite the fact that they didn't know each other before entering the Maze, shared interests and cultural bonds from which the ernani were excluded.

"Stym was always the quiet one. My mother says he is the child of his grandsire, our tribal chieftain, while I favor my granddam. She it was who taught our tribe to read and write and speak your language, for she was known as Kara of Pelion."

Obviously, Jarod was proud of his grandmother's connection to Pelion, as well he should be. Here was the reason the twins' knowledge was advanced far beyond the other ernani. Putting aside that idea, Reddin concentrated on Jarod's explanation.

"Stym lost his tongue because of this place. He is accustomed to being a leader of our tribe, but here, among the men of Pelion, he grows shy and uneasy."

Reddin was quick to disagree.

"He's still a leader! No one equals his abilities in the arena. Dysponteus, the fastest runner in Pelion, rarely bests Stym." Reddin couldn't prevent the bitterness of his next words. "Having witnessed my performance in the arena, Stym knows how gifted he is."

"He sees only that you read books we cannot begin to understand, that Adrastus speaks knowledgeably about . . .," Jarod stumbled over the next few words, ". . . stress points . . . cantilevers . . . weight-bearing surfaces, while Dysponteus speaks of metallurgy and melting points. These words have no meaning for us."

"Adrastus trained as an engineer. Dysponteus apprenticed at the Forge. I have as little knowledge as you about the construction and design of buildings or the refining of metals."

"Ah, but you have concepts for these words, while we have none! We see only that we are barbarians. This is difficult for my brother," he added, "and myself."

There was a sound of finality in his last observation and also a note of reproach. Gathering up his tablet and pen, Jarod returned to his brother. As he murmured the explanation of the formula, Stym lifted his head to gaze steadily across the table at Reddin. Made uneasy by Stym's measured stare, Reddin dropped his eyes to his book.

The door to the library opened and shut again, and Strato, Head Trainer of the Maze stood before them. A grizzled Legion veteran of some fifty years, his thick torso, long arms, short legs and even shorter temper caused the men to dub him "The Bear." A hush came over the room as he surveyed them, his great scruffy head moving slowly from side to side to observe them. Satisfied he had their attention, he began issuing orders in a loud rumble emanating from deep within his chest.

"Men of the Maze, this afternoon begins a scheduled change in our procedure. You will proceed to the arena as usual. Instead of disrobing at the gates, you may retain some or all of your clothing. If you choose to strip down, you must retain your loincloths."

A buzz of muted conversation followed his announcement, causing a look of distinct annoyance to appear on his weather-beaten face. Choosing to ignore the interruption, he continued to address them in a voice much more suited to roaring in the arena than speaking in the library's small enclosure.

"As of today, several newcomers will train with us in the arena. I expect your normal performances; no favoritism will be shown to either you or the newcomers." Strato must have sensed the interest generated by his mysterious announcement, but, old soldier that he was, he overrode it by increasing his volume. "Two more rules: you are absolutely forbidden to engage in any physical contact with the newcomers, and the only valid topic for conversation is information concerning the event underway. Is that understood?"

When Dorian, the wiry candidate from Pelion who finished third in the Trial spoke up, the men quickly smothered their laughter. A full member of the Chartists guild before competing in the Trial, Dorian proved himself a mimic of genius and regularly entertained them after the evening meal with imitations of themselves and assorted Maze personnel, most of them good-hearted and all of them displaying his gift for acute observation. Dorian was doing his "Bear" imitation as he growled out a question in an over-loud voice.

"Trainer, might we know the identity of these 'newcomers'?"

Some of the men were laughing openly at this point. Strato shot them a poisonous look, which only increased their mirth. Hands on his hips, he shook his head slowly from side to side (which only increased his likeness to the animal they chose as his namesake), and uttered a single word.

"Women."

The laughter died. For a moment the only sound was the tutor who worked solely with Keret, the ernani from The Flowering Lands, trying to explain to him the new rules. Keret's vocabulary might be small, but his ability to absorb information was astonishing, and already he could speak in broken sentences. The tutor must have reached the end of Strato's speech, for suddenly a white-toothed grin spread across Keret's ebony face as he announced in a booming voice:

"Women. Good!"

At that single adjective, all the men collapsed in laughter, slapping their thighs, the backs of chairs, the books open on the tables before them, their neighbors—anyone or anything within reach. For twenty days they had lived solely in the company of other men, although the ernani spent time each day with a hetaera who instructed them in joining, sessions from which the candidates from Pelion were exempt since they received instruction in the House of Hetaeras during adolescence. Strato's announcement produced giddy anticipation, for the women they saw today might eventually be escorted to the cells waiting for them in the deeper recesses of the Maze.

As the roar of laughter subsided, replaced by hiccoughs and much clearing of throats, Strato regarded them with an expression of utter disgust. Stroking his stubbled chin, his eyes flicked from man to man.

"All this energy convinces me I've been too easy on you." A quick round of denials greeted his observations. "That must be it; too easy by half." His decision made, he barked out an order. "We'll have ten extra laps at the conclusion of this afternoon's session," he paused, taking great delight in his pronouncement, "after the women leave the grounds."

With no indication that he heard the groans emanating from twenty throats, he issued the last bit of information necessary before their trip to the arena.

"The women will compete in running and archery, although other events may be added. One word of caution." He paused. "You've heard the rules and they'll be strictly enforced. You'll meet your partner soon enough; it would be folly to consider this anything but a normal part of your Preparation."

THE RUCKUS THAT erupted after Strato's exit could be heard halfway down the hall. Shaking his head at the men's antics, he let the grin he'd swallowed in the library spread over his face. The Eighteenth Mother helped him prepare his speech at noon after Prax spent all morning with him in an attempt to foresee any problems that might arise. Strato himself was cautiously supportive of what Prax proposed. He'd been the Head Trainer for seven years and would be among the first to admit that nothing was perfect, for he'd had his failures, as had all the personnel within the Maze.

It was the session with the Eighteenth Mother that convinced him the changes could work as planned. He knew her father and watched her grow up around the other sons and daughters of cavalry officers. Facing her across the round table in her tower chamber, all thoughts of her youth vanished as she outlined not just what he was to say, but how he was to present it to the men.

"You must strike the right note with them, Strato. We forget that this class has no knowledge of our procedures in the past. What you outline today is simply a duly scheduled change, no more, no less, and certainly not a matter for comment or discussion. Give them the rules and then announce the consequence of disobedience."

Mischief danced in her eyes as he remembered her audacity when it came to riding. She had always been a fearless child on horseback.

"It might be helpful to give them something other than the women to remember about this day. After all, Strato," she added, "you're the most hated man in the Maze. We must do everything possible to maintain your reputation."

It worked like a charm. He couldn't read them individually, but he'd opened himself to their emotions and they'd gone through every stage she'd predicted—resistance, suspicion, and finally, after the release of laughter, his last words were met with understanding. They knew what they risked if they broke the rules, and even Dorian (whose impression flattered Strato immensely) sobered at his warning.

Strato reached the gates and threw them wide, viewing the empty arena with vast pride. This training ground had prepared some of the finest Legion officers ever to wear the brown cloaks, a raft of ernani skilled in weaponry destined to keep their lands free of the tyranny of Agave, and two members of the current Council of Pelion. If women were to be the next trainees, Strato, for one, would welcome them. Rubbing his hands together, for the afternoon was chilly, he heard the men and their monitors approach and bawled out his usual command:

"Let the session begin!"

WE ARE TRULY a motley crew, Reddin decided as he ran his eyes over the men scattered about the arena. Naked bodies created an impression of anonymity; today each man's choice of apparel gave him a certain identity, an insight, Reddin thought, into how they perceived their bodies when in the presence of women.

The Lapithians were fully clothed in the brown breeches and blouses that were standard issue and retained their boots, although Stym removed his for purposes of running. Manthur of Endlin, too, was fully dressed and had even wrapped a cloak around him while he waited to take up his longbow. The mountain man, Altug, was stripped to the waist, his long mustache brushing the middle of his chest.

The men of Pelion were either less modest, or more flamboyant, each of them stripped down to a loincloth. Of all the ernani, Keret wore the least, and even that small piece of cloth was worn over his loud, if incomprehensible, objections. Despite Keret's protests to the contrary, his monitor finally tied a loincloth around his hips and shoved him through the gates.

The opportunity to observe the others was broken by a bellow from Strato, who was personally overseeing the archery session.

"Archers approach! Prepare!"

This was the first round, normally reserved for light-weight bows. Reddin took his usual position, stringing his bow, aware that one of the women was taking her place directly to his right. Each woman was dressed in loose cotton breeches with a gathered waist tied with a drawstring and a full-cut blouse tucked into the top of their breeches. The woman beside him had rolled up her sleeves nearly to her shoulders in order to free her arms. Reddin's curiosity was aroused when he observed that her darkly-tanned

skin ended at a distinct line near her elbow. He hadn't meant to stare, but
she must have sensed his inspection for she turned two icy blue eyes toward
him and pointedly rolled down her sleeves. Embarrassed, he looked away,
reminding himself to tend to business.

"Shoot at will!"

Reddin still lacked the upper body strength necessary to pull one of the
longbows used by Jarod, Stym, and Manthur, although his accuracy had
improved after twenty days of regular practice sessions. Taking his time, he
pulled, aimed, and released, trying not to be distracted by the woman beside
him who was shooting three times as quickly, sending shaft after shaft directly
into the middle of the target. The unmistakable twang of sinew against flesh
made him lower his bow, listening with growing astonishment to a string
of profanities so graphic he could hardly credit the fact that they issued from
a woman's mouth.

She dropped her bow and was hopping up and down, her short curls
bouncing in rhythm, her right hand grasping the inside of her left forearm.
Once he'd overcome his shock at her language (for some of her curses were
inventive to a degree) he walked over to her, fighting his impulse to pull
away her hand and examine the place struck by the snapped bowstring.

"Let me see."

Her face twisted in a grimace, she thrust out her arm. Midway between
her wrist and her elbow a bruise was forming. Already a deep angry red,
by tomorrow it would be a purple welt.

"There's a healer on duty by the gate."

He pointed out a figure lounging near the reviewing stands. Nodding
her understanding, she retracted her arm and reached for her empty quiver
and bow. As she straightened, he noticed she was almost exactly his height,
with long legs and square shoulders. She was heading for the stands when
he thought of something that might help prevent another injury.

"Ernani," he called after her, "ask them for an arm-guard before you shoot
again."

She stopped dead in her tracks and turned slowly to stare at him, her
expression solemn and decidedly unfriendly.

"What makes you think I'm an ernani?"

It was nothing more than a lucky guess, although after hearing her speak,
her accent marked by a soft sibilance different from any native of the city,
there was no need for her to confirm her identity. Now his problem was to
convey to this foul-mouthed barbarian that no self-respecting woman (or
man, for that matter) swore in quite such an uninhibited manner, especially
in the presence of the opposite sex.

"Your speech is more . . . colorful . . . than that of a woman of Pelion."

She must not have discerned the disapproval in his voice, for she wasn't insulted in the least. In fact, it was as if he'd offered her a compliment. A tinge of pink colored her cheeks and she laughed outright. He didn't find her attractive in the least, for she was slim as a boy and her features seemed overlarge for such a thin face. Her laughter did nothing to change his impression, for it transformed her into a creature of bold impertinence, not a quality he valued in a woman. In the next moment she was off, her stride long and purposeful. Soon she was running, her head catching a stray shaft of sunlight, setting her hair aglow like the flame of a lighted candle.

A slight shiver ran over him as a cloud covered the sun. A blanket was thrown over his bare shoulders.

"Strato is . . .," Flavius grimaced, "I believe the polite expression is 'annoyed.' I'm to report exactly what transpired."

It wasn't Flavius' fault that Strato was a tyrant; even so, Reddin couldn't hide his resentment at being continually observed by so many watchful eyes. In twenty days they'd stripped him of his freedom, his privacy, and his ability to study in any concentrated matter. Now they wanted to know every word that passed his lips.

"Her bowstring snapped and struck her forearm. I directed her to a healer."

His delivery was rapid, flat, and purposefully void of emotion. A long, low whistle drew his attention. Flavius was staring at the woman's target. She'd loosed twenty arrows. All but one was buried in either the black center or the red second circle. A single shaft resided in the outer circles, the result, no doubt, of her injury. Reddin had never shot so well in his life.

A mighty thump on his back nearly set him face-down in the dirt, an explosion of raucous laughter greeting his grunt of pained surprise. The four candidates from Pelion surrounded him with identical expressions of excitement.

"We saw you speak to her!"

"Come, man, don't keep it to yourself!"

"Reddin, we're waiting!"

"By the Makers, who is she?"

Reddin bit back the words on the tip of his tongue. It had been a hateful, bothersome day. Any anger on his part would only worsen the ones to follow. These men shared his condition. If he gave in to the exasperation he felt for the pointless physical and weapons training for which they had nothing but approval, he would only make his situation more miserable.

"She's an ernani."

They waited expectantly for him to continue. When he stood mute, Adrastus threw an arm around his shoulder in a great show of camaraderie.

"Surely a great scholar like you observed more than that simple fact!"

Shrugging off Adrastus' arm, Reddin turned to face them.

"For my part, you are welcome to her, since her behavior suits me not at all."

He turned on his heel to leave them, groaning as he heard Strato yell out a command that the men approach the track. Mastering his rebellion, he approached the starting line, readying himself for ten more laps around the arena.

Daily he asked himself what he was accomplishing. Daily the remembrance of Orrin's wordless description of what he sought provided a reason for continuance.

Chapter 11

The Moon of Joining

CLEAN FROM THEIR scalps to their toes, damp hair hanging in limp ribbons down shoulders draped in freshly-laundered nightgowns, the troubles of the day washed down the drains, the women gathered each evening to pass the few remaining hours before the torches were put out. Despite the similarity of their attire, they differed in size, shape, and color as do the autumn leaves of twenty fall-struck trees. Like flocks of starlings who swarm before migrating en masse toward warmer climes, their formations swerved and shifted constantly—here a group of two or three bent over a book or drawing; there, a group involved in an animated discussion ending in shrieks of laughter or an eddy of moans and giggles; small groups dispersing to form larger ones; larger ones scattering to spread some bit of news or amusing anecdote. Some evenings the women of Pelion sang songs of the city, celebrating its glories with dense, six-layered harmonies as the ernani sat rapt and silent. Other nights the ernani spun tales of lives lived far beyond city walls, their descriptions leaving the city-dwellers wide-eyed and wondering.

This night would be their last together. Tomorrow, the evening trumpet would find them in a cell with a man they had never met, a stranger with whom they would take their first hesitant step toward what was promised. A kind of wistfulness haunted the sleeping chamber, for thirty days bound them together, some as sisters, some as helpmates, friends, or confidants. They said no farewells, for they would meet tomorrow morning in the dayroom, yet never again would they gather in the dormitory, and that knowledge muted the evening's revelries. One by one they drifted toward their beds, placing their heads of jet, copper, bronze, and gold to rest on scented pillows. A sole figure in grey wandered the hall, extinguishing the torches, while they lay together in silence, the light of the full moon drenching the room as it fell through the high windows.

"Awake are you, Lillas?"

"Yes."

"I ask myself, `Halys, what waits tomorrow?'"

There was a long silence.

"Scared are you?"

"I . . . I try not to think about it."

"Scared am I."

"It's no use being frightened. If you don't care for him, you can end the contract at the next full moon."

Halys' response was barely a whisper.

"Of not wanting him, I worry only a little. Of not being wanted, of this I have great fear."

Lillas could hardly credit what she was hearing. Halys, who ran like the wind, her hair streaming behind her like a flag as she passed the other runners on the track. Halys, whose diligence over every task put Lillas' feeble efforts to shame. No one worked harder to please than Halys, pouring over books and figures, her fingernails orange crescents from her work with the clay she chose as her craft; yet tonight she lay sleepless, worried that somehow she might be found unworthy.

Lillas' response was fierce.

"You are everything a man could want and more than he deserves!"

"To be like you," Halys sighed, "you who fear nothing. Miss you, I will."

With a grim smile, Lillas punched the pillow and rearranged it beneath her head. She hadn't lied to Halys. It was true she'd thought little about what tomorrow would bring, for it was always her way to avoid the unpleasant, to bury the painful. If it weren't for the dream, she thought, my doubts would disappear. If it weren't for the dream . . . Sighing, she closed her eyes, pressed her lips together, and forced herself to think of other things.

THEY WENT THROUGH the lists together, five heads bent over stacks of papers and charts. Tomorrow brought with it the Day of Joining, a rite by which they would place another forty souls on the Path of Preparation. One among them, Kazur, had undergone that day as a participant. Tonight was his first time to partake in this, the most solemn duty of the Council of Pelion.

Hesione reached for a goblet of wine and sipped its sweet fruitiness gratefully. Prax was off to the west again, tightening the net he wove to trap the beast that was Agave—meeting with his spies, retrieving and organizing necessary information while Hesione tended the girl around whom all his plans revolved. Replacing the goblet on its silver tray, she introduced the subject they had danced around all night.

"What of Lillas? I sense reluctance on Chryse's part to discuss her. Is there something we should know?"

The hour was late and the hetaera had unbound her hair, its raven darkness lying in heavy waves around her slim shoulders. Clear brown eyes rose from the papers strewn in front of her. She spoke, as always, simply and from the heart.

"I fear for her."

Hesione considered the evidence, running her mind over daily reports that offered nothing but good news about the ernani from Agave. In the past ten days she'd been born again as the Lillas described in Phoron's journals. Headstrong and impatient, she labored resentfully over the studies demanded of her, moving her teachers to despair on a regular basis. Energetic and totally without fear, she climbed the ropes forbidden her, dangling playfully thirty feet above the arena and frightening Strato nearly to death. Her sense of humor emerged as well, the stories of her pranks in the Hall of Women scandalizing even the most broad-minded of monitors—a bowl of gooey porridge dumped on Phoebe's head in an act of delayed but effective revenge, games of dice (at which she was a master) played until dawn, and fits of swearing that left the prim women of Pelion open-mouthed with horror.

Her recklessness and temper aside, she also revealed her loyalty and sense of honor. With a persistence no one suspected she possessed, she would sit for hours with Halys and Fenja, giving them the chance to converse freely with one who was neither tutor nor critic, teaching them by example, correcting their errors without seeming to do so. A woman of her word, she plugged away at the lessons they placed before her every morning so as to run free in the arena every afternoon.

Still, Chryse was fearful and Hesione respected that fear. The Mistress of Joining had the ability to intuit troubles of the spirit unexplained by studies of behavior.

"Show us what your fear."

At Hesione's command, Chryse closed her eyes and invited them within, transporting them to the library, the site of her meetings with the female ernani where she schooled them in the techniques of joining, inspiring confidence in the five women who sat gathered around the table. An adept of lesser talents would have shown them the moment as they experienced it in the fixed chronology of time. Chryse's mind was infinitely more flexible, shifted them easily from image to image as she built for them the reason for her fears.

They were subtle observations: Lillas wincing when Chryse described how a man's arousal might be increased or delayed. When Chryse assured them that they need not join their bodies with their partner during the first moon, relief flooded Lillas' face. During another session, they saw Lillas struggle with a waking dream that left her unable to rejoin the discussion. In time Chryse returned them to the tower chamber, leaving them alone with their individual thoughts.

"We know her to be a virgin. Are her reactions unlike those who share her condition?"

It was a thoughtful question because Kazur was always, unfailingly, thoughtful. Hesione smiled inside herself, gratified that he was beginning to take the initiative in their discussions. His question was directed to Chryse. Nadia intervened.

"I must qualify something here. Phoron was explicit in his journals. At no time during his tenure did she join with another. He kept careful records of her monthly flow, yet never had occasion to examine her. My examination yielded no confirmation of your assumption that she is, indeed, a virgin. There is no hymen, although many women, especially those who are physically active, lose their maidenheads at an early age or simply lack one from birth."

"Still, Kazur's question is a fair one." There was a short pause as Chryse explored the memories of her years as Mistress of Joining. "It has been my experience that virgins are often frightened of what I teach. Here is the difference: Lillas hides her reactions. You experienced it with me, a half-formed impression that her reluctance is based on something she conceals from us, and, more dangerously, from herself."

Nadia took the floor now to report on her patient.

"There is an additional problem beyond the one Chryse describes. I hoped exercise would restore Lillas' natural balance, but she has yet to experience a monthly flow, making it impossible for me to chart her cycle. Until I can do so, I can't set the correct dosages of the medicines which will prevent conception. For this reason, her partner must refrain from joining with her, something he must be told immediately."

Nadia's concern was well-founded and shared by everyone around the table. Hesione took a deep breath. This was more complicated than she'd realized.

"We must consider Reddin in this matter. Do we have any indication of how he will react to our demand that he refrain from the act of joining?"

There was no response to her query. Privately, she cursed the Trial and the limitations it forced upon them. Year after year they struggled through this night, their knowledge of the women candidates strong and sure from interviews with family, friends, teachers and fellow-workers, as well as countless sessions with the candidates themselves. Their knowledge of the male candidates was limited to two brief interviews, one of them hindered by the presence of a President, all of whom were infamous for asking the most mundane questions imaginable. Reddin was chosen on the basis of Chryse's intuition and Ranier's brief observations, neither of which helped them with their present dilemma.

The judgment Hesione sought came from an unexpected source, for Kazur's knowledge of Reddin was limited to his performance in the Trial. Fingering his earrings, Kazur recited from memory:

"'He is endurance, patient and eternal.' So Chryse said and so he proved himself in the Trial. Ranier spoke of the strength of his desire for the gift; Orrin told us of his longing for a mate of his heart. What more is necessary? We move forward. We trust."

With that, the Council put aside their papers and charts. Humbled and heartened by their newest member, they passed out of the tower chamber and into the sleeping world of Pelion.

REDDIN'S STOMACH WAS fast becoming a knot. An unexpected interview with the Mistress of Joining this morning didn't help matters. Disruption of the menstrual cycle was a common occurrence among young women, but it added to his uneasiness. Since no other choice presented itself, he promised to refrain from joining until the ernani's healer was convinced there would be no issue from their bodies. Part of him was relieved; another part remained troubled, for somehow he must bind this ernani to him in the first moon or risk her deciding to end their contract. What little confidence he could muster resided in his ability to please a woman.

Catching himself listening to every footfall passing down the corridor beyond the locked door, he cast about for something to do. His skin and hair were still wet from his bath. The air in the cell was cool, a quick shiver convincing him that he'd catch a chill if he didn't dry himself thoroughly. After removing his damp blouse and breeches and spreading them out to dry, he squatted by the fireplace, struck a spark on the flint and lit a fire. Soon he was toasting himself in front of a friendly blaze, his mood improving as warmth began to permeate the cell. Once his hair was dry, he made a leisurely tour of the room, exploring the place he would spend every night for the next four moons.

Appropriately named a cell, it was more dismal than he'd imagined. It was also small, perhaps fifteen paces long and ten wide, with a low-raftered wooden ceiling and stone walls. A high narrow window covered with iron bars ran along the wall opposite the iron door. What furniture there was—a wardrobe, bed, two chests, a table, two high-backed chairs and a three-legged stool—was constructed of serviceable oak, old-fashioned and reeking of recently applied wax. Crockery, utensils, cooking pots, and various herbs and spices were either hung or stored in an orderly fashion against the walls on either side of the hearth, which stood to the left of the iron door. The table and chairs were arranged to form a tiny eating area, which might serve as a suitable place for studying, he decided, surveying the placement of the furniture with a critical eye. The wardrobe stood at the end of the room farthest from the door. Upon closer inspection, he discovered it held two woolen dresses, a long-sleeved nightgown, and a hooded cloak dyed a deep midnight blue. His own clothing was folded and stacked in a brass-bound chest beside the wardrobe; his books (brought from the attic as Flavius promised) were neatly shelved along the wall beneath the window.

Considering this morning's developments, there was a certain irony to be found in the placement of the bed. Unlike most sleeping chambers, it was not pushed against a wall, but stood in the center of the room, dominating the floor. To move anywhere in the room, one was forced to circumnavigate its indomitable, unwieldy presence. The frame was solid, the mattress thick, the headboard without decoration of any kind. Down-filled pillows rested upon a faded coverlet that had once been blue but now was faded to a faint pearl grey. Two striped blankets rested on a low chest at the foot of the bed. Opening the chest, he found it lined with cedar and filled with an abundance of linens and woolen blankets. A chamber pot sat under the bed, a not-so-gentle reminder of the intimacy of the situation in which he found himself. Having pushed aside the overhanging coverlet to view the chamber pot, he discovered, to his amazement, that the bed was bolted to the floor. Someone had drilled holes into the stone floor and run four large screw bolts through an L-shaped iron bracket attached to each of the bed's four legs. The first explanation that came to mind was that the bed, for some reason which escaped him, must remain exactly where it was. The second explanation came more slowly. Did someone actually think the exertions of the two bodies within the bed might be enough to lift it from the floor? A tide of color overcame him at the thought of such presumption.

Well, there was little hope of that particular prediction coming true in the near future. With a resentful shrug, he strode to the shelf, located the book he'd been forced to put aside thirty days ago, and lowered himself into one of the two high-backed chairs facing the hearth. The fire barely provided enough light by which to read. Squinting in an effort to make out the lines that jumped with every flicker of the flames, he had just become immersed in the text when someone slid the bolt and opened the door.

"Help, or I'll surely drop them!"

A woman appeared at the cell door, her arms cradled around a flat wooden crate she was struggling to maneuver through the narrow opening. Responding to the urgency of her request, Reddin threw down his book and hurried to offer his assistance. He was halfway across the cell when the door swung shut behind her, caught her shoulder as she stepped over the threshold and upset her already precarious balance. As he extended his arms, the woman gave a sharp cry, pitched forward onto the floor at his feet, the box dropped into his waiting hands, and the bolt slid back into place.

A stream of profanity, each curse fouler than the last, rose steadily in pitch and volume until the woman was shouting, so angry was she at the clumsy monitor who escorted her to the cell. Steadying his grip on the box, which was unwieldy but not particularly heavy, a twisted smile of recognition appeared on Reddin's face. He wondered at the breadth of her repertoire until she began to repeat herself, at which time he found himself moved to laughter.

Fearing he might hurt her feelings, he tried to smother his mirth, when to his everlasting surprise, the woman, still sprawled face down on the hard stone floor, began to giggle. Soon she, too, was laughing, her shoulders shaking as she picked herself up from the floor. Her gown was plain; heavy wool dyed a nondescript shade of blue, the neckline rising to the hollow of her throat, the tight bodice laced at the sides. The severity of the style made her appear thin and waspish, confirming his impression of her in the arena. Swatting at her full skirts, sending them flying up around her to reveal the petticoat beneath, she righted herself, regarding him for the first time. These same eyes had surveyed him in the arena, blue as a cloudless day in high summer.

"I . . . I thought you were an ernani!"

He bristled for a moment, his pride injured, until he reminded himself there were no means by which she could ascertain his identity in the arena. He'd spoken a few brief sentences. Perhaps her ear for accents was not as finely tuned as his. He shook his head, watching her confusion grow.

"You're so dark! The women from Pelion are . . ." she faltered, no doubt responding to his scowl, ". . . are much . . .," she finished limply, "lighter."

Controlling his temper with difficulty, he managed a civil reply:

"Then I suppose I'm living proof that in Pelion, skin of all colors exists."

At least she had the decency to blush.

"I meant no harm."

Reddin calmed himself. His own sensitivity on the subject made him snap at her. Perhaps it was an honest mistake. His gaze dropped to the box in his arms.

"What did I rescue from falling?"

"Candles." She seemed grateful for the change in subject. "The Instructor gave each of us some candles before we left. I was afraid the pottery would break."

"The Instructor?"

Reddin had never met anyone with that particular title.

"Why, yes!" Seeing no recognition on his face, she sought to enlighten him. "She teaches us. She's lovely, dark braids she wears like a crown, dresses in robes of yellow hues . . ."

"Ah! You mean the Mistress of Joining!"

Reddin had met her twice, once on the day of his first interview and again this morning. The description was an apt one, for she was a beautiful woman, far more beautiful than this ernani could ever hope to be.

"We call her the Instructor," she insisted with a stubborn frown.

He hesitated, considering whether he should inform her of the Mistress of Joining's profession before discarding the idea. It was not his intention to correct all her misapprehensions in a single night. Sighing inwardly, he placed the box on the bed. When he turned back to her, she quickly averted her eyes, reminding him that he had stripped to his loincloth. Although this was exactly what he'd worn in the arena, her reaction suggested she found his bare torso intimidating in the close confines of the cell. Since there was no sense in making this evening more awkward than it already was, he reached for his clothes. He was pulling up his breeches when she asked, or rather, demanded: "Why did you remove them?"

Ignoring her tone, he gave a civil answer as he continued to dress. "They were damp from my bath. The cell was cold and dank, so I lit a fire to warm the room and dry my clothes. Your arrival . . .," he paused briefly, ". . . came unexpectedly, and I had no time to dress."

He was buttoning his breeches when he turned to find a strange look on her face.

"It seems I must offer you another apology. It's just that I thought . . ."

"You thought I was going to throw you on the floor and ravish you?" This struck him as particularly ironic when he considered the promise he'd made that morning. "I assure you," he added, with what he hoped was a reassuring grin, "that was never my intention."

She didn't return his smile. Instead, she grew suddenly intent.

"Wasn't it?"

He didn't know whether to be amused or annoyed.

"I have no interest in forcing my attentions on you."

"Why not?"

What kind of game was she playing? He couldn't tell if she was insulted or relieved.

"I've never forced a woman. I don't plan on starting now."

She mulled that over for a while.

"Why should I believe you?"

He sensed he had reached a turning point with her, that they were striking a bargain of some sort, one he didn't entirely understand.

"Because I'm a man of my word."

It seemed he passed the first test. She extended her hand to him, favoring him with a smile of such warmth that for the first time he thought of her as something other than a savage.

"I am called Lillas."

He touched her for the first time, a quick brush of his palm against hers.
"I am Reddin."

SQUAT CANDLES IN pottery bowls lined the mantle and the narrow ledge
beneath the window, adding a diffused glow to the tiny cell. When a meal
was pushed through the grate beneath the door, they ate hungrily, spared
the ordeal of conversation as they cleaned the bowls of stew with pieces of
bread. She finished first and wandered about the cell, exploring each nook
and cranny as he had done before her arrival. He sat in the high-backed
chair, watching as she demolished the carefully arranged order of the room.
Each chest she opened was rifled and abandoned; his books were scanned
and quickly ignored; the wardrobe door hung open, most of the clothes
within it fallen from their pegs or thrown carelessly onto the floor. She was
by the door now, examining the hinges and then kneeling to thrust her arm
through the grate as if trying to reach the bolt on the other side. A muttered
curse announced her lack of success. At last she turned to face him, arms
akimbo, her hair a tousled mass of light brown curls turned to gold by the
firelight.

"What are we to do?"

There was a touch of desperation in her demand, completing his picture
of her as an untamed animal pacing the boundaries of its cage, seeking some
means of escape.

"We can clean off the table, wash and dry the dishes, and redd up the
room before we retire."

"Redd up?"

"Put into order," he translated, wondering if she understood this was the
root word of his name: 'Reddin, one who puts things in order.'

"Aren't there servants to do such things? There were servants in the
dormitory."

Surely the caretakers told her what to expect? While Reddin considered
the matter, she flounced over to the unoccupied chair and dropped into it,
pulling up her legs under her skirts so she sat cross-legged.

"There are no servants here. Only you and I will ever enter these four
walls. Between the evening trumpet and the morning bell no one may disturb
us. Tonight we were supplied with a meal. Beginning tomorrow, we must
prepare whatever is provided."

A disgusted snort interrupted his recital.

"I have little liking for cookery."

Her chin lifted and he could see a challenge forming in her eyes. Quickly deciding that he should take her at her word, he offered the first solution that came to mind.

"Then perhaps it would be wise to eat large meals in the morning and at midday."

His suggestion must have surprised her, for she frowned. Still frowning, she regarded the cell.

"And I care not a whit about cleaning."

Nodding, he surveyed the disarray she'd created in only a few minutes, hiding his dismay at the messy surroundings. He was always orderly in his habits, the added discipline of The House of Healing making him almost obsessively neat. Sighing on the inside, he envisioned the chaos this woman promised him. His other option was to cook and clean for her, although his intuition told him that if he did so, she would despise him for it.

"Then we'll not clean away the meal or redd up the room."

For his part, the subject was closed and he picked up the book he'd discarded. After a brief pause she interrupted him.

"What if we need fresh linens? Are we expected to launder our clothes as well?"

His irritation growing at her unending complaints and disagreeable mood, he refused to lift his eyes from the page, answering her in what he hoped was a matter-of-fact manner.

"We may leave such items outside the door every morning and they will be returned by nightfall."

After a few minutes of silence, she interrupted him again.

"What is it you read?"

He hadn't heard her approach. Glancing down at the floor, he saw bare toes peeking out from beneath her dress. Leaning over his shoulder to take advantage of the firelight, she scanned the page, giving him a moment to consider her unobserved. There was an arrogant cast to her features—a thin-bridged nose and a jutting chin, as well as the suggestion of sensuality in her full lips. No one would describe her as pretty, but in her was an energy that fueled her eyes, which snapped and sparkled at him. At that thought he realized he hadn't responded to her question, for her eyes had lifted from the page and were glaring fixedly at him.

"It's a study of human anatomy."

Her blank look revealed her unfamiliarity with the term. Turning the pages, he found an illustration and held it out for her to examine. The drawing detailed the musculature of the shoulder, arm, and hand. He thought it might interest her; instead, she pushed it away and made a face.

"Ugh! He hasn't any skin!"

Hiding his amusement at her wrinkled nose and pursed lips, he retrieved the book and began to read again. The fabric of her skirt rubbed against the back of his chair as she walked away; her petticoats rustled as she seated herself, wool rubbing against wood as she shifted her position. Despite the irritating noises she was making, he continued to read. A half-hearted sigh broke his concentration again. When he looked up, a woebegone face regarded him with a child's misery at being left to play alone.

"I haven't anything to do!"

Rising, he went to the shelf and selected a slim volume handsomely bound in scarlet leather. Walking to her chair, he placed it in her lap. She was looking down so he couldn't see her face. As her hands began to turn the pages, he heard her quick intake of breath. Smiling, he waited for the reaction he knew would follow.

"I've never seen a book like this before! It's . . . it's . . .," she stopped, not knowing how to proceed.

"It's printed, not written out by hand. Individual letters are cast and then arranged in a kind of tray to form a single page. The letters are covered with a thin film of ink and then paper is placed over them and pressed by a heavy weight. Each page is printed in the same manner and then bound."

He understood her awe for he had felt it himself. His parents were members of the Guild of Printers and this volume was their first book, put into print nearly twenty years ago. He inherited his love of books from them, although he had no interest in pursuing their craft. His sister was continuing the family business, having completed the printing of her first book last year.

"But it must be rare and costly!"

"The wonder of these books is that they can be quickly printed and many copies of each page made from a single tray of letters. The cost is much less than a book copied by a scribe."

Resuming his seat, he watched her settle herself more comfortably into her chair, take a deep breath and start to read the page open before her. Holding her forefinger under each word to mark her place, she mouthed every word in turn as she worked across the line of text, her face darkening.

"What is `troth'?"

"It means to give your word, to swear."

Without acknowledging his help, she continued down the page. Mesmerized by her difficulties, for he read as easily as he breathed or slept, he watched her struggle on, answering her questions without comment, his interest in his own book forgotten. After almost an hour of intense effort, she lifted her eyes to him. They were bleak.

"Did you enjoy the poem?"

"Enjoy?!" She clearly thought him daft. "How can I enjoy what I can't understand?" Her eyes grew dark and stormy. "Nothing makes any sense!"

"Perhaps it would help if you read it aloud."

To his surprise, she didn't lash out at his suggestion, but after considering him thoughtfully for a moment, settled deeper into the chair and began to real aloud.

> I wonder, by my . . . troth, what thou, and I . . .

Each word was sounded out slowly and with great difficulty, broken by hesitations and much chewing on her bottom lip. When he could stand it no longer, he took the book from her hands. Holding it closed between his palms, he recited from memory:

> For love, all love of other sights controules,
> And makes one little roome, an every where.
> Let sea-discoverers to new worlds have gone,
> Let Maps to other, worlds on worlds have showne,
> Let us possesse one world, each hath one, and is one.

The book must have opened of its own accord, for this was a favorite poem of his, one of the few he ever troubled to memorize. Her eyes widened as he began, then he saw her listen as if for the first time to the words she'd read only moments ago. When he finished the last stanza, he paused, stroking the leather spine, lost in thought until she posed a quiet question.

"Why did you learn it by heart?"

Here was the opportunity to tell her why he had come, to undertake the role the Eighteenth Mother described in the Sanctum, but he could find no words to speak to this stranger with her bare feet, profanity, and lamentable ignorance. Avoidance and evasion were his first line of retreat, so he answered her with a shrug. An uncomfortable silence stretched between them as he searched for a way to bridge the gap.

"Did you understand the poem when I recited it?" A quick nod was accompanied by a stain of color washing over her cheeks. "Perhaps it was too advanced for you to read and comprehend on your own. I never meant to embarrass you." The apology was an afterthought, although she took no offense.

"No," she sighed, "I never thought you did." Sensing she was trying to share something with him, he listened carefully as she continued. "I always understand what the tutor reads aloud; it's only when I have to read it myself that I'm lost. And the others . . . the others are more skilled. . .

". . . so you act as if you understand rather than asking for help."

Her cheeks were aflame with guilt, her face that of a child caught stealing a freshly-baked sweet left to cool on a window sill. He couldn't swallow a smile at her duplicity.   Instantly, she was on the defensive, her voice shrill with derision.

"You can't know what it's like to be the worst at something!"

A straw target appeared before his eyes.

"On the contrary, I know exactly what it's like. You'll get no pity from me," seeing her bridle, he hurried on to complete his thought, "but if your tutor allows it, you can bring your books to the cell and we'll study together. When you need help, you have merely to ask me."

Her eyes narrowed and she hunched her shoulders, making herself more unattractive than ever. He'd expected eager assent; instead she was clearly suspicious.

"What do you want in return?"

"What do you have to offer?"

He'd made a proposal in good faith. Why should she question his motives? Was everything with this woman to be some kind of commercial exchange?

"I own nothing."

"You own yourself."

Her eyes blinked rapidly before becoming a calculated stare.

"True enough."

Slowly it dawned on him. She thought he wanted to join with her in exchange for teaching her to read! What kind of world had she come from! Disgusted, he returned the books to the shelf, strode to the side of the bed nearest the door and began removing his clothing. His blouse was off and he was unbuttoning his breeches when he heard her chair scrape against the stone floor.

"What do you think you're doing?!"

Perhaps it was the ugly tone of her voice, or the fact that she so completely misread him; or maybe it was none of these things and he was fed up with people demanding that he justify everything he said or did in this wretched place. For once he refused to edit his words as they spilled out of his tightly-clenched lips.

"I'm going to bed and I don't give a damn whether you join me or not. Sleep on the floor, in a chair, or stay awake guarding your precious chastity. It matters not to me."

Her eyes shot blue bolts of lightning at him.

"For your information, I am not a virgin!"

He met her fire with ice.

"Nor, I assure you, am I."

Reddin didn't wait for her reaction. Removing his loincloth with a flourish, he dropped it on the floor and climbed into bed. So angry that he was panting, he pulled the pillow over his head, wanting to shut out the sound of her movements in the cell, unwilling to give her presence as much as a thought.

This is my reward for friendliness and offers of assistance, he thought—suspicion and a haughty disregard for my feelings. He'd learned his lesson; she would have to deserve his help before he ever offered it again.

LILLAS SLID THROUGH the door of the cell. Upon hearing the bolt slide shut, she leaned back against the door, shutting her eyes against the shambles confronting her. In the passage of a mere five days the cell had become a monster, taking pleasure in hiding whatever she sought. This morning she looked everywhere for a clean shift, finding one in a pile under her sweat-stained training clothes, and was forced to wear it despite its moldy smell. Last night the disorder sprang to life, for she heard the unmistakable sounds of mice munching on the crumbs and uneaten leftovers still lying on the unwashed plates and bowls from their meal four nights ago. Not frightened by the mice but nevertheless affected by the sounds of eating, she lay curled up in a ball, hoping that the growls emanating from her belly would not be heard by the man sleeping beside her.

The slight semicircle surrounding Reddin's chest of clothes was the single orderly place in the entire room, for although he stuck to their agreement to the letter when it came to cooking and cleaning, he kept his personal items arranged and folded and never failed to leave his laundry wrapped in a tidy ball outside the door each morning. She could tell the mess was a constant source of irritation to him, for his mouth went white around the lips last night when he found his precious book of poetry lying face-down on a dirty plate. Taking up a rag, he tried to wipe away the grease stains, only succeeding in smearing the lettering. She hadn't meant to damage it, and apologized profusely, offering to buy him another copy to replace it. That only made him angrier. He'd locked those dark, judgmental eyes of his on her and spoken so severely she wanted to run away and hide.

"Some things can't be replaced. Another book would not be the one given to me by my parents on the first day of my twelfth year, nor would it be inscribed by them. Besides. . ." he added, which increased her shame, ". . . four days ago you said you owned nothing. Have you received an inheritance of late?"

So many times she regretted what she'd said that first evening. At first she thought him a typical representative of Pelion, with high and mighty airs, flaunting his superior intellect, overwhelming her with his vocabulary and technical knowledge of printing, anatomy, and other things that left her feeling like an illiterate slave rather than a princess of Agave. Not until he lost his temper at her insinuation that he was trying to manipulate her into joining with him did she realize his offer was well-meaning and undeniably generous. True to his word, he never so much as touched her, but slept on his side at the farthest edge of the bed. Yet at the same time, he never tried to hide himself from her, dressing and undressing without seeming to notice her presence, relieving himself in the chamber pot before retiring, and rubbing an oily salve on his shoulders, arms, and thighs every evening. Far from upsetting her, she'd become accustomed to his rituals, although she found herself inexplicably modest around him, sequestering herself behind the wardrobe door while she disrobed, fearful that he watched her and more fearful that he wouldn't try. Last night, in a moment she blushed to recall, she caught herself admiring the sheen of his coppery skin underneath the light coating of oil.

She hadn't meant to insult him by referring to the color of his skin. How was she to know he was sensitive about such things? When she first saw him in the arena, she found him exotic-looking, so much so that she decided he was an ernani and thus not destined to share a cell with her. With his long unbound hair hanging straight and thick around his face and his white teeth exposed in a grimace as he pulled his bow, he'd been unlike any other man in the arena.

Suddenly she knew what had been troubling her all day, upsetting her to the point that she'd asked to leave the arena before her scheduled time, earning a damning frown from Strato and a puzzled expression on her monitor's face as he escorted her to the cell, a detour from her normal evening path to the Hall of Women and an evening bath. From the moment she saw Reddin in the arena, she'd wanted to know him. With a nagging fear she realized that she knew no more of him today than she did five days ago. In a single night she'd ruined everything. Although he always answered her questions in that calm, collected manner of his, never once had he introduced a subject on his own or shown the slightest interest in anything other than his books.

It was Halys who pointed out Lillas' problem without knowing she was doing so. She'd been happy of late, a quiet happiness that shone in her eyes whenever she mentioned Dysponteus, a long-legged fellow who Lillas knew from running heats with him on the track. He'd smiled at her once or twice in the past few days, a friendly smile that told Lillas he knew of her from Halys, for the moon of joining did nothing to diminish the two women's friendship. This morning, while studying in the dayroom, Halys asked her a question that put everything into perspective.

"Know you Reddin a healer is?" When Lillas made no reply, Halys continued without noticing her silence. "Dysponteus names him 'scholar.'" She was beaming at Lillas now, gesturing to the open book on the table before them. "To read so well a wonder is! But to heal . . !" Halys shook her head in wordless admiration.

Lillas' stomach executed an abrupt somersault. She knew not the slightest thing about Reddin, nor had she thought to ask why he read so voraciously, taking notes on a tablet with firm strokes of a pen that never seemed to blot the page or dye his fingers.

With a defiant shake of her curls and a resolute lift of her chin, Lillas swore to herself that by the close of this evening, she would know more about Reddin than her best friend did.

The first thing she must do was attack the monster lying in wait for her, a monster of her own making. Pulling the back of her skirt up between her legs, she borrowed a belt from Reddin's chest and wrapped it around her waist to hold the heavy weight of her skirts off the dirty floor. A doubt caught hold of her, for she'd never cleaned a room in her life and possessed only the dimmest notions of exactly how to begin. Don't be such a coward, she scolded (addressing herself in stronger language than was needful). If a slave can do it, then a princess certainly can! Her confidence restored, Lillas set about 'redding up' the cell.

REDDIN FOLLOWED FLAVIUS' broad back down the corridor, readying himself to enter the cell that had changed from dismal to slovenly in five short days. Try as he might to rise above the chaos of his surroundings, it was beginning to depress him, and worst of all, starting to make him hate Lillas for insisting he live in such a pig-sty. His control was slipping; of that there could be little doubt. Last night he'd snapped at her, speaking so cruelly that there were tears in her eyes when he taunted her about her poverty. He didn't sleep a wink all night, torturing himself with the fact that she'd probably never possessed coins enough to buy food, never mind a leather-bound book. Added to his guilt was the knowledge that she had not slept either, but curled herself up into a ball as if dreading the fact that he might somehow touch her while she slept.

Without any warning, Flavius stopped at a door along a corridor of identical doors, which after five days Reddin was still unable to recognize as his, and slid the bolt.

Almost immediately, Lillas appeared at the threshold, her arms full of what appeared to be laundry. Before Reddin could take in the fact that she was absolutely filthy, her bodice smeared with what looked to be grease, a streak of ashes across her forehead and right cheek, and her hair tangled and wet with perspiration, she bestowed a bright smile on both he and Flavius as she dropped bags of laundry at their feet.

"I thought I'd leave this outside so I won't forget it tomorrow morning."

Before either man could respond, she vanished back inside the cell. Reddin wondered if his face was as astonished as that of Flavius. The smell of roasted fowl wafted out of the open doorway, causing Reddin's mouth to water at the welcome prospect of an evening meal. He'd taken his own advice, eating as much as he could stuff into his stomach for the two meals served in the dining hall. Even so, the absence of sustenance from noon to dawn took its toll on his performance in the arena and made him irritable to boot. With a quick nod to Flavius, he entered the cell and stood transfixed.

The bed was made. He could tell at a glance that she'd changed the bedclothes, fluffed the pillows and shaken the coverlet. The floor was cleared of her clothing and the wardrobe door was closed for the first time since her arrival. The crockery had been washed and cleared away, the floor swept. She must have scrubbed the floor in front of the hearth, if for no other reason that her skirt and petticoats were sopping wet and he could imagine no other way she could possibly get so dirty. Yet she was standing as if she was the queen of some mighty kingdom, rather than a bedraggled street urchin begging for a coin, her eyes alight with fun as she bent to stir something bubbling in an iron pot hung beside the spit on which a plump fowl cooked. His open-mouthed stare must have been disconcerting, for she gestured quickly to a pile of books and papers on the table.

"I didn't want to disturb your things, so I left them for you to sort and put away." When he made no move to obey, she put her hands on her hips and frowned at him. "Reddin, you must clear the table or we can't have our evening meal!"

Spurred into action, he leapt to the table and hurriedly sorted through notebooks and tablets, talking to her over his shoulder while he worked.

"I never meant for you to do all the cooking and cleaning. If you'd waited for me, I would have helped."

A clear burst of laughter was followed immediately by a playful threat.

"It's my intention that you clean up every pot and dish I've dirtied, and woe betide you, healer, if you spill so much as a single crumb on the floor!"

Reddin froze, his hands still holding the books he was carrying to the shelf.

"What did you call me?"

"What?"

"Healer."

The spoon stopped its regular stirring against the sides of the pot.

"Someone must have mentioned it in passing. I can't remember who . . ."

That she was lying was readily apparent, although he had no idea why she felt it necessary to do so. Still, if she preferred to keep her source of information a secret he had no intention of prying it out of her.

"Not only will I attend to cleaning up the meal, I'll also heat some water so you can bathe. There's only the basin, but we can put a cloth on the floor in front of the hearth so you won't be chilled."

They stood a shoulder breadth away from each other, their chins level with the mantel over the fireplace. There was something in her expression he'd never seen before, a resolve of some kind and also a kind of pleading. Searching his face with those clear blue eyes of hers, she took her bottom lip between her teeth. For the first time, despite the dirty face and tangled mop of hair, he thought her attractive, if for no other reason than he could sense her attempt to cross the barrier they had unwittingly built between them.

"After the meal I'll bathe and . . . and . . . during the meal, perhaps we could talk?"

Afraid he might break the spell of their first moment of true companionship, he nodded wordlessly and heard her sigh. Then as quickly as the moment had come upon them, it was gone. Abruptly, she turned back to the hearth.

"If you'll ready the table, we'll eat in a moment."

"What have you prepared?"

Again she laughed, a sweet trill that gladdened his heart.

"Roasted quail, herbed rice, and a recipe for greens taught me by an old hermit called Timon."

SNUGGLING DEEPER INTO the crisp sheets, Lillas watched the waning moon climb high into the heavens. Her arms ached from lifting and carrying and her back was sore from bending over the hearth. Even so, her spirit was as refreshed and clean as if she had scrubbed it rather than the stone floor. For the first time since this moon began, she welcomed sleep without fear, trusting that neither hunger nor bad dreams would disturb her rest.

Their first meal together was glorious, not only because the food was tasty and well-prepared, but because they talked and laughed and then talked some more. Reddin described the House of Healing in such detail that she could have walked its corridors without losing her way. Patients, teachers, fellow practitioners, all was made known to her. Yet more than the knowledge of the place where he pursued his calling, he revealed what it meant to him. His dark eyes glowing at her from across the table, his fine white teeth flashing in a smile of happiness, his layers of reserve were stripped away, making him seem younger, almost boyish.

It gave her pause, this love of his craft, this need of his to share his gifts with others, for it was something she had never experienced. There was a moment when she would have given everything she possessed to desire something so badly that she would devote years of training and the rest of her life to gain mastery of her profession, until she remembered that she could barely read or write even the simplest of sentences. All the tutors she'd dismissed, all the lessons she'd left unlearned, all the subjects she'd never explored rose up to haunt her. In true Lillas-fashion, she pushed them away, unwilling to confront the meaningless life she'd lived without any thought except her comfort, her will, and the flight of a falcon who took to the air at her command, killing whatever game she fancied.

There was also a difference in the way he'd looked at her tonight, nothing lustful or passionate (for men had turned hungry eyes on her before) but a thoughtful expression which implied he wasn't judging her or finding her incomplete. Clearing the table with a rapidity and skillful competence that convinced her he'd truly meant his offer to cook and clean, he prepared a place for her to bathe before the fire and then left her alone, sitting with his back to her on the bed as he worked over a book and papers he'd spread over the coverlet. The moment she wrapped herself in a loose robe, retiring to her wardrobe in order to don her nightgown and dry her hair, the floor was wiped, the contents of the basin dumped into the waste bucket, and the candles snuffed.

Now, as he lay beside her, she was aware that he did not sleep. Adjusting her head on the pillow, she could see him lying flat on his back, his arms cradling his head, the whites of his eyes gleaming in the darkness of the cell. Her movement must have caught his attention, for he turned to face her, his elbow resting upon the mattress, his chin resting on his open palm.

"Too tired to sleep?"

His voice was no louder than a whisper, his teeth glistening against the dusky skin of his face. A brief nod was all the answer she could manage. He regarded her for a long minute while she held her breath, fearful he might ruin the happiness this night had brought her.

"Lillas, let me prove my skills to you."

"What s . . . skills?"

He shook his head, the hair swinging free from his shoulders, chiding her softly.

"You've nothing to fear, blue-eyes. There's nothing of joining in what I offer, only sleep. Give me leave to touch you."

Blue-eyes. The love name of her father for her mother, a name used solely in the privacy of their chambers and one that brought quick tears to her eyes. Surely no one who could speak that name with such gentleness would harm her.

"You have my leave."

At her whisper, he turned her over on her back and arranged her head on the pillow so that she faced the window. He stroked her neck and shoulders lightly, his hands warm against the cotton of her gown. As she relaxed, his hands became more powerful, rubbing away the soreness in her upper and lower back and running down the length of each arm. As he promised, her eyelids grew heavy, and she was almost asleep when she felt him tuck the coverlet around her shoulders. Sighing with contentment, Lillas turned onto her side.

"May we share each other's warmth tonight?"

His breath swept the back of her neck. She smiled to herself, moved at the thought that even now he honored his word.

"Yes. Let's watch the moon together."

She leaned back against his chest, knowing somehow that he would be there to support her, feeling his loins against her hips, his thighs against the backs of her legs. Slipping her feet between his calves, she felt the smooth texture of his skin against hers. There was nothing frightening about him being close to her, nothing but comfort and companionship in the enormous, moonlit bed.

Lillas was soon fast asleep and so never knew that the healer broke his word that night. Without asking her permission, Reddin's lips touched Lillas' hair as it lay shining in the moonlight.

Chapter 12

Conundrum

"W̲E'LL WAIT TO review the current situation until Prax arrives. Until that time, let's turn our attention to events inside the Maze. Has anyone a matter that deserves consideration by the Council?"

Relieved that he need not respond, Kazur leaned back in his chair, waiting for the others to take up the Eighteenth Mother's request. His duties, like those of Prax, lay outside the walls of the city. His knowledge of the ernani and candidates within the Maze was limited to his responsibilities concerning the records of Transformation. Prax's return to Pelion was long overdue, and despite the Eighteenth Mother's studied air of calm, Kazur read the worry and fatigue written on her youthful face. This moon dragged by as if harnessed to sea slugs, immense adipose worms which occasionally washed up on the shores of the Eastern Sea where Kazur spent his boyhood. The Eighteenth Mother was not the only victim of this moon's difficulties; each member of the Council looked the worse for wear.

Strato's bulk was wedged into a chair he clearly found uncomfortable and Flavius looked no happier than the Head Trainer, both men obviously ill-at-ease with their new positions as advisors to the Council. A sad wistfulness hung over Chryse, although Kazur guessed that the fast approach of the Day of Choice was explanation enough for her mood. The first moon of joining had always been, and probably always would be, a time of anxiety for all the caretakers of the Maze, for none of them, not even Kazur, ever forgot that far beneath this tower chamber, hidden away in a maze, twenty couples strove to unite their bodies and their minds.

When no one responded to her request, the Eighteenth Mother tried another approach.

"Chryse, with three days left in this moon, what are your impressions of this group as a whole?"

It was not the Eighteenth Mother's way to pin Council members in this manner, for she was usually content to let them provide the topics for discussion rather than ruling the sessions as was her right. Tired as we all may be, she insists we continue functioning normally, Kazur thought. The only outward sign of her turmoil was the nervous twirling of a silver ring.

Chryse seemed flustered for a moment, then recovered enough to respond to her superior's request.

"Each class has its special flavor, but this class is . . . more volatile than most. The monitor's reports convey proof of my assessment, especially in the number of complaints, violations of minor rules, and competition in study and work sessions."

After a thoughtful nod, the Eighteenth Mother addressed the Head Trainer.

"Have you seen evidence of what Chryse describes during training sessions, Strato?"

His shaggy head nodded several times on his thick neck. Kazur thought him finished until he began speaking in a voice hoarse from its daily occupation of shouting.

"Not being the most sensitive of adepts, still I . . .", he ran his fingers through his unruly hair, ". . . I sense there's something different. . ."

Kazur leaned back into the chair to wait since it was clear that Strato was going to chew on this matter for a while.

"I'm thinking it might be the women." Before anyone could mount a protest, Strato raised a callused palm in self-defense. "Lest you think me an old war horse who's not agreeable to change, let me assure you that no one enjoys the women's presence in the arena more than me. In fact. . ." his eyes twinkled merrily, ". . . I look forward to the afternoon sessions for exactly that reason."

Ranier guffawed. Nadia shot her mate a withering glance, while Flavius strove, without much success, to keep his lips from twitching. Chryse caught Kazur's eye, nodding her enjoyment of Strato's declaration. The Eighteenth Mother remained impassive.

"Still, it's a strain on the men we've never had to bargain with before. If the Mistress of Joining says `volatile', I'm not one to disagree, although I'd say it was a question of tension."

Kazur's interest sparked. For five moons he'd trained in that arena. At last he could satisfy his curiosity as to the effect of the women's presence on that all-male preserve.

"How so, Strato? What's the nature of this tension?"

The Head Trainer regarded him steadily.

"It was titillating in the first moon, a game of sorts. Now that they're joined, it's hardest on the mated couples. Dysponteus handles it best, although if truth be told, Halys has never beaten him, nor do I think it's in her nature to try. Jarod has a hard time of it, not because of competition, for Thaisa uses a light-weight bow and so has never shot against him. Despite his good humor, he's a Lapith born and bred and tenses every time he sees her near another man. Thaisa herself has grown careful, rarely speaking to anyone besides Halys or Lillas inside the arena."

The Eighteenth Mother's eyes narrowed.

"And Reddin?"

Pursing his lips, Strato considered his clasped hands.

"He's hard for me to read. Maybe it's safer to speak of Lillas."

Clearly, Strato was being evasive, although Kazur couldn't imagine why.

"First off, she's a wonder and no mistake. The girl's never known fear, adores competition of any sort, and has physical stamina the likes of which I rarely see. She's taken to the javelin like my mother took to gambling in her old age, barely a one can defeat her in the sprint heats, and Altug is her only competitor with the light-weight bow. Today she was after me to learn wrestling and I was hard-pressed to deny her."

"And Reddin?"

While the trainer frowned, Kazur found himself remembering the stories of Strato carrying the Eighteenth Mother pig-a-back on the grounds of the Cavalry officers' headquarters. Strato had known her since she was born, his appointment as Head Trainer of the Maze one of the Eighteenth Mother's first acts of office. Put out of sorts by her determination that he supply information he obviously preferred to withhold, he growled out a grudging reply.

"What do you want to know? He does his best and never calls quits, something I can't say about some of the others."

Strato was finished. The Eighteenth Mother was not.

"Flavius?"

A flush rose to the monitor's face. Kazur decided the monitor was not so much embarrassed as reluctant to comment on Reddin in the presence of Strato, although the authority of the Eighteenth Mother's request brought his entire body to attention.

"He . . .uh, he worries, Mother."

"Can you be more specific?"

Taking a deep breath, Flavius made a good soldier's report.

"He worries about Lillas constantly in the arena, so much so that he's often inattentive to his own performance. I don't think the question of competition bothers him, for he thinks little of it himself, and Strato . . .," Flavius glanced nervously at Strato, who refused to lift his eyes from their furious contemplation of the table top, "Strato makes sure they're scheduled separately, thus avoiding the issue."

It was no wonder that Strato turned ornery when Reddin's name was mentioned. The men dubbed him "The Bear"; little did they know the tender heart of the man who oversaw their physical training. The much-hated trainer might storm and shout, but he protected his cubs as best he could in the cave called the arena.

"It's her safety that concerns him. Yesterday he was nearly beside himself when she made a bad landing in the long jump. I, uh, I had to hold him back. He swore at me as another healer hurried to her aid."

Soft-voiced Nadia added support to Flavius' observations.

"He requested a meeting with me a few days ago. Knowing his background, I guessed what concerned him. There's still no sign of her monthly flow and, being a healer, he shares my fear that this might be symptomatic of a more serious ailment."

The Eighteenth Mother was instantly on the offensive.

"What kind of ailment?"

"A tumor on the ovary or the pituitary gland, an imbalance of hormones; many diagnoses and many treatments, some of them involving surgery."

Chryse's reaction was immediate. In her own way, the Mistress of Joining was as protective as her counterpart in the arena.

"Surely you didn't convey this to Reddin, Nadia! His mating with Lillas is difficult enough without adding these concerns."

"There was no need to inform him," Nadia stated firmly and without apology. "These were his thoughts before he asked for counsel. He was an excellent student and continues to study, never forgetting what he hopes to achieve after leaving the Maze. As Flavius reported, he fears a fall or more serious injury might exacerbate her condition. With this in mind, he asked me if I would consider curtailing her activities in the arena."

"And your answer?"

"My answer to him is the same one I share with you: Ranier and I believe that if she misses another moon, she must enter the House of Healing. We also believe that to end her participation in the arena would result in the depression she suffered before."

Nadia paused, seeming to weigh something in her mind. Hers was an aged face, all wrinkles and sagging skin, for she was well beyond her sixtieth year. Despite her age, or, more probably, because of it, she possessed an inner serenity unmatched by anyone at the table, including her mate. No Council member's opinion was more valued than Nadia's, partly because of the rarity with which she offered it. That she did so now reflected the importance she placed on her recent meeting with Reddin.

"He was remote at first, speaking about Lillas as if she existed in the pages of a textbook, an object of his study rather than a living, breathing woman whose life has been joined with his. As we spoke, he revealed his talents as a healer, as well as the coldness indicated by his teachers. Assuredly, there was selfishness in his request, for to lose her to the House of Healing means delaying their giving of gifts. Yet there was a hint of change within him — an honest concern for her well-being, a connection he has never experienced with any of his patients, feelings which threaten him to the point that he prefers not to acknowledge them."

A chuckle escaped her.

"Doubtlessly, he's worried, and perhaps with good cause, but what steps he has taken in a single moon! Despite my continuing concern for Lillas' health, I have dismissed my misgivings as to the fitness of their joining."

Long after this night passed, Kazur would remember the quiet satisfaction of his fellows at the conclusion of Nadia's remarks, for they were the last moments of calm before the rising winds threw open the chamber doors to announce the coming of the long-awaited storm.

A figure stood in the doorway, the light of the torches in the hallway throwing a vast shadow onto the floor. A hooded thickly-woven robe revealed no hint of gender. A mask of the kind worn by desert travelers covered the nose and mouth. Kazur's intellect reminded him that no stranger could have successfully bypassed the numerous guards stationed between the outer doors and the Eighteenth Mother's private chambers. Despite that knowledge, the aggressive stance of the intruder—legs spread wide and hands planted firmly on hips—caused Kazur to inch his right hand toward a pocket hidden in the lining of his robes. Tightening his grip on his throwing knife, Kazur tensed as the stranger untied the mask and threw back the hood.

The Council beheld a merchant of Endlin, his hair arranged in an intricate pattern of braids, two rings of beaten gold dangling from his left earlobe and a single ruby gleaming in his right nostril. This newcomer might have been Kazur's uncle or cousin, a dealer in spice or fragrant woods, his many-layered robes under the voluminous cloak announcing his lineage, his ring-covered fingers indicating his wealth and status. As Kazur registered all of these details, the alarm bell in his mind stopped ringing. Making sure his face betrayed nothing, Kazur loosened his grip on the knife.

Crossing the room in three strides to sit next to the Eighteenth Mother, the stranger began divesting himself of wig and jewelry. The bald dome that emerged could only belong to Prax, as could the mischievous glint in his eye as he regarded the Head Scribe.

"Convincing, huh, Kazur? I saw your hand move for your knife, so you needn't deny I fooled you."

"The ruby is a trifle much, Prax. A merchant might wear a carnelian."

Prax snorted, delivered a good-natured curse, and reached for a goblet of wine. Surveying the others, he announced:

"I've news for the Council's ears. Strato. Flavius. You're dismissed."

When the door shut behind them, Prax dropped the mask of good humor he'd worn under the merchant's disguise. After taking a long pull of wine, the master dissembler presented a worried face to the Council of Pelion.

"The Aeson is dying."

And so die all our plans, thought Kazur.

"There's more. Seth is tightening his hold. No one moves in or out without a stamped pass that's impossible to duplicate since it's changed daily. The slavers are out in force; Spence counted no less than twenty chains heading from the scrublands to the desert since he assumed the post Hume assigned him two weeks ago."

Prax took another gulp of wine and passed the back of his hand over his mouth. Sand and dirt were imbedded in his seamed skin, his eyes bleary from constant watchfulness on the long road from Agave.

"Rumors and discontent fly through the city. This should be the rainy season, but not a drop has fallen and the wells are low. My guess is that the push for slaves is to increase the water deliveries from the northwest. One rumor is true: Agave is forming an army, although no one knows for what purpose. They were signing up anyone who could prove free-born status and the lines were long."

Each pronouncement added to Kazur's sense of doom. This was his specialty—the politics of Agave, a female oligarchy ruled by a male figurehead—the subject of six years of study at the request of the newly ascended Eighteenth Mother. Kazur was unsurprised that Scarphe made her bid for power through her son. The shock lay in the quickness of her move. All their plans were built around the girl; if the present Aeson's power was usurped now, they might lose the battle before it began.

"Who confirmed the Aeson's illness, or is it common knowledge in the city?"

Kazur's remaining hope was that, as had happened many times before, Prax's informants might be mistaken or misled. Imarus was nearly impenetrable. It took a full year of well-placed bribes and subtle conditioning to obtain a place for Phoron in Lillas' household.

"Who says he's ill?" was Prax's grim reply.

When Prax's eyes locked onto his, Kazur was first to break away, brooding over the machinations of a woman who had murdered two male first cousins, not resting until she was content that her younger brother would offer her no trouble until her own offspring came of age. The female line might be barred from officially wielding Agave's considerable clout, but the women of Imarus had constituted the power behind the throne for generations. Scarphe's uniqueness lay not in her ambitions, but in the heartlessness of her methods.

"Poison. She uses poison again, just as she did before. Did Phoron confirm this?"

"Charis brought him into the sickroom without Scarphe's knowledge. It appears to be a wasting disease. Phoron said the pain is agonizing." Prax's voice sank to its lowest registers. "The Aeson begged him for a quick release."

A hush fell over the tower chamber, and in that special quiet that haunts the hours after moonrise, the Council of Pelion pondered the agony of one who lay in the arms of an apprentice hetaera who had relinquished her daughter and, friendless and alone, faced the death of her mate.

"Is there nothing else, Prax?"

With infinite care, the Eighteenth Mother turned them away from sorrow. Prax's puzzled expression indicated his belief that the news conveyed thus far must certainly suffice. Discipline prevailed, however, and he cast back into his memories of the past moon, sifting through the interviews held with each agent of Pelion currently working in Agave or its surrounding lands.

"One item of no particular interest, or at least I attached no special significance to it, although. . .," he frowned, ". . . now that I think of it, everyone reported the same occurrence."

A tremendous surge of energy emanated from the mind of the black-robed woman who sat frozen, her hands outstretched and rigid on the table, the narrow silver band reflecting the glow of tallow candles. Five heads rose around the table.

"Tremors. They're used to them in the west, but even the old-timers commented that they've been stronger and more frequent of late. Buildings collapsed two weeks ago in a village southwest of Agave. A deep fissure farther to the south flooded a quarry and brought work to a standstill."

Pushing back her chair, the Eighteenth Mother of Pelion rose to her feet and formally addressed her Council, speaking with voice and mind, her small figure pregnant with power and surety. Kazur's thoughts leapt to join her, finding within her an energy that pulsated and throbbed in the cool night air, dispelling his former gloom and binding him close to the core of her vision.

"Then Prax's news speaks not of despair. The beast slumbers on yet soon will wake. With that waking, what was promised will be revealed. We cannot pause to grieve or wonder, nor will we vary our plans. The course is set, the journey plotted. We work our way through the labyrinth of change."

LILLAS POUNDED DOWN the corridor toward the arena, her ears ringing with the complaints of her tutor in reading and writing, the corrections of the heavy-set dowager who was instructing her in knitting (the craft she'd selected because she hated it least), and the snide venom of Phoebe, who'd taken great delight in ridiculing Lillas' efforts with paints and brushes. It wasn't that Lillas fancied herself a painter; she would be the first to admit that an array of brilliantly colored pots of paint lured her to the easel, coupled with the teacher's suggestion that she experiment in shape and color rather than concentrating on duplicating realistic objects. Those art lessons were often the only thing capable of keeping Lillas within the stultifying confines of the dayroom. If the Instructor hadn't been present, Lillas would have boxed Phoebe's ears for her uninvited lecture on visual "aesthetics," another word Lillas didn't understand, although, as usual, she'd hidden her ignorance from her tormentor.

Her monitor huffed along behind her as usual, causing Lillas to wish for the hundredth time that she'd been assigned someone as personable as Flavius. Anyway, she thought rebelliously, why do I need a monitor? As long as she kept to the routes she'd memorized between the Hall of Women, the arena, and the cell, she had no fear of losing her way.

The dull ache at the back of her right thigh soon took her mind off the petty annoyances she was forced to endure on a daily basis. Her timing off as she approached the long-jump, the awkwardness of her landing pulled a muscle and knocked the breath out of her for a moment. She feared the injury might prevent her from running in the "favor" race Strato announced for this afternoon. Her healer, an old woman named Nadia, thought otherwise. Presenting Lillas with a pungent salve, she promised that if the leg was kept rested and wrapped for two days, Lillas would be able to compete.

The favor matches were something new, introduced by Strato as a means whereby a favor might be earned by the winner of each event taught within the arena. The favor requested by the winner could break none of the rules or regulations of the Maze. Even so, they remained a prize worth serious effort on the part of the participants. Most of the men asked for such things as permission to leave training an hour before the evening trumpet or the privilege of choosing their partner in arms training. The women never had the chance to request a favor since they had yet to win an event. Altug, the mountain man Lillas believed to be a bandit before entering the Maze, beat her in the final round of the archery meet for lightweight bows. Even though she'd improved with the javelin, there was no hope of winning against the larger-bodied men. Halys came in third behind Stym and Dysponteus in the long distance run and Thaisa was disqualified in the second round of the archery meet. It was left for Lillas to win for the women and she had every intention of doing so today in the final heat of the short run.

Arriving at the wooden gates, she did a few stretching exercises while she waited for the monitor to catch up with her. The leg was a trifle stiff, but she was confident that if she warmed up slowly it would serve her well enough when the time came. Reddin wrapped it for her each night, his long-fingered hands deft and businesslike. He rubbed the salve onto the back of her thigh, his touch firm and knowledgeable, as if he knew her body so well that he could actually feel what would give her pain and what would cause her to relax. No one had ever touched her that way. Lying face-down on the bed, her nightshift pulled up as far as decency allowed, she found herself wondering where his hands might travel if she gave him leave to touch her where he pleased.

Frowning, she shoved that thought away, rejecting what it promised. Besides, she reminded herself, he's never given any indication of arousal in my presence. That thought brought with it an even uglier scowl, for the possibility that she did not attract him nagged at her. With a toss of her head to prove to herself how little she cared, she passed through the gates, surveying the sole place within this warren of locked doors she felt confident and comparatively free.

The afternoon was bright and warm enough that several of the men removed their blouses, hungry for the feel of sun on skin already bleached to winter's pallor. Casting her eyes around the arena, she picked out Reddin easily, feeling her stomach twist and her skin burn as she noticed him smile at Thaisa, a pert, snub-nosed woman whose tiny size belied her abilities with a bow. Reddin was laughing now, his hair falling in front of his eyes, then tossed back again with a quick jerk of his head. Thaisa reached suddenly for his arm, shaking her head as Jarod swaggered over to join them. Lillas strolled closer to the archery targets, struggling to hear the conversation in progress.

". . . to share with me the cause for laughter?"

Reddin's head barely met the top of Jarod's shoulder, forcing him to look up as he addressed this warrior of Lapith. He must have observed, as Lillas did, the smoldering fury in Jarod's face. Even so, there was no trace of embarrassment or discomfort in Reddin's steady, measuring gaze.

"Thaisa was reminding me of my performance in the Trial."

Reddin's teeth flashed as he smiled again at Thaisa. Jarod's fists clenched.

"What is this Trial?"

Jarod's question was directed toward Reddin. Thaisa chose to answer it, her manner seeming to both beg and warn her mate to regain control of his temper.

"The men of Pelion compete in eight events for the privilege of entering the Maze. Because so many wish to undergo Preparation, they must prove their abilities in front of the entire city. After the competition, a vote is taken and the winners are announced."

There was a clear note of admonition in Thaisa's voice; she was taking pains to inform her partner that the residents of Pelion placed a high value on the gift offered to those who entered the Maze. Jarod's jaw set, proof that he would not be placated or detoured from his present line of inquiry.

"Were your efforts so laughable?"

Reddin stiffened, the smile leaving his face. Glancing quickly at Thaisa, who seemed to plead with him silently, he swallowed hard before answering his surly questioner.

"Some were laughable. Others made me proud."

"How many men took part in this Trial?"

Though Jarod's belligerence was calculated to insult, Reddin showed no signs of affront.

"Over a hundred men applied for Preparation. Twenty-four were selected for competition. The first five were allowed to enter."

"Of the five, which place was yours?"

"Fifth."

A sneer rose on Jarod's lips. As he opened his mouth to reply, Thaisa ripped into him, her arms crossed firmly over her breasts, her brown eyes flashing out a warning that he had gone too far.

"Yes, Jarod, fifth! Fifth out of a hundred! How many men in your tribe did you compete against for the honor of coming here?"

Lillas expected to see the huge, heavily muscled warrior of Lapith wrap his hands around Thaisa's slender throat and shake her like a dog shakes a rat. Instead, a flush of color suffused his face. Tentatively, he raised a forefinger to brush aside a strand of hair that had come loose from Thaisa's braids.

"Apologies, little one. I heard your laughter and . . .," remembering Reddin's presence, his color deepened. Thaisa continued her intent perusal of her mate's face. Swallowing hard, Jarod offered Reddin a clumsy apology.

"Pardon my . . . my bad temper. I . . . I thought . . ."

"You gave me no offense, Jarod."

As Reddin moved away, Lillas witnessed the slow upward curve of Thaisa's lips. Placing a dimpled hand on her partner's chest, she regarded Jarod with pride, understanding, as did Lillas, what that apology cost him. Lillas might have seen more if a familiar face had not appeared before her.

"How fares your leg?"

Worried that he'd caught her eavesdropping, embarrassed at the thought that he'd exerted so much effort to be here when her presence was the product of a dead prophet's promise and a selfish whim, she dropped to the ground and rubbed her leg, hoping her hair covered her guilty face.

"Stiff, but no pain. I'll make sure it's limber before the race."

He was squatting in front of her now, tracing a series of circles in the dirt.

"There will be other races, Lillas. Must you push yourself so hard?"

Her first indignant response was tempered by the concern she read in his face.

"But this is a favor race, Reddin, and I want so badly to win! This is the last chance for the women to win a victory."

She thought she heard him sigh. He straightened, looking down at her.

"Then I must wish you luck, blue eyes."

With that he was gone, his slim figure disappearing into a group of men gathered around the wrestling ring. It was a struggle not to heed his well-meaning advice, for there was a harried look about him she'd noticed before. What reason he had for worry escaped her, although she'd never thought to ask him. Even after almost thirty days of sharing the cell, their relations were often strained. Without making a conscious decision to do so, she found herself purposefully goading him, turning contrary at the slightest hint of kindness, rebuffing his efforts to help her with her studies, hoping she could break through his air of reserve and push him past the self-restraint that was a continual source of annoyance to her. Try as she might, he refused to be baited, turning silent when she gave vent to curses, opening a book to shield himself from her sarcasm.

When Strato's roar penetrated her busy thoughts, she began removing her outer garments in preparation for the race. With an effort she removed Reddin from her thoughts. She had no time for needless distractions. The race was on.

FROM HIS PERCH in the viewing stand near the finish line, Strato watched the race in progress. Two earlier heats eliminated the slower contestants. The eight runners who made the final cut were those Strato would have chosen without the necessity of trial runs. Dysponteus and Reddin were the sole representatives of Pelion; Stym, Jarod, and Halys (what Strato thought of as the Lapithian contingent) were out in full force; Clive of Cottyo, Po of Tek, and Lillas made up the field. Squinting through the dust, Strato could see the pack spread out behind Dysponteus, not surprising since he preferred running in the lead and set a brutal pace from the outset to demoralize his competition. His strategy succeeded with Po and Clive, who were already out of the running. Jarod was making a poor showing, his mind on other things, most probably on Thaisa, thought Strato, having witnessed their encounter on the archery field.

Stym was making his move. Dysponteus' lead shrank to two strides as they rounded the final turn into the straightaway. Halys and Reddin followed close behind Stym, both of them running easily and showing no signs of fatigue.

Lillas was not running her normal race since, like Dysponteus, she loved being out in front. Today she'd stayed well behind him, finding a place for herself on the outside of the flying wedge and sticking close to Stym's off side. Her slim frame hidden by Stym's bulk, Strato nearly missed her, then almost whooped aloud when he realized that for once Lillas was running not a race of speed, but of strategy. That had always been her failing before. Against male runners she had not the length of stride necessary to set a grueling pace. Strato felt a surge of admiration for her spunk as she let Stym take the lead, pulling directly behind him in front of a flagging Dysponteus. Stym was pulling away from the others now, his eyes on the finish line a few strides ahead. Strato guessed he was already considering his favor when Lillas made her move.

With a sudden burst of speed she pulled around Stym, his head jerking around in surprise since he had not been aware of her presence behind him. She timed it to perfection, waiting until the last possible instant, sure that if she took the lead any earlier, he'd have time to overtake her with his longer-legged strides. With two more strides she was over the line, winning by a nose, and dropped over at the waist, her hands resting on her thighs as she panted for breath. Dysponteus came in third, with Reddin and Halys a close fourth and fifth. Reddin slowed his pace and circled back toward Lillas, who was rubbing the back of her thigh and grimacing as she limped toward the reviewing stand.

Strato made his way down the stairs, pushing a pathway through the onlookers and checking with the trainers at the finish line to corroborate Lillas' win. The runners gathered around him, all of them breathing hard and dripping with sweat.

"The win goes to Lillas!" Strato brayed, noting Stym's glower and Dysponteus' dejection with inward glee. A clear infectious laugh, soaring up into the afternoon brightness, brought grudging smiles to the faces gathered around the girl with bright color burning in her cheeks and wind-tossed hair. Her laugh carried with it the sound of pure delight, an outpouring of personal triumph and sheer bravado. She was hugging Halys and Thaisa now, both of them supporting her slight frame as she stood with her right leg balanced on the tip of her toe. Reddin's face held no answering smile as he stood stiffly behind her, considering her injured leg.

"What is your favor, ernani?"

The smile greeting his question was euphoric. Strato prepared himself for her response, never guessing what burst from her lips.

"I want to wrestle!"

A chorus of groans and intermittent laughter erupted from the group, giving Strato time to sort out his thoughts. By the time the crowd settled, he was ready.

"You know the rules, Lillas. Women may not have bodily contact with men." Before Lillas could protest, Strato turned his attention to the women at her side. "Halys, Thaisa, are either of you interested in learning to wrestle?"

Their faces answered him without necessity of words, although Halys shook her head and Thaisa spoke a quiet, "No."

Abruptly, Lillas disengaged herself from her female companions. In doing so, she would have fallen if Reddin had not steadied her by grasping her about the waist. His presence must have lent her inspiration for her next foray against the rules.

"Would anyone object if I trained with Reddin?"

This time the crowd's reaction was slower and considerably more vocal. Several of the men slapped Reddin's back with raised eyebrows and leering grins. Reddin went perfectly still, his expression inscrutable. Strato was stymied, and almost ready to contact the Eighteenth Mother for guidance when he considered the events of last night's Council meeting. If Nadia trusted Reddin, that was good enough for Strato.

"I have no objections if your partner is agreeable. What say you, Reddin?"

Forty-odd faces of ernani, candidates of Pelion, monitors, and trainers turned toward the slim, dark-skinned man who had not loosed his grip on Lillas' waist. She turned her face around to regard him, seemingly confident of his reply. Slowly, he lowered his hands to his sides.

"I am not agreeable."

Lillas' head jerked as if he had slapped her. A murmur of speculative comments flowed over those assembled as Reddin pushed his way through them, his back ramrod straight, ears deaf to the growing tide of conversation. In the next moment Lillas regained her composure, a spot of color burning on each cheek.

"My favor is to leave the arena."

Three full hours of training remained scheduled for the afternoon, the favor race being the first event of the day. Strato grunted agreement.

"See your healer before you return to the cell."

Lillas gave no indication that she heard him. Her monitor was already at her side, lifting her arm around his shoulder and helping her off the field.

Clearing his throat, Strato bellowed:

"Archery sessions begin at the north end of the track. Check your equipment and take your place. Move!"

As the crowd dispersed, Strato sent a swift thought to Chryse, finding her working with the women in the library. She was instantly attentive, receiving his images of what had just transpired with growing uneasiness. Finished conveying everything that occurred, he waited, hoping he had not forced an issue that should have been delayed until two days hence.

When Chryse's assessment came, it contained strength of resolution he rarely attributed to this soft-spoken, elegant hetaera.

"No other decision was possible. They must strike a balance and we cannot buffer them from hurt. Tell Flavius to delay Reddin's return to the cell. They'll need time to ready themselves for tonight's encounter."

THE CELL WAS dark. Lillas lit neither fire nor candle, ignoring the foodstuffs delivered for the evening meal, and sat in the high-backed chair with her leg resting on a low stool. The evening trumpet sounded an hour ago; none of the feet hurrying down the hallway stopped at her door. In the past few hours she'd passed through anger at being betrayed, embarrassment at her public humiliation, hurt at the thought of what little value Reddin placed on her aspirations, and most disturbing of all, a growing fear of her vulnerability at the hands of this cold-hearted healer.

Her healer, Nadia by name, an elderly woman with stooped shoulders and a large portion of grey in her brown braids, soothed her somewhat, not particularly with words, but with a sense of peace that clung to her, causing Lillas to wish she would hold her in her lap as her mother did on the evening of their parting. Her leg rubbed and wrapped in clean linen bands, Lillas accepted Nadia's offer of a massage, and lay quietly on the table, letting the healer's hands play over her, feeling some of her anger disperse as her tense muscles responded to Nadia's ministrations.

"My hands tell me that your body's hurt is nothing to the hurt residing in your heart," the old woman said at parting. "Remember you are not here to run races, but to walk the Path."

Flavius' heavy boots rang down the stone corridor, the bolt slid open, and Reddin stepped lightly into the room. Lillas didn't deign to turn her head, but sat facing the cold hearth. Squatting, Reddin began sweeping away the ashes, laid a fire and used the flint to start a small blaze. He'd donned a white cotton blouse split on the sides that was worn long and nearly reached his thighs. The skin of his hands was slightly wrinkled, as skin will look when it has soaked for hours in a bath, proof that he'd purposefully avoided her, knowledge that only added to her hurt.

The fire crackled and popped. He was lighting the candles now, behaving as if everything was normal, an ordinary evening after an afternoon's exercise. Incensed by his calm, she attacked.

"Why did you shame me?"

He was in the process of lighting a candle, the burning end of the tinder poised over the wick when it stopped moving, continuing to burn without reaching its destination.

"I didn't intend to shame you."

"If that admission is meant to pacify me, I assure you it does not."

"Pacify you?" a tight smile twisted his lips, one that lacked the slightest trace of humor. "Nothing, I think, will pacify you."

A thought she'd never considered crossed her mind. He'd been concerned about her leg before the race; perhaps this was his way of punishing her for disobeying his wishes.

"Do you begrudge my win so much that you must shame me in public?"

Her barb struck deep. A flame ignited in his dark eyes.

"I begrudge you nothing. As to shaming you in public, if you'd told me what you intended beforehand, I could have spared us both the humiliation we suffered today."

What could he possibly mean? The snickers and jibes were meant for her and her alone. Stung that he was depriving her of her martyrdom, she refused to accept his excuses.

"Exactly how were you humiliated? You stood straight as a lance, denied me, and walked away, not even caring to see how I fared. Or were you shamed by the fact that I beat you? Is it truly so hateful to be beaten by a woman?"

Blowing out the tinder, he placed it carefully on the mantle. His hands were shaking, a sight which filled her with satisfaction. Perhaps tonight he would lose the control that made her feel so completely an object of his derision.

"Why do you hesitate? You've boasted that I can ask you anything. Now that I take you at your word, you squirm and stall, avoiding me by hiding in the bath, shielding yourself behind a wall of silence." Her voice grew shrill. "Come, now! Tell me how you came to be shamed!"

The face he turned to her was drained of its natural color. Pale with fury, he stared at her with burning eyes, a vein pulsing in his forehead. This was what she had wanted; to push him to the breaking point. Even as she rejoiced, regret struck her, for in that moment she understood that she wanted him to be different, that she wanted him to be unbreakable.

"What do you think we do here, Lillas? Are we playing games of winning and losing? Games with bows and arrows and throwing sticks, games that children play? I give not a damn if you win or lose. It matters not to me if you can beat the men or are bested by them in turn. What matters to me is that you lie to yourself!"

Lillas found herself tricked into a battle she was unprepared to fight. She'd thought to fight about the loss of face she'd suffered in the arena. He was fighting about their lives together.

"How do I lie to myself?"

Having awakened his rage, she bore the full brunt of his fury.

"You do nothing but lie, to others and to yourself! You lie about not wanting to learn; you want badly to learn but scorn to be taught. You lie about wanting to win for the women; it was not their victory, it was yours alone! When they chose not to participate in your childish whim, you turned away from them, from Halys, who loves you like a sister!" As he paused for breath, Lillas readied herself for the worst. "But today you took your lies to me outside this cell and bandied them about for all to see!"

"I . . . I . . . don't . . ."

His reply was flat.

"Don't trouble to deny it. You've lied to me today and every day since we first met."

Suddenly, he was angry no longer. With a tired sigh, he sat.

"Do you think I don't sense what troubles you? That I'm so ignorant or unfeeling that I can't see how frightened you are of me?" Lillas closed her eyes, wanting him to stop, but he continued speaking, his voice low and vibrant in the quiet cell. "What more can I do to reassure you? I've given you my word and never broken it. I wait every day in the hope you'll give me some word, some sign that your trust in me grows. You accuse me of hiding and perhaps it's true, but you hide as well, mocking me, resenting me, belittling my offers of help. This afternoon in the arena, you wanted to bend me to your will, to show the entire Maze how completely you control me."

Her eyes shut tight against him. He sighed again, more deeply than before.

"I know nothing else to do, Lillas, no other way to reach you. In two days we must choose whether to continue this joining. If we part, another citizen of Pelion will be chosen for you, while I must leave the Maze."

Poignant, full of regret, the last phrase lingered in her ears as tears formed inside her burning eyes.

"I don't want to control you."

It was barely a whisper, but he heard her.

"Then what do you want?"

"I . . . I want . . . I want you to touch me."

When he made no reply, she cringed inside, hating herself for revealing something that left her naked and vulnerable. Now he would laugh, or inform her with a knowing grin that her wish could easily be granted. Summoning her courage, she forced her eyes open.

He crouched in front of her, his hands loose in his lap, his face shadowed as the fire burned behind him, turning his hair more red than black. There was no smile on his lips as she had feared.

"You have only to ask, blue-eyes."

"I . . . I don't know . . .," she stammered, sensing his bewilderment, "... how ... how to ... "

As his brow furrowed in puzzlement, her embarrassment increased.

"Neither of us are virgins, Lillas. Joining is joining." He paused, an idea glimmering in his eyes. "Or did you lie to me that first night?"

Wounded that he doubted her when the pain of her new-found honesty weighed heavily on her heart, she bit her lower lip.

"No, Reddin. I spoke the truth."

A finger lifted her chin until she was looking directly into his eyes.

"Then what concerns you?"

"I . . . I wasn't sure . . . sure that you wanted . . . that you felt . . . "

The finger moved to her lips, silencing her before she could finish her whispered confession.

"So, blue-eyes, we are both to blame: I for my coldness; you for your lies."

She wanted him to hold her. She wanted him to say he desired her. Most of all, she wanted him to say he didn't care that she couldn't comprehend the books he read, that he was proud she won the race, and that he forgave her for the endless list of lies she told to protect herself in a world so unlike her own. A hand touched her hair . . . and then he was rising to his feet.

"I'll prepare the meal. Rest your leg, for when it's healed, I'll teach you what little I know of wrestling. . .," he was smiling now, a rare, teasing smile, "... although I fear that, all too soon, you will be the master and I the student."

And so the peace was made between them, with a caress and a smile and promises unspoken.

JEN AND JENNA knelt on the marble floor, one on each side of Scarphe, their necks bent over their work, their clever hands working busily at her nails, Jen paring while Jenna filed. Some people like their nails cut straight across; Scarphe preferred an oval shape with the touch of a point at the end. Just a touch. Too much and the tips might catch on her silk gowns and ruin them, at which time she would have to slap Jen or Jenna or both across the face so as to leave her mark on their smooth-skinned cheeks.

Her body slaves were always known as "Jen" and "Jenna." It began when a pair of identical twins was given to her on her tenth birthday. True twins were expensive, so as long as the girls closely resembled one another—two light-haired, two dark, an occasional pair of freckled redheads—it was all the same to Scarphe. Not that she didn't have the price of twins, no; she wouldn't have anyone think she wasn't able to afford them. As the Aeson's sister, his elder sister, she was rich beyond measure.

She was also bored, had been all her life. Nothing for an aristocratic female to do except be beautiful, which she was not. She frowned at the thought, her eyes half-shut, like a cat on a cushion warming itself in front of a fire. Too hot for a fire now, the winter over and a quick spring speeding toward summer. A summer to remember, she hoped, once the interminable illness of her brother came to an end. Never, in her cruelest and most satisfying dreams, had she imagined it would take him this long to die.

A sudden cry from an adjoining wing of the palace jolted her upright in her chair. Jerking her hands away from Jen and Jenna's ministrations, Scarphe watched as they scurried away on their hands and knees, heads bowed to the floor, understanding they must leave her presence immediately or suffer for it.

Alone, she reveled in the cries and sobbing that announced the death of the Aeson of Agave. Oh, the sound of it! Would that she could hear it every day! She gloried in it, Charis' cries of grief and utter desolation spreading from the Aeson's private apartments to the greater palace. Scarphe amended that thought quickly: the *former* Aeson's private apartments. She'd known he was close to death; she'd not known how close. The sheer unexpectedness of the event made her so happy she could have danced a jig! Instead, she clapped her hands. The girls' heads appeared between the curtains.

"Summer wine, the Aeson's best! Two glasses. Now!"

Jen and Jenna fled. Scarphe closed her eyes, the better to concentrate on the sound of Charis' sorrow. How she hated her, Charis with her cool beauty and decorous ways, looking down her perfectly-shaped nose at everything and everyone in Imarus. Now she would pay for that haughty manner of hers; Scarphe would see to it, had seen to it already since Charis was on her knees at this very moment, mourning her dead master while Scarphe sipped summer wine.

A cleared throat at the archway that separated her bed chamber from the rest of her rooms brought a beatific smile to her face.

"Mother?" he inquired softly, fearful of waking her from her afternoon slumber.

Such a thoughtful boy, her Seth, and handsome, to boot. Not for nothing had she chosen the most attractive suitor she could find, enduring his stupid arrogance and ridiculous posturing until she could bear him no longer, at which time she mixed poisons that would send him off to live in the deep desert where Death dwells.

Today her brother joined her husband, her "sweet" little brother, as their mother called him. As her father's favorite child for six years before her brother came into the world, Scarphe hated having her position within the family usurped. As she grew in understanding, she hated her brother for reminding her daily that he possessed what she could never have—the power to rule and thus the resulting adulation of the crowd. She resolved at a young age to be powerful, and she was, but this man-boy standing in front of her, reaching down to lift her perfectly manicured hand to his lips, would be the beneficiary of the richest gift she could give him, one she could never enjoy herself.

"Welcome, son. I've ordered refreshments."

She looked around the room, a frown growing between her plucked eyebrows until Jen appeared at the curtains, holding them open so Jenna could hurry forward with a tray. After a quick inspection of blown glass goblets filled with summer wine surrounded by almond pastries and orange slices, Scarphe waved her hand and the girls backed out of the room.

"How thoughtful of you, mother," Seth murmured, handing her a glass.

"Son, allow me to offer you your first toast."

Seth pulled himself up to his full height (he towered over her) and bowed low.

"Mother, I owe everything to you."

Indeed he did, but hearing him say it aloud with such grace and fervor brought warmth to her heart. Lifting her glass to him, she declared:

"The Aeson is dead. Long live the Aeson!"

Scarphe drank first, reveling in the bouquet of peach, pear, and grape that filled her nostrils and delighted her tongue. Her son drank second before looking around for a place to sit.

"May I linger, Mother?"

"You're always welcome, son."

Seated, he nibbled on a pastry, looking so much like his childhood self Scarphe experienced a sudden onset of apprehension. He had been a fractious child, prone to tantrums and willful acts. She tamed him in time, schooling him to obey her will even when it went against his own desires. Or so she thought.

"Did your uncle say anything to you?"

Seth shook his head, sniffing his distaste.

"He was past speech. All he could do was drool." Seth selected an orange slice. "Of course, I wasn't with him at the last."

Seething inside, Scarphe inquired:

"And why was that? I thought we agreed you should stay until the end, the heir apparent standing loyally by until his uncle breathed his last."

"It was Charis' request. She wanted to be alone with him and the healer."

"What healer?"

"I don't know his name. A bondsman. Head of Lillas' household until she ran off. Uncle gave him to Charis."

Seth's nonchalance was becoming a major source of annoyance to his mother. Her poisons were the best money could buy (so Abas assured her) and supposedly untraceable, but the idea of bringing a healer into a dying man's rooms worried her. And there sat Seth, oblivious to it all, stuffing his face with sweets he didn't need, exhibiting a lack of self-discipline Scarphe abhorred. When Seth reached for a second pastry, Scarphe attacked.

"What if this healer detects the poison? What if Charis announces his findings in public? You forget, my son, that the people love her."

That was what galled Scarphe, not Charis' beauty or her hold on the Aeson's affections, but the fact that her appearance in the marketplace could and did bring commerce to a halt. Everyone wanted to see her, smell her, touch her, breathe the same air she breathed, as if she was a goddess.

"Charis would never do something so disobedient. She is dutiful to a degree and always respectful of my person."

Seth closed his eyes, threw back his head, and listened to Charis keening for the dead Aeson. At times she would dissolve into sobs, then her keening would begin again, her voice low and throbbing over the corpse of his uncle. I'd like someone to keen for me, he reflected, although his mind balked at imagining himself dead. She might be twenty years his senior, but she was an achingly beautiful woman capable of extreme loyalty. The perfect slave, Seth thought, or was thinking as his mother interrupted him yet again.

"I've been thinking . . ."

Plotting more likely, Seth thought.

". . . that you should lead the army."

Seth jumped to his feet, choking on a pastry as he did so, coughing and sputtering, the two slave girls appearing from nowhere, patting him on his back and offering him wine, water, whatever he preferred. His mother simply watched. The girls dismissed, his mother leaned toward him and lowered her voice.

"I want you to bring her back."

"Who? Lillas?!"

"Who else?"

"I'd hardly call it an army, Mother! Rather, it's a rag-tag bunch of cutthroats the city is sending out to find their lost princess. They want her back; we don't. If they'll pay for the privilege of hacking about in the wilderness, let them. They'll return with nothing, and we won't have to entertain any more demands that Lillas be restored to Imarus."

"I know that was the plan, but I think we need her, Seth. I think *you* need her."

"But, Mother! "

"I know there's no love lost between you."

"She's a spoiled brat with not half the charm of her mother."

"The people love her."

"And they don't love me. That's what you're really saying, isn't it?"

Scarphe shrugged, but kept her eyes focused on her son, who wilted under her gaze.

"You can take the Imarus Guard with you. They belong to you now and must do your bidding. Unlike the citizenry, we have a good idea of where she was heading."

"We do?"

Sighing at the slowness of her son's mind, Agave maintained her temper.

"The prophet, remember? The one you had killed?"

"Ah, the prophet," he murmured, remember how angry she'd been when she discovered he'd deprived her of a living source of information. On second thought, an adventure away from Imarus might be a welcome change.

Seth nodded; Scarphe smiled.

"Bring her back, son, and eventually, after you've taught her to obey, take her as a mate. Don't sulk. You can have other women, any woman you want. You're the Aeson, remember?"

And in that moment, Seth understood he was, indeed, the Aeson of Agave and could do anything he wanted, with his mother's approval, or without.

Scarphe sipped last summer's wine, oblivious to the fact that she had just placed the keys of the kingdom she intended to rule in her son's hand.

And Charis, wailing over her lost lord, vowed revenge on them both.

Chapter 13

Dark of the Moon

T HERE WAS NO MOON. There was never any moon, only starlight. And there was music, a faint melody floating from the chamber where her father loved to listen to the traveling musicians who were handsomely paid for their visits. The dream always began the same way: no moon, music, and dew-damp grass under the soles of her feet.

She was never afraid. No matter how many times she left the portico and began walking toward the avenue of tall cedars lining the walls of the palace, she never felt the slightest fear, for this was home and she had traveled this route a hundred times before. Sliding her toes through the wet grass of this desert oasis, she walked slowly, savoring the coolness of the evening.

There was also no warning. Time after time she sought to remember if she could have heard her attacker, if she could have sensed his presence by sound or scent or by the heat of his body. But there was never a warning, just a palm stopping her mouth, a hand jerking her blouse over her head and grabbing her breasts, and then falling, an endless plunge to the water-softened earth that squelched as his body fell on top of hers.

In the dream, she never fought. There were bruises on her body the next day, the remnants of skin and blood under her fingernails, cruel scratches on her breasts and thighs proving she resisted him, but in the dream, she never fought.

Nor could she see. Her blindness was far worse than her helplessness. Perhaps if she could see his face, he would have some reality beyond that of a formless, faceless phantom that thrust into her again and again, plundering her flesh, his labored breathing harsh and rasping, his grunts hoarse and ugly as he rutted beast-like on the ground.

Then he was gone. No warning, no words, no face; nothing but the moonless night sky, distant music, and wet grass stained with her blood.

SOMEONE CALLED OUT to her. Again and again, someone repeated her name. Caught between two worlds, she struggled to find her bearings. There was no grass under her back, just the familiar texture of woven cloth. Relieved, she opened her eyes to scream at the sight of a man leaning over her. She'd never been able to see him before, for her blouse always covered her eyes. His shoulders and chest were black, fading into the surrounding darkness, the whites of his eyes and teeth gleaming eerily at her. For once, finding herself able to move her limbs, she fought against him, finally able to defend herself from his attack.

For some reason he wasn't fighting back. Instead, he kept repeating her name. Grabbing hold of her wrists, he pressed them against his chest, holding them tightly, although not so tightly as when he attacked her under the cedar trees. The rest of his body lay on top of her, weighing down her legs. He wasn't inside her, for she could feel the friction of cloth between their bodies.

Time seemed to slow, shift, and reverse directions. Gasping for breath, she looked up into Reddin's face. During the struggle, his hair fell forward, masking his expression. Now he tossed his head back in order to clear his vision, never loosening his grip on her wrists. When she tried again to pull away, he held her fast.

"Lillas, you were dreaming. A nightmare, I think. Are you awake now?"

He spoke quietly and reasonably, as if he was accustomed to being awakened by a screaming woman who, when he tried to wake her, proceeded to attack him. For a moment she wished the stone floor would split asunder so that she could sink beneath it. The thought of him witnessing her in the throes of a dream about an event so horrible that she'd hidden it from everyone, filled her with such shame that tears came to her eyes.

"Lillas, speak to me. Are you awake?"

Nodding, for it was impossible to talk over the lump embedded in her throat, she turned her face away from him and into her pillow. Releasing her, he left the bed, his bare feet padding over the stone floor. Listlessly, she traced his steps in her mind, hearing him blow at the embers in the hearth, place a lighted candle on the window ledge and pour water from a pitcher. Kneeling near her side of the bed, he offered her a tin mug.

"Drink this."

It was an effort to sit up. His arm circled her shoulders, helping her upright. Too exhausted to disobey, she accepted his aid and drank, the water washing away the sour taste of fear in her mouth. When she ran a hand through her hair, it came away wet with perspiration.

"We've too many blankets for such a mild night. I'll put them away."

She'd forgotten how much warmer it was when he slept beside her. Since the night of their peace-making, he no longer asked her leave, but held her fast against him, the steady beating of his heart sending her to sleep almost before she closed her eyes. He must have wrapped his loincloth around his hips when he left the bed, for she could see the whiteness of the fabric against his dark skin. When he bent over her to remove one of the blankets, her stomach turned over. Eight scratches, four on either side of his chest, oozed blood.

"You're bleeding!"

Glancing down, a wry smile twisted his lips.

"I'll tell everyone they're battle wounds from our wrestling sessions."

He tried to make her laugh; instead, she blinked back tears. Taking no notice of the scratches, he continued folding the blankets with practiced skill. Lillas took another sip of water, wishing she could take a bath. Her skin was sticky and the long cotton nightshift felt glued to her legs. After another blanket was removed, Reddin cleared his throat.

"I think we must change the bedclothes and find something else for you to wear."

Following the direction of his gaze, she almost whimpered in dismay. Now that he'd removed the blankets and pulled back the sheets, a crimson stain anointed the center of the bed. Without bothering to inspect the back of her nightshift, she knew it must be soaked through with blood. No longer embarrassed, she passed over into mortification. This was even worse than her repeating dream; a man witnessing her lying in a pool of menstrual blood.

"I'll make the bed while you change." His favorite blouse was pressed into her hand. "Wear this until your gown can be laundered. Flavius can find me another one like it in the stores."

She struggled out of bed, her knees weak, and managed to lodge a protest, hating the thought of him cleaning up something he should never have seen.

"No, Reddin. I'll do the cleaning. You can . . . read, perhaps?"

He grinned at her, lifting one eyebrow as he studied her.

"It's the middle of the night and though you may find it hard to credit, I've no interest in reading. Why should I sit in a chair and calmly watch you do what I've done a hundred times before?"

"This has happened to you before?!"

"Well, not precisely this situation, I must admit," he chuckled. "But remember, I work with the sick," he continued in a more serious vein. "My duties include replacing soiled sheets, changing bandages on wounds, helping women before and after childbirth . . ."

Sickened by the thought of performing even one of these tasks, she must have paled, for he put his hands on her shoulders, his expression softening as he said:

"I was wrong to jest with you, for this is nothing like those other chores. I do this for you, Lillas. Not a stranger."

It occurred to her that she wasn't used to kindness or generosity. Such things were suspect, signs of weakness or servility. No one was kind in Imarus unless they wanted something. Generosity was unheard of, with the single exception of her father. Timon and Hume were generous, but still they demanded something of her, Timon her company and Hume her labor. The Eighteenth Mother blessed her with the water, wine, and oil, then informed her that she, too, wanted something in return. What did Reddin want?

Accepting his offer with a tremulous smile, she shuffled toward the jug and basin resting on the chest filled with his belongings. She could hear him working away, stripping the bed, opening the chest at the foot of the bed to obtain fresh linens and snapping the sheets open. His composure defeated her. In the dead of night he'd been awakened from a sound sleep, scratched and kicked by a screaming dervish, and now was cleaning up a bloody mess and seemingly happy to do it. Doubtful that she'd ever understand him or his motives, she decided it didn't matter. He was here and she was glad of it.

"Are you nearly done?"

Feeling clean and refreshed, she reached for his blouse. The hem brushed the top of her thighs, the fullness of the cut allowing the pale cotton cloth to hang free from her shoulders, reminding her of the less constrictive clothing she'd worn in Imarus. Reddin's scent, an earthy, slightly musky fragrance, permeated the cloth. For once, her sensitive nose didn't object.

"There's only a few more hours until dawn. Come to bed."

Blowing out the candle, she crawled under the clean dry sheets that smelled faintly of lavender. He was lying on his back, his arms under his head as he contemplated the wooden rafters. Lillas felt a pang of guilt, wondering if he'd be able to go back to sleep after such an eventful night. At the thought of sleep she yawned. On impulse, she leaned over and placed a light kiss on his cheek, watching covertly from beneath lowered lashes for his reaction. Eyes widening in surprise, he arched one of his eyebrows and shot her a boyish grin.

"Tell me what I did to deserve that so I may do it again!"

Nothing he could have said or done could have charmed her so completely. She'd worried he might grab her, or worst of all, ignore her. Instead, he told her plainly that her kiss pleased him and waited for her to explain herself. Put at ease by his candor, she smiled back at him.

"Must I have a reason for everything I do?"

He considered her thoughtfully.

"I suppose you must have a reason, but may offer it when you choose."

That struck her as making extremely good sense. As a result, she gave him the reason, which she'd discovered herself only that moment.

"I wanted to thank you for . . . for tonight."

"For what in particular?"

This was harder to put into words. She worked hard at it, forming the ideas carefully, knowing he was watching her even though the darkness of the room made close observation impossible.

"For not asking questions you want to ask. For not being embarrassed, as I was embarrassed."

There was a long thoughtful silence.

"So, there were two reasons . . .?"

Laughing outright at his hopeful tone, she leaned over to reward him with a second kiss. This time he reached up with both hands and pulled her head down to him, placing her mouth within easy reach of his. Lips as soft as the moleskin muzzle of her prize stallion pressed against hers, inviting her to stay. Trusting she was free to stay or go, she chose to stay. Lowering her upper body against his, her fingertips brushed over the skin of his shoulders, which was as smooth as she always guessed it would be. After a few more feather-light kisses, she began experimenting, running her fingers through his thick, gleaming hair, brushing away a strand that lay across his forehead to kiss the crease between his eyebrows that deepened when she teased or irked him, kissing his broad cheekbones and the hollows beneath them, running her forefinger down his straight nose and tracing his lips, which were slightly parted now. His breath came faster until, in one fluid motion, he turned her over, reversing their positions, and lowered his mouth to cover hers.

Opening her eyes to find a body coming down on top of her, she nearly screamed, holding it back by sheer willpower, clenching her fists to prevent herself from beating him away from her. A shudder ran thought her as she turned her face away, lying stiff and motionless beneath him. Responsive to her change of mood, he turned on his side and regarded her with a troubled frown.

"What happened, blue-eyes? Have you some discomfort?"

His hand reached out to stroke her belly. She caught it before it could descend and pushed it away as calmly as she could.

"You're right. I don't feel well. I think I'll sleep now."

His silence suggested he was not fooled. She prayed that for once he wouldn't pursue the fact that she was lying, for this was one truth she couldn't confess. Still studying her, he pulled the pillow under his head and sank down into the mattress.

"Will you promise me you'll visit your healer in the morning?"

With a nod, she turned away from him, took another shaky breath, and settled her head on the pillow.

REDDIN'S AROUSAL CAME on him so quickly it would take awhile before he could sleep. The sight of her long, beautifully-shaped legs under the briefness of his blouse made him catch his breath in admiration. Then, with a single brush of her lips against his cheek, she'd unwittingly reminded him that his promise not to join with her was no longer binding. Having almost given up hope that her menses would begin, it had become increasingly difficult to keep his word, especially after her heart-wrenching admission that she'd hungered for his touch but feared he did not want her. Vowing to prove his willingness yet fearful of initiating anything that might demand a quick curtailment (a situation that might prove even more insulting to her than his former reserve), his solution was to hold her every night, fighting his body's needs after so many moons of celibacy. She seemed unaware of his tension as he held her close, smelling the eastern spice she preferred above all others and one which scented her soap in The Hall of Women.

What a mass of contradictions she was! She'd fought him like a maddened, wounded beast, then surprised him with a gesture so provocative he could think of nothing else but bringing her to the moment of pleasure.

What could she possibly have dreamed that could make her moan in that heartrending manner, waking him from a deep sleep, and then attack him when he sought to wake her? He knew enough about dreams to understand that he had become whomever she was fighting. Her scream was an anguished outpouring of pain and grief. Every muscle of his body had been necessary to prevent her from ripping him apart with her bare hands. Who had hurt her, and why was she grateful he didn't ask?

Had anyone ever kissed him in such a way, with a kind of innocent but seductive wonder as she discovered his face and hair? She swore she was no virgin, but surely only a maiden could be so unconsciously erotic, awakening in him in a few short minutes more desire than he'd experienced after hours of love-play with a trained hetaera. The moment he'd felt her relax against his chest, her breasts straining underneath the mannish blouse that suited her so well, he'd been ready to take her as far as she was willing to go.

Why had she left him? The moan she uttered suggested pain and certainly many women suffered in the first hours of their menses. Yet he'd sensed a lie from her, and then refused to believe she could lie to him only days after they made a pact to continue their joining. Troubled, he turned on his side to face the door, sensing she would reject him if he took her in his arms.

The tidy bundle of discarded bedclothes shone dimly in the unlit cell, for the night was clear and pinpricks of stars gleamed in the early winter sky. Drifting toward sleep, he found himself musing about those bedclothes, now stained with his blood as well, for he had wiped the blood from his chest when her back was turned . . .

Waking with a start, he sat bolt upright, jerking the covers with him. A sleepy complaint came from the tousled head on the pillow beside him as a tanned arm reached up to replace the coverlet that had fallen away from her shoulder.

"Lillas! Lillas, wake up!"

Mumbling, she snuggled deeper into her pillow.

"Lillas, I must speak with you!"

His urgency must have registered with her, for one blue eye struggled open.

"Do you remember asking me what I wanted in exchange for teaching you?"

All of a sudden, she was awake.

"I've decided what I want."

Was it his imagination, or was he seeing the Seventeenth Mother consider his question at the altar, her face intent on his childish request? The scent of the sacred oil drifted past his nostrils and he shook his head to clear it. Lillas was staring at him as if he was possessed.

"I want you to come with me to the Sanctum tomorrow."

"Why?"

"I want to offer my second gift and I want you to watch."

"Your second gift?"

Her face was confused and blurry-eyed. He reminded himself she knew nothing about what he was proposing.

"I wiped my chest with the sheet. You know we must give our gifts. This will be my second, the gift of blood, the first since I was a child."

"But you would be giving my blood as well as yours."

"Just so."

She pulled herself up into a sitting position and ran a hand through her tangled mass of curls. He'd often wondered if her short hair was the result of her first gift, although it would have been impolite to ask.

"Could it count as my gift as well?"

He tried to hide his excitement, afraid that if he pushed her she'd turn contrary just to spite him.

"If you give it of your own free will."

A huge yawn made her cover her mouth with her hand. Nodding sleepily, she slid back down on the mattress.

"Then we'll both do it. It's a deal."

Her indifference came as a highly unpleasant shock. Here he sat, exultant that this strangest of nights had yielded two more steps toward Preparation and she was uncaring to the point of boredom. He thought of her as a barbarian but never fully investigated what the word signified. From her attitude he concluded that she thought his request simple-minded and an easy trade. One of her curses rose to his lips as he punched his pillow and slid down the headboard to lie on his back. What was he going to do with this exasperating, headstrong, and increasingly desirable woman?

Starlight blanketed the bed as his feelings for the ernani sleeping soundly
beside him waxed and waned, mirroring the faces of the moon caught in its
eternal cycle of nightly changes, the same moon that had disappeared tonight
to be reborn tomorrow as a fragile silver crescent. No rule stated that Lillas
must understand. What she gave freely would be accepted. Action trumped
knowledge.

Somehow, Reddin must find contentment in that.

"FORGIVE MY TARDINESS, Mother."

Chryse's flushed cheeks bespoke her rushed journey from the Maze to
the Library, no doubt the result of some unforeseen problem only she could
remedy.

"We've just begun," was Hesione's amiable reply.

The hetaera smoothed her robes and ran a light hand over her braids,
seeming to polish the richness of her dark tresses. Hesione requested no
explanation, but Chryse seemed compelled to offer one.

"Charmian requested counsel. Since she rarely confides in me, I thought
it best to meet with her without an appointment."

This was always Chryse's way, thought Hesione, putting aside her
personal agenda to make time for those in her care. Thus she had put aside
Orrin's entry into her life's work, although their mating continued strong
and unabated. Hesione welcomed the prospect of the Master Hetaera joining
her Council in the near future, judging that the infusion of a masculine
counterpart to the Mistress of Joining might further assist the male ernani's
journey on the Path.

"Come, Chryse, don't keep us on tenterhooks. Why does the unflappable
Charmian need your advice?"

Kazur's teasing brought a smile to the hetaera's face. She responded in
kind, her lips protruding in a slight pout.

"As always, it's the fault of the male ernani. For some reason they don't
always respond as we citizens of Pelion would wish, and have peculiar
customs as regards questions of kinship."

"Let me guess. Could it be our twin giants from Lapith?"

Her smile announced his success. As she settled down to describe the
session, the humor gradually left her face.

"It seems Jarod offered his first gift without sharing that knowledge with
Stym beforehand, appearing at the morning session with shorn locks.
Charmian says Stym returned from afternoon training in a foul mood that
worsened as the night wore on. Even after two moons together, he rarely
speaks to her of things that trouble him. It took hours for her to find out
what bothered him."

"That in itself should not upset Charmian. Stym comes slowly toward her as we predicted, and she spoke lovingly of him on the Day of Choice. What is the crux of her concern?"

Unhappiness made a rare foray over Chryse's features and Hesione readied herself for disappointment since it was clear that the hetaera had been unable to rectify Charmian's problem.

"She hoped he was readying himself to offer his first gift, for he asked her many questions about exactly what the ceremony entails. Now he believes Jarod has 'bested' him by making his offering before Stym. Last night he swore to Charmian that his hair would never feel the knife."

It was for the purpose of recording the gifts of ernani and candidates from Pelion that Hesione was meeting with the Mistress of Joining and the Head Scribe in an alcove of the Greater Library this afternoon. Gifts offered in the first moon of joining were a rarity, although the three-moon contract begun after the Day of Choice brought with it a proliferation of requests for audiences with the Eighteenth Mother on the pedestal before the altar. Hesione received Jarod's gift yesterday and recalled her feelings of exultation as she placed the mass of sun-streaked hair upon the grate.

The twin giants from Ariod's Lake were an experiment of sorts, the first full-blooded relations allowed entry into the same class. The Council was persuaded by a fervent request from their mother, the daughter of Tyre and Kara, a transformed adept who begged that her twin sons not be separated. With this development, Hesione wondered if the nostalgia engendered by the offspring of the founders of the colony at Lapith had unduly swayed the caretakers of the Maze from their mission.

"I'm concerned by Stym's use of the word 'bested,' and I suspect Charmian shares my feelings. To consider the giving of gifts a competition of some sort, a race run between brothers, is not . . ."

"Was that your impression of Jarod when he made his offering?"

Kazur's even-voiced inquiry brought her up short. It was a refreshing, albeit disconcerting, experience for her to be interrupted in mid-sentence. No other member of the Council could do what Kazur did easily and without thinking. Born and bred to the power of the black robes, a native of Pelion would never dream of interrupting her words or thoughts. Perhaps this is why I called him to Council, Hesione thought, smiling inwardly at her newest helper, to guard against complacency and keep me humble.

"I had no such thought and you have my thanks, Kazur, for your reminder. He was solemn-faced and ill-at-ease as he stood before me, but I sensed nothing of a supposed victory over his sibling."

Nodding to himself, Kazur rested his chin on his hand and considered the parchment before him, running his eyes over the neat columns of names and offerings. After a moment he leaned back in his chair to address Chryse.

"Sometimes we forget how little the ernani understand. For instance, has Charmian made it clear to Stym that there is no particular order for the giving of gifts? True, we usually call the offering of hair the first gift, if for no other reason than it is a child's first offering. Perhaps she should point out to Stym that it's impossible for him to know how many gifts Jarod has given since two are offered without visible proof to anyone but the Eighteenth Mother. If Stym can't measure Jarod's progress, no race is possible."

The women sat lost in wordless admiration. Made shy by their gratitude, Kazur ducked his head and hurriedly continued transcribing notes. Soon after, they joined him in the task at hand.

What happened next began with a wisp of a thought flitting across the fabric of Hesione's consciousness. Just as one would swat a gnat, she brushed it aside, taking up her work with Chryse and Kazur again where she had left off.

The second contact came some time later, weak and distant, but with enough substance to be recognized, if not actually identified, by the sense of urgency with which the call was made. Chryse and Kazur remained bent over the records of Transformation, murmuring occasional comments in subdued voices, unaware of anything out of the ordinary as Hesione withdrew her mind from the waking world.

Reaching out her thoughts as if they were fingers, Hesione strove to grasp onto the mind seeking hers and hold it fast. In time, her efforts were rewarded.

"... dead. All dead. Must.. .find. . ."

The smell of rotten leaves. A floor of moist earth. A man, a wounded man, who hid in the darkness, fearful of being found. Pain. Grief. Tears. And then, nothing.

"Chryse, Kazur: join me!"

In the next instant their minds were connected with hers, reviewing the memory of what she had just experienced.

"A man who's badly injured, moving in and out of consciousness as he tries to reach me. That was his second attempt. Pray he makes a third."

Absorbing energy from their linkage with her, she was able to search greater distances, turning by instinct toward the west. Time crept by on all fours as she sought to pierce the darkness, willing this wounded man to persevere, demanding that he fight his way toward her, enjoining him with the simplest of words: "The door is open; you must try again."

Connection came again and with it, identification: It was Didion, a veteran healer currently on duty with Hume's cavalry unit stationed on the western frontier. Hume's men had escorted Hesione to the shallow grave beyond Pelion's boundaries just as they had escorted Lillas, the Lapithians, and Altug through the old forest toward Pelion. Didion served as healer to the most experienced battle-ready unit in the entire Legion.

Searching through Didion's memories, Hesione found Ranier, one of Didion's mentors during his studies at the House of Healing. Quickly locating Ranier and Nadia in the Maze, she included them in her mental circle, Chryse and Kazur supplying them with details while Hesione labored on, sorting through the mass of impressions contained in Didion's fevered thoughts. As Ranier and Nadia attuned their minds to their friend and colleague, Didion's panic lessened, allowing him to focus on the information he was determined to deliver to the Mother of Pelion.

"They came yesterday before dawn. A mass attack, two hundred; maybe more. Killed the outlying sentries before they could warn us. No chance to defend ourselves."

Hesione saw the massacre as Didion had seen it. In blackest night, the moon hid its face as if it could not bear the sight of forty Legionnaires caught unaware by five times their number, most of them roused from a sound sleep, reached groggily for a weapon to be cut down as they rose up from their blankets. Some cried out for mercy; none was offered. Others ran for cover only to find a sword or an axe waiting behind a tree or boulder. And through it all, over the hoarse screams of attackers and attacked, the clang of metal and the solid thud of iron weapons against human flesh and bone, she heard, as Didion heard, the voice of Hume. Like the rolling summer thunder that comes without rain, his shouted commands rose up out of the mayhem, exhorting his dying patrol to regroup even as he roared out his curses at the wanton destruction of his men, until, finally, his voice was stilled.

In the quiet that followed, Didion wept as Hesione braced herself, certain that Didion's tears boded worse things than death.

The image of a man with ginger hair and beard rose before her, squinting with malice as he considered how best to question his captives. Thankfully, the image faded as quickly as it appeared.

"At first light, they . . . they . . . tortured Hume."

Anguished screams rose around her, threatening her self-control. Suddenly, Prax's consciousness joined hers, a soldier forced to listen to the sufferings of his brother-in-arms, Prax's fury like a living flame within him.

"A single question, repeated endlessly, `The girl, where is the girl?' By nightfall, Hume was unconscious."

Silence fell again but Didion wept no longer. Perhaps the healers were the cause of his calm, for Hesione could feel their presence in Didion's mind, moving him away from pain, urging him toward serenity. Whatever the reason, he was more coherent now.

"Their greed saved my life. When someone pointed out that a healer is a valuable commodity in the marketplace, they broke my legs instead of killing me. Once it was dark, I put the guards to sleep, stole a knife, and cut my bonds. I crawled to Hume. He was hemorrhaging inside."

Didion's sorrow carried the force of a sharp blow.

"There was no remedy. I . . . I eased his way."

As if in a dream Hesione felt the others take over, Prax mapping the location of the cave in which Didion hid, assuring him a patrol would be with him shortly; Ranier and Nadia murmuring a song of forgetfulness, wrapping Didion in a web of sleep, keeping him safe until their healing hands could begin their work. Despite their efforts, Didion called for Hesione again, stubbornly intent on delivering his message.

"Hume called her Skat. Even until the last moment he protested that Skat was a lad, a boy of no account. I read their leader. He does not know, but he suspects. It is everywhere in his thoughts: `Pelion,' and though he does not know its meaning, `the gift.' He will continue searching for her. If his search is futile, he will journey south."

Her private musings were ended by Ranier's sharp request that she help the living.

"You have my thanks, Didion. You must rest now and wait for help to arrive. What you did for Hume was a great kindness. I will say the rite this evening for him and for all who gave the city the gift of their lives."

Gently, she detached her mind from his, trusting her Council to begin the activities necessary to find Didion and bring him back to Pelion where he could begin his convalescence in the House of Healing.

Twilight's pall fell over the Greater Library. Sitting alone in the darkening recesses of the alcove (for Chryse and Kazur departed at her request), Hesione considered the papers spread before her, squinting against the gloom in order to locate the name for which forty lives had just been lost. There it was, printed neatly in Kazur's distinctive block capitals: "LILLAS."

In the first years of Hesione's reign, time seemed infinitely extendable, a friend who could grant any favor. Today it became her foe.

The beast had awakened, and with it, fear.

Chapter 14

The Pledge

"WHAT HO, LILLAS! Care to take a turn with me?"

Dorian was in rare form tonight, his face aglow with a high sheen of perspiration, proof that he'd danced with nearly every woman at the Gathering, a plan he announced to those assembled in the dayroom at the beginning of the festivities and one that brought peals of laughter from the women and glares from some of the men. Lillas thought Dorian a flagrant womanizer until she saw his mate, Fenja, her round face wreathed with smiles as she sat among the musicians, a drum held between her thighs, her agile hands tapping out rhythms impossible to ignore, bringing every couple in attendance out onto the polished wooden floor to dance. That Fenja had carved a niche for herself without need of speech brought a smile to Lillas' lips and a quick flood of appreciation for Dorian, who was making the best of his mate's absence.

"Dorian: be warned! I'm twice as fast on the dance floor as I am on the track!"

With a roar of appreciative laughter, he grabbed her tightly around her waist and they were off, blazing a pattern of circles around more slowly moving couples, galloping, romping, and leaping in a series of steps that knew nothing of propriety and succeeded in raising several eyebrows among the more conservative dancers. Careless of censure, carefree and happy enough to defy gravity and float on the melodies of the fiddles and fife, Lillas found herself laughing for no other reason than the fact that she was alive to the tips of each finger and toe, free to gambol about to her heart's content, sure that when she stopped, if she stopped, another would take Dorian's place, whirling her away from cares and worries, every trouble forgotten in the blaze of candlelight and the high-pitched tattoo of Fenja's tight-skinned drum.

Begun the first evening of the second moon of the three-moon contract, the Gatherings offered fellowship in an informal and hospitable setting. Free to come as they chose and leave when they liked, the couples gathered in the dayroom between the evening trumpet and the removal of the torches. Most evenings were spent in casual conversation, communal games that tested memory and observation, or sessions of skill and luck with cards or dice. This evening's dance was a break in routine, having been planned by those who longed for revelries remembered from days past.

The Gatherings changed everything about Lillas' life in the Maze, becoming nearly as important as her daily sessions in the arena. She hadn't known how starved she was for company, for frivolity and light-hearted camaraderie. The Gatherings were nothing like the extravagant entertainments of Imarus, but the music and laughter, the games and friendly rivalries they engendered, fed her spirit and lightened her heart.

At first she'd feared Reddin couldn't be lured from the cell and his beloved books, but he'd offered neither complaint nor excuse and accompanied her whenever she expressed a wish to attend. To his sole request, that she forgo the Gatherings on the night before an examination, she willingly agreed and kept her word, studying with him over the books and figures that were no longer quite so inhibiting, gaining confidence as her tutor complimented her on her achievements, earning the respect of her classmates, and best of all, Reddin's quiet pride as she waved a nearly-perfect paper under his nose.

No announcement requested festive attire, but everyone in attendance tonight wore their finest clothing, most of it either requested from the storehouses or hand-made by the women in their daily sessions. Hair and skin gleamed with health and a wealth of fragrances drifted on the air warmed by torches, braziers, and the heat of bodies striving to match the strenuous rhythms tapped out on the drum, swaying to the inviting melodies sent soaring by flutes and fiddles.

Two dances later, a stitch in her side and a newly-formed blister on the back of her heel, Lillas detached herself from a disappointed Dorian, gasping her excuses, and after removing her shoes, limped over to a trestle table bowed with the weight of pastries, fruit, cheeses, and goblets of sweet wine. She drank thirstily, so thirstily that she choked, then sputtered, and felt a cloth napkin being pressed into her hand.

"Limping and choking! Never have I seen anyone work harder at enjoying herself!"

Running the napkin over her wet lips, she turned to find Reddin grinning at her, his face a picture of impish delight as he took in her wine-spattered bodice and bare feet. A fortnight ago he would have either berated her or been shamed by her state of disrepair. Tonight he was charmed, with traces of heightened color along his cheekbones and a glow of desire in his eyes. He wanted her. Without thinking, she responded to his need. Dropping the napkin, she took a step toward him, closing her eyes against the tumult of the dayroom. His lips brushed against hers, then pressed more insistently, wanting more of her. Sliding her hand up his shoulder and beneath his hair, touching the warm skin at the nape of his neck, she opened her mouth, tasting the wine on his tongue.

"Are you two never done with wrestling?"

Lillas stiffened, pushing Reddin away as she bit back angry words. Turning to the source of annoyance, she found Jarod of Lapith regarding her with an expectant grin. Her temper was legendary in the arena and all the men enjoyed baiting her, hoping they could bring on one of her famous tantrums. Lifting her chin, she declared:

"Practice makes perfect. Our technique improves daily."

Her cool sally brought a round of guffaws at the expense of Jarod. A squeeze of Reddin's hands wrapped around her waist, signaled his enjoyment of the Lapithian's upset.

While Lillas and Reddin were otherwise engaged, four couples gathered around them at the trestle table to partake of much-needed refreshments after their exertions on the dance floor. Lillas often wondered at the fact that the wayfarers of Hume's caravan to Pelion, her first reluctant contact with inhabitants of a world other than Imarus, remained her closest friends. The twins from Lapith stood arm in arm with their mates, looking more alike than ever in matching tunics and tight-fitting breeches. Halys, attired in a gown stitched by her own hands, leaned ever so slightly against Dysponteus, who, for some unknown reason, had stopped visiting the barber, letting his close-cropped hair grow long and slightly shaggy about the ears. Even Altug, whose hard-nosed cynicism was much abated since his joining with Valeria, had become a welcome companion despite his irritating tendency to beat Lillas in the archery matches. Valeria, plump and vivacious, with an infectious laugh geared to cheer the glummest of spirits, was even now offering the mountain man a bite from a ripe plum and wiping the purple juice from his mustache over his protests, which, Lillas observed, were neither forceful nor heartfelt.

One eye cocked impudently at the Lapithian by her side, Thaisa offered Lillas a saucy explanation of his behavior.

"Take no notice of Jarod. I suspect he would like nothing better than for me to join him in the wrestling ring."

At his mate's teasing, Jarod colored and muttered under his breath. Charmian joined the fray by turning to Thaisa with a face pulled long with woe, gesturing to Stym, who wore an expression of wounded masculine pride identical to his brother's.

"It's happened again! Tease one and the other ignites! Shall we ever understand these Lapithian males? Could it be hot tempers are necessitated by cold winter nights? One would think our milder climate might cause them to cool."

It occurred to Lillas that although these two women of Pelion, Charmian and Thaisa, might share few physical attributes, they were nearly interchangeable in temperament and in their methods of expressing themselves. Neither could have spoken without benefit of her hands, which gesticulated like branches dancing on a balmy breeze. Each possessed a certain quality of serenity and each was evidently a source of considerable vexation to their respective mates.

Without losing a beat, Thaisa continued Charmian's train of thought.

"Perhaps it's because they're twins. My maternal aunt raised twins and told me that if one disobeyed and was punished, the other would immediately demand like punishment, even if he'd done nothing to merit her displeasure."

Turning to face the brothers, who were by this time painfully aware of the fact that they had become the center of attention, Thaisa quizzed them:

"Was your mother ever faced with a similar dilemma?"

Slowly, grudgingly, Jarod ground out a reply.

"Once, when we grew taller than her, she tried to punish us by separating us—keeping me with her in the tent and sending Stym to our father who tended the herds. It didn't work as she planned."

The set of Jarod's jaw made it clear he would not be finishing the story. Just as clear was the way Stym avoided looking at his brother. With a triumphant cry, Charmian pounced.

"Confess, Stym! What mischief did you do?"

A rueful smile tugged at Stym's lips.

"I ran away from our father, untied the leather thongs attached to the ground stakes, crawled under the loosened hide, dislodged the central poles, and collapsed the tent"

"Our mother," Jarod interjected, "was not amused."

"Neither was our father," Stym added, "even when our granddam laughed so hard she couldn't speak . . ."

Jarod completed the story with aplomb.

". . . so that our grandsire persuaded our parents not to punish us."

Once the laughter crested and began to dissipate, Lillas noticed that Thaisa, like Jarod's mother, did not appear to be amused.

"Your grandmother couldn't speak for herself?"

Everyone sensed the accusation behind the question. Stym actually took a step forward, advancing on Thaisa, but Jarod threw out an arm to stop him. Stym halted, but continued glaring at Thaisa, who stood her ground admirably, Lillas thought, surrounded as she was by two angry Lapithians.

"You misunderstand," Jarod explained. "My granddam was adored. For my grandsire, the sound of her laughter was better than a fast ride on a good horse. We were rewarded for making her laugh, not keeping her silent, as you implied."

"She came from Pelion," Stym added, "and was much like you," he indicated Thaisa, "and you," he added, turning to gaze at Charmian with something akin to wonder, Lillas thought.

The awkwardness passed in time, the ernani and their mates reminded of the vast differences between them. Some were reaching for refreshments when Reddin offered a casual observation.

"The tendency for twins is passed along from generation to generation. There's a good chance you might father twins of your own."

Expressions of absolute horror appeared on Jarod's and Stym's faces. Their mates dissolved into helpless laughter, although Thaisa was able to gasp out a reply.

"I can think of no better reward for them than to be repaid by their own children!"

Surrounding Thaisa with his arms, Jarod posed a question with an ominous glint in his eyes.

"If the scholar speaks true, you share this trait with my brother and me. If your mother's sister birthed twins, might not that be your fate as well?"

Thaisa's wail caused several heads scattered across the dayroom to turn toward the group around the table. This time Jarod and Stym led the laughter.

Made uncomfortable by all this talk of parenthood, Lillas slipped away from Reddin's arms and reached for another goblet of wine. Unbeknownst to Lillas, a serving woman was refilling trays with fruits and cheeses. As Lillas lifted the goblet, the woman turned, hitting Lillas' outstretched arm and sending liquid flying over the skirt of her already wine-spattered dress. With a foul curse, Lillas grabbed a napkin to sop up the spreading stain.

"You clumsy slave! My dress is ruined!"

The woman stared at her, opened her mouth to speak and then shut it with snap. Taking her tray firmly in her hands, she straightened her shoulders and walked away, her back stiff with indignation. Unsettled by her reaction, Lillas spoke to no one in particular.

"One would think I'd insulted her, when it's she who should apologize to me!"

Absolute silence greeted her complaint. When she turned to observe her companions, she met nine faces with expressions ranging from shock and disgust to pity and frowning disapproval. Confused, ignorant of how she had offended, Lillas turned to Reddin, who broke the uncomfortable silence by offering a quiet observation.

"Indeed, you did insult her, Lillas. She's not a slave, nor is anyone in the city, for we abhor slavery and have rejected it since the founding of Pelion. The servants in the Maze are an elite of sorts and highly paid for their services since they're required to deal directly with those who have no knowledge of our customs."

Damning herself for her quick temper, Lillas tasted Reddin's rebuke with blood from her bitten lips. In a single moment for which she was solely to blame, he became a stranger again, separate and distant, his expression as inscrutable as it had been during the first few days of their joining. Worse than the loss of his approval, her blunder compromised her identity. Charmian's next question reminded her how completely she had revealed herself.

"I know you come from the western lands, Lillas, but I never thought you . . . you might own slaves. Is this so?"

Denial sprang to her lips but guilt made Lillas nod her head in answer, adding:

"Once it was so, but no more."

At her response, the tension in the group lessened, and it struck Lillas they must be thinking that by coming to Pelion she rejected slavery as they did, and had freed her slaves as a result of her beliefs. Much as she disliked the feeling, remorse filled her at the thought that she could deceive them so easily. They wanted to like her and were willing to forgive the slip of her tongue as long as they believed her no longer a slave-owner. Halys spoke up now, her eyes flooded with painful memories.

"My brother, he it was who in the Maze should be. Gone he is four years without a word. Lost he is, my father thinks, to slavers from the south. My turn it was, a daughter sent to travel where only sons may freely go." Tear-filled eyes lifted to Dysponteus and Lillas heard the resolve contained in her next words. "So I must return, to ease my father's grief."

Dysponteus drew her tall, thin form close to him, whispered in her ear, and they withdrew from the group, making their way slowly toward the door and the cell that lay beyond.

Altug cleared his throat noisily and turned toward Lillas, who quailed at the hatred in his eyes.

"I know you think me a bandit and in some ways, your guess is shrewd. My people guard the mountain paths, and it's true we often steal from the caravans traveling between east and west. My skill with a bow comes from hunting men, not just birds and game. We rob merchants, but we kill slavers," the skin over his jaw tightened, "without mercy and without regret."

"What of the slaves, Altug?" asked Valeria, the quaver in her voice revealing her fear at hearing his answer.

Not pausing to acknowledge his mate, Altug continued his address, each word geared to punish Lillas. "We free their bleeding wrists and ankles from the shackles, give them the meager provisions from the slavers' supplies, share with them what we carry, and let them choose their own route home." His tone was deadly now, his eyes tiny slits of malice. "The adults are not the problem. It's the children, many of them ignorant of where they were captured, most of them orphans even if they know where home lies; these are the ones who suffer most. It is our custom for mated couples to adopt these lost ones. I am such a child."

This admission was stated without shame or self-pity and the fire that burned in Altug's eyes announced he would abide no expressions of sympathy. Stym added his testimony to that of the mountain bandit.

"In my grandsire's time the slavers preyed on our people, but he brought back from Pelion knowledge of swords and strategies for battles that keep us free from his day onward. Still, we are vigilant, every man riding patrol from the day of his induction into the warrior clan."

"It's for such knowledge I came," Altug said, then turned back to Lillas. "Know you, Lillas, I hate everything and everyone connected with slavery, which robbed me even as I rob those who cross my path. If you own slaves no longer, I am thankful, for if one person can turn their back on Agave, perhaps there's hope others will do likewise."

With a stiff nod of farewell, Altug left them. Valeria lingered for a moment, breaking the uncomfortable silence that followed her mate's departure.

"You have my thanks, too, Lillas. What you were before entering the Maze is not my concern, but I'm grateful for this evening and what it revealed. You helped Altug; for this I will always be thankful."

The group broke up quickly after Valeria's departure. Lillas was left with a taste of bitterness in her mouth, an acrid mixture of regret and shame. A dry voice broke through her bleak mood.

"Would you care to dance?"

Suddenly the dayroom was hateful to her, the music grating on her ears, and the thumping of feet against the wooden floor adding to the pounding in her head. An hour ago she'd been happier than she'd felt since leaving Imarus; now she was filled with self-loathing, despising herself for her cowardice in not admitting the truth of her situation to people who freely admitted their hopes, their failures, and their beliefs. In comparison with them, her hopes were selfish, her failures rampant, and her beliefs non-existent. Emptiness claimed her as she shook her head, unwilling to meet Reddin's gaze, loathe to witness the contempt with which he must be regarding her.

"I think not. I . . . I have not the heart to dance."

When he said nothing in reply she started for the door. Stepping in front of her, his eyes searched hers. She could read no contempt there, only quiet understanding.

"It will pass, blue-eyes. You spoke in haste and ignorance but faced your punishment without shirking or fighting back, as is your way."

How was it possible that he could forgive her when she was unable to forgive herself? Lost in the wonder of his acceptance, she could think of nothing to say, nothing except her gratitude, but somehow, the words would not come.

"Come, blue-eyes. I, too, have no heart for dancing."

With that, he led her away from the bright lights and boisterous laughter, Lillas willingly relinquishing the music and the dance for the dim silent cell that was no longer a prison, but a place of sanctuary. Bowing her head, Lillas let Reddin lead her home.

THE NIGHT WAS young for they left the Gathering long before the torches were put out and Reddin felt no need for sleep. Lillas was restless, pacing the cell only to examine her studies lying spread on the table for a moment, and then commencing her tour of the cell. Knowing the reason for her distress, and knowing just as well that there was nothing he could say to ease her mind, Reddin disrobed, folding his tunic and breeches for storage in the trunk. Taking up a book, he packed both pillows beneath his head and reclined on the bed, resting the book on his chest and reading by the light of the candles glowing on the window ledge. Becoming involved with the subject at hand, he was only half-aware of Lillas' movements, although he heard the squeak of the wardrobe door and guessed she was finally removing her bedraggled gown. The sound of water being poured in the basin followed and he turned his attention back to his reading, content that her spirit was settling at last.

"May I join you?"

As the result of his refusal to take back the blouse he'd loaned her, it became her nightwear of choice, a development that pleased him in an indefinable way. She wore it now, the ivory color matching the scrubbed skin of her face and neck. Her hair had grown longer since their joining and fell in soft waves below her chin. A vigorous brushing left it silky and somewhat awry, but the air of dishabille suited her. Smiling his welcome, he gestured to his side and offered her a pillow from beneath his head.

Soon she was curled up with her back to him, a pillow tucked under her breasts as she read the story assigned for the next day's studies. The night was mild; there was no need for blankets to shield them from the draft emerging from the barred windows. It was his custom to sleep unclothed, but lately he wore his loincloth, a change in routine that troubled him somewhat, for he tried to be easy with his nudity around her, not flaunting himself, but making no attempt to hide his genitals or bodily functions, wanting her to accustom herself to him. At the same time he had grown more modest, she had been freer of late and no longer hid behind the wardrobe door. Judging that they were approaching middle ground, he dismissed his concerns.

Since the night of her monthly flow, there were other subtle changes between them, a kind of lingering promise, and glancing at her bare legs and

the flawless curve of her hip as it rose from the back of her thighs, he
remembered the taste of wine that had clung to her lips and the feel of her
hand pressed against the back of his neck as she kissed him in the dayroom.
She came toward him without the slightest hesitation, insensible to the people
surrounding them, and he had been exultant, sure that she shared his longing.
At Jarod's interruption, he sensed her growing fury and moved quickly to
calm her. Soon after, he became aware that she made no attempt to remove
his hands from her waist and seemed content to remain encircled by his arms.
Then she cursed the servant and all hopes of what this night might bring
disappeared.

No one was more shocked than Reddin by her outburst. She spoke
infrequently of her origins, but he had heard bits and pieces—a father she
adored, a friend named Phoron, hunts and seemingly pointless games of
dice. At no time did she mention slaves, and he had been appalled and then
furious that she kept such weighty secrets from him. Putting his anger aside,
he watched her struggle for composure, biting her lips, her eyes tear-filled
at Halys' confession, enormous as Altug lashed out at her. His admiration
grew as he realized that this was not the brazen ernani of the first night of
their joining, ready to attack at the slightest sign of weakness, nor the cunning
ernani of the arena, head-strong and arrogant in the face of public censure.
She didn't retaliate or wriggle out of her predicament, but silently bore Altug's
abuse, the twins' outrage, and Halys' sorrow. Tonight he saw proof that she
was changing, and wondered if he, too, was becoming something other than
the man he was before they met.

With that thought, he turned his attention back to his book. The only
sounds were occasional pops from the fire and the rustle of a page being
turned. Lillas readjusted her position from time to time, but he read on,
oblivious to anything but the question of blood circulation and the mechanisms
of the human heart.

A current of air ran over the hand with which he'd offered her the pillow
and left flung out from his body. Ignoring this distraction at first, he became
aware that she was touching the underside of his forearm, following the
tracery of veins under his skin with either her lips or her fingertips. As she
found the tender skin on the inside of his upper arm, he felt the warm moisture
of her breath against him and decided it was her lips that moved gently over
his skin. Lying motionless, afraid she would pull away if he moved, he kept
his eyes glued to the book resting on his chest, trying to push away the tension
that was claiming him.

Reaching his shoulder, she stroked the hair under his arm, a faint giggle
escaping her. He struggled not to react to the tickling sensation he felt to the
tips of his toes. The ends of her hair brushed against his chest and he inhaled
her scent, the faint aroma of sandalwood that clung to her even in their

wrestling sessions. Assuredly she touched him in the arena, but those were different ways of touching, for during their bouts she was tough and merciless, whereas now she was tentative and shy, her lips tasting him for the first time, her fingertips caressing the surface of his skin, which seemed to burn as though touched by flame.

Moving her attention to his torso, she ran her fingers through the fine dark hair on his chest, her position allowing him to observe her for the first time, the book forgotten as he watched her flushed face and a pink tongue between slightly parted lips. Refusing to meet his eyes, her finger circled the dark aureole that held some kind of fascination for her, and as her mouth covered him, he couldn't control the tremor that ran through him. Lifting her head, she regarded him from under lowered lashes.

"Do I disturb you?"

Stifling his amusement at the studied politeness of her inquiry, he answered her as seriously as he could given the novelty of their situation.

"Not at all. It's just that . . . that it's difficult not to respond to such pleasure."

A rosy blush rose to her cheeks and her eyes shone underneath thick sandy lashes.

"Do you mind?"

What possible answer could he give to such a question? Did he mind that she was touching him of her own volition, something he'd dreamed of for weeks? Did he mind that he was already aroused to the point that he could hardly keep his hands off her? Yet she was hiding from him still, eyelashes lowered, her blushes proof of her timidity. As impossible as the prospect seemed, the best course seemed to lie in letting her continue and offering up a prayer that he could hold to his decision.

"I would mind only if you stopped."

Her happy sigh quelled whatever doubts remained. Setting aside the book, he shifted to the center of the bed, replacing the pillow beneath his head and raised his hand to push away the hair that had fallen in his face, intent on watching her if he could not touch her in return.

"Let me do that."

Pushing his hand away, she knelt at his side and brushed aside his hair, smiling down at him as she continued to stroke it away from his face.

"So soft, like black silk touched with red fire."

Her hair gleamed with golden tints, lit from behind by the dying flames flickering in the hearth. He felt himself lost in her eyes, drowning in their depths, for though he'd never seen the ocean, every song and tale he had ever heard convinced him that only the sunlit seas could equal the beauty of her eyes. Her hands slid over him, continuing her voyage, and he learned from her reactions the truth of her innocence, for it was clear she had never felt the pleasure of palms and fingers passing over the flesh of a body unlike her own. Every discovery delighted her, and he joined in her delight, feeling himself being reborn, as if no other women had ever touched him, had ever probed the mystery of him.

When she reached his navel and followed the line of dark hair that ran down into the top of his loincloth, she hesitated, bit her lower lip and removed her hand. Taking that hand in his, he raised it to his mouth and kissed the palm.

"Why do you stop? There's nothing beneath this cloth that you've not seen before."

There was no reason for her to shrink from seeing him. His state was natural, proof of his desire for her, something he couldn't achieve without her participation.

"Untie it. I want you to see my need for you."

Her eyes searched his for a moment, weighing his request, testing his sincerity, and then, satisfied by his assurances, she loosened the fabric tied around his hips. Closing his eyes, he felt her hands move down his loins and a deep sigh of contentment broke from his lips as she touched him lightly, running her hand along the length of him and cupping the softer parts below. Her hands grew no bolder, but moved to his thighs and down each leg. Opening his eyes, he caught her staring at him with an undecipherable expression.

"So, am I different from other men?"

A slight frown cast a shadow across her face and she shook her head. Pulling himself up against the headboard, Reddin watched her closely as he voiced a suggestion.

"Will you let me touch you as you have touched me, freely and without reservation? Would that give you pleasure?"

This time a sudden rush of color tinged her cheeks, face, and covered her neck and the portion of her chest visible beneath the open-necked blouse. He prepared himself for rejection, but with a rush of thanks, he watched as she pulled the blouse over her head and used it to cover her breasts.

"Do you promise to stop if . . . if I ask it of you?"

"Are you frightened of me, or of yourself?" he countered.

"A bit of both," she confessed with a crooked smile, and he smiled at her courage, which never seemed to falter.

"Then I give you my word, just as I did our first night together."

Without taking her eyes off him, she lay down on the mattress and remained stiff as a poker, her face frozen with fear, her eyes wide and slightly glazed, looking like nothing so much as a human sacrifice to a vengeful god. Sighing, he slid down to lay beside her and traced her cheekbone with a single finger.

"I'm not a stranger. I'm Reddin, the same man you kissed tonight in the dayroom, the same man you aroused only moments ago. What do you fear, blue-eyes? Your body is beautiful, long and slim, strong and supple. Surely you feel no shame at your appearance?"

"Do you truly think I'm beautiful?"

He never thought so before tonight, but the moment he said it he knew it to be true. Lovely as a fawn she seemed to him, fine-boned, slender, large-eyed and infinitely desirable.

"How can you doubt me when you've seen how my body yearns for yours? Think you a man can lie about such things?"

Her tension ebbed as he spoke sweet words of longing to her. His fingers played over her shoulders, smoothing away the rigidity of her limbs.

"Your skin is smooth and moist to the touch." Taking hold of the blouse, he pushed it aside. She released her hold on it without a struggle. "Your breasts are tender and fill my palms just so." She flinched and then lay still as he touched her nipples and watched them swell between his fingertips.

"Will you kiss me?"

Her simple request touched him to his heart, and wrapping his arms around her, he pulled her close to him, kissing her soft, full lips. Once she understood what he wanted, her mouth parted, and he kissed her deeply, aware that her body had lost its stiffness and moved willingly towards his. Continuing to kiss her, reveling in the taste of her mouth, the play of her hair over his face, he ran his hand over her ribs and down her loins, feeling the line of her hips and the curve of her buttocks. Her breath came faster now as he kissed a pathway to her breasts, suckling her and hearing for the first time her sounds of pleasure. Taking his time, with infinite care, he ran lips and hands over her, stopping from time to time to refresh her lips with another kiss, reminding her that it was him who touched her with such intimacy, and heard her answering coos of contentment as she stroked his hair and the skin of his neck and shoulders. Taking nothing except what she offered freely, he felt her open to him, unfolding to his hands and mouth leaf by leaf, petal by petal.

Her legs parted of her own accord and he ran his fingers between them, marveling at the satiny texture of her thighs and the strength of her arousal as his hand moved to find her private places, hidden places he guessed no man had touched before. A cry escaped her, signaling her readiness even as she pressed her loins urgently against his hand, wanting more of his touch than his fingers could provide.

They were lying side by side. Now he moved her gently onto her back and raised himself over her, her thighs spreading naturally to receive him, her hips lifting slightly, issuing her welcome, and speaking plainly of her need for him. Just then, her eyes flew open, and instead of the passionate invitation he anticipated, there was only terror.

"Stop!" It was almost a scream as she pushed him away, shouting out a denial of everything her body promised him. "You promised you would stop! Please, please stop!"

Stunned, aghast at her near hysteria, hurt by her rejection, he lifted himself off her and stood by the bed, the stones cold and unforgiving under his bare feet. Taking a blanket from the chest, he wrapped it around his shoulders. She curled up in a tight ball, her arms shielding herself from view. Pity turned to anger, for he had done nothing deserving of such treatment.

"You must explain yourself, Lillas. I didn't force or compel you in any way. You cannot deny that you wanted me."

He could barely make out her response.

"It's true I wanted you."

Tired and troubled, he sat on the bed and willed her to communicate.

"Then you must tell me why you refused me. How am I to know what I did wrong if you say nothing?"

Pulling at the bedclothes scattered at the foot of the bed, she wrapped them tightly about her and then looked at him, blue eyes swimming in tears that remained stubbornly unshed.

"I opened my eyes and you were on top of me. The thought of being . . . covered . . . it frightens me."

"Covered?"

What did she mean by such a word? It was an expression reserved for the mating of animals and caused him to shiver with disgust. There had been nothing bestial about his actions and he resented the accusation. Seeing his reaction, a dry sob shook her and she turned away from him, burying her head in the pillow that had been discarded during their love-play.

"What am I to do, Lillas?"

A few more sobs made her form quake under the bedclothes.

"You . . . you must wait for me."

"Then there is hope that in time you'll come to me?"

"Yes."

"Is that a promise? I need your word, for you've left me with nothing else."

"A promise?"

There was a long pause. At last she spoke.

"I promise I will come to you . . . in time."

As the candles burnt out and the fire crumbled into red-orange ash, despair overcame him as he lay tense and lonely on the huge bed. For the first time since entering the Maze, Reddin despaired, for he could do no more than he had done tonight. For the first time since reaching manhood he sought to give more than he took and still it was not enough. Somewhere he must find patience and compassion, yet everything within him was bruised and painful to the touch. He had failed Lillas, failed her in some way that escaped him, failed her to the point that he doubted he would have the courage to try again. Burying his head in the pillow, he pulled the coverlet around him and settled himself for sleep, hoping that it might quell the emptiness inside him. Without her promise, he might have wept. Holding that pledge like a talisman, he waited for the dawn.

Lillas would come to him . . . in time.

FAR ABOVE THE sleeping city, high on the ramparts that rose like a sheer cliff above the valley floor, a darkened figure haunted the shadows of a watchtower. A white banner, all signs of heraldry hidden by its thick folds, hung limp and lifeless in the thick night air. From time to time a watchman's all clear sang out in the city below as did the occasional jarring cry of a night bird restless for the dawn.

A warning brought her, penetrating her dreams and fitful slumber. As insidious as a fever, as furtive as a hunter silently stalking unsuspecting prey, the strength of her premonition caused her to rise, dress, and mount the tower steps, pulling her robes tight around her, grateful that their black hues blended effortlessly with the murkiness of this ill-favored night.

As her eyes adjusted to the darkness, she squinted toward the northwest, training her eyes over the plotted fields, past the open pastures, and on to the wooded hills beyond, where campfires glowed, fires that had not been there at dusk.

Hesione had hoped for ten days. Seth gave her five.

Chapter 15

The Iron Fist

PUFFING UP THE hundred steps that led to the Eighteenth Mother's private tower, Prax ran over the siege preparations in his mind. Five days since Didion's warning; two since the arrival of Seth's army. Not much time, but warning enough to inform the Guild Assembly, call in the outlying farmers, re-stable the cavalry reserves in makeshift stables erected in the parks, and send out as many patrols as Prax could spare from the defense of the city to reconnoiter to the north and east and form infiltration parties able to watch their jailers at close range. He shed blood over that decision; hating the thought of dividing his forces, yet knowing cunning eyes and ears spread throughout Seth's troops would serve him better than soldiers manning the watchtowers.

The loss of Hume's troop hit him hard, harder than he would have guessed. Over the course of his years as Commander he'd lost men aplenty, some of them friends from childhood or his years spent in the Maze as monitor and trainer, but never forty at one time, and never killed with such vengeful malice. He'd ridden hard with a hand-picked corps of veterans to find Hume's campsite. To a man they'd been sickened by the hacked and mutilated corpses spread at random under the lifeless trees. It was a long-standing custom for the Legion to bring their dead home. Standing among their bloodied remains, he decided they must be fired — seeing them would only increase the grief of their relatives and fan the panic that was already coursing through the city.

So far the panic was controllable — a few incidents of looting, primarily foodstuffs and staples; one fistfight between an irate farmer and the Legionnaire in charge of finding quarters for the flood of immigrants who poured in daily from the surrounding countryside; and assorted family disputes caused by overcrowding. Tubal astonished everyone by voluntarily taking over emergency rationing, water supplies, and was currently issuing mandates concerning the supervision of fuel usage by each residence, shop, and guild. Prax had just passed his rotund, pretentious presence on his way back from the northern gate, and listened as he berated a fellow guild member for hoarding charcoal, Tubal indignant at the thought that a member of his own guild would stoop to such perfidy. Seeing Prax, Tubal halted in mid-rebuke to address him.

"What news, Commander?"

"Nothing's decided, Tubal. When we know, you'll be the first to hear."

"How is she?"

The jerk of Tubal's head toward the northwest tower indicated the subject of his question. Prax mustered up a confident smile.

"Waiting and watching."

"She's very young," was Tubal's even-voiced reply. Prax was instantly on the defensive, narrowing his eyes at the President's implication.

"Young in years, old in wisdom. If you have doubts as to the Eighteenth Mother's competence, you'd best express them now. If the citizens sense hesitation on any of our parts, we'll soon have a worse situation inside the walls than we have beyond them."

Tubal retreated immediately, turning pompous at Prax's insinuation.

"No doubts, Commander, none at all! I, uh, I only suggested that she, uh, she hasn't a great deal of experience concerning a siege of, uh, this proportion."

"Do any of us?"

Quailing under Prax's decidedly unfriendly stare, Tubal adjusted his robes of office and stroked his waxed goatee, clearly anxious to end this unfortunate discussion.

"No, no, of course not! Pardon my oversight."

Not caring if Tubal saw his disgust, Prax continued toward the Maze, hearing over his shoulder a stream of abuse aimed at the hapless man left to receive the considerable weight of Tubal's ire.

Reaching the top of the stairs, Prax paused for a moment, preparing himself, and then marched over to the group gathered around the Eighteenth Mother. A stiff wind blew continually on the towers that rose above the valley. Black, green, and saffron robes fluttered in the wintry breeze. Kazur had abandoned his usual robes and stood attired in regular Legion issue, causing a brief smile to cross Prax's face as he recalled the young ernani from Endlin he met during his first bout of duty in the Maze. Kazur might be a famous scholar, but he was a wicked man with a knife and cagey to boot. Kazur's keen ears heard Prax's approach above the wail of the wind and drew the attention of the others to his return.

The Eighteenth Mother searched his face, her shoulders slumping as she read the failure of his mission. Turning away to resume her watch, she let Kazur lead the questioning.

"What says Seth today?"

"The same as yesterday. The girl or a siege. No treaties, no bargains, no bribes, and no answers to any of my questions. He added a vow that not a single living creature would survive in a ten mile radius around the city. Any travelers, whether citizens or no, will be executed under the same edict."

"Can he do it?"

Prax took his time, re-checking the encampment below where Seth's army had already destroyed every fence and were now making bonfires of the orchards they'd cut down yesterday, the green wood sending columns of acrid smoke billowing up toward the overcast sky. Three hundred cavalry and five hundred on foot, wagon-loads of supplies, easy access to the many streams and brooks that careened down into the valley, free-ranging livestock impossible to house within the city, and wild game in the hills to the west and east. Try as he might, Prax couldn't imagine better conditions for a successful siege, knowledge that sat heavy on his heart.

"In his situation, I could make good his threat. In fact, it's an excellent strategy. Eight hundred men will soon grow restless. With this plan, he'll keep them sharp and fit, sending out different patrols everyday while the bulk remain here, rested and eating better than they ever ate in Agave. He'll have no deserters, of that I'm certain."

"Ranier, you inspected the granaries and water supplies this morning. What did you find?"

The healing partners stood with hands held fast, green robes billowing out from under their heavy cloaks, Nadia composed and mild-eyed, Ranier functioning with his usual efficiency.

"Thanks to the harvest, the granaries are well-stocked. As we speak, the Forge makes cisterns to catch rainwater and every household will be issued one. Well-water must be carefully rationed. Tubal is implementing my suggestion that citizens be asked to curtail baths and limit laundry to one washing every other week. Everyone's been instructed to boil drinking water."

"That will take fuel. We've still one or maybe two moons of cold weather," Prax objected, only to have Ranier observe him with a stern frown.

"Better that we huddle under blankets than face disease raging out of control."

A quiet voice cut through their bickering.

"How long can we survive?"

All heads turned to the Eighteenth Mother, who maintained her position at the battlements, her back straight, hands gripping the stones in front of her. Feeling the others bow to his authority, Prax answered.

"Three moons without undue hardship if everyone cooperates. Two more before starvation sets in. And that long only if we have steady rains. Without them, three at the most."

"And if we fight?"

That calmly spoken question sent a shiver through Prax and elicited a gasp from Chryse, who turned unbelieving eyes on the Eighteenth Mother. Kazur's face turned to rock and the healers bowed their heads, unwilling to countenance such a question. For five hundred years, Pelion had never

engaged in open warfare, never attacked unless provoked beyond their
ability to protect their surrounding citizenry, and never, in those five centuries
of relative peace, had they contemplated marching armed forces out the
gates to fight under their banner. Yet Prax would not deny her an answer.

"A chance at winning if we steal out under cover of night and slaughter
them without mercy, hoping they lose heart and make a run for it. Even so,
it would take every Legionnaire and as many volunteers as we could muster
and still we'd be substantially outnumbered. I'd estimate our casualties at
two hundred dead and twice that number wounded, more if we're discovered
while opening the gates."

Another question was posed, this time to the Head Scribe.

"Kazur, what would happen if Seth were to be killed in such a battle?"

His reply was immediate and flatly decisive.

"Scarphe would be out, another would be in, probably the Aeson's second
cousin on his father's side."

The Eighteenth Mother turned her back on the assembled forces of Agave
and faced her Council, green eyes clear and focused, lacking the indecision
that had haunted her for the past few days. Prax relaxed. Even without
knowing what she would say, he blessed the fact that at last they could settle
on a plan. Nothing troubled him so much as lack of direction.

"Prax, ask Flavius to bring Lillas to me."

Heads jerked up, mouths opened in protest. A raised palm silenced them.
Chryse alone found the courage to override that commanding gesture.

"You can't surrender her to him! For all we know, he plans to kill or
enslave her! It's unworthy of us, of you, a betrayal of everything we believe,
of everything we stand for!"

A look of tenderness and vast affection appeared on the youthful face of
the Eighteenth Mother. She smiled a smile of such warmth and understanding
that Chryse halted her barrage, struggling to understand this enigma robed
in black, a leader who faced mutiny with love in her eyes.

"Chryse of the faithful heart, I'm thankful for your presence among us.
In the face of adversity, you stand unafraid, refusing to set aside our principles
despite conditions that must lead us to destruction or starvation. Like you,
I wrestled in my heart. Now the way is clear, for we have been summoned.
Come."

At that simply stated invitation, the Council of Pelion found themselves
transported to a vista they had never seen, a dark plain unpeopled, unknown,
unimagined, a place lit by a golden sun and crescent moon which hung side
by side in a cloudless, starless sky.

The whispers began concurrently with their arrival, voices hushed with
solemnity, suggesting nothing so much as the wind rustling through dry
leaves, the cascade of water in a fountain, and to Kazur's ears, the rush and

ebb of ocean waves. At first the sounds were nonsensical, at once blurred and synchronous; with the passage of time, which seemed strangely fixed, unconnected with things temporal, individual voices emerged, many of them female, although a lyric tenor sang with them, as did a bass voice resonant with purpose.

"Trust in the prophecy," advised an unknown voice cracked with age, ripe with mysticism. "'The light which flickers like a flame' holds the answer," was spoken in the voice of one beloved by Ranier, Nadia, and Prax, who held their breath at the sound of the Seventeenth Mother's voice. "Watch and wait; fear not the darkness." This woman's speech was measured, lovely bell tones that reminded Chryse of the voice of a teacher she once had. "'The candle of despair will be lit,' so I have written and so it will come to pass," was intoned by another woman and Hesione welcomed the Fifteenth Mother, the source of the prophecy for the new age. Finally, the voices rising to a crescendo were surmounted by a rich bass voice raised in a wordless paean of praise, glorious in its perfect trust in a future for this newest of worlds they inhabited, a world like, yet unlike, the one from which they came. A world the Sowers promised and provided. A world they must make their own.

At the height of this oratorio, the glittering orbs above their heads blinked out, the whispering plain vanished, and they stood again on the stone outpost, the high see of Pelion.

"We will do as they advise and put ourselves in the hands of 'the light that flickers like a flame.' Lillas' decision will be ours. I will speak with her alone."

ALTHOUGH SHE WAS apprised daily of Lillas' well-being, Hesione had not seen the girl since the day she stood restlessly beside Reddin on the pedestal in the Sanctum, shifting her weight from foot to foot, speaking her single phrase of gift-giving after a furtive peek at the man by her side, who nodded his encouragement before turning a radiant face to Hesione, his pride in his success evident in the set of his jaw and his uplifted chin.

The woman who stood before her now was equally as uncomfortable as she had been five weeks ago, her eyes shifting as she tried to avoid acknowledging Hesione's presence, her slim body poised for flight, as if with a single word Hesione could put her in motion and she would rise on the winter wind, wheeling and floating in the perfect freedom she craved. The lives of ten thousand and more rested on her shoulders, which hunched self-consciously under the burden of Hesione's gaze.

"Lillas, I must speak with you, but first I must show you something. Come here, if you please."

Motioning her toward the edge of the battlement, Hesione stepped back at her approach, allowing her a full and unprejudiced look at the scene below them. Hesione watched her hands grip the stone walls and then tighten until the joints whitened from strain. After a silence pregnant with emotions too varied for Hesione to distinguish, Lillas' lips formed words, her voice barely a whisper.

"They've found me."

Dread, desperation, fear, even terror were to be found in those three words. Hesione's pity, already profound, magnified as she considered the ernani who looked down on the fluttering banners of the clenched iron fist.

"Lord Seth of Agave sends us a message. He demands the return of Lillas, the daughter of the Aeson, who, he says, is gravely ill."

Not bothering to comment on the revelation of her true identity, Lillas turned unbelieving eyes to Hesione.

"It can't be true! My father's in the best of health. He's never been sick, and even if he was, my healer serves my mother and could cure any illness he might suffer."

It was on the tip of Hesione's tongue to reveal the true nature of her father's condition. At the last second, she reconsidered. If Lillas was to choose, she must choose without benefit of any other knowledge than that which could be plainly proven.

"So says Lord Seth."

"He lies!" was issued in a snarl of hatred as Lillas returned to her view from the turret, her skirts snapping angrily in the breeze.

"What does he want of you, Lillas?"

"Everything," and then more bitterly, "and nothing."

Hesione waited as the girl struggled to ask the questions on which everything was balanced.

"What will he do if I refuse?"

It was characteristic of Lillas that she never once considered that she might be forced out against her will. Admiring her self-confidence, which even after the blow of seeing Seth was unabated, Hesione settled down to work, offering the facts, intent that she not lead or influence this decision, for it was not hers to make.

"He has sworn to obliterate every sign of life within ten miles of Pelion and hold the city in a state of siege until you are surrendered. No one will be allowed entrance or exit through the gates, and anyone who journeys here, no matter how ignorant they may be of our situation, will be put to the sword."

Wide blue eyes turned to Hesione, pinning her as surely as if Lillas had loosed an arrow at a straw target in the arena.

"And any ernani who comes for the gift. . ."

". . . will be slaughtered on sight."

Her gaze never altered, although she swallowed hard before lifting her chin to a position of rare dignity.

"And so you want me to leave."

Difficult as it was not to advise Lillas to stay within the Maze until the walls caved in from the force of battering rams, Hesione matched her control, replying evenly:

"On the contrary. We are prepared for a siege and should weather it well enough. I brought you here for one reason and one reason alone—to hear your choice, spoken of your own free will. If you tell me you wish to stay, that you are committed to walking the Path, you may stay until the gift is achieved."

"And if it is achieved, what then?"

"Many things will become clearer if you complete the Path, but of none of these may I speak. Also, given time, the situation outside these walls may undergo changes we cannot foretell. We must live day by day, walking through the labyrinth we call life."

Making no reply, Lillas crossed to the other side of the battlement, looking out over the city below, a few inhabitants hurrying along broad tree-lined promenades, the domed roof of the Guild Hall rising against the leaden skies. Here she could hear and see the tumbling waters of the many fountains spread about the city and wondered at the sight of them, for she had never seen a fountain before. Only a waterfall, she reminded herself, and only when I turned south to find this city.

"Is it true? Will you place all of this in jeopardy—the children, the House of Healing, the great libraries and halls of learning, the galleries and theatres, shops and guilds the women speak of—all to be sacrificed for one person, one woman who has never done anything for anyone other than herself?"

In that moment, Hesione blessed Reddin and all he had accomplished. This was not the Lillas who had burst through the door demanding attention four moons ago, nor was it the Lillas who had cursed a serving woman only three days before. The third gift remained, but she had made a transformation of a different kind. This was the wisdom of those on the whispering plain, for truly, Lillas held within herself the answer that would scourge the beast of the west. The way remained unclear, but her feet were firmly planted on the Path.

"We believe the ernani come here for an important, even vital, purpose. For each of them, we would sacrifice the luxuries of our daily lives."

"And if I stay, all the ernani who come, as Halys came, and Fenja, Altug, Jarod, Stym—all of them will be slaughtered and soon the Maze will stand empty." When Hesione made no reply, Lillas shook her head, utterly rejecting the vision she had just described. "I will not be the cause of their deaths nor will I stand between those like Halys who must return to their people. I will go."

"And what will become of Reddin?"

Foolishly, Hesione assumed Lillas forgot him in the contingencies of the moment. When, at the mere utterance of his name, the girl's face turned stark white, Hesione realized the truth. From the first moment Lillas had balanced this decision with her loss of him.

"He must do without me." Her face was stern, seemingly unmoved as she continued on, pushing out the words. "He can't come where I must go. I can't protect him there and he might . . . he might be hurt."

"Will he not be more hurt if you leave the Maze?"

Her eyes were dry and fixed on a point removed from the valley, far beyond the western horizon. "He wants the gift badly, so badly he's willing to put up with me." Her lips trembled as she attempted a smile. "He believes the gift will make him a better healer, and there's nothing he wants so much as the healing of others. He will recover."

"You might be surprised what he wants if you put him to the test . . ."

"No!" Regaining control, Lillas continued more quietly. "No. I want your promise, your solemn oath that you will not tell him who . . ." her voice grew bitter with self-hatred, "or what . . . I am. He needs no test. He is good and true and I will not involve him in a world that has no regard for healers except as expensive slaves reserved for the nobility. Let him stay here, where he can achieve what he deserves."

Hesione spoke as gently as she could, loathe to hurt the girl, but insistent that she fully recognize what her choice would mean to the one left behind.

"But Lillas, surely you see that if you leave, Reddin must return to his home. Two must tread the path together . . ."

Lillas grabbed her hands, a move Hesione was unprepared for and one which unsettled her since her mind instantly reacted to the flesh touching hers. Curbing her thoughts, which strove to cross the barrier and enter a mind forbidden to her, Hesione struggled to regain her composure, hearing the plea already in progress.

". . . and let him come again when he is ready! Surely you could make this happen, especially since it's not his fault! Tell the others you had to promise me this to make me leave! Tell them anything, but don't make him go through another Trial!"

Hesione nodded, sensing the instinctual goodness of Lillas' hasty heart, intent not on her own fate, but that of another.

"If this is what you want, I will make it possible for Reddin to join with another ernani here in the Maze."

Lillas' eyes had been bright with hope, filled with happiness at the thought that she could bestow on Reddin the prize he sought. At the mention of another woman who would live with him, join with him, and with whom he would achieve the gift he hungered for, Lillas winced and closed her eyes, whispering through her agony.

"Truly, it is what I want."

"Then you have my word."

There remained only one question to be discussed.

"Will you tell him, or shall I? I warn you, he will not willingly assent to your decision. Perhaps it would be best to leave without seeing him . . ."

Hesione was cut off.

"No. I must see him one last time. I must make sure he'll forget me."

Beneath the pain of that statement was clear-cut resolve, and Hesione's pity shifted from the girl beside her to the man who would bear the brunt of her decision. How did Lillas plan to make Reddin forget her, a woman he'd lived with for nearly three moons in an intimacy that rivaled few matings other than those of fully adept couples? As she watched Lillas straighten her shoulders and smooth out her gown, the fire of determination in her narrowed, tearless eyes sent a flash of illumination through Hesione's thoughts.

Lillas had resolved to destroy Reddin's love for her in the hope that he would turn quickly toward another. As Lillas ran a steady hand through her tangled hair and strode purposefully toward the tower steps, Hesione doubted not that Reddin would come to hate Lillas by the closing of this day, never suspecting that her greatest gift to him would be the ability to mate with another.

What lengths will we go to protect the beloved? Lillas' unspoken reply echoed in the chambers of Hesione's mind.

"Whatever lengths are necessary."

STRUGGLING AGAINST THE oily limbs wrapped around him, trying to maneuver his legs at the same time his arm was being twisted nearly out of its socket, Reddin heard Altug's grunt from someplace behind his left shoulder blade with a mixture of relief and disgust.

"Give it up, scholar. You're pinned."

The instant Reddin relaxed, the pressure eased and Altug rolled off him, landing lightly on his feet and reaching down to offer a helping hand.

"One thing's for certain, you're more aggressive than you used to be. Is she the cause?"

It took a minute for Reddin to understand the question. After realizing the compliment offered to both Lillas and himself, he acknowledged it with studied neutrality as he brushed off the dirt clinging to his sweat-covered skin.

"If you say so."

"She, Lillas, is . . . remarkable."

Reddin waited as the mountain man shifted his weight, uncomfortable with what he had begun but determined to persevere.

"I didn't mean to hit Lillas quite so hard the other night at the Gathering. Valeria says I was cruel to her."

Altug seemed to want Reddin to disagree. When no comment was forthcoming, he shrugged and reached for a blanket to wrap around his shoulders.

"It was her manner, I think, her tone of command. We mountain people don't take kindly to being told what to do."

Reddin was unwilling to think about that night.

"If you want to beg pardon, you must speak to her. I'm not her errand boy."

His tone must have been sharper than he intended for Altug stepped back as if slapped, turned on his heel, and walked away.

Curse the woman and everything about her! It was not enough that she made his life a misery; she was capable of ruining other people's lives as well. Reddin's irritation grew as he looked around the arena only to discover that she'd not yet arrived, nor had any of the women. After a quick survey of the progress of the other teams, he decided he had time for a brief rest before the next event and wandered over to the sidelines to sit and sulk.

The afternoon was cloudy, dismal and drear, and no one's mood seemed any better than Reddin's. Even Flavius annoyed him this afternoon by rushing him out of the library for no apparent reason at least an hour before his study time was up, although if truth be told, he'd had plenty of time to read lately since Lillas had retreated into a shell, or more descriptively, under a rock. He'd been proud of the way he'd handled himself, matching coolness with coolness, refusing to tease her out of her melancholy, punishing her the way she always punished him, only to lie beside her last night, long after they'd retired, and listen to her cry into her pillow, muffled sounds of woe that made him grit his teeth, unwilling to believe that she, who never cried, never shed a tear in his presence, was actually as miserable as himself.

A long body dropped on the grass beside him, interrupting his guilty thoughts. Dysponteus favored him with a friendly grin that did nothing to improve Reddin's foul humor.

"Where are they, Reddin? Halys? Lillas? Thaisa? I asked Strato and he nearly bit my head off. Did Lillas say anything this morning about not coming?"

Lillas said nothing at all this morning or the last two mornings, but there was no reason for Reddin to confess that fact to Dysponteus. Before he could reply, Adrastus lowered himself beside Dysponteus, grabbing a handful of his shaggy hair to pull back his head and wrapping his other arm around his neck in a playful hold.

"What's the meaning of all this hair? Just because you live with a Lapithian doesn't mean you can't visit a barber once in awhile. Perhaps I need to escort you, or do the deed myself."

Looking decidedly uncomfortable at Adrastus' suggestion, Dysponteus muttered:

"I'm growing it for Halys."

Adrastus roared. Reddin couldn't help smiling at Dysponteus' admission.

"So, Halys prefers long hair, does she?! Likes to have something to hold onto when she's riding, I'll wager!"

At that ribald remark, Dysponteus' eyes narrowed and his voice became dangerously quiet.

"I'm sure I didn't hear you correctly, Adrastus. Perhaps you don't understand that I'm growing my hair so my appearance won't shock her tribe. You saw Jarod and Stym when they arrived. If I'm to live among Halys's people of Eastern Lapith, I must honor their customs."

"Live among them!" Clearly astonished, Adrastus sputtered in alarm. "What about your family, your friends! Think, man! What do you know of riding horses and tending herds? You apprenticed at the Forge! Do you think you'll be content counting sheep and milking goats?"

"I've thought of little else since I first met Halys."

His anger forgotten, Dysponteus rested his back against the wooden planks of the reviewing stand and looked up to the overcast sky, choosing his words as if testing them on his companions, rehearsing, thought Reddin, for the day when he would repeat this speech to his family.

"I won't be herding, of that I'm sure. Once I'm admitted to the tribe, I'll build a forge—my own forge, and soon I'll be making swords, shoeing horses, turning wheel rims, anything and everything that will defend and enrich the tribe. I'll teach not only how to forge iron, but how to fight slavers with swords and shields."

"Won't you be lonely, Dysponteus?" asked Reddin, suddenly intent on hearing that particular question answered.

"Lonely?" Dysponteus dismissed Reddin's question with a quick shake of his shaggy head. "I'll never be lonely with Halys by my side. And besides," he grinned at them, "perhaps I didn't mention that I'll be a chieftain's son! Yes, Dysponteus of Pelion, the ordinary son of an ordinary man, will be a leader of the tribe, responsible for their well-being and continued survival: master of my own forge, a chieftain, Halys' mate, and the father of her children."

Reddin closed his eyes, envy twisting around his heart. Dysponteus had just broken the silence each man feared to break, confessing that he and Halys had offered the third gift. Now they waited at the end of the Path, trusting that the gift would be given as promised.

With an excited yelp, Dorian threw himself onto a patch of dead grass near Adrastus.

"Have you heard the latest rumors?"

Adrastus' vexation matched Reddin's. Even on the best of days, Dorian was a pest.

"We've no interest in your gossip. Besides, Dysponteus' news is all I care to handle in the course of one day."

"What news, Dysponteus?"

"I'm going to Lapith to live with Halys' tribe."

"Felicitations! Maybe we can travel east together!"

Adrastus turned to the wiry prankster who liked nothing better than to make mischief.

"That isn't funny, Dorian. Don't jest about such serious matters."

Offended, Dorian remembered he'd never liked the ever-haughty Adrastus. It was time to take him down a peg.

"Who's jesting, oh mighty engineer? Do you think Dysponteus is the only one eager to see new lands, new peoples? By the end of this year I'll be lying on the sand, listening to the waves, able to handle a boat as easily as I jump a hurdle. From what Fenja tells me, it's unlike anything I've ever imagined—islands dotting the ocean, waves breaking against white powder beaches, exotic flowers and strange animals we've never heard of. And I'll catalogue every island, explore every cave and inlet!"

Crowing in delight, he turned a backward somersault and walked on his hands.

"Think of it! An Chartist mapping new lands!" Tumbling to the ground, he grew more serious. "Of course I'll teach her people to read and write our language, and try to evolve a system to record their language if I can. Fenja teaches me, but without a dictionary or a grammar, it's tough work."

Reddin hadn't thought it possible to become more depressed, but Dorian's energetic recital pushed him into the slough of despondency. Adrastus, struck dumb by these new developments, rose to his feet, his back stiff with disapproval, and strode off. Dysponteus chuckled to himself before addressing Dorian, who was currently trying to place his legs over his shoulders and grunting under the strain of his contortions.

"What rumors, Dorian?"

"Ah! I nearly forgot." Looking around, he drew closer and dropped his voice. "There's something wrong in the city. I overheard the servants talking after the midday meal and caught something about rationing before they saw me. I tried to worm it out of them but Strato came along and chewed me up and spit me out. If you want my opinion, they're keeping mute to hide something the Eighteenth Mother doesn't want known."

"You know the rules," Reddin snapped, his patience gone. "No information in or out for five moons, or as long as it takes to complete the Path. If the Eighteenth Mother doesn't want it discussed, I suggest you keep your mouth shut."

Offended by Reddin's unaccustomed bluntness, Dorian turned to Dysponteus with a frown.

"What's wrong with the scholar?"

"The same thing that's wrong with everyone here. We're changing, changing in ways we never dreamed. Now, lay off him and move on. I'm going to rest and pray that Strato forgets my existence in the course of the general chaos."

Dorian had been gone a quarter of an hour before Reddin gathered courage enough to speak.

"Did Halys ask you, Dysponteus, or did you offer?"

One eye opened and then shut again. There was a long silence and then a low-voiced reply.

"It happened without words. We were . . . we were joined together, you see, and then we knew. It wasn't one giving or another taking. We were one."

The arena echoed with the noise of training, male noises—bellows and shouting, curses and grunts. The women's absence brought out the worst in them, Reddin decided, even though Lillas could swear with the best of them and often did. Still, the women's presence, elusive as it might be to describe, made the arena less sterile, less rough and primitive. His thoughts wandering over these speculations, he came at last to an understanding, something that had stymied him for the past three days. Dysponteus expressed it as something different from giving and taking; Reddin reinterpreted it in his own terms. He had thought Lillas the competitive one, intent on winning despite the cost. Now he discovered that he was equally as competitive, thinking only of winning her—her compliance, her affections, and the delights of her body, all of the things necessary to obtain the gift. Yet there could be no winner in what they attempted, for the simple reason that there could be no loser. Somehow, they must become one.

AS THE FAINT brassy notes of the evening trumpet invaded the quiet of the cell, Lillas lifted her head from the pillow where she'd lain for the past few hours, alone on the great bed, awaiting Reddin's return. The Eighteenth Mother gave her permission to take any or all of her possessions, but she had reached the sad conclusion that there was nothing here she needed. The only thing she wanted was Reddin, and he must be left behind.

The pillow was damp with her tears. Fluffing it with a few pats, she tossed the wet side against the headboard. Rising, she examined her wrinkled gown and decided half-heartedly that she must change. It was time to resume her game, the one she played upon leaving Imarus, and it would not do for Reddin to find her tear-stained and mussed. In the interminable slowness of these afternoon hours, she'd studied her victim, laid her plans, and determined her role.

Knowing him as she did, it was heart-breakingly simple, to choose the course of action that would best make him despise her. And worst of all, the events of the past three days, days that she'd passed in search of her soul, eliminating everything but the core of her being, uncovering the secret place where lived Lillas of Agave, these melancholy days would prove to him the finality of her actions rather than the monumental discovery she'd made on a journey into her inner self. Reddin would never know that in the last three days she had at last understood that she loved him, an emotion she fought against, denied, ridiculed, and ignored, but something that made her better than she was without him. With Reddin, for the first time, she knew completeness.

Her eyes burned again with another surge of tears and she wiped them away, helpless to dam the tide of misery that claimed her. It had ever been a point of pride with her that she never cried, yet in the past few days her eyes continually filled with tears, making her wonder if there was some point at which all tears must end, if finally there would be no moisture left within her, for once Reddin passed the threshold, there could be no more tears.

Rinsing her face with water, she blotted her eyes with a cloth, and paused in front of the wardrobe, listlessly eyeing the dresses hanging from the pegs, not caring what she wore.

An overpowering feeling of loneliness overcame her as she donned a grey-blue gown, trusting the color to conceal her gloom. Brushing out her hair, curling the ends around her fingers so they formed thick ringlets that dangled about her ears, she heard the first sounds of footsteps in the corridor and readied herself for the door to open.

Lillas never noticed that in the charade to follow, no drop of moisture threatened her disguise.

IMPATIENT WITH FLAVIUS' slowness, Reddin pushed open the door and walked confidently into the room, searching the cell until he found her, standing restlessly by the unlit hearth.

"I missed you this afternoon. Where were you?"

"Do I owe you explanations for my actions?"

The coldness of her reply made him retreat a step. Running his fingers through his hair, still wet from his bath, he studied her. She'd turned away with a toss of her head and was noisily stacking her books and tablets, cleaning the nib of her quill pen, and tightening the cover on the inkwell. This done, she gathered everything in her arms and deposited them next to his papers.

"Have you finished your studies for tomorrow?" came his more careful observation, answered this time by a derisive snort.

"Yes, I've finished. Finished forever."

Something in her manner disturbed him even more than the thought that she had for some reason decided to end her studies. He'd thought she'd begun to enjoy them, for her mind was sharp and she quickly grasped concepts if they were clearly explained, but something must have happened, some setback or disaster in the classroom for her to react in this manner.

"Forever . . . ?"

"I need study no longer, and for that I'm grateful. It was a tiring affair. I'll have no need of books in the future."

"In the future . . . ?"

Like a simpleton, he kept repeating her last words, for he found himself totally at sea, a sea that threatened to drown him.

"Stop questioning me! I've had enough of questions and soul-searching, demands and judgments. In the past few days I've made my decision. I spoke to the Eighteenth Mother this afternoon. I'm leaving the Maze."

He found himself sitting on the bed, unsure of how he came to be there. It was unthinkable, absolutely incredible, to think that she could leave, could even consider leaving, without discussing such a step with him.

"Why . . . why would you do such a thing?"

Her reply was sharp and he cringed under its biting sting.

"What reasons have I to stay? I'm tired, I tell you, tired of having my will forever denied, tired of rules and regulations and senseless requests. I've no use for this gift, if, indeed there is a gift, and so it seems pointless to stay."

If she had attacked him, he would have welcomed it, knowing he was partially to blame for the wretchedness of the past few days. For her to question the gift infuriated him. No matter that she had given her second gift; she remained a barbarian. With all the self-control he could muster, he set aside his anger, knowing from experience that nothing would be gained by responding to her insults. He must reason with her.

"And what of us, Lillas, and our joining? Does it mean as little to you as the gift?"

She'd turned to the wardrobe and opened the door, busily searching through the clothes for something. Her answer was thrown carelessly over her shoulder.

"Since the reason for our joining was a requirement of the gift, I see no reason to continue. I've known since the first day in the arena you found me not to your taste and you're certainly not the man I would have chosen for myself. We'll both be better off, free to find someone more to our liking."

She removed her cloak from the back peg and was beating it, cleaning off the dust that had gathered over the course of three moons. In four running steps he was across the room, pulling it away from her, grabbing her upper arms and shaking her, too furious to credit what he was hearing.

"You see no reason to continue? You dismiss our time together with a careless shrug and a toss of your head? Do you dismiss your promise as easily, the only promise you've ever given me?"

He stopped shaking her so as to hear her response, but kept a tight grip on her, fearing she'd run or hide or somehow escape his anger. Instead, she raised crystal clear eyes to him, lifted her chin, and replied:

"I made it under duress. You pressured me and it was the only way I could avoid joining with you. I don't consider such a promise binding."

Searching those eyes, full of disdain for a memory he'd come to cherish, his rage turned to loathing. Then, using the same superior tones she'd used to berate the serving woman at the Gathering, she ordered him to let her go.

"Remove your hands, healer."

Opening his hands, he watched her slide away. He looked at his empty palms, almost choking on a rising flood of bitterness. She had played him for a fool from their first moment together, letting him believe she wanted something more than her own willfulness, seeming to change while underneath she remained the arrogant, vulgar, slave-owning savage he'd first seen loosing arrows into a straw target. Like an inexperienced schoolboy, he'd taken everything at face value, never dreaming that a woman could be as heartless and uncaring as this one, who was now draping the cloak around her shoulders and heading casually for the door, taking no more than a few minutes to end what had taken three moons to create. Hating that retreating back, he spit out an order of his own.

"Wait. I have a parting gift for you."

She froze, her back toward him. Congratulating himself on the fact that she responded instantly to his icy command, he grabbed up a book from the shelf and threw it at her, the missile striking her back and falling to the floor. It must have hurt, for he'd thrown it with all his force, but she gave no cry of pain and knelt to retrieve it. As she looked up at him, the hood of the cloak framing her curls, her deceptive face still touched with loveliness, his stomach convulsed and it was all he could do to keep from retching.

"It's your book of poetry." After cradling it in her arms for a moment, her fingers running over the gilt-lettered spine, she held it out to him.

"It's yours, for I'll never read it again. The poet speaks true, it seems, but until today I didn't understand."

At her confused frown, he recited from the last stanza:

"'Whatever dyes, was not mixt equally.' We are not mixed equally and so we die."

Her face paled, and he was glad of it, proud of hurting her, of piercing through the hardness he had never truly seen until today.

Without a word she left him, the door opening instantly at her knock, and he was alone, left with nothing but the urge to rip apart the cell with his bare hands, to shred her clothing, destroy her books, pull the bed loose from its moorings and consign every memory of every moment he'd spent with her to the flames. Then, drawing a shaky, trembling breath, he found his self-control and seated himself carefully in the high-backed chair, willing his racing heart to slow and resume its regular beating.

Lillas was gone, he must leave the Maze, and the gift would not be his. But he would survive. He would never open his heart to another woman, trust a stranger, or read a love poem, but he swore to himself that he would survive.

AT THE SIXTH hour after midday, on the eighth day of the third moon of the new year, the northern gates of Pelion swung open. A hooded figure walked over the muddy ground, picking her way neatly around the puddles of standing water caused by the downpour that began at dusk and continued to drench the violated landscape of the valley of the castle. A small party of armed guards accompanied her, their leader, a bald man who wore no headgear despite the rain, carried a white flag of parley. The woman walked before them, seeming to lead them forward, her shoulders straight, her long legs carrying her swiftly toward the richly-appointed tent that stood under the banner of the iron fist.

The siege of Pelion was ended.

Chapter 16

Mother of All

STAMPING THE SNOW off his boots, Orrin rapped on the door. It was the fifth hour after midday and a late winter storm darkened the city streets. Snow flurries danced attendance on their master, the wind, which sang as it rounded the corner of each tile-covered roof. The houses, identically-shaped boxes draped in ivory velvet, resembled miniature lanterns, each of them illuminated from within by the amber blaze of tallow candles and oil-burning lamps.

Not even an unexpected cold snap could blight the spirits of the citizens of Pelion. Seven days since the end of the siege and some were still celebrating. A party of wandering revelers caroled joyfully, oblivious to the cutting wind that threw their voices back over their shoulders. Waving happily to Orrin, wishing him a good eventide, the piping of their flute reached his ears long after they passed down the street.

The door swung open. Shutting it hurriedly behind him to keep out the wind's greedy fingers, Orrin brushed melting snow off his garments. Unclasping the fastenings at the neck of his cloak, his greeting died in his throat as he observed his mother's careworn face.

"Go to him. Take no notice of his evasions."

"What is it, mother?"

Tightening her lips, she shook her head and motioned to the attic stairs. "Judge for yourself."

Bounding up the stairs, he paused at the door that normally stood open, but now was shut. When he attempted to lift the latch, he found it locked from the inside.

"Reddin, it's Orrin. Let me in."

"Come another time. I'm in no mood for visitors."

Working the latch, Orrin shoved the door with his shoulder. It didn't budge. Annoyed, and doubly so because the staircase was drafty and his feet were wet, he leaned against the door, shouting through it:

"Damn your stubbornness! If I catch a chill from the draft blowing through this accursed hallway, you'll have mother to answer to!"

Footsteps tread heavily across the floor, the door was unlatched, and the footsteps retraced their path. Shoving the door open, Orrin stepped into the attic room. Taking in the disarray which greeted him with one sweeping glance, his attention was claimed by the room's sole occupant, who sat in the leather chair before the fireplace, an ancient quilt wrapped about his shoulders.

The room was shock enough, the bed unmade, clothes and trays of uneaten food littering the floor, the desk a ramshackle of books and papers that looked as if they'd been tossed by the north wind. If the room signaled upset, the man sitting in the chair did nothing to calm Orrin's misgivings, for he seemed a ghost of his former self, his face gaunt and lined with exhaustion, as if he had not slept since leaving the Maze. An unshaven and unwashed Reddin stared aimlessly into the fire, an enormous blaze that blasted heat into every corner of the room, yet still he held the quilt together tightly at his throat as if to ward off the cold.

After removing a pile of dirty clothes from a chair at the desk, Orrin dragged it over to the hearth and sat with his legs astride, resting his forearms on the high back, studying his brother, who didn't remove his gaze from the flames. Since beginning his duties in the Maze the day after Reddin left, Orrin had been an infrequent visitor to his parent' home. The two times he'd come, long after the evening meal, Reddin hadn't answered his hesitant knock. Assuming his brother was asleep, he'd crept back down the stairs. Now he cursed himself for his inattentiveness, for he should have sensed Reddin was avoiding him on purpose. His work this afternoon was disturbed by a mental call from his mother, something she did with such rarity that he'd cancelled a counseling session and run for home, unsure of what to expect.

Nothing prepared him for the phantom who sat hunched and lifeless, staring blankly at the grate and seemingly unaware of his presence.

"Are you ill, Reddin? Should we send for a healer?"

There was no response, not the blink of an eyelid.

"If you don't answer me, I swear I'll pick you up whether you will or no, and carry you through this infernal blizzard to the House of Healing! Now, again, are you ill?"

A flicker of consciousness ran over Reddin's face, his lips twisted in a bitter smile. His mouth worked without emitting a sound, as if he couldn't recall the mechanisms of speech. At last, he rasped out a hoarse, "No."

Unconvinced, Orrin continued his interrogation.

"You look awful, smell worse, and appear not to have eaten or slept in days. If you aren't ill, what ails you?"

Bloodshot eyes found his before closing wearily, shutting out the world.

"Go away, Orrin. Leave me alone."

Wood scraped against wood as Orrin threw his chair across the room. Kneeling down, he jerked Reddin's chair away from the fire, forcing his brother to look directly at him.

"I'm not leaving, so there's no use shutting me out. If you won't answer me now, so be it. I'll camp here until you do."

Reddin grimaced, obviously believing the threat.

"You can't sit dumb forever. Sooner or later, you'll have to talk to someone, and I'd sooner it be me. So, tell me, what ails you?"

Thoughts whirled behind Reddin's eyes. Orrin considered touching those thoughts with his mind, but held back. Having left the Maze, Reddin's thoughts were no longer forbidden to members of the Council, and surely this constituted an emergency, yet Orrin felt strongly that to touch his brother in that manner would be a violation of some sort. A shiver ran down his spine as if it were being stroked by a warning hand. The feeling was strong and he obeyed it.

Ever so softly, Reddin spoke at last.

"I . . . I think I'm going mad."

Falling back onto his haunches, Orrin closed his mouth with an audible snap. Orrin knew his brother. This was no bid for pity, but a trained healer offering an honest diagnosis. Calming himself, he decided to explore that diagnosis.

"Now that you've said it, you must explain. You're a healer. Report on your condition."

Reddin had loosed his hold on the quilt and held his hands clenched in fists. At Orrin's request, he spread his fingers, wincing as if they pained him, and began to list his symptoms.

"I've no appetite. I can't read or study. I lie abed, but can't seem to sleep," He considered his hands before adding, "and the touch of another human being sickens me."

The last admission was by far the most troubling. Unsure as to how to proceed, Orrin frowned. This is your vocation, he reminded himself sternly; it's time to earn your keep.

"I know mother and father touch you rarely and you've come to understand why they refrain from doing so. Who has touched you in the past week?"

"I. . . ," he croaked, his face tight with misery, "I visited the House of Hetaeras. "

Orrin nodded, sympathetic toward the difficulties of this particular confession.

"I thought it might help somehow."

"Did you go for joining or for companionship?"

"It had been so long, you understand, so long since I . . ."

There was a painful pause. Orrin held his tongue.

"She's someone I visited before, a warm-hearted woman, quiet and understanding."

Orrin knew the hetaera Reddin was describing and agreed with his assessment. Sensing that to interrupt this story might end it before it began, he waited for Reddin to continue.

"I was fine as we began to talk, she about the siege and everyone's relief at waking to find the army gone. Then . . . then we disrobed, and I . . . I . . ."

Orrin interrupted, hoping to spare his brother's feelings.

"There's nothing abnormal about occasional impotence."

Reddin showed the first sign of life since Orrin entered the room.

"No!" he shook his head from side to side, fidgeting uncomfortably in the chair, "No, you don't understand! I . . . we never got that far. She . . she began to stroke me, love-play we've enjoyed before, and I . . . I . . .," his lips whitened and his voice lowered to a whisper, "I couldn't bear her touch. It was a ghastly sensation, bringing on a kind of nausea. My skin crawled and I could do nothing to stop it nor could I bring myself to touch her in return. When it became unbearable, I grabbed my clothes and left, unable to explain or excuse my rudeness."

"Did she remind you in some way of the ernani?"

Orrin purposefully refrained from using her name, although he knew it from Kazur's records. Reddin reacted as if he'd screamed it aloud. Rising shakily from the chair, he pulled the quilt tightly around him.

"She's nothing like Lillas! Nothing like her, I say! Do you think I'd go to a woman who reminded me of her? This has nothing to do with Lillas! She's gone and I'm well rid of her!"

He was pacing now, his bare feet kicking away the clothes and papers, shouting denials in a voice hoarse not from disuse, but from hate.

"Calm yourself and pardon my mistake. I'm relieved to hear you have no feelings for her."

Orrin wasn't much of a liar. Reddin didn't seem to be listening to him in any case. He continued pacing about the room, muttering all the while. With a sinking heart, Orrin realized that his brother resembled nothing so much as a raving madman.

"Come here and sit down. You've explained the touching. Now tell me why you can't study."

Orrin's ploy successful, Reddin returned to the chair, a ragged sigh escaping him as he readjusted the quilt.

"It's my mind. I can't explain it very well, but I'm gradually losing my ability to concentrate. I read and comprehend, and in the next moment I can't remember what I've read, as though the thoughts pass through my mind without registering in my memory."

At this point, Orrin was ready to make good his original threat and escort his brother to the House of Healing without delay. It was only as he heard the response to his next question that he began to understand what Reddin was describing.

"Now tell me why you can't sleep."

Reddin squirmed in the chair, his reluctance clear. When he tried to avoid the question by turning his head back to the fire, Orrin would have none of it.

"You've told me all the rest. Now tell me why for seven nights you've not enjoyed a moment's rest."

Grudgingly, Reddin lifted his head, not moving his eyes from the flames.

"I can't sleep because she calls to me."

"She?"

"Lillas."

"But you said you have no feelings for her . . ."

Again, flat denial.

"I've none, other than betrayal, anger, and regret for the entire time we spent together."

"Then why . . ?"

Tight lips spewed out Reddin's resentment.

"I don't know why! I only know that the moment I close my eyes to search for sleep, she's there, calling to me, crying. . . ," his voice broke, ". . . even sobbing out my name, an endless refrain that tears me apart, for she didn't want me, had no use for me, and left me like a stranger who says farewell to an acquaintance met on a journey of no account."

His tortured gaze fixed on Orrin.

"The Maze has ruined me—robbed me of my sanity, my sleep, and the ability to practice my profession. I'm a healer who can't touch the sick and a scholar who can't read a book; in other words, I'm not Reddin anymore. Now, brother, who wonders why I hide in the attic behind a locked door, tell me: what else am I to do?"

Orrin rose from the floor, towering over the figure slumped in the chair and took matters in hand.

"First, I'll draw a bath and help you shave and dress. Then, we'll wrap ourselves in every cloak mother can provide and walk to the Sanctum."

A grim smile twisted Reddin's lips.

"I feel no urge to give a gift."

"We're not going to the Sanctum for that. We're going to a meeting of the Council of Pelion."

"For what purpose?"

Catching the faint glimmer of hope in that cautious question, Orrin smiled.

"So you can tell the Eighteenth Mother exactly what you've just told me."

* * *

ORRIN SEEMED CONVINCED of the rightness of his decision, so much so that Reddin dared to hope. But now, sitting on the hard bench outside the Eighteenth Mother's private apartments, his feelings of despair returned. No sounds escaped the heavy door guarded by two dour Legionnaires. Unexpectedly, and much more quickly than he would have guessed given the personages responsible for the decision to meet with him, the door opened and he was ushered inside.

He recognized Ranier and Nadia, the High Healers of his guild, and the Mistress of Joining, who smiled and nodded at him. Grateful for her presence, he managed to smile back. A man who strongly resembled Manthur of Endlin looked him over carefully, as did a bald fellow whose stiff-backed carriage announced a lifetime spent in the Legion. Last of all, he saw the Eighteenth Mother and the empty chair beside her. As he had been taught, he bowed his head to show his respect, and was rewarded by a tinkle of laughter.

"Come, Reddin! We keep no formalities here. Some of us you know, but let me introduce Kazur, Head Scribe of the Greater Library, and Prax, Commander of the Legion." Two heads nodded at him, Kazur offering a brief smile, the Commander looking grim and exceedingly vexed. Without taking any notice of the Commander's disapproving presence, the Eighteenth Mother waved Reddin to the empty chair. Thankfully, Reddin found Orrin seated on his other side.

"Orrin has advised us of your troubles. Before you share them with us, I'd like to make a suggestion. You may, of course, refuse what I suggest, but I think you should consider it before we continue."

Reddin heard the happiness in her voice, a richness of pleasure at his presence, as if he had brought her a gift of exceedingly great value. Almost frightened by her aura of joy, he nodded his head to indicate his willingness.

"Orrin says that in your present condition, you believe you've lost your purpose. My suggestion is really an offering of sorts, for I can assure you that if you choose to return, a place in the Maze will be made for you without necessity of undergoing another Trial."

She was watching him intently, her gray-green eyes bright and observant. His first thought was elation, the next total disbelief, and finally, a growing suspicion that this was a trick of some kind.

"Is it the custom for such an offer to be made to someone who leaves the Maze?"

If she was hiding something from him, she did it well, because he could have sworn she was speaking with absolute honesty.

"No, it is not. Due to the nature of your circumstances, an exception will be made. Tubal has been informed and agrees that you may enter with the next class, or any class in the future."

"Why are my circumstances special?"

"Because I gave my word that I would offer you this option."

Sounds of alarms went off inside his head.

"Who asked you for your word?"

Her reply was gentle, but firm.

"Lillas."

The room rocked for a moment, the faces around the polished table floating, and Reddin guessed he was even closer to insanity than he'd feared. This made no sense at all! Why would Lillas leave him so callously, yet at the same time beg the Eighteenth Mother to break the rules on his behalf? And why would the Eighteenth Mother grant such a request to an ernani who was leaving of her own free will, announcing to him her disbelief in the entire purpose of the Maze? Nothing made sense. His head ached as he tried to sort out facts that fit no discernible pattern.

"There's no need for an answer tonight. I wanted you to understand that if your desire for the greatest of gifts is unchanged, we hold a place for you."

Rattled by her revelations, he spoke without thinking, even without embarrassment, careless of the strangers gathered around the table.

"I could never, ever do that again. I . . . I'm ruined somehow, dead inside. I've nothing to offer another woman."

Nodding slowly, she leaned back in her chair, sitting quietly, as did the rest of the Council. After a quick glance at Orrin, who nodded his encouragement, Reddin relaxed for a moment. A sudden wave of fatigue washed over him, emptying him of the ability to concentrate on this or any other problem. Without Orrin's help he would never have been able to wash or dress. He'd been nothing but a nuisance on the snowy walk to the Sanctum, stumbling and nearly falling several times, Orrin supporting him for the last hundred steps.

It took him forever to understand what the Eighteenth Mother was saying, although he could see her lips moving. His head grew so heavy that he could hardly hold it upright on his neck. Gratefully, he heard the Eighteenth Mother give him permission to rest.

". . . and help you sleep. Rest your head on your arms now, and think of nothing. No one will harm you. We'll be here when you wake; Orrin, and all of us will care for you, for we want you to regain your health and peace of mind."

He couldn't have offered resistance if he'd wanted to. All he wanted was to listen to her hypnotic voice caressing him, lulling him to sleep, promising him freedom from the haunting that made the nights times of torment.

". . . and think of nothing, nothing at all. Soon I will touch you, Reddin, a light touch on your forehead. It will not make you ill or affect you as the other touches did. You are not to blame, Reddin, of that I assure you . . ."

The woman in black didn't lie, for he felt her cool, dry fingers against his brow. As he sighed with relief at the thought that perhaps he was not mad after all, he was gently led into darkness and knew no more.

THEY LINKED THEIR minds with her after she entered his thoughts, waiting respectfully as she calmed his fears and brought him toward acceptance. One look at him as he walked into the chamber revealed he would have little strength with which to fight her. As she hoped, he offered no resistance, following her as faithfully as a child, grateful for the rest she promised. At her unspoken request, Orrin removed the leather jerkin and unbuttoned the loose-fitting shirt, pulling it down to bare his neck and shoulders. Kazur and Prax laid his inert body on the backless couch that stood between several lighted braziers while Orrin arranged Reddin's limbs more comfortably. Hesione placed herself at the end of the couch, taking his upper body onto her lap so she could more easily maintain her hold on him. When everything was accomplished, she instructed her Council.

"What we do tonight may be dangerous. The warning Orrin felt when he considered crossing the barrier may apply to my probing as well. I could go alone, but decided I need your help. Orrin knows Reddin better than anyone here; Kazur and Prax have both gone through Transformation, something we born adepts can never experience as anything but onlookers.

"As much as you can, I want you to shadow me, keeping on the fringes of my thoughts, suppressing as much of your individuality as you can. If you feel you can offer something of use, do so without breaking my concentration. Now, have you questions?"

There were none.

Hesione put aside the need for words and all other requirements of the waking world. Flexing her mind, she ran through a series of exercises that led her to the place of inner tranquility. Then, with a single thought, more delicately spun than spider's silk, she probed the mind of the man asleep on her lap, concentrating on sensing anything that resembled a warning against further trespass. Finding none, she gathered her strength, asking for and receiving the energy of the flames in the braziers surrounding her. Then, placing her hands firmly on either side of Reddin's bare shoulders, she leapt the darkness, landing lightly in the corridors of his mind.

HE HAD BEEN asleep only a few minutes when she entered, yet already she could feel pulsations, vibrations of a sort that ran through his thoughts at irregular intervals. Their meaning was unclear, and rather than searching for their source, she decided to explore her surroundings in order to better understand the nature of the man held tightly between her earthly hands.

Her first thought was to wonder at the expanse of his mind. Knowledge and memories resided behind each of the doorways in the corridor in which she stood, ready to open at his need for them. At once, she was struck by the fact that here, in the entryway of his thoughts, a place usually marked by wide open doors and bright light, rooms that traditionally were much-used, or much-cherished by their owner, more doors were shut than open. Puzzled, she began exploring what lay behind those closed doors. After many such visits, a pattern emerged.

Lillas lived behind each of them. Down hallways and byways, opening doors as she passed, Hesione would swing a door wide to find Lillas' bright-haired figure within. Here she sat studying in the cell, her fingers dyed blue-black with ink, a smudge anointing her nose as she eyed her scribbles with disgust, ripped out a blotted page, crumpled it into a ball and threw it into the fire with a filthy curse. Waves of gentle humor indicated Reddin's reaction as he observed her struggles, waiting patiently for her to request his assistance. In another room, the air ripe with sensuality, a bare white leg extended from beneath Lillas' nightshift as she lay on her stomach, her eyes closed as Reddin's hands traveled up and down the smoothness of her flesh, his state of arousal clear from the intentness with which he rubbed the oily salve into that long, perfectly-shaped limb. Here Lillas could be found shaking dice in a cup, peering wickedly across a table at Reddin's rapidly diminishing pile of markers, glorying in his defeat, never suspecting that the reason he played so badly was his inability to concentrate on anything besides her glowing face. In time Hesione discovered there was no rhyme or reason to the closed doors, for they were ruled solely by Reddin's delight in his companion coupled with his need to purge her from his thoughts.

As she moved deeper into the labyrinth, a place usually reserved for difficult memories, ones that gave pain or ones troublesome to the point that they must be contained under lock and key, Hesione's uneasiness grew. Prepared to find doors half-open, or entirely shut, here, too, in the dim light of forgetfulness and rejection, many doors stood wide-open, the painful disturbances within them radiating out into the hall. From one came the sound of music, a jolly dance tune that seemed inappropriate to this darkened, narrow corridor. Hesione peered within, hearing Lillas' voice grate across the dayroom, seeing the offended stare of the serving woman, feeling Reddin's sudden surge of anger, jarring against the rhythms and sounds of people hard at play.

And here, at last, she found the room she dreaded entering, the room in which Reddin was forced to live and re-live Lillas' departure, his emotions wracked, his beliefs twisted, everything left to ferment and fester as her hooded form receded into darkness. His illness was mysterious no longer.

His lack of concentration, his inability to think of anything except Lillas could be explained by the impossibility of him finding a place within himself where he might escape her presence. This in itself could indicate a sickness of the mind, a solution that became unacceptable given the other evidence Orrin supplied.

Without warning, another vibration ran through the chambers of Reddin's mind. Hesione's worldly body called to her. Fixing herself in this place, she used her earthly eyes to watch Reddin's face convulse and felt the muscles underneath her palms tense, jerk, and attempt to fling her hands away from him. Grappling with him, for it was imperative that she be physically connected with him in order to probe this deeply, another quake shook their linked minds. Then, strangely, mysteriously, the light within his mind began to shimmer with waves of energy that pulsated and quivered. Incredibly, in a manner she had never experienced before, another mind reached out, groping toward them. Blindly, awkwardly, it hovered there awhile. In that moment, Hesione felt the touch of Lillas' thoughts although she was certain Lillas was unaware that she had reached the one she sought across long distances of time and space.

She was calling to him, without words and without consciousness, the call initiating, Hesione realized, from the substance of Lillas' dreams. As the intensity of her call increased, a violent shudder ran through Reddin's body. Suddenly, he was fighting with Hesione, desperate to rid himself of her hands. She fell with him, struggling with him on the stone floor, almost losing her grip on his shoulders when someone stopped his progress across the floor. Now that he was immobilized, she clutched him more tightly, panting from her exertions. Despite this interruption, her contact remained unbroken. Taking a deep breath, she returned to the shimmering corridor.

The air around Hesione was heavy, suffocating them both with the weight of Lillas' need. To remain here was nothing short of agony since there existed no place to hide from Lillas' all-encompassing yearning for the healer who writhed in Hesione's arms. Unable to wake because of Hesione's presence, unable to bear the touch of hands that were not those of the one who searched for him, Reddin was trapped, thrashing and screaming for relief.

The breath of an anonymous thought washed over Hesione.

"This is the first stage of Transformation. You must leave or upset the process irrevocably. They may both be harmed if you stay."

She must go, but first she must find a place for Reddin to rest. His condition made it imperative that she shield him from this torment, if only for a few hours. The vibrations ceased, and taking advantage of their respite, Hesione took Reddin with her, away from this place that shimmered with pain and into the corridors that marked her place of entry. Fearing to place him in one of the chambers containing Lillas, she hesitated. Another mind offered a solution.

"We will find a place where he may dwell in safety. Rest while we search."

Grateful for their care, she held Reddin gently in her thoughts, soothing him and feeling his tension dissipate. A presence joined her, a woman, although she didn't expend the energy necessary to identify Nadia or Chryse, for to do so might have reduced her ability to guide Reddin in the direction they were being led.

Hesione was tiring now, her mind aching from Lillas' assault, her body sore from its struggles with Reddin. It was tempting to leave him here, to free herself and escape the entrapment of his troubled mind, but her courage rose and she faced a door which stood only slightly ajar, calling on the others to aid her, willing that it open and provide a haven for the man in her arms. The opening became larger, the light within spilling out onto the floor of the corridor. With a final joint effort, it swung open to embrace the suppliants.

A woman, dark-haired and dark-skinned, sat in a cushioned chair, a lighted candle beside her on a small table. She was reading as they entered, but looked up with a smile and motioned to her feet. A small boy, of age no more than three or four years, entered the room. That she was his mother was evident from their resemblance, as was the loving look with which she greeted him, although she made no motion to touch him as a mother might, neither pushing away the tangled hair from his face, nor kissing his dirty cheek. Instead, she waited patiently as he sat cross-legged on a cushion in front of her. Clasping her hands together in her lap, she began telling him a story.

As she spoke, Hesione sensed the man with whom she was linked being drawn forward, passing over the threshold into a room well-known and a memory well-loved. The tale over, the boy slept, his chubby arms and legs sprawled out over the tufted pillow he rested upon. The woman rose, tiptoed to his side and knelt beside him. Now that he slept she could touch him without fear, and she did so lovingly, tracing the lines and curves of his sturdy body, stroking his hair, and finally leaning over to kiss his forehead.

"Sleep, my child."

The boy's eyes flew open, perhaps awakened by her unaccustomed touch, and he smiled up at her. Withdrawing her hands, she folded her lips together and sat beside him silently, watching him with loving eyes, but touching him no more. Wistfulness hung in the room, but with it peace and security.

Hesione left Reddin asleep with his mother standing guard.

THE SMELL OF yeast woke him, the unforgettable aroma of bread newly-baked; also liver and onions and mint-laced tea. His eyelashes seemed glued to his eyes. He lifted them with an effort, hearing his stomach growl, a loud, empty rumbling signifying ravenous hunger. Orrin's face came into view, his left eye bruised and swollen and a satisfied grin on his face.

"The sleeper wakes! Much longer and I was going to eat everything myself!"

His limbs stiff and his shoulders sore, Reddin struggled into a sitting position and began rubbing his neck, trying to loosen muscles that seemed not to have moved for at least a week. How long had he slept? After a quick glance around the room, he realized he was no longer in the tower chamber.

"When it was clear you were going to sleep for awhile, we moved you into my quarters in the Maze."

"You live in the Maze?"

Reddin knew he was groggy, but this bit of information didn't fit with the way things had been before he slept. Orrin spoke cautiously, anxiously scanning Reddin's face as he did so.

"I'm the Master of Joining and the newest member of the Council."

"Then the Mistress of Joining . . .?"

". . . is the mate of my heart."

Too many changes, too many developments, Reddin's mind cried. When the memory of his interview with the Eighteenth Mother came flooding back he was lost again, reality flickering around him, threatening his composure. Dropping his aching head into his hands, he heard Orrin say:

"Slowly, Reddin, take it slowly. You've slept a night and a day. It's time for the evening meal and you're hungry. Concentrate on the food and put the other things away for a time."

The food was good, better than any he'd ever tasted, the rolls soft and dripping with butter, the onions translucent against the browned liver, the figs sweet and rich on his tongue. As he ate, balance was restored. After a time he shifted his attention from the food to his brother.

"Who blacked your eye? Has an ernani attacked you already?"

A smile tugged at the corners of Orrin's mouth.

"Actually, it was a candidate from Pelion."

Something in the way Orrin was looking at him, a certain glint of barely suppressed laughter, made Reddin suspicious. He stiffened, immediately defensive and on the alert.

"What are you saying?"

"I'm only teasing. Your elbow caught my eye by mistake. My carelessness is to blame."

The food lay heavy in his stomach as Reddin considered that he had made a fool of himself in front of his brother and the entire Council of Pelion. It would have been better to stay in the attic since it was clear that in his present state he couldn't prevent humiliating himself in public. Embittered and embarrassed, he wiped his hands on the napkin and swung his legs over the side of the bed, intent on exiting the room as quickly as he could, only to be prevented from rising by two hands that dropped heavily on his shoulders.

"Reddin, accept my apology. I've managed this poorly, telling you nothing and teasing you for something you couldn't help. Please, I beg you, forget everything I've said and let's start afresh."

No one could have resisted such a heartfelt appeal. Reddin leaned back against the pillows as his brother pulled a footstool to the side of the bed. Now that their peace was made, Orrin seemed to be having difficulties deciding how to begin. When his eyes lifted to Reddin's, they were thoughtful, as if trying to gauge how to proceed given his brother's troubled state of mind.

"Before I begin, I must ask you a question, a difficult question for me to ask and you to answer. Perhaps it would be best if you think of me not as your brother, but as a caretaker of the Maze." After Reddin's wary nod of agreement, he continued. "I speak for the Council, not for myself. We know from the records that neither you nor Lillas offered a third gift." Reddin tensed, guessing the question before it was spoken. Orrin forged on. "I must ask if you joined your bodies together. I need no explanations or details; a simple answer will suffice."

"Why do you ask? What difference does it make?"

Reddin could hear the hostility in his voice, but could do nothing to stop it, for the wound Orrin touched was raw and he couldn't bear to explore it with anyone, not even his brother.

"I ask because the Eighteenth Mother judged me best equipped to question you without fear of giving offense. The difference it makes is more difficult to convey, although it is connected to your present state."

It was hard to maintain antagonism in the face of such good-hearted concern. His defenses crumbled. What difference did it make if Orrin knew, if the entire Council knew? His joining with Lillas was a failure. Why not own up to his responsibilities?

"No," he sighed, "we never joined together."

"Yet you wanted this to transpire, you felt desire for her and she for you?"

Had he felt desire for her? It seemed so long ago, but he made himself look back, past her betrayal, past her rejection, and remembered her hands running lightly over him, her arousal as he caressed her, the joy he felt when her need answered his.

"We desired each other, yes . . ."

His voice broke as he shook away those thoughts, only to see a slow smile rise on his brother's lips.

"Then I must tell you this: a wondrous thing has happened, a miracle of which you are a part. For the first time, a couple in the Maze has begun

Transformation without the giving of a third gift. Last night we confirmed you are not mad. You are experiencing the first signs of the gift."

As Reddin started to protest, Orrin's jaw set, announcing he would not be stopped.

"If you were both in the Maze, you would be in each other's presence constantly and there would be no pain, no inability to be touched, for her hands would touch you daily. As the process went forward, Flavius would mark your door and you would be excused from all activities, able to remove yourself from the world and find a new world inside each other."

"But this process has gone awry, and so she calls you, and you her, both of you experiencing the pain of your separation. This is why you must go to her, for she cannot come to you."

"Go to her? I don't know where she is or even if she wants me."

Reddin was trying desperately to accommodate this new information, elated at the thought that the gift was within his grasp, yet at the same time filled with trepidation. Orrin's eyes filled with understanding, but he would allow no self-pity.

"You can doubt no longer that she wants you, or that she is equally as miserable as you have been since her departure. We have records, Reddin, records of every couple who has ever undergone Transformation. Ranier searched them today, trying to find anything that resembled your situation. He found it not long ago. Forty years ago a male ernani broke his leg in the arena and had to be removed to the House of Healing. He and his mate had shown no signs of Transformation, but that night it began. His reactions were dismissed as the result of shock, but she was found in the cell the next morning in convulsions, her arms bruised and bleeding from where she had beaten them against the cell, trying to reach him through the locked door."

"And Lillas could be. . ."

He couldn't finish because of the lump that rose in his throat as he pictured Lillas, the strong one, the fleet of foot, the keen of eye, battered and broken in some unknown place.

"Rest assured she is not hurt. Ranier and Nadia believe that since you have been separated by time and distance, the process has slowed. Even so, once that couple was united, they recovered and emerged from the House of Healing as transformed adepts."

Suddenly, it was breathtakingly simple. Lillas wanted him. With that certainty all doubts faded to be replaced with a rush of anticipation.

"Then I must go to her. Where is she, Orrin?"

For the first time Reddin caught an undercurrent of sadness in his brother's voice.

"It will be more difficult than you imagine. Her home is far away, and to journey there will mean considerable danger to you and those who travel with you, for you cannot go alone."

"Why not?"

"Because without an adept to lead you to rest as the Eighteenth Mother did, you'll weaken and your illness will return."

Something else was lurking behind Orrin's eyes, something that frightened this self-assured brother of his. Reddin guessed what remained unsaid.

"And if we cannot find one another, if the process cannot continue, we'll lose our sanity?"

"We do not know, for none have ever been separated before," his voice lowered, "but we fear it may be so."

There was nothing else to be done but find acceptance. For such a gift he would give his life. Reddin would persevere.

"You've still not told me where Lillas has gone."

Orrin's reply came slowly, and with great reluctance.

"You must travel west. Lillas awaits you in Agave."

"HIS ANSWER?"

"They have never joined together. He gave no reason and I asked for none, although he added that they have shared desire."

"Ah! Then it must be that for them, it is enough."

There was a reflective silence, then another question.

"He understands and accepts?'

"He begins to understand. He accepts without hesitation."

"He sleeps?"

The Master of Joining sighed.

"He was shy of my touch, but suffered it. His resistance and my inexperience made me clumsy, but I found the door and left him within. It will grow easier with time."

The Eighteenth Mother turned to the High Healers.

"What of his health, Ranier?"

"Better than we could have hoped. The arena has saved him, giving him the stamina to endure. After a few days of sleep and food, he should weather the journey without difficulty."

"Nadia?"

"I contacted Phoron and instructed him on a like procedure with Lillas. Work with an injured mind is a great love of his, second only to herb lore, and he's anxious to begin. Seth's company is expected in Imarus next week. When she arrives, Phoron will be ready. Once Lillas' mind finds rest, Reddin's ability to concentrate should return."

Every member of the Council sat still and hushed, sensing the Eighteenth Mother's mind gathering the information necessary to proceed, feeling her tension, her excitement kept barely in check.

"Your decision, Prax?"

"No more than three. Even that small number may draw undue attention. My agents are fearful, my most experienced patrol in that area turned to ash, and Pelion, the place that stole the Aeson's daughter, a hated name throughout the marketplace. They must go disguised, the more foreign the better."

The silence which followed was broken by Kazur's unique brand of nasal laughter.

"Then I suppose I must volunteer, although I'd thought to do so before Prax so aptly described me, for I've longed to walk the streets of the city I've studied these six years. Think you a prince of Endlin will suffice, Commander?"

A slap on his back was his answer. A soft escape of breath from Chryse brought all eyes to her face, which had taken on a softer glow in the past week, due they knew, to the man seated beside her whose hand never left hers.

"We have a volunteer, although he doesn't know the circumstances of this trip. I had not recalled him until Kazur spoke just now."

"Tell us, Chryse."

"It's Flavius, Mother. He caught a glimpse of Reddin as he left Ranier's healing chamber and must have run the Maze in record time to accost me in the dayroom. I could not answer his questions as fully as he wished, but his statement was flat and brooked no argument. 'Tell the Eighteenth Mother I've invested too much time in them not to see them newly transformed.'"

Nodding, well-pleased, her grey-green eyes sparked flashes of emerald. The Council basked in her happiness; Prax, alone, seemed unaffected by her mood. He sat brooding, lost in the net of strategies he had woven with his own hands. Soon he was thinking aloud, working through the changes that had come upon them unannounced.

"They'll head due north first, to put any watchers off their track, and then turn west at the old forest. We'll form a web to protect them, although once they cross the scrublands and meet the desert, they'll be beyond our protection. Somehow," he groaned and rolled his eyes, "we'll get a pass so they can enter Agave. There's an inn I frequent that will serve our purposes, a trifle run-down, but serviceable, and more open than most to strangers." He shifted his attention to the Eighteenth Mother. "How to smuggle him into Imarus escapes me. Phoron travels to and fro with a pass stamped daily and is well-known by the guards. Even in disguise, Reddin could never be mistaken for Phoron, and my guess is that Seth won't let Lillas out of his sight. My question is this: how shall we bring them together?"

Six heads turned in Hesione's direction, expecting instant illumination. They were met by a face stark with the power of prophecy, her voice like the sound of a muted gong.

"It is finally right, my friends. The siege distressed me, for I could not find it anywhere and it haunted me as surely as Lillas haunts Reddin. But now we progress, we go forward toward the battle I have seen in tiny scraps and half-forgotten fragments of dreams and visions of the whispering plain. The two rings I see, the voice of the prophet I have heard, the flame has passed into the wet lands, and the beast has awakened. We stand at a crossroads, having become complacent, trusting in former times and former solutions. We must not falter, but press on, regardless of risks, questions unanswered, or problems unsolved. We must leave the city so as to share our gift with the world. And so we will go, to the west, to the city of madness, to Agave!"

She stood revealed, the Mother of All, robed and armed for battle, the emblazoned banner flying above her head as she spread wide the city gates, her weapons compassion, rectitude, and a slender, dark-skinned man who journeyed toward the city of slaves, his mind attuned to a light that flickered like a flame, drawing him onward with a promise that would change the world.

Chapter 17

Masquerade

REDDIN FELT A FOOL. Worse, he knew he looked one. His stubble-covered jaw itched, his earlobe ached, and his head throbbed from the unfamiliar pressure of tightly-pulled braids. Kazur's mate, Eluria, oversaw the ear-piercing and the braiding, two indisputable (and therefore unavoidable) hallmarks of an adult clansman of Endlin. The saving grace of the entire affair was Kazur's grudging concession that Reddin's nostril need not be pierced; in his present mood that injury could not have been borne. Added to these indignities was the costume he must wear, a multitude of brightly-colored scarf-like robes layered to reveal wide lapels of richly-worked embroidery. Unaccustomed as he was to wearing skirts, the simple act of walking became an exercise to be practiced daily under Kazur's judgmental gaze. The slick, silky fabric continually dogged his mobility, threatening to fly open despite the voluminous sash that bound everything together in a laborious composite of folds and pleats. Kazur, who wore these same robes with careless majesty, demanded a like perfection from his student.

Matters of appearance merely scratched the surface of what Reddin was expected to learn. Kazur schooled him in the rigid hierarchies of courteous behavior based on rank and male privilege that ruled all private and commercial exchanges in the lands neighboring the eastern sea, aspects of a way of life foreign to any native of Pelion. Prax, the dour Commander, kept him bent over maps, memorizing routes to and from places he'd never heard of and assigned Flavius to act as examiner. Once, in a decidedly rebellious state-of-mind, Reddin made so bold as to question his teacher. The result was, to say the least, discomforting.

"Why must I learn these routes if my escort knows the way?"

"If you're separated, you'll need to know how to proceed alone."

When a sarcastic scowl greeted this reasoning (for Reddin had no intention of becoming separated) the Commander of the Legion replied bluntly:

"People die or disappear regularly between here and Agave. Study hard, healer. Your life may depend on it."

At first Reddin quailed at the thought of memorizing anything, sure that his inability to concentrate would plague his efforts. But recently, for some reason he didn't understand and no one bothered to explain, his mind cleared, and he crammed the information into his head, no longer resentful because of his thanks that he was returning to normal. Only at night, as he settled himself for sleep, could he sense the disturbances of the early days. At a single touch of Orrin's hand, he found relief and blissfully peaceful sleep.

His days were full, packed with activities too numerous to allow him time to brood or grow fearful of what he attempted. A voice inside him whispered that this was the Eighteenth Mother's intention. Even so, he let himself be sucked into the whirlwind of preparations, grateful for any ploy that prevented introspection. His books lay forgotten in the attic room and he lived in the upper levels of the Maze, far away from the cells. Forbidden contact with his former companions, none of whom were aware of his presence, he might have been lonely except for the company of his brother and Chryse.

Flavius, too, was a mainstay in his life, his hearty cheerfulness never flagging as he taught Reddin the basics of riding each morning at the Cavalry stables. Afternoons were spent studying with Kazur or Prax; every evening he stripped to a loincloth and joined Strato in the deserted, torch lit weapon's room. There the Head Trainer drilled him in knife fighting, teaching him dirty tricks Strato had learned from countless ernani and a few he'd invented on his own. The difference between this training and that of his previous training with the ernani was neither subtle nor difficult to understand. Strato wasn't teaching the artistry of the craft, the sense of balance, the subtlety of feints and passes, or the strategies necessary to disarm his opponent; Strato was teaching him to kill. It worried Reddin, who'd taken a healer's oath. Strato's vicious attacks left little time to ponder ethics. Putting his reservations aside, Reddin left them half-buried, but not forgotten.

Two days ago came a new game for him to play and one that left him badly shaken. Without warning, Kazur and Flavius appeared in the training room, both of them stripped, like Strato, for action. On a signal Reddin neither saw nor heard, all three men jumped him. They were unarmed, as was he. Nevertheless, he found himself fighting for his life, unable to think of anything except freeing himself from forearms locked around his throat, legs that tightened around his waist, and knees that aimed unerringly for his groin. When the first bout was over and he lay flat on the ground, straddled by Flavius and panting hard, Strato eyed him with disgust:

"If you can't do better than that, you're finished before you start. Out there, a second thought means death. Again!"

And so he tried again, this time fighting in pairs, another time one on one, until at last he lost his temper and went after Strato with a vengeance. After pinning him to the ground, Reddin earned his first compliment from any of his teachers.

"That's it, man! Put aside those healing ways and concentrate on staying alive!"

AND THEN THERE was the question of his identity.

Kazur posed it to him last night, when Reddin visited his home for the purpose of receiving his braided locks. Kazur's mate, Eluria, was beautiful as the women of Pelion were beautiful, with olive skin, brown eyes, and masses of luxuriant hair falling unbound to her waist. Their home was a striking mixture of eastern ornamentation and Pelion simplicity, functionally furnished yet adorned with touches of surprising elegance, among them, a series of woven tapestries adorning the timbered walls, fantastic landscapes of sea and sky, of a glistening citadel perched above sheer cliffs against which waves crashed and foamed and interior views of vast rooms peopled with men and women bedecked in the same strange garb Reddin was learning to wear. When Reddin expressed his admiration, Eluria moved swiftly to his side.

"That is the place of Kazur's birth and a thousand times more lovely than the tapestry suggests."

"You've visited there?"

His surprise came when he considered the distance. His journey to Agave would take twenty-odd days; a caravan to Endlin would constitute three moons or more.

"We went after the birth of each child so his father could accept our children formally into the clan of the Kwanlonhon. They are of an ancient lineage and such things are customary among them."

Turning to Kazur, for he had thought the sessions in which he'd been taught to address Kazur as prince were strictly fabrications for purposes of security, Reddin asked:

"Are you truly a prince, Kazur?"

As he wrapped an arm around Eluria's shoulder, a lazy smile indicated that the question amused the Head Scribe greatly.

"I am Eluria's prince. No more; no less."

It was strange being among them in the privacy of their home, witnessing the blending of their pasts, reminding himself that once they were strangers united in a cell, taking the identical pathway begun by Reddin and a woman he sometimes despaired of seeing again. Something of his mood must have fallen on his hosts, for Kazur motioned to large cushions that served as chairs and Eluria handed around a warm drink with a spicy aroma and a hint of citrus. After a brief lull, Kazur asked him what name he would use. Reddin suggested 'Manthur', since with the exception of Kazur, Manthur was the only person from Endlin he'd ever known.

Dismissing his suggestion with a wave of his hand, Kazur instructed him in the realities of their situation.

"Manthur comes from another branch of my family and his name might be known abroad. No, we must choose something likely, but unknown." He paused, fingering the two hoops hanging from his earlobe until his face lit with a smile. "You will be Ryzan, the eldest son of my brother, a strong line of kinship that will explain your presence and your silence, for your father would give you to me after your passage into manhood, trusting me to instruct you in obedience in the presence of your elders. In Endlin, it is forbidden for a parent to strike his child. An uncle suffers no such constraints."

A tinkle of laughter from Eluria indicated that Reddin's opinion of the custom described must have shown on his face. She was quick to reassure him.

"You are fortunate in your coloring, Reddin, for the Endlinese are dark-skinned and dark-eyed. And your hair," her eyes twinkled, "will look fine in braids."

Groaning inwardly, Reddin nodded politely. Soon he was sitting between her knees as she began her work.

"Did you learn to do this on your travels?"

Another laugh issued from her throat.

"I learned this under Kazur's tutelage, for he wore his hair in this fashion until long after we left the Maze. It is a sign of rank, you see, and indicates that a man has many concubines. For a clansman to braid his own hair is taboo."

"Concubines?"

Kazur cleared his throat. Eluria continued, undeterred by her mate's expression of something akin to embarrassment.

"Haven't you told Reddin about the mating customs of Endlin?" She was teasing now, although there was concern in her voice, Reddin decided, and a touch of anger. "What if someone were to ask him the size of his uncle's harem? Would you have him answer honestly, thus making a lie of your disguise and his?"

"I . . . I never thought to instruct him in such matters."

"Surely you've informed him as to the meaning of his earring!"

Eluria was clearly indignant. Anxious that he not be the cause of discord, Reddin interrupted, "I assumed it signifies a man who is as yet unmated. Is the second ring added at the time of mating?"

His question earned a decided look of amusement from Eluria, and a dispirited groan from Kazur.

"I fear I have not been the best of tutors. For this I ask your pardon."

Kazur shot a baleful glance at his mate, although his lips twitched, suggesting that his irritation was half-hearted at best. In the next moment he remembered Reddin and hurried to explain.

"The clansmen of Endlin are polygamous. There, a man's rank is figured not only by wealth or the status of his family, but by the number of children he has fathered. A poor man might have only one or two women in his household; a prince would have no less than thirty. The second ring is inserted after the birth of a clansman's first child, who, whether male or female, is called a "sa'ab". All children belong solely to the father. Indeed, we have no word which means 'parent' in the sense of shared parentage. The word we use translates as 'he who mounts,' since conception and the prevention of conception is entirely the responsibility of the male."

Another voice, solemn now and strangely sad, took up the explanation.

"And so a woman is honored by her lord if she is selected as a worthy vessel for his seed. She is mother, yet never parent; a partner for joining, yet never a mate; her value figured by the perfection of her beauty and the fertility of her womb. Hers is a life of ease and riches beyond comprehension, yet without rights or privileges, even so much as the care and nurturing of her children."

Words ceased and a hush lingered over the room. Within that silence Reddin sensed a wealth of anguish and compromise, understanding at last the truth of Kazur's rank. For Eluria's sake, Kazur chose to dwell in a land not his own, for he could not be both a rightful prince of Endlin and the prince of Eluria's heart. At last, the silence was broken.

"My thanks for your interest in my pupil, beloved."

"It is nothing, my prince."

When her fingers finally stopped their work and Eluria handed him a glass, Reddin could see her watching him intently over his shoulder as he considered the strangeness of his reflection. Her farewell was serious, but heartening.

"Kazur will guide you well, never fear. May your Transformation make you truly one with your ernani, as I am one with mine."

KAZUR WAS INSPECTING him now, running a critical eye over every detail of Reddin's disguise. His inspection finished, Kazur turned to address the Commander.

"He would fool me, Prax. I can do no better."

Kazur's approval seemed a signal of sorts, for suddenly Reddin was surrounded by well-wishers, the caretakers of the Maze gathered around him as he stood at the northern gate. His horse, a dun gelding of Lapithian stock, stood head down, cropping at a few last mouthfuls of grass, seemingly free of the nervousness that was fast claiming Reddin.

Events began to blur around him: a nod from Orrin; a warm smile from
Chryse; Strato's gruff reminder to watch his back; the High Healers of Pelion
standing with hands entwined, their words of parting seeming to emanate
from a single mouth. The Eighteenth Mother, small and slightly forlorn, came
forward at last, her eyes searching his as she gestured that he move away
from the others and join her for a private farewell.

"You've said nothing, Reddin, but I must ask. Are you sure of this decision?"

He nodded his head, for his throat was tight with emotion and he could
not trust his voice. Her answering smile was wan, he thought, and did not
reach her eyes.

"We've told you next to nothing, sending you beyond the walls with no
more than your faith and our hopes. Remember your vows, the oaths you
rendered when you chose to walk the Path."

"I . . . I wish I knew more about . . . " he could not speak Lillas' name aloud,
but she seemed to guess his subject before he could force the word out of his
mouth.

"This much I may say: the decision to leave was entirely her own. It was
an act of generosity, demanding courage and self-sacrifice, the first a quality
she has never lacked, the second something she learned from her time with
you. Her first and last thoughts were of you, that you might not lose the
thing you treasured most. Thus she demanded my promise that with the
greatest of gifts you might heal the world of its wounds."

"She was wrong."

Bitterness overcame him as he reflected how brutally Lillas had left him,
how her departure complicated everything concerning the achievement of
the gift, and how frightened he was of this journey.

"Was she?" Again, her eyes searched his. "Was she wrong to choose
selflessness over selfishness? Was she wrong in her belief that you value the
gift more than her, that your first thought was the loss of the gift rather than
the loss of Lillas?" At his startled frown, she shook her head reproachfully.
"Transformation may have begun but the third gift stands before you. You
must forgive her, as you have doubtless done many times before. But more
than this, you must come to value what is distinctly hers."

She paused, considering him a moment, and then continued softly, her
voice weaving a spell, conjuring a vision of Lillas as his nostrils flared at a
faint aroma of sandalwood drifting about him.

"There are two kinds of courage, Reddin, that of the just cause and that
of the cause that seems lost. Both require bravery, but the bravery of the latter
outshines all human endeavors. Lillas stands before me, straight of shoulder
and clear of eye, acknowledging her hopes only to set them aside for the
sake of others. . .," her voice dropped to a whisper, ". . . for her flame will not
be extinguished and she will light the candle of despair."

Her sorcery ceased, the vision fled, and the woman in black raised her hand in benediction.

"Follow the Path, Reddin of Pelion."

KAZUR DROPPED AN armful of logs on the fire, for the night was clear and unseasonably cold. Brushing off his hands, he settled down on his sleeping robes and pulled a blanket over his shoulders. They had made good time today, the trail clear and well-marked, the wind brisk, the horses fresh and high-spirited as the city walls receded and finally disappeared from view. Flavius dozed off an hour ago, his snores deep and regular. Kazur appeared tired, but gazed fixedly into the flames, his thoughts obviously many miles to the south. Reddin posed the question that had troubled him all day.

"Does it bother you, Kazur? Leaving Eluria behind?"

Kazur's response was immediate.

"She travels with me. We are one."

It was the same phrase Dysponteus had used. Hearing it again, spoken with such easy confidence, caused Reddin to fret over what this journey boded. As relieved as he had been to have his mind restored in these past few days, there had also been a sense of loss. Transformation may have begun, but he no longer carried the proof of it within his thoughts and that lack bothered him.

Kazur pulled his saddle underneath his head to serve as a pillow before issuing the invitation Reddin had been waiting to hear with a mixture of shame and anxiety. He'd grown accustomed to Orrin's touch each night. The thought of a stranger entering his mind filled him with revulsion. Kazur stated it as a matter of fact, something that deserved no comment.

"Call me when you have need of me."

Perhaps the beauty of the night inspired him, or perhaps he was simply being obstinate. Whatever the cause, Reddin chose not to accept Kazur's offer. Determined that dreamless rest would be his, he buried his head in his arms.

Surrendering himself to the weariness of his body, he was soon on the fringes of sleep, stepping forward into the darkness to be hailed by an unknown voice, sneering yet ruthless in its intensity.

"... for the time is past that you may protest. Nor will I tolerate disobedience of any kind. He is dead and buried. You belong to me now and must act accordingly."

This was a dream within a dream, for Reddin knew that he slept and dimly accepted the unspoken guarantee that he was free from threat, yet there was another presence within him he could not explain, a presence who feared these words and the man who spoke them. Other perceptions made their way into his dreaming state, small observations that seemed clues of some sort, although the words themselves did little except confuse him. The man spoke with a sibilant accent reminiscent of Lillas' speech, although in this speaker's mouth the lisping elided consonants lost their charm, becoming sounds of liquid spite.

"You will accompany me whenever I visit the city, and best you play your part well. Remember Charis, and know I will not be trifled with. Your behavior determines her fate."

Rising from the mists came a face, at first shadowy and indistinct, the major impression one of a halo of ginger-colored ringlets that grew in shape and form to become the outlines of a man's hair and beard. On another person, these carefully arranged curls and ringlets might have suggested frivolity or affectation, but the severity of his face, the menace that turned his pale bluish eyes almost colorless with the force of his dislike, belied his perfectly groomed appearance. As the blurred outlines of Reddin's vision shifted and came into clearer focus, so the presence he had sensed grew in clarity, for with a sudden certainty, he knew this was Lillas' vision as well, and she was paralyzed by fear. Although Reddin had no understanding of the nature of the speaker's threat, the recognition of her fear disturbed him, for his Lillas feared nothing. Even when he shook her, bent on seeing her cowed and submissive, she'd squared her shoulders and lifted her chin, daring him to strike her.

The man was gloating now. With each of his pronouncements, Lillas' mind retreated as from a flurry of blows.

"You may keep your apartments until I decide otherwise, but make no attempt to leave the palace walls. Remember, lest your adventures have caused you to forget, that your willfulness will no longer be tolerated."

As the vision faded, the agony began. It caught Reddin unprepared, turning the waking dream into a return of his nightmares. Alone now, and terrified of the ginger-haired man's power over her, all of Lillas' thoughts were of Reddin. She mourned over the loss of him, her need for him increasing until he felt himself wrenched apart—his body in the scrublands, his mind far to the west where a bright light shone, a dream woven by Lillas, but a dream that, lacking Reddin's physical presence, was gradually becoming a nightmare, her need to touch him, to feel the reassurance of his flesh pressed against hers growing so powerful that Reddin stood on the brink of madness, struggling against her, his mind thrashing and writhing as Lillas' cries became his.

"Wake, you must wake!'

Hands of steel gripped his shoulders, shaking him, and the nausea returned, stronger than it had ever been before, making him rebel against the domination of those unwelcome hands.

"Reddin, return! That way madness lies!"

Something or someone wrenched him free from Lillas' nightmare, away from the violent brightness of that light. Reddin stared up at a stranger with braided hair, a pearl gleaming in his right nostril, a pair of golden rings dangling from his left ear. Disoriented from the force of the nightmare, he struggled for a means by which to identify the foreigner leaning over him. Flavius came into view, crouching beside Reddin to offer him a battered tin cup. With the reassurance of his solid, kindly presence, reality returned.

"Drink. Your throat must be raw."

After a quick swallow, the bitter tea painful as it coursed down his throat, he realized the screams within his mind must have pierced the silence of the camp. Humiliated and remorseful, he waited for Kazur's rebuke. It never came.

"You're not to blame. If it's anyone's fault, it's mine," Kazur said, obviously furious with himself. "I should have made this part of our studies, so that when the time came you would have some reason to trust me." He continued more calmly. "Like all ernani who walk the Path, I received the gift late in life. As a group, we tend to be more reticent than born adepts, perhaps because even now, twenty years later, it remains a mystery to me, something I speak of rarely; something I share only with my mate, my children, and the Council."

Kazur had been crouching by his side. Now he lowered himself to the ground and sat cross-legged, regarding the fire.

"I don't know what your brother told you, but this you must believe. Even though you've left the Maze, the rules of privacy remain intact. I will never enter your thoughts without your permission. Once I am invited to enter, I will take you quickly to the place of rest and leave you there. I interfered tonight because you gave me no choice."

A silence followed in which Kazur seemed to make a decision. Turning to Reddin with a quick move of his head that caused his braids to swing against his face, he spoke with quiet deliberation.

"We hoped to protect you from worry. I have come to believe such ignorance is dangerous, for you must understand the consequences of what you undertake and resist the temptation to search for Lillas. As you learned tonight, you lack the strength to break her hold. She will be caught as well, made helpless by your mutual need. This need will grow stronger as we approach Agave, of that Ranier and Nadia are certain. For this reason, we may not linger. Once we reach Agave, it is possible that I may not be able to free you if you attempt again what you did tonight."

"Why must it be so painful?" Reddin asked with a tired sigh.

"It need not be so." Kazur's expression softened. "It is my most precious memory, those days of private harmony spent together in our cell. As the mind opens, you find yourself within her and she in you. In time, you are no longer alone. It is a joining beyond the body, beyond the mereness of language, beyond time and place."

Hesitantly, Reddin hazarded a question that had plagued him for weeks. "But what of your home, Kazur? To leave everything behind. To leave Endlin . . ." he paused, thinking of Dysponteus and Dorian, thinking of himself, ". . . to leave Pelion forever . . ."

The Head Scribe wrapped his arms about his knees and lifted his head to consider the stars. He gave no sign that he had heard the question, seemingly engaged in some private contemplation Reddin was loathe to disturb. His eyelids growing heavy, his mood sad, Reddin slumped down into his sleeping robes. At last, Kazur spoke:

"Home. My earliest memories—my ayah, my pets, my playfellows in the harem. The year I reached manhood, the heat rising within me, the youthful ardor of man discovering woman. Lessons studied, punishments received, obedience learned. My father's face. These places I visit in my memories and so can never be lost."

Reddin mumbled something incoherent, Kazur's words rhythmic, lyrical, quatrains of poetry singing him to sleep, working as a tonic, a sleeping potion mixed with words rather than herbs.

"Then there is the home of my spirit, which abides with my Eluria, nestled safely against her heart. She is with me now, my other self; for long ago I left Kazur behind. We are and ever shall be Kazur/Eluria, Eluria/Kazur."

The words were slowing now, sinking inside him, plunging into the depths of Reddin's dreams.

"Finally, there is the city called Pelion, the Realm of the Gift, where in time, all will journey. From the wind-swept ends of the world, across seas that bear no names, they will come, until all speak mind to mind, and the world will be remade."

As a hand brushed over his forehead, Reddin sank into untroubled dreams. Kazur's litany tumbled down with him, echoing around him as he fell head over heels down the long black tunnel that led him toward sleep.

"I have not left my home, Reddin of Pelion. I was allowed to find it."

"TOMORROW WE BEGIN the last stretch, leaving water, grazing, and shelter behind as we pass out onto the face of the desert. Drink your fill in the morning and drink sparingly from the water skins throughout the day. We'll not reach the first well until dusk, and with the drought, it may prove dry."

"What of the horses?"

It was evident that Flavius' question weighed on Kazur's mind.

"I'm reluctant to bring them since we lack the guarantee of water, yet we have need for haste. What think you?"

Scratching his beard, Flavius squinted into the campfire, weighing the necessity for speed against the death of three fine horses.

"I think we must take them. If the first well proves dry, we'll release them tomorrow night. They'll make for water and likely head back from whence we came."

Nodding his agreement, Kazur took a sip of the bitter tea brewed nightly in the hope it might mitigate the chilly night breezes.

"The time has passed that we may speak of Pelion. Tomorrow begins the masquerade of a prince of Endlin, his nephew, and their squire in search of skilled slaves to service my racing stables in the east. Both of you will speak only when addressed by me, Flavius with lowered eyes and Ryzan with a careful regard for my exalted position."

Flavius greeted this dictum with a grunt of enjoyment and was immediately in character.

"Great lord, will we meet strangers on this route, and if so, will we join with them in caravan? Your humble servant begs enlightenment."

"If it pleases me to do so, you will be informed," came Kazur's lofty reply, to which Flavius bowed his head, uttering a grateful sigh that his question merited a response. Reddin laughed aloud at the spectacle of Flavius' transformation into a submissive menial complete with rounded shoulders and meek demeanor. An immediate and haughty reprimand issued by his new-found uncle brought him up short.

"Does it amuse you, nephew, to witness the correct behavior of a servant to his lord and master? It would behoove you to study Flavius' manner, for your mirth displeases me and spoils my peace."

It was Flavius' turn to laugh and he nearly split the seams of his jerkin, so heartily did he enjoy the sight of Reddin's comeuppance. Helpless to do anything except join in the spirit of Flavius' fun, Reddin wiped tears from his eyes. Flavius was trying to regain his composure and Reddin was having even less success, when, with a disgusted wave of his ring-covered hand, Kazur shooed them off to their assigned duties.

"Since by your noise you signal your unrest, see to the horses and the fire. I give you leave to depart my presence."

"I'll check the horses, Ryzan," Flavius drawled the name, causing Reddin to stifle another burst of laughter, "if you'll bank the fire. I tossed some kindling on the other side of those bushes."

Following Flavius' pointed finger, Reddin made his way to the outer fringes of the camp and began searching for the stack of wood gathered by Flavius in the early hours of dusk after Kazur called a halt to the day's travels. Sensible and uncomplaining, Flavius was an ideal traveling companion, willing to talk or keep silent depending on the mood at hand. More than once he'd helped Reddin over the rough spots, teaching him some of the finer points of riding, and with a few well-aimed jests, helped him place some distance between himself and what lay ahead in Agave.

Reddin's eyes were adjusting to the darkness beyond the campfire when he stumbled over the firewood, a move that may have saved his life. The swish of a knife slashing the empty air over his head and a muttered curse made him continue his fall forward, freeing his knife as he tucked and curled, coming up from a body roll with a cry to alert the others and a dagger poised and ready to defend himself. Before he could locate his opponent, who must have hidden himself in the low breaks and bushes since they'd long since passed the timbered lands, a hairy forearm wrapped around his throat, a raspy voice demanding:

"Drop it!"

Since this request suggested that his attacker had no intention of killing him, Reddin's immediate reaction was to obey. In that instant, he heard Strato bellowing at him. Lowering his knife, feeling the tension in the man's arm relax, he ducked and bent, throwing the man over his shoulder in a move that might have broken Reddin's neck if the man had been either heavier or wiser.

His assailant landed hard and Reddin was quickly on top of him, his knife at the man's throat. Later he would remember the man's eyes, grim and expecting death, but in that moment two events informed his decision, a cut-off cry from Flavius and the sound of someone sneaking into position behind him. It was as Strato warned him: if he paused to reflect on the morality of his action, he would surely meet his death, and so he killed quickly and efficiently. Severing the throat with one precise gesture, he could identify each muscle, tendon, artery and vein as he slid the silvery, razor-sharp blade across the man's flesh. Waiting tensely for the body behind him to leap on his unsuspecting back, he turned at the last moment, impaling his assailant on his outstretched knife, twisting it brutally inside the lower abdomen, knowing he was ripping through the coils of intestines, hearing the man scream as he was disemboweled.

Pushing aside the still-twitching body, Reddin was off toward the site of Flavius' scream, hearing Kazur's gasp of relief as he determined Reddin's identity and with a sharp pull of his arm, freed his knife from a body slumped beside him on his sleeping robes. Kazur joined his sprint across the camp, a flaming log in his hand as they ran toward the horses, both men painfully aware that no sounds were coming from that direction.

"Flavius!"

Reddin could hear the stark fear in his voice, but it mattered not. The night was dark, the moon a pale slipper shedding such little light that he could barely make out the shapes of the horses, who shied at his shout, one of them neighing in fear, the others pawing at the ground and snorting their distress.

"No sense spooking the horses. They've had a rough night."

No one but Flavius would be considerate of the horses after having fought for his life. Once Reddin located him, resting his back against a rock as he cradled his injured arm, he saw a body sprawled a few paces off, Flavius' knife buried in his heart, open eyes gazing blankly at the night sky. Dropping to his knees, Reddin set aside the hand Flavius was using to hold the sides of the wound together, and in the light of Kazur's torch, examined the sliced forearm. The incision was a curving slash, bleeding freely, and in need of stitches. Painful though it might be, it was hardly life-threatening, and with care taken against infection, Flavius would quickly recover its use. Relief flooded Reddin and with it, a fit of trembling, as if he'd caught the nervousness of the horses, which were shaking their heads, their eyes rolled back in their heads. Flavius cut through the still night air with a dry observation.

"I trust you found the kindling?"

When Reddin nodded his head in answer, Flavius regarded him with a keen-eyed gaze.

"How many?"

"I . . . I killed two."

An eyebrow raised as Flavius considered him. Kazur spoke a quiet question.

"Were they the only ones you saw, Reddin, or were there more?"

"I'm not sure. I never got a good look at the one who made the first move. He could have been the second man I killed, though there might have been a third."

Kazur and Flavius exchanged glances. Handing the torch to Reddin, Kazur stepped into the darkness, disappearing in the direction from which Reddin had come.

"Why does he worry, Flavius? We're alive! If there are others, they've fled by now."

"Because we've no way of knowing how long they listened or what they heard. Consider, if you will, what Kazur said after we'd cleared away the meal and gathered at the fire."

Reddin cast back over what seemed like hours ago, although it had been a matter of minutes, until he remembered: "'The time has passed that we may speak of Pelion.'"

"Which is more than enough to hang us all."

* * *

A JEWEL-BEDECKED HAND tossed aside the silken draperies that guarded the privacy of Scarphe's inner room. Her son swaggered into her chamber, hands on hips, his annoyance stamped on his furrowed brow. Pleased at his bad humor, well-satisfied that she could manipulate his emotions as easily as ever, she let nothing of her satisfaction read on her face, hiding her thoughts behind a mask that had served her well for sixty years.

"What is so important that I must be dragged from the hall? Abas would tell me nothing; like a blinded worm he twists and turns. Phaugh! He disgusts me!"

With a grimace, Lord Seth spat out his distaste. Scarphe responded with soft laughter that contained not a jot of humor.

"What choice do you give me, son, when it seems my presence holds no joy for you? As to Abas, I remember well, as should you, that your revulsion has not prevented him from rendering you services of, how should I phrase it, a somewhat. . . ," her voice hardened, ". . . disgusting nature."

To her delight, he froze, an ugly red flush rising from the neckline of his satin robes. Enjoying his fury, she made a quick inventory of his appearance, proud of his flamboyant style of dress, his perfect coiffure and studied air of elegance. He might lack the commanding presence of his lately departed uncle, but heads turned whenever he appeared.

With an airy wave of her hand she dismissed his anger, fixing on her face a charming smile.

"No matter, my son, no matter. You are here and I rejoice in your presence."

Mollified, he reclined in his usual place, carefully arranging his garments so they fell in graceful folds. The Aeson's medallion swung from his neck. She noted he wore blue sapphires to adorn his fingers, chosen no doubt to accentuate the indigo satin of his robes. As her glance lingered over him, she came back to the color of his clothing with a start. He's been wearing blue, this special shade of blue, quite often of late.

"What news of the lovely Charis, my son? Has she left off her mourning for her master? It troubled me to see her lost in grief, for, you must admit, black ill becomes her beauty."

Her eyes narrowed, although her voice revealed nothing of her anger as her son stretched and licked his lips, unaware that his expression was nothing short of greedy, a gluttonous, salivating boy masquerading in a man's body, the picture of a husband she had detested, then rendered impotent after the birth of her son. Unaware of her reaction, her son began to wax eloquent, every word grating against her ears, threatening her ability to conceal her hatred of the detestable slave who had nearly ruined all her plans.

"I convinced her to set aside her mourning when Lillas returned, advising her that it was no longer fitting for her to swathe herself in black once her daughter was rescued. Unlike her daughter, Charis is obedience itself."

Seth snickered, well-pleased with himself.

Scarphe's lips curled into a wintry smile.

"Have you found another apartment for her, my son? It hardly seems fitting that a slave should retain such, uh, lavish, quarters."

"You forget yourself, mother!" His eyes had gone small and piggy, always the first sign of his temper. "She is my slave and she will live where it pleases me to let her live!"

Scarphe continued smoothly, not deigning to respond to his insulting tone, although by rights she should have slapped his insolence away, something she had done with regularity until the death of her brother.

"I would think she would be happiest with her daughter in the apartments nearest the gardens, and thus you could see her whenever you visit your betrothed."

"Charis stays in her chambers. . .," muttering under his breath, Seth completed his thought, ". . . as far away from that hellcat as is possible."

Fool! Scarphe screamed inside herself, have I taken you this far for you to throw it all away for a worthless slave who by rights should be dead? Shall you lust after a woman twice your age whose days of breeding are past? And shall that blue-eyed slattern take my rightful place beside you in the halls of Imarus? For an instant, her mask slipped, and he must have read the murder in her eyes.

"I warn you, mother, if anything untimely should befall Charis, an illness or injury of any kind, be assured that I will hold you personally responsible."

He fingered the medallion briefly, purposefully, as he fixed his cold blue eyes upon her, eyes that matched her cruelty with his own, eyes that gloated over her, announcing his power, power she had given him and power she could never share. Hating him, she turned away, a disinterested wave of her hand indicating her submission to his will.

"You mistake my concern. If you want Charis for a plaything, so be it, although I never thought your taste ran to leftovers from another man's plate."

Her sneer had its intended effect and his temper blazed.

"Silence! I've had my fill of your carping! Tell me why I'm here or let me return to the entertainment!"

Another approach was necessary to keep him in the room. Swallowing her venom, she reached for a goblet of wine and wet her lips, readying herself for their next bout.

"Forgive me, my son. Time weighs heavily on my hands and old woman that I am, you must pardon my tendency to nag." His eyes flickered, but he made no response. Carefully, she provided the bait. "I called for you because something interesting came to my ears, and I thought you might appreciate some information."

"Information concerning what?" A tapping foot indicated his boredom.

She paused, making him wait, enjoying the cast of the lure.

"Pelion."

How he hated the word! She could hear his teeth grind as he remembered his return from the campaign, furious that the city elders met his terms and returned the girl without a protest, robbing him of the chance to wreak destruction on a city he held responsible for the drop in slave traffic, the growing unrest of the populace, and worst of all, the decrease of his coffers. Scarphe made him see the need for the girl, for a dynastic marriage that would silence the whispers of treachery connected to her father's death, but his intention was that the army he led would crush Pelion. He never dreamed the rulers of Pelion would capitulate without a fight, forcing him to retreat despite his wish to punish them for their prosperity. Had the army been completely in his employ, he would have persevered. Still, his greed made him unwilling to drain his private purse so he appealed to Agave's business leaders for funds. Every soldier under his command knew the terms of the contract with the Aeson. Once their darling was rescued, Seth lacked the power to demand further actions for which the city would not pay.

He sulked for days after his return, harassing the girl for information concerning this "gift" promised by the black prophet, sure that this secret would unlock the mystery of a city that had not existed until fifty years ago, yet threatened the very existence of slavery, and by extension, the glory of Seth. But the girl could not, or would not, provide the information he needed, and he had dismissed her from his presence in a fit of rage. Now he spoke from between clenched teeth.

"Tell all, mother."

Triumphant, relishing the ease of her victory and the return of his dependence on her, Scarphe wove the story with care.

"A party of slavers working the scrublands to the northeast came upon three travelers, eastern by their dress. They overheard several odd phrases: a reference to Pelion, the word `masquerade,' and one man, apparently a servant, who spoke with the accent of the south. According to my source, they seemed in a hurry, although they mentioned no destination."

Knowing better than to question her sources, he waited for her to proceed, tugging impatiently at the chain around his neck.

"Alas," she sighed, "the slavers were incompetent. Four were killed; the fifth escaped."

He was fidgeting now, glowering at her, and she reveled in it.

"Of what possible use is this drivel from the lips of a coward?"

"Patience, patience, my son!"

She nearly laughed at his ferocious scowl, knowing better than he who truly held the reins of power.

"This coward saw them enter the gates of Agave today at dusk and followed them to an inn. Knowing my generosity for any bit of news that concerns the welfare and interests of my son, he contacted Abas tonight."

In a single move Seth was on his feet spouting orders, the exact orders she had issued over an hour ago.

"Capture them alive. Tell Abas to keep them in Agave until they've been tamed a bit. I'll question them myself."

"As you wish, my son," came her demure response.

At the entrance to her chambers, he paused, turning back to her with a grudging smile.

"My thanks for your help, mother."

"It is nothing, my son. It pleases me to offer you my assistance."

"Perhaps. . . perhaps you'd be my special guest at this evening's entertainment?"

She rose and glided toward him, accepting his arm and sweeping grandly through the silken drapes and down the marble passageway.

"Could your source remember the exact reference to Pelion?"

Smiling inwardly at his attempt at nonchalance, she offered him the prize, a prize she would have kept to herself had he not offered to escort her to the hall.

"'The time has passed that we may speak of Pelion.'"

Chapter 18

The Pits of Agave

STREET NOISE, A dreadful din of screams, shouts, and general mayhem, woke Flavius. Without thinking, his hand shot under the pillow, searching for his dagger, until, his memories catching up with his reflexes, he registered the street noise for exactly what it was: the usual morning sounds of a city called Agave. Fully awake, he paused for a moment to wonder at how quickly he'd come to detest this place. In the time it took to have their pass stamped, walk under the forbidding sandstone gateway, push and claw their way through the unwashed masses, locate the inn, and tumble exhausted into lumpy cots whose mattresses stank and undoubtedly were the breeding ground of countless fleas, he'd called himself a fool, and worse than a fool, a thousand times. Who else but a Legionnaire with an overdeveloped sense of duty and a fatal case of heroism would voluntarily enter this shit-hole?

For that matter, who else but a pea-brained idiot like himself could listen to a woman like Dana (an ernani from the west who had traveled a hundred leagues out of her way to avoid Agave) inform him that he had finally lost what little sanity he'd ever possessed, and then kiss her indulgently, assuring her that her fears were exaggerated. She'd planted an elbow in his stomach, boxed his ears, and sent him on his way with her curses ringing in those same ears. Mournfully, he scratched a fleabite and burped the wretched fare they'd purchased last night for three times the price of a decent meal in Pelion, considering the fact that at this moment Dana was dressing their son, feeding him her famous linked sausages and hot, spicy eggs, and undoubtedly smoothing his disobedient red curls, curls the exact shade of his mother's hair. Damn you anyway, Flavius, what were you thinking of?

The stitches in his arm itched. Turning his head, he examined the scar with pride. No healer had ever worked over him so diligently or followed his recovery with such attentiveness as had Reddin. He'd guessed that about him from the first day he saw him standing on the reviewing stand. Serious, unsmiling, reserved as a priest, Reddin was the only person who could have inspired Flavius to pass through Agave's gates of his own free will. At that thought his confidence returned. His arm was healing and would soon be as good as new, Kazur was as savvy a leader as any soldier could wish for, and Reddin's spirits rose with every mile they traveled toward Agave. In two or three days he'd shake the sand from his boots and make a beeline for Dana, knowing from experience that by the time he returned her anger would have run its course. And maybe, he thought, chuckling to himself, maybe they'd start work on creating that red-headed daughter he'd always wanted, a perfect copy of rough and tumble Dana, the long-suffering mate of a dim-witted fool of a Legionnaire.

His bladder close to bursting, he tossed off the yellowed sheets, scratched and stretched, and made his way toward the stinking slop bucket. Glancing over at the two narrow cots beside his, he noticed for the first time that they were empty. Hell and damnation, what was going on? He was always the first to rise! In the next moment he was checking the sun's position through the open window, relieving himself, throwing on his clothes, grabbing his dagger and money-belt, and lacing his boots. Then it came to him. He'd drunk some local beer last night, Reddin and Kazur abstaining, and could dimly remember being helped up the steps with Kazur frowning on one side and Reddin smiling on the other. Doubtless they'd decided to let him sleep it off. Cursing himself far more viciously that he'd cursed Agave, Flavius pounded down the three flights of steps and entered the common room, searching for two heads of braided hair bowed over their morning meal.

Except for a fellow sweeping out refuse into the open sewer that passed for a city street and a one-eyed tom-cat who hissed at his approach, the room was empty. In a split second his head cleared, his eyes focused, and Flavius went into action.

"Innkeeper, I was wondering if you've seen my master and his nephew? They broke their fast together this morning, if I'm not mistaken."

He kept his delivery purposefully submissive, remembering Prax's admonitions that in Agave there was little difference between a slave, a bondsman, or a servant. The free-born of Agave were a touchy lot. Nothing infuriated them more than an uppity menial.

The innkeeper glanced at him over his shoulder, shrugged, and continued his half-hearted sweeping, an air of futility hanging over him like a shroud.

"The older man left at dawn. The younger came down an hour ago."

Flavius' heart stopped beating. Then, with a rush, it started pounding so loudly Flavius was surprised the innkeeper didn't turn back to him and ask for quiet. That Kazur had left at first light didn't surprise him. There were agents to visit, plans to make, routes to survey, and Kazur was anxious to familiarize himself with the city as quickly as he could. But to think that Reddin had left . . . no, it wasn't possible! He'd been cautioned repeatedly about the danger of wandering about alone and had given his word he'd not leave the inn without either Flavius or Kazur in attendance.

"Begging your pardon, but did you happen to see which way my young master headed?" Flavius started building his cover story, wheedling and whining with his tail between his legs, hoping the innkeeper was more observant than he seemed. "He's been ill of late and took the desert travel hard."

The innkeeper was nodding, his face morose, a grave-digger's face, Flavius thought absently.

"He took ill again and could barely stand. His friends helped him outside to catch a breath of fresh air."

It took every particle of Flavius' training not to grab this scarecrow of a man around the throat and shake the information out of him. But Prax was a hard taskmaster and his briefing for this mission covered every possible set of alternatives. Calm yourself, Flavius, he told himself. Panic makes mistakes, and a mistake could cost you that red-headed daughter of yours.

"Might I trouble you for a roll and tea?"

The innkeeper's ears flapped at the sound of two coins being rubbed together. In no more than a minute Flavius was choking down a stale roll and lukewarm tea with all the flavor of pond scum.

Affable, everybody's favorite squire, Flavius commented on the lamentable lack of rain, commiserating with the innkeeper over the high cost of water, gradually moving the conversation back to the regrettable illness of his young master. Without a moment's hesitation, he invaded the man's mind, keeping him talking with a series of grunts and smiles as he searched for memories of Reddin.

He saw it all, choking back his fury when he realized that the innkeeper had seen the bandy-legged man work his slight-of-hand, dropping the powder into Reddin's tea before it ever left the counter, and watched as Reddin passed his hand over his eyes, shaking his head as if it pained him, and then staggered groggily to his feet, trying to make his way up the stairs. Up the stairs to me, Flavius thought, up the stairs to his monitor, obeying the rules the way he always had in the Maze, trusting that Flavius would keep him on his feet and, if necessary, carry him away from the finish line.

Someone else was there instead. Not Flavius, a useless drunk scratching fleabites in his sleep, but a bandy-legged spy and a squint-eyed monster of a man. They'd pulled Reddin away from the staircase, their arms cradled around his shoulders, calling him by name as they helped him out to the street, the smaller man throwing the innkeeper a few coins to assure his silence. "Ryzan" they called him. Now Flavius knew the worst.

Sick with guilt, crazy with worry, he smiled broadly at the innkeeper, patted his belly, and announced his intention to meet his master at the slave market. His tip was lavish, his walk unhurried as he sauntered out into the city of madness, everything about him indicating confidence and good humor, while inside his mind he considered his knife and the heavy purse secreted underneath his belt. Their mission was a shambles, their identities known and traced to the inn, and all their lives not worth the price of a cup of Agavean well water.

"REDDIN IS GONE and we cannot find him!"
The mind reaching out to them was reeling and dangerously close to hysteria.
"Report, Kazur! Report, I say! Hold together, man, or we'll lose you as well!"
Something shifted as Prax assumed command. A chord was touched, moving Kazur's thoughts closer to rationality.
"It happened as you said it might. There was a fifth man. They drugged Reddin at the inn. Flavius and I contacted your agents and we've worked the crowds all day searching for the men who took him."
"Abort, Kazur!"
There was no response.
"Do you understand me? Abort! Ditch the clothes and trade the jewels. Buy the shackles and exchange roles as we practiced. They're looking for an eastern merchant and a bearded squire. They won't look twice at a clean-shaven farmer and a slave in chains. The gates close at dusk. Move!"
"I won't leave him."
This from Flavius, bull-headed despite his terror.
"Flavius, this is a direct order. You'll never find him and you can't save him even if you did. His welfare is no longer your responsibility. We knew this might happen. There were no guarantees. There are never any guarantees."
"Flavius, Kazur, hear me."
At the touch of the Mother of Pelion's thoughts, their worries calmed, for she took their guilt away, putting it on her shoulders, absolving them of their sins, whether real or imagined.
"You must not grieve for him. You fear that he is dead; I know he lives. Leave quickly and quietly as Prax advises. Your duties are finished."
Breaking the contact, Hesione leaned back in her chair.
"Prax?"
He started, lifting his head from his hands and regarded her with a look bleaker than the desert wastelands.
"I leave at dawn."
Nodding slowly he turned away from her, staring sightlessly at the stone walls. After a long silence in which she felt him taste defeat, she spoke again, willing him to listen.
"I need you, Prax."

His clenched fist smashed down onto the table, a fist that could have shattered bone but left not the slightest indentation on the scarred surface of the round table.

"Which Prax do you need? A Commander who's lost one too many men and can't seem to shake the ghosts that haunt him, a strategist for a war we've nearly lost, or a Council member who hasn't made a single worthwhile contribution, so bound is he to old ideas, old ways of doing things?"

"I want none of these."

"Neither do I, Hesione. Neither do I."

Hearing her name on his lips, she smiled, knowing that to Prax she would always be Hesione, knowing that it indicated not a lack of respect, but recognition of their special bond. Much as he revered the black robes, he had come to love her as a father loves a bright, willful daughter, despairing of her youthful enthusiasms, protective of her shortcomings, steadfast through times of trouble.

"I want the son of a man whose back proclaimed him a slave. I want the young Legionnaire who stood by the Seventeenth Mother's side during the Selection Protest. Most of all, I want the man who removed this silver ring from the hand of a dead girl."

"I . . . I'm not sure he exists anymore."

"But he's here," she protested, refusing to let him give in to self-pity, "sitting beside me while the others hurry home to family and friends, the happy, oblivious citizenry of Pelion he adores, having devoted his life to keeping them safe and free from harm or worry. Tomorrow, he will ride west with me, offering me the use of his good right arm."

"And likely lead you to your death," he muttered.

Smiling, she rose and walked across the room, whirling around to face him, laughing aloud at his astonished stare.

"Say rather that you escort me to my bridegroom!"

Uttering a disbelieving grunt, he continued staring at her, his mouth open in wordless surprise.

"Nothing else can be achieved in Pelion. I've known this since the day Lillas left the Maze. You've sensed it, too, although you ignore it at every opportunity. I was chosen for this moment: the youngest Eighteenth Mother in history, healthy, keen of eye, a woman reared outside city walls, a child who rode before she walked. Small and dowdy I may be, but who will fear me, or give me a second glance when we pass through the sandstone walls?"

"This is my destiny, Prax: to bring Agave to heel, to muzzle the beast. Too long have we hidden here, safe and comfortable in our walled domain, waiting for the world to come to us. I will be the first of many black-robed women to pass beyond the city walls. Lukash was my prophet; you are my disciple. And if I live. . ., " she paused, her lips curving into a smile of something akin to both joy and sadness, ". . . if I live, I will look back with fondness on the days to come, knowing that nothing in my life will compare to the adventure we begin today."

Long ago he had knelt at her feet on a floor of leaves and pledged his obedience. Today he knelt on a floor of stone and offered her his life.

REDDIN'S JAILERS DRAGGED him down the dingy corridors as he shivered and shook from the rough dousing they administered in a horse-trough. Desperate to quench his raging thirst, he managed to swallow some of the water in the trough only to vomit it up, earning a blow and a curse from the nameless ones who brought him out of the pit. Begrudging the fact that they had to smell and touch his foulness, they ducked him again and again under the stagnant water, rinsing off the worst of the vomit and excrement that covered him, the result of the drug that had nearly killed him as he lay retching and moaning in the fetid straw, helpless to control the bouts of nausea and flux that kept his stomach and bowels in a constant state of twisted torment. Too ill to care where they were taking him or what he would face upon arrival, he hung limply between them, his sodden, filthy braids slapping him in the face, his head pounding with every step they took.

He lost all sense of time as he lay in the pit, moving through various stages of wakefulness and unconsciousness as the poison coursed through his system. He was in a room now, being pushed in front of a thick pole that he could lean against for support, his arms pulled around the pole and tied behind his back. Resting, grateful for an end to the misery of movement, he must have dozed. All at once someone was snarling at him, slapping him awake.

"Time for questions and answers."

He forced his eyes open, willing them to focus. The jailer's face retreated, a new face replacing his, a face frowning with displeasure.

"I said tame, not kill. What have you done?"

"I, uh, I misjudged his weight, my lord. It wasn't until we stripped him that I realized I'd used too much."

There was the sound of a slap, a whimper, and the frowning face reappeared in front of Reddin.

"Do you hear me, spy?"

Reddin heard but could not bring himself to understand.

"When I speak, you will answer!"

As punishment for his lack of response, Reddin was struck a fierce, backhanded blow. A line of fire burned across his cheekbone and warm liquid dripped down his sliced cheek. Over the sound of his retching, for the blow reawakened his nausea, he heard a squeal of outrage and received a slap to the other side of his face.

"You filthy pig, you've ruined my gown!"

The man was cleaning blood off the diamond rings lining the knuckles of his right hand and blotting the front of his elegant robes with a silken handkerchief.

"Come, my lord, it is an old gown, and I've often thought you should replace it. The color does not flatter."

It was a woman's voice, beautifully modulated and carefully cajoling. A pleased look crossed the man's face as he turned away to address someone standing beyond Reddin's view.

"Think you so? Had you told me before, it would have been immediately consigned to rags."

As they conversed, the man simpering and the woman beguiling, Reddin's vision cleared. As he stared at the back of his tormentor's head, the elaborately arranged ringlets seemed somehow familiar. Try though he might, he could not pierce the fog surrounding his memory.

"Now, slave, tell me what you know of Pelion."

When the sickness came upon him in the inn, he'd dimly heard them call him Ryzan. Too dazed to fight them as they half-carried, half-dragged him out of the inn, he'd been only partially aware of what that name signified. As his mind began to clear, he knew they were betrayed and mourned over Flavius and Kazur, sharing his captivity, enduring like treatment in some other dirty cell.

"I . . .," he croaked, ". . . I passed that way on my travels."

A knee landed full in his unprotected groin. Denied breath enough to scream, he groaned as his vision exploded into bursts of violent white light. As he pitched forward, the rope around his hands pulled tightly against the pole, digging into his wrists as he was held forcibly upright.

"I've no time for games. Your masquerade is over. Tell me what I want to know or the past two days will seem restful in comparison with what will follow. Serve me well and you may yet live."

Through the layers of pain, Reddin heard the lie. This man spoke no truths, believed no truths. A fist closed on the back of his braids, jerking his head up and back. Even with his eyes clenched shut, he knew the deviousness of this man, the danger written in his cold pale eyes.

"What is the gift?"

"The gift?"

Numbly, he repeated the phrase, mumbling words that tasted of despair.

"Yes, you miserable cretin! The gift the prophet promised, the gift that will destroy Agave! Deny me, and you'll beg for death!" The voice paused, considering some private evil, and then continued, dripping with honeyed deceit. "Tell me and I'll free your friends."

Something died inside Reddin at the mention of his companions, yet he could not, would not, answer this madman. Any mention of the gift in this wretched place soiled its memory, befouling what Reddin had sworn to protect. He was not a brave man, but he would honor his oath. Armed with that thought he roused himself to look full into his questioner's face.

"What you ask cannot be answered."

With a high-pitched scream of fury, his questioner struck him full in the face. His teeth catching his lip, he tasted his own blood. Sweet and salty, it seeped down his throat, causing the nausea to return full force.

"Put an end to his infernal insolence!"

Retching as his body slid down the pole, helpless to avoid the attack which followed his inquisitor's command, Reddin writhed on the floor as heavy boots kicked him, the blows landing unerringly on his belly, his ribs, his groin, his torturers working on either side of his prostrate body, taking turns, offering no respite. The sounds of cries and groans floated around him, but they seemed unassociated with him for he was waiting now, sure that relief could not be far off. Soon he was slipping away, the pain a fiery river bearing him toward a blessed land of nothingness. In front of his face, a foot pulled back. In slow motion he saw it travel through the air and land, felt the stabbing agony of ribs cracking, and rejected a world that offered nothing but pain.

"IS HE DEAD?"

Seth loved the boredom in her voice, the artistic phrasing of her casual inquiry. Charis was nothing short of perfection with her perfectly shaped eyebrows set like wings above her glorious indigo eyes. It surprised him that she wanted to accompany him to the city, but then she had sought his presence repeatedly in the past several days. He was exultant, positive that she was turning to him at last, putting aside her show of mourning for the old man whose affections she'd been forced to endure for so long. Seth had wanted her for years, lusting from afar, confident that she returned his feelings but feared her owner's jealousy.

She was gazing coolly down at the naked, stinking, dark-skinned man who lay on his side, his legs drawn up in a pitiful attempt to shield his genitals. His face was hidden by those ghastly braids that made Seth shudder whenever he saw one of those insufferably proud easterners in the marketplace. Blood stained the floor near his face. Just as Seth was about to answer with an affirmative, Abas crouched by the body and searched for a pulse. Backing away from the inert form, he turned mournful eyes to his lord and master.

"He lives, Lord Seth."

This worthless excuse for a servant had not only botched the capture of the other two men, but seemed incapable of carrying out the simplest of requests. Still, it would not do to make a fuss in front of Charis. Sensitive to her status, she became uncomfortable when he disciplined his slaves in front of her. He would match her manner of haughty disregard toward clumsy and inept attendants.

"Have him executed in the marketplace at noon."

Extending his arm to her, he sensed her disapproval as she accepted it, and was immediately suspicious.

"Have you feelings for this insolent dog?"

When a bright bubble of laughter lifted musically from her throat, he was instantly reassured. She smiled up at him, her perfect teeth shining against the pinkness of her full, pouting lips.

"Oh, my lord, how ridiculous you must think me! Be assured that I care nothing for your enemies. I merely thought ... please excuse my effrontery ...," at his gracious nod she continued, ". . . I thought another public execution might speak poorly of your reputation in the city. After all, he will most likely die on his own, will he not? And who could blame Lord Seth then?"

She fluttered her coal black lashes, looking kittenish and utterly desirable. He was on fire for her and would have done anything to please her, although he was flattered by her interest in his affairs. This was exactly the kind of suggestion that would have occurred to his mother. Admiring her all the more for her shrewdness, he patted her hand and turned to Abas.

"Put him back in the pit. I never want to see or hear of him again. Use your own judgment as to how to dispose of the body."

Abas nodded vigorously, bowing and smirking, grateful no doubt that it was not his wretched carcass that was to be thrown into the pit.

"You are wise in the ways of men, my lord," she whispered in his ear.

"And you, my precious one, are all that I desire."

She looked up at that, for it was the first time he'd put his desire for her into words. He thought she paled, but she quickly lowered her eyes, and he smiled contentedly to himself, charmed by her shyness. After all, she'd known no one but his dearly departed uncle. As they walked out of the sandstone fortress that housed the Aeson's prison, Seth decided that it was time for Charis to experience the delights possible with a younger and more virile man.

A ROTUND, BALDING fellow puffed loudly as he pushed his way through the crowd of beggars lining the rear entrance to the Aeson's prison. It was not a much frequented street, but beggars were licensed in Agave, and the poorest of the poor had to settle for a street whose lease they could afford. Children with ancient eyes pushed their bowls toward him, wailing true stories of infirmity and abuse. The blind took up the chant, empty sockets turned uselessly upward toward the harsh light of day. This morning their pitiful prayers were answered, for a copper coin found its way into every bowl, and they praised him, singing their adoration to the skies, for today they would drink, and if the day continued fair, by evening they might eat.

Stopping at the guard-post, a ramshackle hut where two men played dice, the man produced his papers.

"A bargain-hunter, eh?"

Nodding, smiling, stammering tales of a stingy lord, the man's belly shook with nervousness. The guards laughed and passed him through.

They did not look over their shoulders as he walked toward the pits, and so they missed a remarkable transformation as the bumbling bookkeeper straightened, pulled a heavy belt complete with dagger and purse from underneath his robes and strapped it around his considerable girth, all of this accomplished without altering the rhythm of his march. A heavy signet ring found its way onto his forefinger, and he was now a steward, a highly-respected employee of a ruling house, brought here by the underground traffic in unlicensed slaves, for this Aeson was not bound by his own rules. Since Lord Seth's ascension to the high seat, a small fortune had been made on transactions not hindered by taxes and fees.

The pits were aptly named. Perfectly square they were, some twenty feet deep, with sheer walls impossible to climb covered by iron grates fastened with padlocks. Rumor had it they had been dug by quarry slaves, all of whom had been left to die in the tombs they'd fashioned with their bleeding hands. The morning was warm, but not yet sweltering, so the inhabitants were quieter than usual. On the blazing days of high summer, when the sun beat down unmercifully through the grate, their screams for water rose to disturb the residents of the surrounding neighborhood, a fact which made these rents some of the cheapest in Agave. This morning their noise was a kind of dull moan as they waited for the water-carriers to make their sole visit of the day, lowering down a tin bucket of water to their grasping hands, careful that the rope be removed lest a body be found hanging the following morning, for after all, the pit-dwellers were not just prisoners, they were merchandise, and Agave was a city founded on solid principles of trade.

The steward stopped to ask directions from a water-carrier and was directed to a bandy-legged man standing on the edge of a pit aiming an arching spray of amber urine through the grate. As he heard the steward approach, his hands moved frantically to button his breeches. His fingers were nimble, so that by the time he turned, he was decent, at least in dress.

"I was told I might find a slave here of particular talents."

The steward was brusque, but the bandy-legged man was accustomed to brusqueness. Bowing and fawning, his eyes taking in the purse, ring, and dagger, he nearly scraped the ground in his willingness to serve.

"What talents, my lord? We have so many residents." With a sweeping gesture he indicated the surrounding pits. The steward shook his head impatiently.

"This is a special case, one that came to my attention through a highly-placed source." With a single raised eyebrow he indicated Imarus. The bandy-legged man nearly capered with delight. The steward continued, lowering his voice to the tones of conspiracy. "My master has need of a letter written, a letter of, shall we say, a sensitive nature. He needs a learned man, preferably one who will not live long enough to betray his secrets."

It was a common enough story; the bandy-legged man had heard it before. Scribes were expensive, too expensive to kill for the writing of a single letter.

"My source says you have one who reads and writes, for he comes from Pelion."

The final word was uttered in a low whisper, the steward's head turning from side to side as if well-aware that this name was a curse in these parts. Cautiously, the bandy-legged man nodded, his eyes crafty since he smelled a deal and a rich deal at that. Here was a way to earn a profit at the same time he obeyed his master.

"I know the one of whom you speak. I don't know if he writes."

Eagerly, the steward grasped his arm.

"Come, man, let me examine him! I've no time to spare and my master is generous toward those who assist him."

The purse jingled as the steward shook it. A ladder appeared, a key unlocked the grate before them, and both men climbed down into the pit.

The interior was dim, for the sun wasn't high enough to illuminate its depths. The foul stench of vomit, excrement, and fresh urine rose from the filthy straw, a new layer set down with each new prisoner, the old layers left to mold and decay. A single pit-dweller was in evidence. Sprawled on his stomach, it appeared that he lay as he had fallen or been thrown, his face buried under a mass of tangled braids, his arm thrown up and over his head. He made no move as the two men drew near him, and might have been dead except for the sound of labored gasps that more often than not ended in moans.

Streaks of filth were smeared across his buttocks and down the back of his thighs as were a multitude of bruises, not so much purple as black against his earth-colored skin. With a practiced nudge of his foot, the bandy-legged man rolled him over, the man limp and unresisting. Once on his back, more grievous injuries could be seen. A deep gash oozing blood was painted across his right cheek. Above it, his eye was swollen shut. Rusty stains anointed his cracked lips and a swollen tongue emerged from his open mouth.

"When did he last drink?"

"Uh, yesterday. Perhaps the day before."

"I need water in order to question him." The steward selected a silver coin from his purse and flipped it into the jailor's grasping hands. "That should buy a bucket and leave some left over for your trouble."

The next moment the bandy-legged man was scurrying up the ladder. The steward knelt down in the straw, leaning over the motionless body.

"What have they done to you?" he muttered, running his hands quickly over the hot, dry skin, noting the sunken eyes and cheeks. When his skilled fingers found the swelling over the ribcage, the moans from the injured man's parched throat increased. When the steward's hand brushed against the prisoner's swollen testicles, a whimper escaped him and a shudder ran down his body. The shudder became trembling and suddenly the prisoner was shaking with chills, his hands flexing as if he reached for an imagined blanket to ward off the cold.

The steward's eyes shut tight, then flew open as he heard the grate being lifted and feet scuttled down the ladder rungs. A battered tin cup was placed in his outstretched hand. Reaching underneath the neck to supporting the prisoner's head, he began dribbling water into the open mouth.

There was no reaction as the liquid dribbled down his chin. In time there was a slight response, his mouth opening, his tongue moving to beg sips of water as the steward doled them out, careful that his charge not choke. As the cup emptied, his eyelashes fluttered. When the gift of water ended, he uttered a sigh, then gagged and vomited, his violent movements awakening the agony of the beating. The steward closed his ears against the sound of his groans.

Frowning, he looked up at the jailor.

"How long has he been like this? I want someone who's fit enough to compose a letter. This one will be dead by sunset."

"It's the drug."

"What drug?" The steward's frown grew deeper.

"Something we use to make the new ones more obedient."

"Show me."

The bandy-legged man burrowed in his pockets and produced a small envelope. Snatching it away from him, the steward opened it, sniffed at its contents, then wet his finger and inserted it into the powder, tasting it with the tip of his tongue. Grimacing, he spat, dipped the cup back in the bucket, rinsed his mouth and spat again, his disapproval clear.

"Hold his head and we'll try again."

With grim persistence the steward forced the prisoner to drink. Finally, some of the water made its way into him without being expelled. He was rousing again, his good eye open and attempting to focus on the figure bending over him. The steward went to work.

"Would you like more water?"

The prisoner struggled to understand, the steward repeating the question, aware that his bandy-legged companion listened attentively to every word. At his hesitant nod, the steward continued.

"I'll give you more in a minute. But first, you must do something for me."

"Y . . . e . . . s."

It was a single word rasped in a low whisper, but for the first time the prisoner displayed a glimmer of consciousness.

"I was told you can write. Is this so? Can you write?"

A troubled frown greeted his question, as if the prisoner was afraid to admit such a talent, fearing that such an admission might bring more punishment. The steward urged him on, demanding his compliance.

"I want you to write. Do you understand? I want you to write some words for me. If you do, I'll give you more water."

The prisoner nodded once and closed his eyes. Reading assent in that gesture, the steward quickly cleared away the straw from a small area of the floor in order to find the sand below. Taking hold of the prisoner's clenched right hand, the steward extended his forefinger, lowering it until it touched the sand.

"Now, write each word I say." The finger moved slowly, obediently, tracing the letters into the sand. "Water." "Wine." "Oil." A look of peace came gradually over the prisoner's drawn features. The last three letters formed, his hand dropped palm up in the sand, and he lay quiet.

The steward rose, brushing off his garments, and reached for his purse.

"He will do nicely."

He chose a single golden coin and placed it in the jailor's hand, noting his look of sheer disbelief. The steward listed his additional demands in a firm, no-nonsense manner.

"This payment includes his removal from the pit and men enough to carry him to my carriage two streets away." With these words came images geared to instill deep fears, the steward intent that the bandy-legged man would never remember this day without recalling the vivid nature of his threats. "You will say nothing about my purchase. There are stiff penalties for what we do here. If you betray me, I swear I'll take you with me to the mines or worse."

The bandy-legged man sputtered protestations, but the steward was no longer listening.

* * *

"DON'T HAGGLE WITH Abas; it will weaken your position in his eyes. Reward him well and then frighten him. This is the way Scarphe treats him and he will respond by force of habit."

After placing the purse in Phoron's hands, Charis turned away, staring out of the slatted blinds already pulled against the brightness of the morning sun. Her hair, still wet from her bath, hung in a blue-black ribbon down her back, dripping down the sheer robe tied loosely around her waist. Tall and statuesque, she seemed carved from stone. Phoron wondered at her stillness, at limbs which could remain motionless without tension. She is waiting, he thought to himself, but for what? And then she was speaking again, her voice remote as she focused on something beyond the gardens below her window.

"I have bought you seven days time. Seth hunts to the northwest, vowing to bring me back the skins from his kill. He is besotted."

This was delivered in a tone of quiet observation rather than contempt. In the face of her utter calm, Phoron saw Charis as she must have stood on the platform so many years ago. This was how she would have appeared, perfection rising above the ugliness surrounding her, untainted by the squalor of the steaming, voracious crowds. Gracefully she turned to him, the horizontal bands of light striking against the white, slender column of her neck to reveal bruises ringing her throat before disappearing into the line of fabric covering her breasts.

"You must not let him hurt you, Charis! Prax can get you out. Sacrifice has its limits."

It was a time-worn subject between them. As always, she smiled at him, touched by his concern but puzzled by it, as if he were a wayward child who could not, or would not, understand her reasoning.

"You are wrong, my friend," she said. "There are no limits to sacrifice. I thought so in my youth, but that youth is gone and with it my innocence. We are the sum of our acts with the gifts we are given. So the Seventeenth Mother said, and so I have come to believe. As to hurt," she turned away again, "you, Phoron, of all people, should know that I am beyond hurt and almost beyond life."

He knew it well, knew and accepted it as she had. Even so, he labored to keep her in the world.

"What of Lillas?"

"Yes," she whispered, "Lillas."

"She has need of you, Charis."

"Soon, I think, her need will lessen." She turned to consider him for a moment. "I saw him, healer, as he recognized the lies Seth spoke and protected the truth he holds so dearly that he would die for it. This has always been my role with Lillas, the sayer of difficult truths, the one who will not allow her to hide from things she would deny. He will be her truth-sayer now. He will speak the truth and my daughter. . .," she paused, her profile shadowed with equal parts of love and loss, ". . . my daughter will defend it."

PUSHING ASIDE HIS memory of Charis as he had left her, standing beside her window in the quiet hush of morning, waiting for something she held buried in her heart, Phoron looked down at the man at his feet. Water-carriers were gathering above him, no doubt bribed to leave their duties. He ran over the details in his mind: a short trip to the carriage hired with Charis' gold and the five-mile trek to Imarus where Lillas waited, unaware that her truth-sayer was being brought to her, unaware that the reason for her birth fast approached.

Chapter 19

The Nest

LILLAS LIFTED HER eyes from her book and counted heads. Everyone was involved in adding rows of figures, with the rather large exception of Mia, whose cumbersome body overflowed her chair and whose triple chins wagged as she shelled peas, stripping away the pod in two economical moves before thumbing the green peas into an enormous pottery bowl resting almost daintily on the vast expanse of her lap.

"Mia, have you seen Olwyn?"

The shelling continued, the peas dropping regularly into the bowl as the cook took her time answering. "Phoron asked for him after the morning meal, my lady. I've not seen him since."

Dismissing the empty place at the table with an inward sigh, Lillas leaned back against the pillowed headrest of her armchair and considered the rays of bright sunshine filtering through the silken drapes covering the windows of her antechamber. Such a lovely morning, she found herself musing, just right for a brisk run . . . and abruptly ended her fantasy. Childhood had passed and with it her faith in dreams.

Like a student copying out a hated lesson, she bit her bottom lip, determined to master the lesson her absent teacher had assigned. Her father was dead, dead a fortnight before Seth arrived outside the walls of Pelion. With his death, her freedom vanished. With no rights or privileges other than those grudgingly granted by Seth, she was a prisoner, forbidden to visit her mother or to leave her apartments for any other purpose than to accompany the new Aeson on official visits to Agave. Once she thought the Maze a prison, with its damp stone walls and locked doors, yet freedom of ideas abounded within its routines, rules, and discipline. Imarus seemed to her a prison of a harsher sort, for under its manicured lawns and marble facades all was falsehood and deceit. As a child she had mastered the art of fakery. To put her mask aside meant facing her failures.

Her eyes were those of one newly-born: the pitiful quarters where her slaves slept on hard marble floors, huddled together for warmth in the cool desert nights without a shred of privacy; their lives of routine labor without hope for advancement, denied the chance to learn new skills; their blank, empty faces as they sought to avoid her presence, fearing a sharp reprimand might end in their removal to a far worse place. And in each of them she saw faces of others lost to their families as Altug and Halys' brother were lost, or bound by the shackles of memory as Timon was bound after forty years of freedom. Bitterest of all was the realization that once she could have freed them, but now she could do nothing.

Even so, the Maze had done its work and she carried from it the essentials of freedom: ideas, industry, and self-respect. No longer a believer in the careless shrug of complacency, within her was sparked an energy she had not thought she possessed.

Stingy as he was, Seth maintained the same allowance her father gave her, something to hold over her head, Lillas guessed, if she displeased him. Now, instead of silks, jewels, and precious oils, she ordered cots, mattresses, and durable linens. Jobs were switched and rearranged so duties rotated weekly, each slave learning many skills instead of one. Only Mia received exemption, for she protested that she was too old to learn, and in any case, she asked with a confident grin, were there any complaints about her cooking? There were none, although she found herself with a larger budget, assistants eager to learn her craft, and the prospect of fresh vegetables and herbs from the newly planted gardens taken over by the slaves for their personal use, some of them making decisions for the first time as they pondered what crop they should plant and worried how it should best be tended.

Yet these were cosmetic changes, and Lillas knew the difference between the appearance of change and the struggle to attain inward change, for this had ever been her trial. Bettering their living conditions was one thing; changing the way they thought about themselves was quite another.

At first she tried to join in the household chores, but they froze when she approached and stammered when she attempted to engage them in conversation. She was ever master and they were ever slaves, and here the joys of trade that rule human exchanges came to ruination, for in this transaction one party benefited while the other stood deprived, the cost of their deprivation the loss of self-hood.

Helpless in the face of their helplessness, she acknowledged defeat. Then, one afternoon, she found herself sitting at the large table in the antechamber of her bedroom, fingering a slim volume of scarlet leather. The day was a quiet one, her mood pensive, and the book opened of its own accord to a page marred by a greasy smear. When her eyes wandered down the printed page, coming to rest on a stanza of verse, she heard a petulant voice demand:

"What is 'troth'"

And another voice answer mildly:

"It means to give your word, to swear."

The strangest and most blessed thing of all was that she felt no sadness at remembering Reddin. Rising, she walked to a wooden cabinet unopened for ten of her twenty years and flung wide the doors. There, in stacks dusty with neglect, she found storybooks, primers, grammars, arithmetics, geographies, all of them purchased at exorbitant prices for the education of a single pampered princess; all of them unopened, cast aside with a thoughtless hand or shoved under a bed in the hope they would disappear.

That evening she appeared in the kitchen as the slaves partook of their last meal of the day. Hearing the awkward hush that always greeted her arrival, she announced quietly and without fanfare:

"Tomorrow I will begin studying in my antechamber after the morning meal. I invite you to study with me. I am no scholar, but I can help you with the alphabet, with simple reading and writing, addition and subtraction. We have books. Phoron will purchase tablets, pens and ink tomorrow." Their faces remained blank. Hearing Reddin's first lesson ringing in her ears, she spoke from her heart. "I myself was ignorant of the pleasures to be found in books. Now, I find joy in reading of ideas, of descriptions of places I will never see, and of poetry that sings within my heart. If you share these longings, join me."

And they came, unbelieving at first, hesitant, ashamed of their ignorance, frightened they might make mistakes, shyly grateful for the opportunity to learn. None of them were literate in the common tongue that served Agave, Pelion, and much of the south, yet somehow she managed to teach them what she barely knew herself: reading, writing, and the mysteries of numbers larger than twenty. Sometimes she grew impatient, other times she despaired, but she persevered, measuring her success by their progress, finding her reward in a word correctly spelled or a sum precisely added. With the advancement of her pupils, she saw herself schooled under the gentle tutelage of Reddin. And with her teaching, as inexpert as it might be, she began repayment of a long-standing debt.

That afternoon she began the true healing, the inward growth of a spirit she feared dead. With it came grace, for although she'd set Reddin free, she guarded his memory jealously, punishing herself with daily reprisals and nightly retributions. As she set herself free, her memories became blessings, cherished relics to help her through the days and years of her imprisonment.

For the first few weeks the lessons provided her with an activity to speed her monotonous days. All too soon, her spirits flagged. She could not live on memories and eventually her students would overtake her in the classroom. Pacing the confines of her bedchamber, she wrangled over her lack of purpose, tasting bitterness and resentment over the meagerness of her talents. Finally, she turned to Phoron.

She found him, as ever, in his garden. Spring came early to Imarus, for the winters were mild and rarely did snow sweep over the desert lands. The winter just passed was the driest in memory, reservoirs were low and water was already being rationed in the city. All the waste water of her household continued its service as watering for the newly-planted gardens.

He was setting out seedlings and bulbs, digging irrigation ditches, and acutely annoyed at the sandy quality of the soil, which he was improving with generous handfuls of compost carted from the heap he maintained behind the kitchen. He was conducting a dialogue with himself, muttering of alkaline and acid and proper drainage when she interrupted him.

"What do you plant, Phoron?"

"Herbs for the kitchen: fennel, chervil, coriander, mustard, and hyssop. Chamomile and a curly variety of mint that loves the shade, I fear. Shallot sets, allium ascalonicum, to be exact."

He would likely have continued, but she knelt beside him. When he fixed her with a piercing gaze, she avoided it by asking another question.

"What of the herbs for healing?"

Sinking back on his thick haunches and groaning a little, for his belly had grown in her absence, he wiped away beads of perspiration glistening on his forehead with a faded handkerchief.

"My stores are full for the moment, although I'm in desperate need of elder bark."

"What is that?"

He looked sideways at her.

"Have you five years to devote to the herbalist's art?"

She looked steadily at him and answered:

"I have more than five years. I have a lifetime."

They sat together in the sun-warmed dirt and spoke of healing. As their conversation progressed, she asked him what she had suspected since her first session with Nadia in the Maze.

"You studied in Pelion, did you not, Phoron?"

He gave her a cryptic stare, mumbled something to himself, and looked off into the distance.

"Here's my proposition, Lillas. I'll teach you the rudiments of healing: dirty, thankless work that will probably offend that sensitive nose of yours more than once before you're through. My price is the retention of my privacy."

"I've finished bargaining, with you or with anyone. If you teach me, you'll have my gratitude. As for your privacy, it's yours to keep, not mine to invade."

He nodded slowly, still not meeting her eyes. Bouncing up from the ground, she inspected him with hands on her hips.

"Soon you'll be free of servitude, at which time you'll probably charge me for your services."

She'd intended her words as a jest, but his usual sense of humor seemed lacking. He sat quietly among his seedlings, murmuring "Perhaps another teacher can be found."

At the mention of his departure, loneliness flooded her. In a year he would leave her, his bond paid in full, and she would be friendless and alone and mated to a man who showed daily how thoroughly he detested her. In that moment the world seemed to shrink around her, and she struggled as if drowning, the undertow pulling her away from the shoreline as surely as she fought to reach the land. A friendly hand appeared on her shoulder. As her waking dream faded she wondered at Phoron's touches, more frequent of late and powerful in their ability to provide a calmness she was unable to create within herself. He would leave her, but another teacher might be found, and as she had confessed to him, she had a lifetime before her in which to master her craft.

HER REFLECTIONS WERE broken by a shout for Mia from the direction of the kitchen. Grunting, the cook pried herself out of her chair and waddled toward her domain. Returning to her book, Lillas was interrupted by a cleared throat.

"Lady, c-could you visit the k-kitchen for a moment?"

Olwyn spoke, as always, with a slight stammer, the result of his beating four years ago. His flayed back healed but the scars and stutter were blemishes he would carry with him always.

"What kept you from your studies today, Olwyn? You were missed."

His face shone with earnestness as he offered his excuse.

"Phoron needed me, lady. I promise I'll c-come tomorrow."

Lillas forgave him on the spot. As she headed for the kitchen she reminded herself to scold Phoron for kidnapping her pupil. All other thoughts fled at the sight of Olywn, who must have followed her into the kitchen, running ahead to assist Phoron by taking a human-sized, blanket-covered bundle into his arms. As mysterious as the bundle might be, it was Phoron's face that made her catch her breath, for he was staring fixedly at her, a portly, round-faced man grown suddenly severe.

"I've bought another slave. Tell me if you'll house him or no."

Speechless, she stood there, aware that Mia's face was dark with disapproval, knowing that this action would affect every resident of her household, for the slaves knew as well as she did the precariousness of her relationship with the Aeson. Taking a step closer, she tried to gather her thoughts.

"How badly is he hurt?"

"Badly enough that he'll die without our help."

Her good sense told her she must not allow it even as compassion tugged at her heart. A muffled sound escaped the bundle, indicating the fragility of the life Phoron held in his arms. With it came resolve. If she was to be a healer she must heal. Not for her the endless juggling of careful moralities, the fears for her own well-being, the selfishness of turning her back against the ugliness of the world. If her life was to have meaning, she must begin now or forever be a prisoner of this place.

"Yes."

With the utterance of that single word all doubts fled. Phoron gifted her with one of his rare smiles.

"Come and assist me then, apprentice," he ordered gruffly.

Lillas ran to obey, pulling aside the curtain that covered the storage room that had long since been converted into a healing chamber for the slaves of Imarus. It was greatly changed since Olwyn shivered within its enclosures and now housed a narrow bed instead of meal sacks, shelves that once held foodstuffs lined with Phoron's medicines, braziers and candles arranged to provide light and warmth, and a single window covered with a heavy shade.

Under Phoron's guidance, Olwyn turned the bundle over and lowered it onto the bed. The healer was issuing directions.

"Mia, everything he drinks must be boiled. We'll begin with water. Eventually we'll need clear salty broths. Olwyn, stoke the kitchen fire and light the braziers in here. Lillas, find as many clean rags as you're able."

Mia mounted an immediate objection, for water was dear. Lillas overrode her protests.

"We can use my ration to bathe him, Mia."

The cook eyed her askance, shaking her head at the thought that the Aeson's betrothed might go to her bed unwashed. Her complaints were good-natured as she began rifling through her shelves.

"Lice and fleas he'll have, and you tending him! Stars above, you'll be scratching yourself raw by the end of the day!" A satisfied grunt rewarded her search and she extended a bar of strong-smelling yellow soap. "Here, and mind you wash his hair twice." With a parting grumble she added, "Don't worry, my lady. Somehow we'll find food and water enough for one more."

Accepting the soap with a grateful smile, Lillas gathered rags and a well-worn drying cloth before running to her bedchamber to change into the dress she'd worn when she left Pelion, judging it would be more serviceable than her silks. She returned to the kitchen just in time to receive a basin of clean water from Mia and a searching look from Phoron. He'd pulled the curtain shut behind him and was regarding her thoughtfully, as if testing her in some way.

"Are you sure, Lillas? I won't hold you to our agreement if you choose to wait." The skin around his eyes wrinkled as he smiled at her. Even so, there was something ominous in his voice, a kind of warning that made her hesitate.

"Don't you want my help?"

"Indeed I do, but this won't be easy for you."

"Would it be easier for another?"

When he hesitated before answering her, she sensed his reluctance to let her pass. Sighing, he pulled aside the curtain.

Her first glance revealed a man's naked body sprawled on his stomach. Her second glance blurred and then focused as she saw skin the exact shade of rich earth. Handing the basin to Phoron, who accepted it wordlessly, she dropped to her knees beside the cot, seeing Reddin's battered face and crusted mouth, hearing his labored breathing, feeling the tears she had not shed in all these lonely days running down her cheeks and splashing on his muck-stained shoulder.

She could not think to ask why or how he'd come, she only knew that he was here. At last she found the use of her voice and without taking her eyes from him, whispered:

"Tell me how badly he's injured."

Phoron's hands gripped her shoulders, steadying her.

"The beating was a bad one, but except for some broken ribs, there's no internal damage. His greatest injury is the poison they fed him, a vile concoction that has left him dehydrated. You will begin by bathing him to lower his skin temperature while I mix an antidote."

"Will. . . will he awaken?"

His reply was honestly yet tenderly spoken.

"Everything depends on how quickly we can stop his nausea and introduce the salts and fluids he's lost."

Lillas set to work, conscious that a single wasted moment might cost Reddin his life.

SHE BATHED HIM with her tears and with basins of precious water. She said nothing, not even when the chills shook him or when he raved in fever dreams. She stayed on her knees, as if that posture was a penance of some kind and she was a sinner begging forgiveness. She washed the hair now freed from its braids and cleansed the dry, parched skin with hands that never faltered and eyes that never lifted from her work.

She held him in her arms as the chalky medicine was dribbled into his mouth and cleaned away the vomit as he retched and fought against hands that lovingly insisted he drink and drink again. As minutes turned to hours, she stood the lonely vigil of the night, warding off the powers of darkness as did the brazier that warmed the cool desert air. Hour after hour, she placed the cup to his lips and willed him to drink, until, as darkness became dawn, he drank as if he had become thirst, and she gave him water as do the rains that come in spring.

And never did she speak, not even to call his name when he wandered in delusions that dragged him down corridors of memory too evil to be named. She spoke only with a moist cloth held to a fevered brow and the tender caress of a hand that cleaned away his filth. In time, her touches altered the paths of pain he traveled, setting him on a different course, one that led to her, and he followed her as a flower follows sunlight, bending itself toward the giver of gifts too bounteous to be named.

Only at the pink-tinged coming of the dawn, when he gave her moisture back to her, his skin pouring out the life-giving water as he sank at last into the sleep of peace, only then did she bow her head, kiss his lips, and whisper his name.

And so she found her calling even as she called for Reddin of Pelion. And thus Lillas, the flame of Agave, lit the candle of despair.

THE FIRST TIME Reddin woke, a fight up through layers of pain toward a place someone had promised him in his dreams, he found not the face he sought, but one unfamiliar. A firm hand on his pulse counted the beats of his heart. When his head was lifted from the pillow the right side of his face throbbed. The broth in the pottery mug was warm and slid easily down his throat. Heeding the warnings of his memories, he tensed, waiting for nausea. None appeared. As his head was lowered carefully onto the pillow, he moved his eyes restlessly about his dim surroundings, searching for the one in his dreams.

"Lillas rests now. So must you."

He alternated between sleep and brief sojourns into the waking world, floating in a limbo where figures moved about him, voices were hushed, and a single pair of hands tended him. His burning thirst was finally quenched and he drank whatever was offered. At times he would almost wake, to be pulled down again into the warm and friendly darkness.

The second awakening was gentler than the first, a gradual journey toward light he could feel on his closed eyelids. His eyes still closed, he felt the touch of silk over his body and the pressure of a bandage around his ribs. The silence in the place where he lay was deep and heavy-layered until he heard the unmistakable sound of a page being turned. For a long time he lay undecided until, at last, he opened his eyes.

She was reading in a chair beside a small table on which a candelabrum burned, six candles rising from a solid brass pedestal providing light for the volume lying open in her lap. She was changed, changed in ways he couldn't explain, her hair arranged in careful ringlets rather than flying wildly about her head, her dress exotic and unreal, a Lillas bejeweled and groomed as he had never seen her in a lavishly cut blouse of sun-colored fabric that made her skin shine like polished gold in the soft glow of the candles. There were other, subtler changes; the planes of her face were rounded rather than angular, as well as a generous curve to her neck which he remembered as thin and slightly hollow. That she was Lillas became clearer as he noticed she was sitting cross-legged in the chair, wrapping and re-wrapping a ringlet around her index finger. A tray sat on the table beside the candelabra, a tray like many he prepared in the House of Healing to sit beside the bedsides of invalids with a cup, a basin and a pitcher, salves and cloths, a comb and a brush. As another page turned he shifted his attention back to his companion's face and met blue eyes of a rare and singular beauty.

There was everything to say, but no words with which to speak. She had betrayed him, but called for him; he had denied her, yet came at her call. As the past assaulted him, she paled, her lips trembling, and he read in her eyes her need for his forgiveness. Then, as the woman in black had foretold, he accepted at last the essence of Lillas and began their joining anew.

"What do you read?"

It was difficult to talk, hard to make his mouth and tongue do his bidding. His voice sounded hoarse and raspy to his ears. He winced as the movement of his jaw awakened the pain in his cheek.

She was on her knees beside the bed in an instant, her hand reaching out to touch his forearm.

"Hush, you mustn't speak."

At her touch, recognition coursed through him and he knew his dreams to be true. Her hands had stroked him, cleansed him, held him as he shook and shivered in the dark.

"You're safe now, my love. The fever has broken and you've slept for a day and part of the night."

He heard nothing but the endearment. Her hand slipped down to his and he grasped it tightly, witnessing her answering smile. With her other hand, she brushed away his hair from his face. They let the silence grow between them, relieved that they were free to fill it with whatever they chose. In time, his eyes grew heavy, and then there was only her voice, reciting the words of the poet:

If our two loves be one, or, thou and I
Love so alike that none do slacken, none can die.

*   *   *

REDDIN CAME AWAKE with a start to find a rounded arm flung across his throat and a tousled head buried in the pillow beside him. Disoriented by the presence of a body next to his, his first thought was that he was back in the Maze, lying with Lillas on the enormous bed, and the nightmare he'd lived through had been only that and nothing more. On impulse, he started to sit up. When his body screamed out a warning, he sank back down into the soft mattress and began to consider Lillas' nest.

As his eyes traveled over the large bed beneath them that stretched from wall to wall, filling the tiny room almost to capacity, he nearly laughed, but feared to wake his bedmate. It was no wonder she slept so soundly in the full light of day, for she must have worked through the night. While he slept, she created a cell for them to share. Her taste was unmistakable. The silken bedclothes were her colors, pale pastels of pinks and yellows, a satin coverlet that matched her eyes, and beautifully woven tapestries mounted on the walls. Two bronze braziers stood at the foot of the bed, unlit now; near the entrance she had arranged a small marble table and two matching ottomans. It was an exact copy of their cell in the Maze, but designed by one who loved color and light as much as she detested pallor and damp.

A giggle interrupted his inspection. She was laughing at him, her expression full of mischief.

"We could have taken you to Pelion and back and you wouldn't have awakened!"

When she rose onto her knees he saw she was wearing a blouse very much like the one he'd given her, only this one was made of a silk thin to the point of transparency. With her tousled hair, tawny skin, and glowing eyes she was the picture of health and happiness. He drank in her loveliness, quenching a thirst almost as desperate as the one he'd suffered in the pit.

When she pulled the cloth that covered him down to his waist, he quailed for a moment, not knowing his appearance, but fearing it was horrible. As she reached out to touch him, he recoiled. Her hand stopped in mid-air.

"I won't hurt you."

Her eyes were searching his with a troubled frown. He tried to allay her fears.

"It . . . it was only a reflex."

Her quietness evidenced her disbelief.

"Was it?"

The frown left her face. Instead, she regarded him solemnly, as if reminding him that they began afresh and that honesty must be their constant companion. Acknowledging the rightness of her demand, he explained what he would have preferred to keep hidden.

"I was uncomfortable at the thought of you seeing me . . . this way."

"But I've cared for you from the first moment, bathed you and tended you for two days," she protested. There was a short pause before she added, "Unless you resent my care . . ."

"No, Lillas," he replied, "I cherish your care for me." He closed his eyes, for the effort of conversation was draining his strength. "They . . . they hit me so often, you see. I . . . I saw only the hand, and was afraid it might . . . strike me."

A warm body snuggled close to his, a mass of curls brushing his left cheek as she settled her head on his shoulder. Her hand stroked his chest lightly, pushing away the memories of the hands that had hurt him as he listened to her assurances.

"No one will ever hurt you again, beloved. We are warm and safe in our nest and you will heal in time."

His hand touched her hair.

"How long do we have?"

"Not long," she whispered.

"What shall we do in the time that remains?"

He could hear her quiet confidence.

"We'll make a new joining, one without lies. Each day will be a gift, and we'll stretch minutes into hours and hours into days, so that when they . . ." she faltered, ". . . when they pass away . . . we can live a lifetime on their memories."

They lay quietly together in the comforting light of day.

"I've only one regret, Reddin."

"What is that?"

"That you . . . that you won't receive the gift."

A splash of liquid wet his chest. He smiled, stroking her hair to soothe her.

"Only one ernani can ever live in my heart, blue eyes."

A hand crept up and traced his lips and he kissed the fingertips that caressed him.

"Shall we never part, Reddin?"

He knew what she asked, for death camped outside the door to Lillas' nest. He knew no details, no plots or schemes; he knew only that he was whole now, holding her close to him, and he could not face the thought of losing her a second time.

"Never. We will live as you described and fear no tomorrows."

A tremor ran through her and he held her fast.

"Come, Lillas, we must begin."

"Begin?"

"First, you will tell me from whence came your inheritance, for I see that you can well afford to replace my book."

And with a soft laugh, she began telling the tale of Lillas of Agave.

THE MAN GREW in strength, the woman in loveliness, and the sound of their joy together brought happiness to all who heard them. The slaves lingered in the kitchen, hearing her bright laughter harmonize with the lower tones of the man in whom she took delight. When they emerged from their room from time to time, the man leaning heavily on her shoulder, they wondered at this dark-skinned stranger with flashing white teeth who so visibly adored their mistress. Occasionally Mia would mutter darkly to herself, but even so, they set aside their fears and formed a conspiracy of silence. They varied their habits not a jot, continuing their lessons under Phoron's tutelage, the women smiling as they worked busily at the new tasks their mistress requested, and every night the slight, fair-haired girl who once tended Lillas' bath slept in the empty bedchamber, hoping her presence would reassure any guard who entered unannounced. Slaves from other households sent to Phoron for healing were treated in another room, and during their visits they were watched with hard, distrustful eyes, for the household would allow no one to threaten the bliss of the two who dwelt within.

Seven days had passed since the man's arrival and their fears grew. Three more days passed and they put aside their fears, laughing at their lack of faith. Then, on the fourteenth day, came the news they dreaded.

PHORON CLEARED HIS throat, steadied his nerves, and called:

"Lillas?"

It was mid-morning and he'd waited as long as he dared. Her reply was instantaneous.

"Come, Phoron."

They were sitting at the table, breaking their fast with fruit and fresh rolls from Mia's oven. Lillas was wrapped in a robe; the man bare-chested with a silken square knotted around his waist. Always the professional, Phoron studied Reddin's injuries, noting, with well-deserved pride, that the swelling had left his face. The stitches he removed several days ago had drawn the severed skin over his cheekbone together neatly, a thin scab the sole evidence of the beating. His ribs remained bandaged, but he was moving less stiffly of late and the bruises had all but disappeared from his torso. His skin glowed like burnished copper, causing Phoron to wonder at the change until he realized, with the quick blush of a modest man who had never mated, that Lillas must have rubbed him with oil.

"Yes, Phoron. Reddin is fine and I continue to care for him."

His blush deepened as he realized she'd discerned the reason for his embarrassment. As he pulled himself together, he remembered why he was disturbing them.

"I have some news, Lillas."

She nodded, continuing to peel an apple with a pearl-handled fruit-knife. As the skin came away in an unbroken strip, Phoron wondered at her calm.

"Lord Seth demands your presence tonight in the great hall at a dinner honoring your mother. The message came early today. I pleaded illness and sent the messenger away. A second followed an hour later. You must attend, sickness notwithstanding."

It was the man who reacted. Stiffening at the mention of Seth's name, the lean muscles in Reddin's arms and chest tensed.

"What will he do if you refuse, Lillas?"

Phoron answered, intent that Reddin should understand the danger of her situation.

"He will send the palace guards to fetch her with instructions to drag her there whether she will or no."

Lillas placed the apple on her plate and leaned across the table, concerned for the one she must leave behind.

"Don't fret, Reddin. I must go if for no other reason than to see my mother." She paused, adding, "I have a request of her that has been much on my mind." Lifting her eyes to Phoron, she posed a quiet question.

"Have you bought what I needed in Agave?"

He fought against her with a frown. When her frown matched his, he nodded his acquiescence. Her face cleared, and with a sunny smile she rose from the ottoman and took her place behind Reddin, running her palms lightly over his polished shoulders.

"Thanks for the news. Inform Seth's escort that I'll be ready at sunset." She added as an afterthought, "Tell the women I've chosen the yellow gown with the embroidered sash."

Nodding, Phoron left, pulling the drapes closed behind him, and unashamedly waited to hear what was said within.

"Must you go, blue-eyes?"

"You know that I must."

In the silence that followed, Phoron surmised that Lillas had slid onto Reddin's lap, for her voice was only a murmur.

"What troubles you, beloved? I'll be gone a few hours at most. By moonrise I'll be safely returned to your arms."

"I fear for you."

"But there is no need, no need."

There was the sound of footsteps and the clatter of objects being scattered, a quick curse, and an abrupt question.

"Might I have a razor and a glass before you leave?"

Phoron heard Reddin's frustration with Lillas' decision. But Lillas seemed concerned solely with Reddin's request.

"What . . . what do you think to do?"

He was bleakly sarcastic.

"I thought to cut my throat, but I'll settle instead for shaving off this wretched beard."

"No!" And then more carefully, "No, please, my love. Leave the beard."

"Do you like it?" followed in tones of pure astonishment.

"I adore it. You remind me of a famous prophet . . ."

At which the man cried:

"Oh, Lillas!"

Phoron left at the sound of bare feet running across the marble floor. He pictured them clasped tightly together, their love shimmering like a living presence in the tiny storeroom.

Reddin was correct in his fears and Phoron shared them; not for reasons of danger to Lillas, but the danger of them being separated if for only a few hours. He monitored their progress daily, aided by Nadia/Ranier as he gleaned their minds for every detail of Transformation they had observed for sixteen years with hundreds of couples. He choked back sudden laughter when Reddin referred to the storeroom as "Lillas' nest," for the term applied to this stage of Transformation was "nesting." Since Reddin's awakening, Phoron watched as they opened their lives to one another, talking endlessly of everything they had ever felt, learned, shared, or experienced. Their bodies were in constant contact, their hands caressed each other without self-consciousness and they literally shone with health. There could be no other explanation for the quickness of Reddin's recovery; in three days he was on his feet when any other man would have been bedridden for at least a week.

As to Lillas' reaction to his news, his worst suspicions were confirmed. Clearly, she was not worried, and that lack of worry concerned him more than the news that Seth desired her presence. She was, after all, her mother's daughter, and in her stillness Phoron remembered Charis standing at the window, waiting for who knew what. If he could have read her, everything might be resolved, but he was trapped by his oath and the severity of the Eighteenth Mother's commands.

"We are sending them to you, Phoron, but they are not to be touched. When the temptation grows within you, remember these words: `And yea, they shall be joined as no others before them.'"

In his present mood words of a prophecy were small comfort, but then he had grown accustomed to small comforts after four years in bondage. He volunteered for this mission, and no one could say he hadn't entered Agave without understanding the difficulties of what he attempted. No one told him he would come to love his headstrong charge, even as he had come to love her haughty mother. And certainly no one told him that the responsibility for a miracle would be thrown squarely in his lap. With a silent curse, he picked up his stride, intent on delivering Lillas' messages. An errand boy, he thought with chagrin, a herbalist of repute reduced to carrying messages. What would my pupils think? With an inward laugh he answered his own question.

They would think I am a sentimental old fool. And they would be right.

IT WAS CLOSE to midnight. Phoron stalked the darkened apartments like an expectant father, listening hopefully for the sound of heavy boots treading the path that lead from the great hall. Lillas had been gone for hours and he was starting to despair. Reddin retired three hours ago, his face drawn and his mood grim. The slaves were asleep in their dormitory, the sound of their snores and muttering no different from any other night. Resolving to check on Reddin once more to make certain he slept, Phoron padded through the antechamber and into the kitchen. A light shone through the drapes to the storage room, a light that hadn't been lit at the time of his last visit. He pulled aside the curtains.

Reddin sat on the side of the bed, his hands gripping his head as he keened for her, rocking forward and backward in a hypnotic rhythm that suggested either grief or insanity.

Hardening his resolve, for despite his many talents he was not a particularly brave man, Phoron ran to the dormitory, woke Olwyn with a sharp jab that brought the man rapidly to his senses. Soon the two of them were sneaking past the sleeping guard and running down the flagged walk that led to the Aeson's palace, Olwyn pulling on his boots as they ran. As Phoron feared, the banquet was over, the guests long departed. Only the slaves were still in attendance, cleaning up the debris from a sumptuous meal served to nearly fifty guests. A whispered word to a former patient ended in a pointed finger and then they were running up the stairs toward the west wing. A guard nodded at his post and they tip-toed past him, coming to a stop at a door guarded by someone who immediately indicated his wakefulness by drawing his sword.

"Identify yourselves!"

"Phoron, healer and bondsman to Lady Lillas. I was told she fell ill at the banquet and that I should attend her."

He expected disbelief. Instead, the guard relaxed and the sword was reinserted into its sheath. With difficulty, for the nose guard of the Imarus' guards insured their anonymity, he recognized Paladin, a captain of the guard and a favorite of the late Aeson.

"I'm glad of your presence, healer."

Paladin was clearly worried by what lay within the room he guarded. Phoron decided to proceed with as much truthfulness as was possible.

"I tried to convince Lord Seth that she was ill, but he demanded her presence. Her headaches seem to have worsened since her return."

The guard commiserated with him over her illness, contributing details that added to Phoron's sense of foreboding.

"She took sick a few hours after arriving. I saw her ask the Aeson if she could retire, but he, uh, he seemed to disagree." Phoron noted that Paladin was an astute politician. That Seth was a brute was common knowledge to everyone who dwelt in Imarus. "She grew pale and then began to moan and hold her head as if it pained her. I offered to escort her to her apartments, but was refused." There is anger here, Phoron noted with interest. "At last the Aeson ordered her carried from the hall, but commanded that she be kept here in the hope that she would recover and rejoin the banquet."

"The last guests are gone. May we remove her now? I've a potion that guarantees quick relief."

"With my thanks, healer."

The door was unlocked and swung open. She was ranting, tearing at her hair, her garments falling off her shoulders as if she'd tried without success to remove them. Phoron wrapped a blanket around her and she was swept up into Olywn's younger and stronger arms. With a nod of thanks to Paladin, they retraced their steps, Lillas struggling against arms that weren't Reddin's, Olwyn holding onto her with desperate strength, and Phoron calling madly for Nadia/Ranier.

The moment his mind touched theirs, he fed them everything he'd observed, not bothering to edit or compose but drenching them in the wild outpouring of his thoughts.

"Calm yourself, healer."

It was Nadia, as cool and composed as if she was taking a stroll through the atrium.

"It begins. Their minds are opening; first will come the sharing of dreams and then the sharing of consciousness."

As Ranier began sending in the space of a breath, Phoron marveled again at the union between these born adepts. Few could match the perfect symmetry of their thoughts.

"No one must disturb them for the next twelve hours. As soon as they sense each other's presence, they will calm."

Now the two minds spoke as one.

"Guard them well, for at this stage they are particularly vulnerable, as you have seen. In the Maze, the cell protects them from outsiders, for we join them only in the last few minutes in order to shepherd them through the newness of their gift. You are blessed, Phoron. Few have seen what you will witness."

They left him and he picked up the pace. The guard snored on, insensible to their entrance into the apartment. Phoron blessed Seth's stinginess. Reducing wages might have bought on a mutiny; instead, he'd increased duty hours with the result that sleeping at their posts had become a regular occurrence within the ranks of the Imarus Guard.

Entering the storage room, he indicated that Olwyn should place Lillas on the bed and raised a finger to his lips to indicate silence. He went to Reddin first, stripping off the cloth tied about his waist and pushing him down onto the bed, motioning Olwyn to hold him there. The moment Olwyn touched Reddin he began fighting him off, but in his present state he could do little but flail harmlessly against Olwyn's bulk. Lillas was next. Phoron worked impatiently at her sash, then reached for scissors from the table. With two cuts of the blades she was freed of the gown. The camisole and briefs were removed as quickly as he could cut the straps and drawstring. When Olwyn averted his eyes, reluctant to witness the nakedness of his mistress, Phoron muttered at him under his breath.

"Don't be a fool! This is the only way to help them."

With Olwyn's help, he positioned them on their sides facing one another, placing free arms around shoulders and breasts and entwining their legs. As Ranier promised, they seemed to sense each other's presence by touch alone, for their eyes remained shut even as they began to calm. Musing for a moment, Phoron wondered at their beauty, two bodies almost identical in length and weight, both of them slender, although Lillas' breasts and hips were more rounded of late. As Phoron watched, it seemed they began to merge together, Lillas' head dropping onto Reddin's shoulder as he moved his loins closer to hers. Unable to witness their desperate intimacy, Phoron lifted the silken sheet and floated it over their bodies. Quietly, he ushered Olwyn out of the room and pulled the curtain tightly shut.

Taking up his post in the kitchen, he pulled a stool from beneath the counter and commenced his watch. In time he heard the sounds of their joining, the muted cries of their loving, and it seemed to him that music could not have been sweeter. Phoron reveled in the beauty of the night as Lillas and Reddin gave the third gift.

*   *   *

SHE WAS KISSING him, her lips covering him with moist testimonials of her love. How she had come to him he knew not, but she had left him and was miraculously restored, and he held her fast, swearing fiercely he would never let her go. Her kisses sang to him a melody of a pledge maintained, telling him that she had come to him at last and wanted him inside her. Stroking away the hair from her face, he watched his image floating in twin orbs of blue. That he wanted her was undeniable, but still he held back. Feeling the evidence of his desire pressed against her flesh, she wondered at his dishonesty. He could not bear her sadness, and whispered softly what kept him from her:

"Blue-eyes, you are no longer in your healer's care. If we join together, there might be a child."

Her face lit with a radiance he had never seen before.

"What better gift to a dying world than this, beloved?"

All this time she had wondered at his reticence, but she carried that secret deep inside her heart. Her wants voiced, his fears forgotten, they surrendered themselves to the urgency of their need and satisfied their craving for each other, their mouths and hands tasting and touching as they nestled side by side on the silken sheets. Memories of other joinings fled his thoughts and she left her fears to wither on the blood-stained grass. There was only their arousal, the fragile beauty of their hopeless cause, and the shafts of moonlight drenching them in its watery beams.

He entered her, hearing her cry out as her hips began to dance against his loins. She welcomed him joyously, feeling him pulse with the rhythm of dancing flames as the fire of life was kindled in her womb. He gave himself to her and she yielded herself up to him, and in their joining there was no bargaining, but only their need to climb together toward the heights of something promised. They rose together until, at the apex of their journey, they cried and shuddered their success while the night hushed around them.

And in their hearts they heard the poet's words, for their troth was plighted, and together they bid good-morrow to their waking souls.

Chapter 20

The Prophetess

LATER, MANY WOULD boast of witnessing her entrance into Agave, hindsight rather than memory guiding their beliefs. Much later, self-styled mystics would shake their heads, place a finger to the side of their nose, and announce that they had predicted every event that followed. In the historical accounts of this day, texts written centuries after the fact by scholars trained in economics, politics, and the intricate processes of historical change, it would become evident to even the simplest mind that no other course could ever have been possible. With detailed maps and demographics, they would either twist their theories to encompass the historical event, or skew the truth of the events so their theories could stand unaltered.

The truth of the matter was that no one noticed the Eighteenth Mother's arrival in Agave for the simple reason that she chose not to be noticed. She entered at first light, leading her horse, her robes bleached grey from sun and sand, her face burned brown and a permanent line etched between her far-seeing eyes. Her companion, a man never mentioned by the ballad singers who would turn this day into song, was equally travel-stained and weary. Their race toward the west shortened a twenty-day journey to sixteen, the man's horse foundering before reaching the last well. The final day they trudged over burning sands, spelling the exhausted horse that carried the last of their supplies.

Even at dawn there was a sizable group gathered outside the gates, eager to get about their business and leave before nightfall, no one so foolhardy as to stay any longer than was absolutely necessary in a city famous for its inhospitality toward strangers. In such a crowd, one drably-dressed woman and a bald-headed man, who bore no weapons but possessed the dangerous air of a hired mercenary, brought not a single curious glance. If anything, they were notable for their silence, although even this quality went unnoticed in the tumult that followed their entrance into Agave on a warmish morning in mid-spring.

They had just surrendered their passes to a surly guard when the first wave of tremors caused the sand to ripple underfoot and a muted sound like rolling thunder washed across them. The woman would have lost her balance if the man hadn't grabbed her; they stood together silently as prayers to indifferent gods were screamed around them in a babble of foreign tongues. Together, they waited for destruction, hearing the ominous creaks as the enormous sandstone walls shifted on their foundations, watching the tiny cracks of their surfaces widen into fissures, then dwindle again into cracks.

But the walls did not tumble, destruction being scheduled for some other day. In the moments which followed, the ground ceased shaking, became firm under their feet, and once desperate prayers subsided into indifferent shrugs as the world was put to rights.

Later, the balladeers would say that she made her first prophecy at exactly this place and a granite marker, now unreadable, still marks the spot. But this, again, is folly, the work of sentimentalists unversed in the realities of her situation, for the Eighteenth Mother made no prophecy other than whispering to her companion in a voice hoarse from thirst, "We are in time."

If truth be told, she made only one pronouncement and at the time appointed, for she was tired unto death and wanted no more than to find a quiet inn and rest until she was needed. There is no marker at the inn, now long demolished, where she bathed her face and hands, partook of a tasteless meal, and lowered her aching body into an ancient chair. There is also no mention of the fact that she did not sleep, but fell into a kind of trance while her hard-faced companion guarded her without seeming to do so. One poor soul, who knew nothing of mysticism, history, or ballad-making and thus never received credit for his observations, noticed her as she sat mumbling to herself, twirling a silver ring on her middle finger. Dismissing her as touched in the head, he went about his daily work of slicing cabbages and onions for the meatless midday soup.

The hard fact of that day, one that is easily forgotten and consistently omitted, is that no one, not the agents of Pelion, the dwellers of Imarus, or the citizenry of Agave, knew that the Eighteenth Mother of Pelion, the first of her line to travel openly in the world as it was then known, a woman who would become revered in words and songs as the Prophetess of Agave, kept her vigil in a deserted inn as she waited to be told the reason for her presence.

THE FIRST TREMOR was less strong in Imarus, but strong enough to elicit wails of despair from the slaves, the sole inmates of that elegant court who were awake at such an early hour. They huddled in terrified groups, most of them prostrate on the shifting marble tiles they polished on hands and knees, the stable floors thick with dung where they dodged the dangerous hooves of maddened horses, or the flooded grates of the palace laundry. Their cries woke the less industrious inhabitants of Imarus, most of them recuperating from the debaucheries of the night before.

One so awakened was Lord Seth, whose head ached from too much wine and who emitted a strangled cry when Charis rose to open the blinds, allowing unwelcome sunshine into her bedchamber. The light stabbed him between his eyes, and at his groan she flew to his side, whispering words of abject apology and running for a cold cloth with which to bathe his forehead. Soon he was purring under her ministrations. Only then did he think to ask what happened.

"A tremor, my lord, a stronger one than usual. Forgive my thoughtlessness in disturbing your rest. My intention was to assure you there was no danger."

Sweet, submissive, Charis. Had a woman ever been more beautiful, more charming, or more skilled in the arts of pleasure? No wonder his uncle kept her like a sacred treasure in his household. Seth considered himself a virile and lusty man, but last night she had elicited such heights of ecstasy from him that he found himself pleasantly sated and in the best of moods.

At the dinner he'd given in her honor, his first public acknowledgement of her new place as his favorite, she had been winsome, lovely, and altogether delightful, flattering the guests he wanted flattered and inducing jealousy in those he wanted to spite. All of this was accomplished without a hint of the domination he suffered under his mother's hands. Scarphe nearly underwent an apoplectic fit when she saw him bestow on Charis a passionate kiss and a diamond pendant that put a sizable dent in his treasury. The fact that a gift given to a slave was a gift that could be reclaimed at any time was neither here nor there. His gesture was perceived as beneficent and added to its reception was the pleasure he'd felt at insulting Lillas, who was seated next to her mother at the banquet. He became aware that Charis was chattering about her daughter.

". . . as if she thinks we're unaware of her dealings with that. . . that. . . !"

Her full, luscious lips pressed together in disapproval, the word Charis was searching for remaining unspoken. "She brings dishonor to you, to me, and to the memory of her late father." She was pouting now, stroking Seth's stomach and playing delightful games with his navel. "I often think you are too permissive, my lord."

"What dealings?"

His question was decidedly disinterested since the play of her fingers over his flesh made it difficult to concentrate. As she spoke, he felt the first onslaught of misgiving.

"Why, her dealings with that slave, of course."

"What slave?"

When she dismissed his question with a careless shrug, it became evident that the identity of the slave mattered not at all.

"Everyone knows that the ladies of Imarus sometimes enjoy the company of particularly attractive members of their household, but to take a slave as a permanent bedmate . . .!"

Seth wasn't listening anymore; he was fighting back a storm of temper that threatened to explode between his ears. Taking a punishing hold on Charis' shoulders, he forced her down onto the floor, spitting out questions as she trembled and quaked.

"Do you mean to tell me that Lillas is sleeping openly with a slave? My intended bride shaming me in front of all Imarus? And you've said nothing?!"

She was sobbing with terror, her eyes wide with fright as she mumbled apologies and protestations. In between her sobs he caught occasional words and phrases which only served to fuel his anger.

". . . thought you knew . . . for many days now . . . gossip among the slaves . . . told me last night . . ."

The last comment stopped him dead, the pulse throbbing behind his eyes slowing as his fury changed to hate.

"She told you herself, boasted her crime in a public place?!"

"Indeed it is a crime, my lord, a crime against the Aeson!"

She was blubbering now, desperate to placate him. Shoving her aside, he strode to the ottoman and retrieved his clothing. She lay where he discarded her, groveling on the floor, her hair flying wildly about her naked shoulders as she began to beg. Her fear of reprisal was strangely pleasing, demanding that he act, demanding a plan.

"Please, my lord, forgive me! I live only for your favor! Don't let my daughter's foolish actions alter your feelings for me!"

The plan took on dimension as he attended to his toilette, grooming his hair and beard at Charis' dressing table, using her cosmetics to cover the bites on his neck. As he fingered the evidence of her passion, he smiled, remembering her efforts on his behalf the night before and the resulting outrage of his mother. Soon he was humming tunelessly to himself as Charis continued to plead for forgiveness. As he arranged the folds of his gown, he spoke carelessly over his shoulder.

"Bathe and dress yourself in the most luxurious of your gowns. We leave Imarus within the hour."

"Where . . . where . . . do we go, my lord?"

He turned to her, hoping his voice sounded normal but afraid it might be a trifle high-pitched.

"We go to Agave, where your whore of a daughter will be sentenced for crimes against the Aeson. I'm tired of the city's love for her ill-mannered, shrewish behavior. After a public admission of her wrong-doings with a slave, they'll abandon her like a mangy dog." He smiled again, loving the perfection of it all. "Then, my darling Charis, I will raise you in her stead."

With a thankful cry, she crawled toward him and kissed his feet. As she did so he saw the stretch marks from childbearing on her body and swallowed his repulsion. She was twice his age, it was true, but her talents would serve him until he tired of her. Until that time, she was nearly as popular with the crowds as her daughter, and nothing else he could do would annoy his manipulative mother quite so much. Kicking Charis aside, he exited the bedchamber in a mood of high anticipation. In a few more hours he would be rid of Lillas, foil his mother's plans, and be free to enjoy the afternoon with his submissive and undeniably sensuous slave.

After Seth's departure, Charis rose from the floor and walked with quiet deliberation to her wardrobe. Throwing open the doors, she searched through a multitude of glorious gowns, most of them in shades of a particular and expensive blue dye, until she found the one she sought. Pulling it free from the confines of the wardrobe, she laid it over the bed after smoothing out the rumpled bedclothes. Next, she moved to her dressing table and sank onto the ottoman, observing the bruises that marred her ivory complexion with a half-smile that held within it sadness and a hint of remorse. Last night she had used her body as a drug, an aphrodisiac intended to enslave her master as surely as she was enslaved. Picking up her brush, she cleaned it of several ginger-colored hairs before polishing her blue-black mane. Twenty years of palace intrigues had taught her to hold her tongue against the ever-present threat of eavesdroppers. For once, she spoke aloud, her words containing the sound of purest thanksgiving.

"It is finished."

IN THE DREAM they were swimming, an incredible and completely unimaginable sensation, one that seemed nothing short of miraculous, for Lillas had never swum in a pool, a river, or a lake, and knew not the slightest thing about moving her body through water deeper than her ankles. Yet in the dream she swam like one born to the water, a nymph sprung from waves and sea-foam. Beside her swam Reddin, splashing at her in fun, his sleek, wet head thrown back and laughing, his teeth flashing like the sunlight that danced upon the waters.

They played and dived and loved in the water, never tiring, never thinking to stop and rest from their exertions, for like the creatures of the sea they had found their element. Within it they defied gravity, escaping all things earthbound.

Dream time is unreliable and impossible to recall. It seemed to Lillas that they had swum for days and perhaps for many moons before a destination appeared, a place toward which their travels took them. They swam abreast, their arms and legs moving in unison toward a bank that rose before them, its shoreline peopled with friends and strangers. Mouths were open; no sounds emerged. Hands gesticulated insistently for the swimmers to approach the shore. And then, quite unexpectedly, it became difficult to move, as if the water was congealing and Lillas was swimming not through liquid but through heavy mud. Before she had time to struggle or grow fearful, a trembling ran through the water and a giant wave, the crests of which resembled rearing horses, threatened to overtake them. The wave coursed on, growing larger as it sucked up the water in front of it, and she and Reddin were being sucked up into it . . .

And she woke, the bed shaking and trembling beneath them, a silver tray bouncing off the table, clattering and scattering its contents all over the floor. The slaves were screaming, as she might have been if Reddin had not been holding her so tightly she could barely draw breath. She heard the marble walls groaning under the strain of remaining upright as well as a low rumble emanating from deep inside the earth, as if it hungered and sought to quench its appetite by gobbling up everything resting on its surface.

Just as had happened in her dream, there was no time to grow fearful, and in the next breath it was over. The bed came to rest with a thump and they were thrown back against the head board, bumping their heads against wood. They lay still, counting their slowing heartbeats, until Reddin managed to ask:

"Are you often awakened in such an . . . abrupt . . . manner?"

Nestling close to him, she shook her head. With that motion, which cleared her head of thoughts of earthquakes and strange dreams, she remembered the night they had passed and pulled the silken sheet up to her chin, suddenly fearful of the clear light of day.

A hand with long, finely-shaped fingers moved toward her face, lifting her chin so she was forced to meet his eyes, and he smiled at her, a smile of tenderness that put her fears to rest. He loosened her fingers, which clutched the sheet to her breasts, and pulled her up into a sitting position. With her hips fast against his loins and her back resting on his chest, he enfolded her with his arms, resting his chin lightly on the top of her shoulder. She was loathe to broach the topic of last night, for to do so might tarnish its memory. It seemed he shared her reluctance to mention what had passed between them. In this way, they rested in quiet intimacy, listening as the battered world came slowly back to life.

"I had the strangest dream, Lillas." Even with her back to him she knew he was frowning. "We were swimming, you and I," he paused, "and although I don't know how to swim, I was unafraid."

"That was my dream as well."

She spoke matter-of-factly, for it seemed natural that they should have similar dreams after what they shared the night before. He tensed beneath her, turning her around in his arms, his eyes searching hers.

"In my dream there were faces; was it so in yours?"

Surprised by his intensity, she nodded.

"Describe them."

She bridled at his tone, for she had never been one to obey orders, but there was something odd about him, as if he was trying to suppress excitement of some kind. She decided to humor him.

"Most of them were people from the Maze: Nadia, Strato, the Instructor with a man I didn't recognize. . ."

"My brother, Orrin," he murmured under his breath.

"Reddin, what. . .?"

"Never mind. Continue, blue-eyes. Don't let me frighten you."

Disturbed, for his arms were like iron bands around her shoulders, she struggled to comply.

"Timon, the hermit I told you about. . ."

"An elderly man with a full beard and ragged clothing?"

She nodded as she strove to remember, ". . . and a woman standing off by herself, away from the others, who reminded me of you."

"My mother."

She opened her mouth to have a palm cover it. He shook his head at her, willing her to be silent. He closed his eyes and when at last he opened them, there was a kind of wild recklessness within them.

"What happened at the end of your dream?"

She frowned, growing mulish as he refused to explain the meaning of his excitement. He motioned insistently for her to continue.

"The water . . . thickened, and then there was a wave . . ."

". . . with churning foam made of horses' heads. . ."

". . . and it grew larger. . ."

". . . sucking up the water in front of it. . ."

". . . and I woke!"

She was more than annoyed, she was furious, whereas he seemed ebullient to the point of inebriation. Setting her carefully aside, he rose from the bed, stretching out his limbs, wincing as his ribs pained him, and began to pace at the foot of the bed.

"What is it!?"

At her question, his exhilaration ebbed. He scrutinized her with a worried frown.

"I . . . I . . .," He let fly an obscenity she had never heard him use and one she'd doubted he knew, only to realize (proudly) he'd learned it from her. He was pacing again, clearly fighting with himself and losing the battle. Finally, he faced her.

"I can't tell you."

"What!!"

It wasn't a scream; it was a screech. He ducked as if warding off a blow.

"I made a promise before I met you, and much as I long to tell you, I cannot break my oath."

He was earnestness itself, speaking with a truthfulness almost painful to the ears. Not bothered that he loved truth as much or even more than he loved her, she opened her arms to him, glorying in his steadfastness and resolve, content at last that he saw her clearly, yet loved her still.

He came full into her arms, knocking her over with his exuberance, covering her with kisses from her head to her toes, paying special attention to the places he knew would arouse her. His pace slowed as she began to respond, stretching out full length on the silken sheets, feeling languid and sensuous and at ease with him, no longer shy of the daylight and the passions it might reveal. His body was over hers and heat radiated from him, warming her flesh as he kissed her eyelids, and very slowly and very thoroughly, kissed her open mouth. When she could breathe again, she ran her fingernails lightly up his flanks, back, and shoulders, hearing his quick gasp of pleasure, and whispered softly in his ear:

"Can we make the bed move again, my love?'

To which he replied:

"We can only try."

DESPITE PALADIN'S ORDER for a surprise attack, his cadre's entrance into the Lady Lillas' apartment was regrettably noisy since the slaves seemed intent on giving loud and frequent warnings to their mistress. One of them, the bondsman who had tricked him last night, actually put up a fight until he was silenced with a single blow. Paladin was in no mood for this assignment. The thought that a slave might interfere with the execution of his duties was unacceptable.

A quick search by his men of the antechamber and slave quarters revealed nothing. Paladin's attention riveted on a cloth draped over a doorway off the kitchen. Holding his sword loosely in his right hand, since if this slave was bold enough to sleep openly with the former Aeson's daughter, he might be foolish enough to defend himself, Paladin thrust aside the heavy drape.

They were waiting for him. Clearly, he had disturbed them in the midst of joining. Trained eyes went first to the slave's hands, noting that they held only the woman, who seemed to be speaking softly to him. Both of them were naked, although a white bandage was wrapped around the slave's ribs. One of his men loosed a long, low, appreciative whistle at the abundant charms of the Lady Lillas. Paladin silenced him with a glare and issued a quick command.

"Cover yourselves."

A sheet was quickly wrapped around them. Neither made any other move. The Lady Lillas seemed actually to relax, leaning back into the slave's arms so as to rest her tousled head against his chest. Paladin wondered at her brazenness until he saw the slave tighten his arms around her and kiss her shoulder, the tenderness of his caress unmistakable even to the world-weary eyes of a captain of the Imarus guard.

"Lady Lillas, you are charged with adultery against the Aeson. You are to be taken to Agave, where at midday you will be publicly sentenced for your crimes. Dress now and we will escort you to the palace."

She took it bravely, as Paladin knew she would. A tingle of admiration ran through him, for this was the well-beloved child of a man he had served with pride. He could tell she recognized him, for her eyes warmed, but she made no motion to obey.

"Tell me, captain, what are your orders concerning Reddin?"

Since he knew of no Reddin, he assumed she meant the slave.

"I have no orders concerning him, lady."

She nodded thoughtfully, the slave still quiet although he threw back his head to clear the hair from his eyes, transferring his gaze from the woman to Paladin.

"Do your orders specify in what manner I'm to be transported to Agave?"

Caught off guard, for his orders consisted of nothing other than what he had repeated to her, he tried to guess what was in her mind. Her expression revealed nothing save mild curiosity.

"My orders were brief, lady. I thought to take you in a cart."

A soft laugh escaped her as she shook her head.

"That's out of the question, captain. Please inform the stable that my carriage should be made ready. Have them harness the matched grays, please. At two hours before midday, we'll emerge and dutifully accompany you to Agave. Until that time, you may circle my apartments with your guards to prevent any attempts at escape."

Paladin was caught between irritation and amazement. Far from being frightened, she was at least two steps in front of him at every turn. Without orders to the contrary he was unable to treat her as anything but a high-ranking member of the nobility, and she was clearly determined to be considered nothing less than the daughter of a former Aeson until the moment of her sentencing. It was at this point that he remembered something that sounded suspiciously like trouble.

"We?"

"Why, of course, captain! Do you think I'll leave my household behind when my fate determines all their futures? I am their mistress. They will accompany me. For this reason we leave two hours before midday, for they must walk to Agave."

He felt his mouth gape at what she described, but she had not finished. With a beckoning hand, she indicated a pile of sun-colored silk lying on the floor.

"Would you be good enough to hand me my gown?"

As if in a trance, he moved to obey, standing mute as she extracted a piece of parchment from a pocket sewn on the inside of the delicate fabric and handed it to him.

"Perhaps you would read it aloud, captain?" she suggested politely. He did so, the words sticking in his throat.

> Be it known that the slaves of Imarus will accompany my daughter whenever and wherever she commands.
>
> Charis, Head of the Household of Lord Seth

What Lillas planned was nothing short of an insurrection. She was asking him to lead a party of several hundred slaves to Agave, knowing that if the slaves left, the nobles would follow en masse, and so insuring the attendance of the entire population of Imarus at her sentencing. Lost in admiration for her strategy, which was nothing less than the battle plan of an astute and wily commander, he managed to voice a single objection.

"Your mother accompanies the Aeson, lady."

"Her absence does not negate her orders. All of Imarus witnessed the power entrusted in her by Lord Seth at last night's banquet. She rules his household and that household comprises all of Imarus."

What was she planning? In that moment he knew. In the next he decided to support her. Perhaps he was prompted by devotion to her father and dislike of his present employer. Perhaps he was a soldier to the marrow of his bones and the call to battle was one that made his blood sing. It was also possible that he was tired of secret arrests, bloody interrogations, and other deeds of a shameful nature that made a lie of his training and placed a shadow on his soul.

Later, in a tavern and drunk on cheap wine, Paladin would confess that it was none of those reasons. When his compatriots urged him to divulge the truth, he would remember a pair of sky blue eyes asking him to do what was right, and he would cry a little into his cups and hold his peace.

SHE WAFTED FROM his arms with an airy grace that was new to her and wrapped herself in the ruined gown. Surveying the disordered room, she sighed, and knelt to clean up the mess of strewn clothing and the objects that had fallen during the earthquake and littered the floor. As the sound of tramping boots faded away, she disappeared beyond the curtained doorway where he could hear her issuing instructions to the slaves, one of the younger girls sobbing with fright. Her voice was gentle, and soon they quieted. There was the scuttle of bare feet on marble tile, a few whispered words he couldn't understand, and she returned to him, standing at the foot of the bed with her arms full of silk, a wrapped parcel held in her right hand.

He was waiting, as he had waited through the interview with the captain, her earnest plea that he do nothing restraining him from fighting to the death for her, for there would be death today, of that he was certain. He tasted it in the air as they awoke, a taste of ashes and woeful loss. He feared death, as all who live fear death, but more than this he feared the death of Lillas, who stood in tousled, poignant beauty, and who had come to him at last.

The curtain parted and a copper tub was carried inside and duly filled with steaming water. She flung aside the gown, and with it the last of her modesty in his presence, and he watched her bathe, soaping her limbs with a priceless sponge brought by caravans from the eastern shores, washing her hair with scented soap that cast the smell of sandalwood into every corner of their silk-draped nest. Rinsing and drying herself, she smiled a wordless invitation. He accepted willingly, content to have her unwind the bandage from his ribs and bathe him as if he were a child again, the bath one of the few times his mother had ever touched him.

Still he waited, knowing she would tell him in time, confidant that in her seeming contradictions lay her strength. As he waited, he grieved for the gift that was rapidly approaching but would find them too late. They had come so close, the giving of their last gift vibrant and pure, the sharing of their dreams promising the gradual merging of their thoughts. Closing his eyes against the knowledge of that loss, he let her wash away his sorrow.

Clean and dry, he stood before her. Placing two pieces of silk in his arms, she broke her silence.

"These are for you, my love."

He had ever dressed somberly, at first for want of money, and then for reasons of practicality in the House of Healing. Now he held in his arms silk of the finest quality, cool and weightless, of pure and spotless white. Tongue-tied, he watched her don a gown of matching white shot through with silver threads, the thin fabric draped around her slim waist and clinging to her breasts and hips, and gasped as she turned to face him. Reading his praises in his eyes, a rare blush bloomed on her cheeks and she turned away to busy herself with the parcel. He dressed quickly, stepping into wide-legged breeches that gathered and tied at his waist and pulling on a full-cut, lavishly embroidered robe that reached his ankles. As he looked around for a sash to tie it closed, a laugh escaped her.

"It's worn open, my love." A slight frown wrinkled her brow as she bit her bottom lip. "Are your ribs well enough that you might leave off the bandage today?"

When he nodded, she came towards him, adjusting the line of the shoulder seams and arranging the front panels so that they hung in perfect folds. There was something wistful about her as she arranged the drape of his robes. Not meeting his eyes, she asked:

"I know so little about your customs. Do your people celebrate births or matings?"

It seemed an odd question, but no odder than their present circumstances. As a result he thought little about it, glad to talk of anything other than what awaited them outside this room.

"Births are a private affair. The Mother of Pelion is summoned to bless the child with the giving of the water, wine, and oil. As to mating, the country-dwellers hold elaborate celebrations, with singing and dancing and feasting for everyone in the village. City-dwellers are more . . . ."

"Sophisticated?"

"I was going to say `circumspect.' Sometimes there is a gathering. Often it's nothing more than friends and family members who bring a meal to their home and leave gifts of bread, salt, and wine."

She had moved behind him now, still tugging at the hem of his robe. Something about her silence puzzled him.

"What of your customs, Lillas?"

Her reply was cheerful, yet forced, causing him to wonder what she was hiding.

"I fear you might find them extravagant. We love festivals and holidays, for on those days the markets close. The mating celebration is . . .," her voice caught, ". . . is arranged by the mother of the woman who mates, for on that day the betrothal ring she gave her daughter is moved from the second to the third finger of her left hand." There was longing beneath those words, as well as a growing dreaminess. "The couple to be mated are always dressed in white, and they wend their way through the guests, who throw flowers at them in the moons of warmth, and sprinkle their heads and shoulders with water in the moons of winter."

The silken robe billowed about him as he turned to face her.

"Your women have sewn these garments especially for this day, have they not?" She nodded assent. "You have always known it would come to this. You were surprised at nothing the captain said, in fact, you welcomed his arrival. I could feel relief course through you as I held you in my arms." He spoke more quietly now, watching as her eyes filled with tears. "Is this what you've planned, Lillas, my Lillas of the lost cause? That today will be our mating celebration? That we will walk through the slave market together, our invited guests the slaves of Imarus, our greetings cries of 'lecher' and 'whore', our flowers the spit and curses of angry crowds?"

"Yes," she whispered.

"And my beard which could not be shaved?"

"Will be curled into ringlets, as will be your hair and mine, for such is the custom with both the rich and poor who dwell in the western lands, that those who mate are adorned not with jewels, but the simple beauties of their bodies."

"Have you a ring?"

Her skin matched her gown and her lips trembled, but her tears remained unshed. Awe-struck, he marveled at her fortitude, at the terrible strength to be found in her, a strength he did not share.

"My mother is a slave and thus I received no ring from her hand. Instead, I have found these rings for our ceremony."

In her hand she held a pair of manacles. Touching their cold, menacing steel, a shiver ran through him.

"You are still safe, Reddin, and need not go. Imarus will be emptied of guards, the stables deserted, and Mia can pack enough food and water to take you over the desert and beyond. You told me Prax made you memorize the route and Phoron bought a dagger at the same time he purchased the manacles."

Here was her generosity, her hugeness of heart that she would plot his escape even as she planned this macabre ceremony of mating wherein the honored guests were victims, sacrifices to be thrown to the mob. Gently, he took the manacles from her, noting that his hands shook, unashamed of his fear. Snapping the ring shut around his right wrist, he inserted the key and turned it until it locked.

"Come, blue-eyes. Our time grows short."

He kissed the wrist of her left arm, the skin satin smooth beneath his lips, and then placed the manacle around it. The key turned again, the scrape of metal rubbing against metal jarring in the stillness of their nest, and they were joined together, their arms braceleted with silver rings that insured they need never part.

WORD SPREAD, LISPED behind manicured hands of the privileged, enjoyed as a choice bit of gossip that might add zest to their pointless days before filtering down to the merchants, who cursed and railed against business being spoilt. The inn and tavern keepers, who were the next recipients of the news, exulted, for tonight their rooms would be full to bursting with travelers forced to spend hard coin on an extra night's meager fare and filthy lodging. Beggars and thieves spread the news to the slaves and all rejoiced, the former because coins might be thrown and purses might be cut, the latter because their prayers had been answered and they would not be sold today.

By noon the marketplace was bedlam and still the people gathered, pushing, cramming, forcing their way toward the place where the banners of the iron fist were raised. Across from the Aeson's platform, bannered and festooned as if for a holiday, stood a platform strangely empty, its sole decoration the two sturdy poles from which chains dangled and from which recalcitrant slaves were hung to be stripped and examined by prospective buyers. It was toward this place, chosen because it was nearly central to the slave market whose only roof was the cruel desert sky, that the crowds fought and shoved, for on its rough boards would stand the criminals waiting to be condemned.

Two people, their heads bowed and their hands linked, were propelled forward by the tremendous force of the hundreds of bodies behind them. The woman's head barely reaching the shoulder of the brawny man beside her, her small size making her an easy target for those determined to usurp her place. Several times she was forced onto her knees, to be pulled up like one drowning by the man whose curses were unheard and ineffective in the din of a thousand voices raised in a continual scream of excited expectation. No words could be heard over the sounds of the crowd's madness, but something was exchanged between them, for from beneath his cloak the man produced a hardwood stave. Shoving the woman into position behind him, her fingers gripping tightly to the back of his belt, the man began to use the stick with a fierce and frightening intensity, deaf to the cries of those he beat and buffeted as he thrust his body like a battering ram through the crowds, thrusting himself and his companion onward toward the heart of the slave market.

He reached their destination, stopping at a stand neighboring the empty platform across from the Aeson. When the women gestured frantically up, up toward the sky, he lifted his eyes to the place she indicated and nodded, his jaw set and the swelled veins in his neck pulsing. Taking the staff firmly between his meaty hands, he began to push aside those who barred his way, their bodies falling off the steps as he led the woman up, ever upward, until they reached the top of the stairs. By now his stick was bloodied and the swarm of watchers gathered on the platform made haste to give him room. The woman tugged on his belt, content with their position, and again, without words being exchanged, he squatted while she scrambled up onto his shoulders. With a grunt, he straightened, a strong man with the body of a bull, and lifted his burden up to the skies.

It was in this way, and no other, that the Prophetess of Agave came to view the events of that day. The ballads sing of a silent parting of the crowds as she approached, a thousand heads bowed in silent unison at the sight of her commanding presence. The mystics prefer a more miraculous version, speaking knowledgeably of a timely descent from the skies, while the historians mention this part of the event not at all. But in truth, the Eighteenth Mother of Pelion reached the platform on which legends rest through the efforts of one man, and one man alone, and was raised above the crowds on the broad back of a slave's son.

There, a head and shoulders higher than the assembled throng, she was the first to see Lord Seth mount the steps and the first to catch a glimpse of the woman, Charis, who followed him, her cloak of indigo blue trailing elegantly behind her as she ascended the staircase, careless that the priceless fabric dragged across rough-hewn timbers. With a leisurely gesture Lord Seth indicated her place, a gilt-covered chair placed slightly to his left. Disdaining to sit, Charis shook her head with a captivating smile and took her rightful place beside him. The crowds erupted, screaming their pleasure at her beauty, remembering how often they had seen her beside their former Aeson, a man well-loved for his fairness, singing out their praises that she had given her master and their former lord a child, a child who once had made their lot easier to bear.

From her vantage point, the keen-eyed woman in dusty robes marked the glitter of Charis' eyes, saw the heightened unnatural color of her cheeks and the tension of hands clenched in fists. And only the woman in black thought to wonder, on this warm day in the midst of the stinking heat generated by thousands of unwashed bodies, why Charis' cloak remained fastened at her throat with a jewel-encrusted brooch.

Even as Hesione wondered, her attention turned toward one of the many archways that fed the inhabitants into the hub of the marketplace. Long before the groundlings or even those lucky enough to obtain a place on one of the many platforms became aware of the procession wending its way toward the center of the marketplace, her sharp eyes caught a flash of white and the sparkle of silver and her keen ears caught the singing of the slaves of Imarus. As her senses perceived their coming, her heart lifted up, for it was only at this moment, as the horse-drawn carriage with its mounted escorts drew slowly toward her, that Hesione understood Lillas' plan.

Five hundred voices strong, the slaves of Imarus kept time with the beating of their bare feet on hard-packed sand, their hands clapping out the rhythm as they lifted their jubilant song on high. No longer angry, no longer intent on witnessing the public sentencing and death of some unknown criminal by their tight-fisted ruler, the crowds became joyful, even ecstatic. There, in her magnificent carriage and clothed in a gown of silver, rode Lillas, the only child of their former lord. Beside her sat a stranger to their curious eyes, but a man bedecked in the white of one who would mate. The crowd came to witness a hanging. Instead, Lillas brought them a mating celebration. Even the poorest among them remembered the heat of the curling iron turning unruly locks to ringlets and the hoarded coins spent on lengths of white fabric they could ill afford. Those who had once loved, those who loved still, and those who hoped to love someday, saw themselves in this glorious couple and their wedding party of singing slaves. The sentimental souls among them wished they had brought flowers, for it seemed an injustice that Lillas and her betrothed should come unheralded by the bright blooms that signified the most precious commodity in Agave, a surfeit of water. Even the foreigners, for there were outsiders in the crowd that day, understood the nature of this procession, for as the carriage passed slowly through the crowds, its occupants seemed to shine with a radiance of love and health so bright that even the most hard-hearted could not find it in themselves to scoff or jeer.

It was in this mood of festivity that the crowds parted, clearing a pathway to the empty platform where Lady Lillas and her chosen mate mounted the steps and stood side by side in front of the Aeson of Agave.

And no one, not those who were in attendance on this fateful day, nor the mystics, the balladeers, or the historians; none of them, not even Prax, on whose shoulders Hesione perched, knew that the Prophetess of Agave spoke aloud for the second time that day, saying simply:

"It begins."

Chapter 21

The Fountainhead

IT IS A truism that stories grow with the telling, for who among us can resist adding details to a story long-established, a deviation from the original harmless in and of itself, especially when it is precisely this invention which kindles delight in the eyes of the child on our knee, causing her to demand with the imperious voice of one who will not be denied, that we tell it just so for the next twenty tellings? Who will not admit the pride of a slight exaggeration, minuscule embroidery of an event or a character, when it elicits a cackle of enjoyment from a grandfather whose days are measured by a rivulet of sand in an hour-glass of pain? These are, after all, our stories, and perhaps it is just and right that we, by means of our creativity and individual powers of observation, take ownership of our cultural memories and become artists in our own right. Yet we must ask ourselves, over the course of time measured in generations upon generations, if in our charity toward our hearers we perjure our heritage.

The events of this particular day have suffered in the telling, have become fraught with senseless details and exaggerations of a harmful nature, the first dangerous because it fastens on a simple object, a wooden stave, let us say, and inflates its importance far beyond the dictates of the story; the second threatening in its power to reduce the truly miraculous, overshadowing the truth with fanciful imaginings to the end that a fountain becomes a geyser or a stream an ocean, whereas we have only to consult a map to discover that there exists no geyser and no ocean, and thus the entire tale shrivels to be blown away by the brisk winds of skepticism.

To be sure, miracles occurred, but they did not spring from magical staves or hundred-foot geysers shooting loftily into the blazing desert air. The miracles were these: that Death came but took up no permanent abode; that the earth reclaimed a forgotten child; and most importantly, that for a fleeting second, the more precious because of its brevity, the eyes of humanity blinked open.

That those eyes shut again is the reason the tale must be retold.

* * *

"REMOVE THAT SLAVE!" Seth shouted, but no one heard him over the noise of the crowd. He lifted his hands, demanding silence, but still the crowd's roar did not subside. Intent on learning the identity of this dark-skinned stranger who accompanied Lady Lillas, they ignored their new Aeson's attempt to quiet them.

For they were cautious, these citizens of Agave, and proud as only the guilty are proud, their love of profit and its tangible rewards admitted openly and without apology, always conscious that their name was a curse to half the inhabitants of the world. Lillas' suitor won their approval at first sight, not the least because he had embraced their customs, assuming the time-honored ringlets of hair and beard and clothed in the white robes of a male desiring to mate. They thought him a foreign prince and rejoiced, certain that his title would lend them much-needed respectability. Agave could benefit from the acceptance of their nobility as fit and proper mates by those from far-off lands since the residents of Imarus rarely looked beyond their palace walls for purposes of mating. There were whispers from the mouths of midwives that more bad babes than good were birthed in those marbled halls. All things told, this foreign prince might lack the elegance of the current Aeson and the command of the former, but there was an aloofness about him, a formality of character that appealed to their guilty pride and their sense of failure as a culture.

"Remove that slave!!"

Lord Seth repeated his directive, hearing the crowd react with murmurs of disbelief, repugnance, and hotly growing anger. They had been robbed, and though thieves and cut-purses had been working the crowds since the marketplace began to fill, robbing them of items of a far more personal nature than a foreign suitor to Lady Lillas, they scorned this imposter, this slave, with his conniving ways and false posturing. They parted with good grace as a member of the Imarus Guard, a captain by the name of Paladin, dismounted his horse and ascended the steps to obey the Aeson's command.

As Paladin trod heavily up the stairs toward Lady Lillas, the crowd hummed as wasps do when their paper-thin nests are disturbed by a random breeze.

Paladin, his eyes locked with those of Lady Lillas, asked quietly:

"What would you have me do, Lady?

To which Lillas responded:

"Do what you must, Captain. We stand ready."

Moving to Lillas' left (for they stood as if for the mating ceremony, Lillas on the right as she faced her mother on the opposing platform, Reddin on her left) Paladin took a firm hold on Reddin's shoulders, pulling him forcefully away from Lillas' side.

What happened next came to be a staple of the lore of Agave, for whom but a populace of free-born and enslaved, those who forged and wore the bracelets of slavery, could be so affected by two who wore shackles of their own free will? They were parted roughly, so roughly that Lillas stifled a scream, her torn wrist dripping crimson tears onto her immaculate gown.

"Lillas, you bleed!" cried Reddin, but Lillas shook her head at him.

"Show them! Make them see!"

Frightened as he was, Reddin could not, would not, gainsay his Lillas, who seemed to him a woman clad in silver armor, thrusting her arm high in the air so all might see the manacles, inviting the midday sun to sparkle on their metal rings. No coward he, Reddin mustered his courage and matched her attempt to touch the desert sky. Upon the sight of their bloody wrists raised in protest, from the throats of the crowd came a sigh that brought silence to a marketplace that had never known silence before.

Into that silence Lord Seth screamed "Cut off his hand!!"

Lillas' wail lifted straight up to the heavens, a sound of such tormented woe that those who heard it, many of whom had mutilated slaves with their own hands, felt their neck-hairs rise. Even the nobles of Imarus, the ones most repelled by the thought of a slave tainting their bloodlines, remained silent and respectful in the face of Lillas' grief.

Silenced hovered as Lillas' cry ended. All at once, she was speaking, sending her voice like a clarion throughout the marketplace. In her they saw her father re-born, her shoulders squared, her chin raised, her bleeding arm held high, forcing all to bear witness to her circumstance.

"I will not be parted from this man! I say again, I will not be parted from the mate of my heart! He who stands beside me is not a slave, but is freeborn, enslaved by Seth because he comes from Pelion, the walled city to the south."

This mention of Pelion disturbed the citizens of Agave since they had mounted a great force at enormous expense to rescue her. Individual voices shouted out a protest, but Lillas would not be silenced.

"I was not kidnapped nor imprisoned against my will as you were told. Some of you remember the prophet who spoke of a gift freely sought that would be freely given. A year ago he was murdered near this very spot by order of my cousin Seth."

Her mention of the prophet reminded them of old rumors about a body found in an alleyway the day after the murder, the dead man's face smashed beyond recognition, on his back a bow and quiver, in his tunic a pay slip from the Imarus Guard. Though it was bitter medicine to learn Lillas' rescue was a sham, they swallowed and listened on.

"I traveled by my own volition to Pelion, hoping to find the gift the prophet described. I found it there," she paused to gaze lovingly at the man by her side, "with this healer who taught me everything I know about honesty and the sharing of self.

"My cousin would have you believe that our mating is a crime against his rights as my betrothed, but I ask you this: when did you see a betrothal ring on my finger? He accuses me of wantonness with this healer from Pelion, yet here we stand, eager to speak our mating vows in the presence of my mother. I do not deny the sharing of my body with him, for even now my womb is rich with our first child, whose birth will come with the winter solstice, the time when rains fall on our dry lands, for this child will be a blessing as are waters from the sky!"

Lillas placed her right hand upon her womb where it would soon swell with the fullness of unborn life, her second gesture of the day and one that never failed to be recounted by the fable-tellers when they told and retold the tale. When Reddin placed his left hand upon hers, from the radiance of their faces one would have thought the babe leapt up at their touch.

There is something wondrous in the fact that Lillas was able to speak without interruption for so long a time, since many in the crowd believed a slave a slave despite his place of birth or the unproven boast of his fertility.

Someone shouted: "Is he a slave or is he not?"

More people took up the chant until the Aeson, his face cold with hatred for Lillas, who never once in the course of her address referred to him as Lord Seth or the Aeson, shouted:

"He is my slave, an agent of Pelion arrested on my orders and thus my property!"

"Am I, too, your slave, cousin?"

It was not the question Seth expected, nor one he wished to answer. As the daughter of a slave, Lillas' status was unquestionable, yet these legal technicalities would be of little interest to a crowd who seemed to love her still.

Seth turned to Charis, who stood silent and motionless during her daughter's speech to the crowd.

"Hear from the lips of this liar's mother the truth of her crimes! Charis will tell you in her own words of her daughter's abduction from Imarus, describe our private ceremony of betrothal in the days following her return, and confess her shame at her daughter's promiscuous behavior with this vicious lecher who plays the loving father to a non-existent child. You know her well; her beauty is famous throughout the land."

Seth motioned for Charis to step forward and as she did so, reached out to unfasten the clasp at her throat. Obediently, Charis suffered her master's touch.

"I give you – Charis!"

As Seth loosened her cloak, Charis was beauty incarnate. As the cloak drifted down to lie like a discarded rag upon the sweat-stained boards of the slave platform, Seth's gasp became one with the crowd's.

No longer attired in splendid fabrics shot through with threads of precious metals, gowns dyed as many shades of blue as existed in the ocean and the sky, Charis appeared before them in the drab of mourning. Her former glory had been traded for a lusterless grey gown unadorned save for an iron ring clasped about her neck, an accoutrement of slavery that harkened to former days when slaves wore iron bands circling their necks as well as wrists and ankles, a custom long since abandoned.

Her beauty vanished as the cloak fell, leaving only its ravaged remains. Her hair fell dull and lifeless over her shoulders, her skin hung wrinkled and pallid. Here was a different Charis, one who willingly paid the price for her life-long loveliness by offering up proof of her loss to those who stood in the square that day, for all could read in her ravaged face her days and months of unending grief, witnessing as she did the agonizing slowness of the former Aeson's death. To compare Lillas and Charis, daughter and mother, separated by twelve spans and twenty years, was to compare the maiden with the crone, the fruitful with the barren, the moons of warmth with those of bitterest chill. Only Charis' indigo eyes lived on.

Charis' life-long loveliness was lost, but in compensation for its loss, she acquired a new and powerful voice. Her accent pure, lacking the lisping affectations of the nobility of Imarus, the vowels rounded, the consonants sounded clearly and with great deliberation, Charis began to speak:

"There was no abduction; my daughter left Agave of her own free will! There is no betrothal; my daughter would wed Reddin of Pelion and no other! As to this man who stands beside me, this liar and brute, he is to blame for the death of his uncle, the Aeson, my master and the father of my child!"

Seth took a step forward in a belated attempt to stop Charis' "song" as it became known in later days, but a member of the Imarus Guard elbowed his way between his master and Charis, seemingly to protect his master from a slave gone mad. Unstoppable now, Charis sang of the painful, lingering death of a monarch poisoned by his ambitious sister and her power-hungry son, of a prophet murdered in the marketplace by a paid assassin, of the healer from Pelion, captured, tortured and left to die in the pits. The Imarus Guard looked on, torn between their loyalty to their former master and their duty to the hated Seth. Lillas stood frozen by the horror of her mother's tale.

"And so I beg you," Charis said, hands outstretched in supplication to the crowd, her gray-clad figure mournful beyond simple grief or sadness, "I entreat you to punish him and his vicious, scheming mother! Scarphe, the snake, with her poisoned tongue! Cowardly Seth, who pays others to kill for him! I protest the death of the Aeson, who honored me and my child! I beg for justice!"

The crowd stood transfixed, uncertain as to what action they should take given these unproven claims. In that moment of doubt, Seth proved Charis' honesty not with words, but with deeds. The guard pushed roughly aside, his jeweled dagger moved in a long, curving arc, passing swiftly through the fabric of Charis' gown, puncturing the skin above her left breast, and entered her beating heart. She made no cry, her voice stilled as she crumpled at the feet of her lord and executioner.

Charis' death-scream came from another source and one that figured strongly in the pandemonium that followed. Much later, long after the crowd dispersed, Scarphe's body was found near the rear of the Aeson's platform, the back of her lavish robes rock-hard with dried blood from the knife blade buried in her back. Her murderer was never found, a bandy-legged man known as Abas, someone suggested. But to everyone in the marketplace that day it seemed a disembodied voice screamed out a protest at Charis' passing. Soon, in an ever-growing voice of rage and betrayal, Scarphe's death-scream became the crowd's.

Like a raging flood sweeps clear whatever lies in its path, they attacked the Aeson while the Imarus Guard looked on in careful solemnity, the memory of other executions foremost in their minds as they stood witness to Lord Seth's end. Deaf to his commands, unmoved when those commands became screams of rage, uncaring when rage became agony, they stood immobile as the crowd wreaked its vengeance, tearing the living flesh from the bones of the last man to wear the medallion of the Aeson of Agave.

When they finished their bloodletting, the flood of their anger having run its course, it was this medallion they offered to Lady Lillas as she stood half-supported by the former slave whose tormentor lay ripped to pieces, his blood seeping down into the greedy, moisture-starved earth. Old debts settled, their consciences clear, the crowd waited expectantly, eager to forge a new and lasting bond with their favorite, whose silver-clad body held the promise of a child who would inherit the legacy they freely offered. She would continue to be their delight, gracing the halls of Imarus, bringing fame to their city, and they passed the medallion hand over hand toward the slave platform, its heavy gold links gradually cleansed of human blood by the repeated touch of so many willing hands.

It reached across the bloody chasm until at last it was held by a man whose head reached the top of the platform. Standing on tip-toe, he stretched his arm up, up, straining to reach her right hand, which hung at her side.

"Take it, Lady Lillas!" he shouted, the crowd holding its breath, tense with anticipation.

Lillas turned her head to regard the man chained to her wrist, saying: "We need not be as he was."

To which he replied with the terrible honesty of which he was capable: "How long could we resist?"

Heeding her truth-sayer, Lady Lillas put aside her grief for her mother, her horror of the crowd, and her fear for her unborn child. She had come to fight a lost cause and that battle she had won. A just cause remained. Again her courage rose within her, her voice like the blast of a trumpet raised to blow the signal for attack.

"I will not rule as my father ruled, for I am done with slavery!"

Her insult stung the citizens of Agave like a lash. Would she take from them their sole means of support, the only riches they possessed in this barren land? When she spoke again, the crowd's anger changed to derision.

"I know a place which offers a gift to all who seek it. With this gift, Agave can free itself from the bonds of slavery. You believe the poor unfortunates who occupy these platforms are the only ones enslaved, but you are wrong. You are enslaved as surely as those in chains, for with every shackle you forge, every family you separate, every soul you torment, you lessen yourselves even as you enrich your purse."

Their humorless laughter filled the marketplace, resounding against the buildings surrounding them and bouncing back from the unyielding sandstone walls. She would take away their livelihood, offering a nameless gift instead. Shouts and accusations began before their laughter ended, demanding again and again for her to give this gift a name.

Lady Lillas stood mute while their cries filled the air. When a visible trembling seized her, the crowd rejoiced, proud that they had quelled her madness, satisfied that she shook with fear.

"Reddin, what is it? Oh, my love, what is it!"

"Lillas, come into my arms! It is time!"

As Reddin's voice reverberated in her ears, a Door opened inside her mind, inviting her to cross its threshold and move toward a bright light promising something wondrous, something unimaginable. She knew her body stood in the marketplace, of that she had no doubt, for Reddin held her fast in his arms even as the waking world began to fade. Every instinct urged her to push forward toward that light, as if she had grown wings and circled a flame, anticipating the glory of what had been promised to her and the man who stood by her side. Soon she must cross over into light, but something held her back, a woman's voice speaking inside her mind, asking her for one final act.

"This is the moment. A single task awaits you, Lillas of the West and Reddin of Pelion. You must invite the people of Agave to witness your Transformation, and by doing so, allow them a taste of the Sowers' gift."

"How, Mother?" Lillas asked, suddenly aware of the crowd's leers and shouted insults, for she and Reddin stood alone and helpless in the marketplace, surrounded by many whose hands still bore the rusty stains of Seth's blood.

"Fear nothing, daughter of Agave. For this moment were you born."

The angry crowd raged around them, screaming their questions into the dust-filled air of the Agavean marketplace.

"What is this gift?" "Where is the profit?" "What should we gain?"

Upon hearing their cries mixed with greed and despair, Lillas, the flame of the West, knew what to do.

"Think of my people, Reddin. Help me take them with us to the Door. They cannot pass through, but they can taste a tiny bit of what is promised. Let us wrap them in our thoughts, slaves and masters, nobles of Imarus and the hopeless poor alike. It is time for them, like us, to walk a new Path."

As she knew he would, Reddin gripped her ever more tightly, holding her fast against his chest, their hearts beating as one, their minds wrapped around the screaming populace of Agave, the healer and his mate leading them inevitably, unavoidably toward the Door.

The crowd mumbled to themselves, uneasy at the sight of a man and a woman being transformed into a statue of living marble, their limbs entwined, their forms blending into light and shadow as they embraced. An unearthly glow shimmered and quivered in the air around them as the sun reached its zenith, its vertical rays bouncing off the surface of their white and silver robes. A new voice, one the crowd had never heard before, proclaimed:

"Silence, Agave! The gift stands before you! Witness the miracle of two who become one!"

A woman dressed in dusty black robes addressed them from the top of the platform on which the couple stood. The crowd muttered their astonishment, for she had not stood there earlier, and they wondered at the power of her voice to reach their ears and their minds with such clarity of purpose. A stave was clenched in her right hand, and some spoke afterwards of an emblazoned banner which furled from the end of this staff, as if there blew a strong breeze, although the air that day lay still and heavy over the marketplace. But they knew her not, this small woman of indifferent looks, and their furor grew despite her warning that they be silent. Her staff raised and lowered three times, the wood striking the timbers of the platform with a hollow pounding, and she spoke for the second time:

"Hear me, Agave! You roar as the prophecy foretold and at last you shall be silenced! Your bride awaits you! Come and meet her at last!"

In a violent contraction of light, time, and space, Lillas and Reddin passed through the Door. In that same moment, Agave met Pelion in all her glory.

Bride though she was, Pelion appeared to them not as one arrayed for the ceremony of mating, but in the garb of all those who inhabited the marketplace of Agave. For in the instant following Lillas and Reddin's Transformation, the thousand souls gathered under the desert sun looked into each other's minds, finding as they did so their other self. Noble became beggar, merchant became slave, orphaned child became ruthless slaver, while the blinded looked through the eyes of those who had placed the white-hot poker against their flesh. Their minds trapped in another's body, the newly-crippled writhed in torment, while those sound of body for the first time, lifted their arms to the sky in a show of triumph. Some minds screamed as they were transported; others struggled vainly to retain what they had always held as truths; more than one sobbed aloud at the joy of liberty restored or the agony of freedom denied. And as their frenzy rose, they clamored for a means to end their captivity, until they heard, as one being, the third proclamation of the Prophetess of Agave:

"The people thirst and their thirst shall be quenched! From the depths is born the fountain from which all may drink! This is your gift, Agave, that you need thirst no more!"

Their minds freed, captives no longer, their eyes opened to find the woman in black standing not on the platform but on the sand below, and watched as she lifted her staff again to strike the earth three times. At the third blow, the earth shook, its second and strongest tremor of the day.

This time there were no prayers to gods and no screams for succor, for somehow they understood that the earth beneath their feet, this good earth, the gift of the Sowers, no longer sought to destroy them. Instead, it offered up precious liquid from its churning bowels. From the ground escaped a trickle of water, at first a tiny bubble of liquid that was immediately consumed by the thirsty sand. The bubbles grew as the sand darkened, and as if the sand had drunk enough and delighted in its drinking, a spray of water burst forth, a fountain twice as tall as a man, and the sunlight played and danced on its cascades.

Slowly, inch by inch, the people of Agave crept forward, reaching with open palms to catch the sunlit drops of water, faces lifted to the bright sky, the cool spray of the fountain washing away the salty tracks of their tears. Many wept, some dropping to their knees in a thankful pose, others backing away, struck dumb with sheer disbelief, still more coming forward, awestruck, mouths agape, to see something they had never seen before—water, cold and clean, spewing freely from the ground on which they stood.

The Prophetess of Agave spoke the last words they would remember hearing:

"This is the fountain of Charis. From its waters all may drink without cost or reckoning. Even now, all around us, fountainheads spring up from inside the earth. In time, streams and brooks, rivers and lakes, will grace your lands. The earth alters its complexion; so must Agave!"

Thus was the possibility of a New Agave revealed.

LILLAS FOUND REDDIN in the gardens, walking in solitary contemplation amongst the flowers of Imarus, his head lowered to drink in the heavy perfumes rising from the blooms of early summer. She reveled in the sight of him as he wandered among the lush mazes where lovers once lingered for their trysts, the evergreen hedges shielding them from the watchful eyes of the palace. He was clean-shaven now, slender as always under silken robes, his hair straight and thick, his arms crossed over his bare chest as he paused to admire a particularly full-blown peony bush. Gathering her skirts in her hands, she broke into a run, her long legs carrying her swiftly to his side. As always, his eyes ignited at her arrival, a clear flame burning in their depths. By the time she reached him, she was gasping with excitement and mirth. An answering smile rose to his lips.

"What news, Lillas-quick-of-foot? Did the Session disband or has Kazur resigned in disgust?"

There was irony in his question, as well as a certain amount of longing. Lillas might have rejected the medallion, but old habits die hard. Forty days had passed since the death of Seth, yet still the people clamored for her attendance as they strove to rule themselves. Half the population had already departed; slaves to find families, nobles to seek more hospitable lands. Those who remained squabbled over rights to land and water, parceling out the surrounding countryside to those whose participation in the miracle convinced them that Agave had received a blessing destined to fill their purses and bellies in new and undreamed of ways.

In time they came to respect Kazur, a third party necessary to negotiate agreements between groups of widely diverse interests; a foreigner who never failed to amaze them with his breadth of knowledge about their past. Even so, it was Lillas' judgment they trusted, never dreaming that most of her decisions were forged by two minds instead of one. She urged Reddin, even begged him, to sit by her side in the Aeson's great palace in Imarus, emptied now of its former inhabitants, which served as a meeting place while Agave was rebuilt. Despite her pleas, he refused. His opinions he would share, and share gladly, always willing to consider the latest issue being discussed around the negotiating table. But sit with her he would not, nor did he offer any reason for his refusal other than his desire to practice his profession. These days, he was most often found in a wing of the palace devoted to healing. There, by Phoron's side, he labored over the wretched of Agave; turning his hand to the craft he loved above all others. The days were full, their hours together few, and although they resided in Lillas' nest, they were constantly denied the peace that haven once offered.

Phoron was not the only teacher in Imarus, for the Eighteenth Mother instructed them daily in the ways of their new-found gift, taking them with her through the passageways and corridors of their linked minds, building their confidence in the possibilities of what they shared, easing them toward the true intimacy of adept mates. Hers was not an easy task, for Lillas balked at entering certain rooms locked tightly against demons she refused to acknowledge, while Reddin shied away from admissions he preferred not to make. This week she cancelled their sessions, her grey-green eyes shrouded in mystery, causing them to wonder at her refusal to teach them. Even so, patients and elected representatives of the populace demanded their help, and they turned gladly towards others to escape what they could not bring themselves to face.

Reddin's question lingered in her ears and Lillas laughed again, color rising to her cheeks. The healer raised a speculative eyebrow, aware that his self-assured mate was not given to meaningless blushes.

"I came to tell you that I am indeed with child!"

Both eyebrows lifted now as he regarded her, a smile playing about his lips.

"It would be remarkable if you weren't, since sixty days have passed since your last flow."

His calm authority deflated her excitement, for she had only just counted the days herself. A frown growing between her brows, she gave way to her sharp tongue.

"How can you know that? You were on the desert at the time!"

"I asked Phoron."

"Do you always count the days so carefully?" she demanded, displeased at learning that her monthly cycle was a topic of conversation among the society of healers.

"Always," came his smug reply, his eyes gleaming with laughter although his lips refused to smile.

An idea was born as she watched his enjoyment at her upset.

"Did you count the days of my cycle from the day of our first meeting?" Sensing his reluctance to answer, she decided to tease him. "Could this be the reason you boasted about your experience in joining, but refrained from offering me any proof?"

He muttered a half-hearted disclaimer. She laughed aloud, her faith in him restored. Taking her arm in his, he guided her through the garden and out onto the lawn, less manicured of late, but bright green and dustless in the late afternoon sunshine. A marble bench, the weeds growing high around it, beckoned to them and they sat enjoying the spectacle of the sinking sun.

"Reddin, will you deliver the child?"

Her question must have surprised him for his eyes blinked rapidly for a moment.

"I thought so, although if you prefer someone else . . . "

With a pang in her heart she realized she'd unintentionally hurt him. She nearly stumbled over her tongue in her rush to explain.

"Of course I want you to do it! How could you think otherwise? It's just that I don't know how things are done in Pelion."

Reassured, he took her hand.

"If we were in Pelion, when your pains began we would go to the House of Healing." His hand tightened on hers as he addressed her fears. "The first child often comes slowly, but I'll help you bear the pain. Once the child is well-placed, we'll speed its birth together."

She nodded, satisfied, until another thought crossed her mind.

"Will we be alone?"

"In Pelion," he replied slowly, almost reluctantly, "the mothers of both mates are usually present in the birthing room."

"Won't your mother be there?" she asked, puzzled by his reaction.

"My mother?" he asked, seemingly dumbfounded by her question.

Lillas' world turned upside down, her mind suddenly intent on problems she had never considered. Would Reddin's mother resent her because she was not native born? Would their child be shunned? Her voice shrill with worry, she demanded:

"Tell me truthfully: will your mother deny her grandchild because of me?"

"We can't ask my mother to travel here! She's quite elderly and has never left Pelion."

Convinced that he was avoiding her question by offering up excuses that made no sense, she replied: "Don't be ridiculous! No one's asking your mother to travel! We'll be in Pelion long before the child is born! What are you thinking of?"

"We'll . . . we'll be in Pelion . . .?" he repeated, looking dazed and confused and altogether idiotic. Half-afraid she was being teased, she resorted to sarcasm.

"Is there some other place we can learn adept healing?"

Now he was staring at her as if she was speaking a foreign tongue, which annoyed her almost past bearing.

"And don't think I've forgotten my question, for I assure you I haven't! Why wouldn't your mother want to attend the birth of our first child?"

By this time she'd risen from the bench, planting her fists firmly on her silk-clad hips, giving vent to her fury as she hadn't done for days. Few would have recognized her unless they knew the Lillas of old. With a joyful cry, Reddin jumped to his feet, grabbing her around her waist and twirling her anger away as his laughter filled the sunlit afternoon.

"You never told me, blue-eyes! I've wanted to say something for so long, but you were always busy with your people and I had not the heart to suggest that you leave."

"This is why you've brooded of late? Why you hid yourself away in the infirmary? Oh, Reddin, how could you doubt me?"

His eyes darkened with tenderness as he held her close, then proceeded to apologize by covering her face with kisses, an apology that never failed to earn her forgiveness.

"And your mother?" she insisted through his kisses.

"My mother will be more than pleased, she'll be ecstatic!" He paused, relishing the thought. "It's odd that her youngest child should give her the first grandchild."

"Are you so confident that Orrin and Chryse don't share our situation?"

"I hadn't thought of that," he replied, bemused as always by her quickness.

"You could ask him," she reminded him. "The Eighteenth Mother must have told him we received the gift. Perhaps he waits for your call, expecting you to contact him when you're ready."

She was nudging him, as she would be the first to admit, but having no siblings, she found she wanted some. In their sessions with the Eighteenth Mother she warmed to Reddin's memories of Orrin, finding in him the brother she never had. For she had been orphaned by Agave as surely as the abandoned slave children being housed in makeshift schools across the city. Everything in her bright and exuberant spirit yearned for Reddin's family to welcome her with the love she felt for him.

Accepting her advice without hesitation, he nodded.

"I'll do as you suggest, blue-eyes."

They strolled on through the garden as dusk gathered around them, Lillas content and Reddin thoughtful.

"Our training together will last a year. Have you considered beginning your studies in the sciences? They would take three years and perhaps four, but I'll help you."

She shook her head, having gone over these realities many times in the past moon.

"I have neither the background nor the aptitude for such a difficult course of study. I came to learning too late to excel, which is no one's fault but my own."

At this, she sighed, for the honest examination of self was new to her and exceedingly painful. Pushing away regrets, she described the life she envisioned for herself.

"I'll be your healing partner, assisting with those patients who require shared attunement. You can do everything you've longed to do—diagnosing ailments, recommending treatments, and prescribing medicines. When you need me, I'll be there to recall them to life or ease their passing, as the case may be."

He did not push her, as she feared he might, but accepted her decision with grave seriousness.

"These things you will do as no one else can, beloved, for these hands gave me back my life."

After kissing the crescent-shaped scar on her wrist, the place where the shackles had dug into her flesh, he held her palms against his cheeks, just as she had held him during the dark times. As memories swirled around her she withdrew her hands, unwilling to surrender the beauty of the afternoon to painful remembrances. Sharing her delight in the gardens, he took her arm again and led her onward.

They were approaching a line of cedar trees, their branches permanently bent away from the steady winds that blew from the west, their odor unmistakably sharp and pungent. She stopped as they drew near, her heart beating faster, her pulse quickening, her entire body tensed as she prepared to flee.

"What do you fear?"

"I have no liking for this place."

"Why is that?"

It was a quiet question as he searched her face with troubled eyes. A hundred lies flew to her lips. Before she could blurt out even one, he said:

"Take me with you, Lillas. It's time."

They were the same words he'd spoken when he'd held her on the platform, stilling her fears as he wrapped her in his arms. Together they left the howling mobs behind, reentering the world of their dreams where they swam in blue waters of enchantment, guided to shore by those waiting to assist their crossing.

What had she to fear with him by her side, with Reddin, who helped her face the maddened crowds, his presence strong and true, never failing in his wisdom as he asked her to consider what the medallion promised, knowing as she did that their lives might be the cost of her refusal to don that golden chain. She had rejected the darkness once before. Now he asked that she do so again. With a sigh, she opened her memories to him, finding herself in front of the door she'd feared to open.

There were no words here, only Reddin's tenderness and a world of understanding for whatever lay behind this locked door. The light was dim along this corridor of her mind, for here resided the loss of her father and the murder of her mother, grievous memories still too painful to be explored. The last door, the one directly in front of her was closed and bolted fast. With Reddin's help, she swung the door open, hearing the creak of rusty hinges. Slowly, fearfully, she stepped across the threshold.

The night wind sighed through cedar branches, the strains of music from the great hall drifting over the dew-heavy grass. She walked along familiar paths, but this time she did not walk alone.

The grass wet under her bare feet, she dangled her sandals in her hands, enjoying the squelch of the water-rich earth between her toes.

There was never any warning in her dream, and this time, too, there was none, a discovery that filled her with relief even as a hand reached out to grab her, stopping her mouth as it always did. Unable to cry out, she heard the silent scream from within, the scream of a girl of barely fourteen years being raped by a stranger whose face she never saw.

In her dreams she never fought. In her dreams she was passive, inert, unable to mount the slightest resistance against her attacker. Now she found herself fighting wildly, scratching and tearing at him, hearing his curses as he fell on top of her, his weight pinning her beneath him. Her legs pushed open by a knee, she felt the searing pain as he ripped through her maidenhead. Warm, sticky blood flowed from between her thighs, but still she fought the man who covered her face as he assaulted her, holding her with a savage strength she couldn't overcome. She was dying underneath him, pain and shame her sole companions, when, after his final thrust, he left her sobbing on wet grass stained with the blood of her virginity.

And then she was in Reddin's arms.

"No shame, Lillas, no shame. He gave you no warning and you fought him with all the strength you possessed. Even when another might have given up, you fought on."

She continued to cry, shaking in his arms, unable to quench the fear inside her.

"Put a name to your fear."

"That he might come back."

Reddin nodded, lost in thought.

"We must return."

"What!?"

"Take me back with you."

Lillas hesitated until she remembered something the Eighteenth Mother said during their lessons together:

"You must practice experiencing the world with your senses combined. It's not just seeing with four eyes. It's one of you hearing the sound of wind through empty branches, while the other feels the crunch of dry leaves underfoot. When you are One, you are doubled—twice as sensitive, twice as perceptive of the world around you as you are by yourself."

With Reddin, Lillas felt the night wind, smelt cedar, heard music, touched the dewy grass with bare feet. Everything proceeded as it had before, save, just as the attacker pulled her down and before he lifted her blouse over her head, for the briefest of moments, she caught a whiff of the thin, rancid odor of male perspiration.

Struck hard by memory, Lillas found herself in the courtyard of her father's palace, panting at the finish line, the winner of a childhood race. Her cousins, male and female, were making a huge ruckus, fighting over bets, swapping coins and generally misbehaving, when Seth approached her, dripping with sweat, his eyes icy with dislike.

"There's always another race, Seth," she crowed, happy at having beaten him.

"You'll be sorry," he growled as he limped away, leaving behind him the stench of his sweat.

"Seth!" she cried aloud, breaking her connection with Reddin, horrified at discovering the identity of her rapist, yet acknowledging it as true to his character. And then she was crying again and Reddin was saying:

"Hush, blue-eyes, it will pass. No more nightmares, no more fears of cedar trees and moonless nights."

They sank together onto the uncut grass as the crickets began their evening calls. He held her against his heart as she wept. As her sobs quieted, he pulled her into the cradle of his arms so they might watch the ascent of the moon to the heavens.

Working as the healing partners they would become, they healed themselves. Reddin found his home in Lillas, who would be his helpmate as they tended the wounds of Agave, for Reddin never doubted they would return. And Lillas faced, and in time would forget, the demons that brought fear to one who, by all that was just, should fear nothing, having stood staunchly against the beast that was Agave.

They had become one, and with the birth of their child they would offer the proof of their final gift, offered on a night when all hopes seemed futile, their joining an act of faith in a despairing world. And in time, the Eighteenth Mother of Pelion would place on the altar a cloth wet with the milk from Lillas' breasts.

* * *

HESIONE MOVED AWAY from the window to regard Prax, who was watching her without seeming to do so. He yawned and stretched, still made uncomfortable by padded ottomans and cushioned lounges, preferring the feel of solid wood beneath his backside.

"Are they coming back to Pelion with us?"

"It would seem so."

Prax nodded over another yawn, tired of this fledgling democracy and the resulting bureaucracy Kazur thrived on. *What I need is a saddle under my arse*, he thought to himself. In a mood of rare reflection he decided that the Eighteenth Mother was acting strangely of late, a strain around her eyes he didn't like the look of. It came to him that she must be worried about her pupils.

"Don't worry about them. The first moon of the gift is always hard. Some things are difficult to share."

"I worry about them no longer. My concern for Lillas and Reddin ceased when they crossed over. Their mating was not an easy one, but as Chryse predicted, they have struck a balance. They and their children will bring such joy to this place as it has never known before."

This interested Prax, since he'd come to despise this marble hothouse known as Imarus almost as much as he hated Agave. It never occurred to him, as it often did to Hesione, that the chains linking Prax to Pelion were unbreakable. He could never have left, as Reddin, Dysponteus, Dorian, and others would leave, to join his ernani in another land, sharing his talents with those who needed them far more than those who dwelt in the walled city to the south.

As Hesione reviewed her inventory of the male candidates of Pelion, she sighed upon remembering that Adrastus, the apprentice engineer, had left the Maze, his joining a failure. Even now, his ernani, Gwyn of Cyme, waited for another candidate to enter her cell. It was a grim reality, the failure of the Trial, and one that could now be set aside, if not this year or the year after, then certainly within the time of her reign. She was not fool enough to believe that slavery would end, for that had never been promised. What had been promised was that Agave would be translated, that a name once used as a curse would become a blessing. In time, those who drank from Charis' fountain would become renowned for their hospitality and the pledge of a citizen of Agave would become synonymous with honesty itself.

Prax interrupted her thoughts, as he often did, although the man who single-handedly cleared her path in the slave market could never merit her wrath. She put aside her contemplations to attend him.

"What's to become of Imarus?"

His question brought a smile from her, knowing full well his fascination with the things of the future. She was careful to guard the visions that came to her out of the whispering plain, but for once she spoke freely, still under the influence of the drama she had just witnessed from the window, a window facing a row of windswept cedar trees.

"In time it will surpass the House of Healing with its reputation for advances in healing techniques, although the House of Healing will remain the school where healers learn their craft."

It irked him a little to think that Pelion might be surpassed in any endeavor, but he chewed on it for a time.

"And Agave?"

This answer was more difficult, for the way was fraught with hardship and might take centuries to reach fulfillment. She shared what she could.

"Once the tremors end, and they may last throughout this year and into the next, the courses of the brooks and streams will settle. Off to the southwest, where once there were fissures, there will be a series of deep lakes. What used to be the scrublands to the northeast and the barren lands to the south will become part of a fertile crescent reaching from the Western Ridge to the valley of Pelion." She teased him and watched him bristle. "Your maps will have to be re-drawn by the Chartists, I fear, not to mention the fact that your patrols will have to cover five times the territory, escorting ernani from the lands far to the west of Agave, those who have never dared the journey until now."

"How far beyond Agave?!"

"Prax, Prax," she said, hiding her amusement at the shocked look on his face, "we have only just begun! Did you think we can rest now? Our labors have been tiny compared to what we face in the future! You've lived in the Maze. Did it ever occur to you to wonder why it was built to house a hundred couples and more while our classes rarely reach twenty? Did the builders overshoot the mark, or do you believe, as I do, that in the decades to follow it will be full to bursting, bringing on a score of other problems I am just beginning to consider?"

"Is that why you've been worried of late?"

Hesione sank onto an ottoman, wondering if others saw through her as Prax did, his hazel eyes pinning her beneath their weight, a stern father interviewing a guilty child.

"I have no worries about the Maze."

"What, then?"

There was a long silence.

"I've seen my death. It weighs heavily on me."

"I knew you thought to die in Agave, but your vision erred for once. For that I was glad."

He knew but said nothing. Even so, he'd offered her his powerful arms, thinking all the while those same arms would bear her lifeless body away from the city of madness. Day in and day out, she held her secret close, trying to keep her fear at bay.

"How will you die?"

She closed her eyes at the force of her vision. Mastering her terror, she replied steadily, "By violence, a blow struck by someone maddened who froths at the mouth like a diseased animal."

The room darkened around them, the shadows from the draperies billowing in the evening breeze casting ghostly designs on the marble floor.

"My death I can accept, for death shuts one door so another may be opened."

"If you don't fear death, what do you fear?"

The urge to confess the answer to Prax's question was the greatest temptation Hesione would ever face, greater than her longing to remain safely in Pelion, greater even than her overwhelming urge to flee the slovenly inn where she'd waited for enlightenment, only to face the marketplace empty-handed, bereft of vision. The words of the prophecy came to her without foreknowledge—she opened her mouth and the words burst forth. In that soul-searing moment, she became for the second time, a Prophet of Pelion.

How badly she needed to confess her fears to this giant of a man, the single person in Pelion who could see beyond her office, the only one capable of lulling her fears as Reddin comforted Lillas as they lay together on the grassy lawn. Should she tell him that she feared not the manner of her death, but that death might come too quickly, robbing Pelion and all the world of her successor, as the Seventeenth Mother had nearly robbed her? To think the chain of eighteen generations might be broken was a thought too bitter to be borne. In the days since the miracle in Agave she'd reached out blindly for solace, finding the chilly hand of despair.

But this secret was not hers to confess. She understood the weightiness of this, the greatest burden she would carry in the heart that beat under the black robes. Such was the price of power, to behold the night yet struggle on to greet the day. With that realization, a voice inside her head whispered: *"Lillas."*

Everything had hung on the utterance of a single word, but somehow Meliope spoke and somehow Hesione heard. With that hearing, all had been accomplished.

Hesione ushered this secret into her heart, placing it next to the vision of her death.

Rising, she smiled at Prax, surprising him with her energy, answering his question not with the truth in her heart, but with the truth of her love for him.

"What do I fear, old friend? What else but the loss of your company?"

He gawked at her and blushed, shamefaced and ill-at-ease in the face of her unexpected sentimentality.

"Come, Commander," she patted his shoulder in a wordless apology. "Mia calls us to supper. I fear for our lives if her meat pie is spoilt by our tardiness."

With a grunt, he rose to his feet, his stomach rumbling as he passed her by, breaking into a jog as he considered the flakiness of Mia's crusts.

The cook's freedom changed nothing about her. From daybreak to sunset she cooked contentedly for the hungry ones of Imarus, content to fill empty stomachs for the rest of her life, confident that her talents would never go unappreciated in a land that would soon be rich with farmlands, herds, and an everlasting supply of spring-fed water.

THE EIGHTEENTH MOTHER of Pelion, the Keeper of the Flame, and the Bride of Agave, lifted her arms to the evening sky, the silver ring on her third finger twinkling like an earthbound star. In the silence of twilight her ears seemed to catch the distant murmur of Charis' fountain, a fanciful thought, due no doubt to the seductive beauty of the evening. She-Who-Was-Hesione welcomed nightfall, trusting dawn would follow.

Appendix I

Chronology of 1 - 51 A.T.

1   The Sixteenth Mother (She-Who-Was-Nerissa) sends out the Third Wave of Searchers to find voluntary ernani of both genders.

5   Ground is broken for the addition of the Hall of Men to the Maze.

14   Stanis of Pelion's *The Search for Ernani* is catalogued in The Great Library.

18   The Sixteenth Mother's *Revisions* are added to the *Legislation for Preparation* and catalogued in The Great Library.

19   The first class of all-voluntary ernani begins Preparation.

20   An addition to The Maze (the men's refractory and dormitory) is completed.

21   Ascension of the Seventeenth Mother (She-Who-Was-Meliope).

24   The so-called "Selection Protest" occurs. In answer to the request of the people, the Seventeenth Mother institutes the Trial, a method by which males of Pelion can   compete for Preparation.

25   The first Trial occurs in the tenth moon.

29   Charis is escorted to Agave.

30   Birth of Lillas.

43   Ascension of the Eighteenth Mother (She-Who-Was-Hesione).

45   The Guild of Printers is founded by Elan and Pasiphae of Pelion. The first book reproduced by mechanical means, *Poetica Antiqua,* is catalogued in the Great Library.

46   The Eighteenth Mother institutes Pelion's war on Agave (the ninth moon).

47   Phoron of Pelion leaves for Agave (sixth moon). Water tax levied by Seth in Agave (seventh moon). Lillas charms the angry crowds of Agave (eighth moon).

50   Lukash/Selena's *The First Generation* catalogued in The Great Library. The passing of Lukash (the eighth moon). Reddin competes in the Trial (the last day of the tenth moon). Lillas arrives in Pelion (the second day of the eleventh moon).

51   The Siege of Pelion occurs when forces from Agave surround Pelion
      and demand the surrender of an ernani undergoing Preparation in
      the Maze. On the morning of the fourth day, the citizens of Pelion
      awake to find their valley deserted and the siege lifted (third moon).
      Preparations and journeys to Agave (fourth moon). The possibility
      of a New Agave is revealed (fifth moon).

Appendix II

The Agave Translation

. . . and so the days shall pass until the beast wakes, and lo, the land shall wither, even to the last blade of grass. On the anvil of the sun, two silver rings are forged.

The prophet speaks, but only one shall heed his call. The flame of the west shall pass into the wet lands where it will not be extinguished. The candle of despair shall be lit, and yea, they shall be joined as no others before or after.

As the beast roars, so shall the people thirst, until their thirst at last is quenched. The staff lifts, falls, and lo, the earth rumbles and shakes. From the depths spurts forth the fountain from which all may drink. And all will drink.

One ring will pass away; one will abide with you forever.

Agave shall be translated and Pelion will wed.

Attributed to the Fifteenth Mother

No part of the ancient *Book of Mothers* has so captured the popular imagination as this entry, commonly known as *The Agave Translation*. A favorite subject of artists for a millennium, its events have seemingly been plumbed dry in one era only to be discovered anew by succeeding generations fascinated by this most dramatic (some would say romantic) episode in the first decades of post-Transformation. One has only to consider the so-called Agavean Renaissance (circa 250-320 A.T.), an outpouring of creativity that yielded Tourne's fabled stone portals of the Agave Session with their carved multitudes of enraptured souls, or Cynthia/Elena's masterwork, *Charissong*, scored for soprano and strings, to understand the immense imaginative influence of an event represented by these few short lines of text. Even Swiasa, a place unknown to first-century dwellers of Pelion, contributed to the storehouse of treasures concerning the events of 50 A.T., its foremost offering being Ashwal/Nihana's Revivalist Tragedy, *The Anvil* (A.T. 687). Time seems not to lessen the evocative nature of the tale, as is evidenced by Lucien/Branwyn's free-standing sculpture, *Staff on Sand*, commissioned by the Folklorists of Pelion and installed in the foyer of The School of Antiquity in 1005 A.T. as part of the commemorative activities celebrating the millennium.[1]

There exist several primary sources which offer first-hand accounts related to the events of 50 A. T., among them: Kazur/Eluria's *Foundation of the Agave Session*, (Great Library of Pelion, 63 A.T.) and *The Journals of Phoron*, (Great Library of Pelion, 67 A.T.). Although historians still debate its authenticity, an anonymous parchment (the so-called "Lillas Transcript"), discovered in the second century A.T. and housed in the Great Library of Agave, offers what seems to be a hand-written transcription of Lillas of Agave's address to the multitudes. The *Record of Transformation* contains a single entry on the subject that establishes Lillas/Reddin as one-time residents of the Maze. Local folklorists of Agave insist that Lillas/Reddin established Imarus House. No documents corroborating this claim survive.

For those who specialize in the centuries immediately preceding and following Transformation, *The Agave Translation* presents several troublesome references, one of the most confusing being that of the prophet's gender, identified as "he". Since the Eighteenth Mother has been irrefutably established as the Prophetess of Agave, Rowra/Crosus (*Assigning Authors: "The Book of Mothers"*, Great Library of Endlin, 1040 A.T.) contend that a scribe's error caused the apparent discrepancy. Another mysterious reference, that of the second ring, is less easily explained. The first ring, which "will abide with you forever," refers to the silver band worn by succeeding generations of Mothers, but the identity of the second ring (designated as the one that "shall pass away") continues to elude present-day scholarship.

Almost nothing is known of the Eighteenth Mother due to her relatively short reign (ca.43 - ca.53 A.T.) although her presence in Agave provides the first recorded journey of a wearer of the black robes beyond the walls of Pelion. Her immediate successor is more widely known for her travels to outlying areas.[2] Still, credit must be given to the Eighteenth Mother for breaking what must have been an especially rigid tradition, having stood unchallenged since the founding of Pelion five centuries earlier. Another event of note during her reign was the Siege of Pelion, of which almost nothing is known other than the fact that it lasted three days, ending abruptly and without incident.

These considerations aside, *The Agave Translation* remains a powerful testament to the advances made toward enlightenment within the first century after Transformation. No less a personage than Hyperia of Tek, philosopher and member of the Thirty-Second Mother's Council, proclaimed it to be:

> . . . the most influential legend in our history, combining as it does the secular with the sacred, the simple with the profound, the singular with the plural. At no other time and in no other place does the private Transformation become public. I, like my sisters and brothers in ancient Agave, stand open-mouthed, awed as my chains drop off of their own accord, allowing me to wet my feet in the waters of change.[3]

[1] The interested reader should consult *Ten Centuries of the Agave Translation* (compiled by the Folklorists of Pelion, Great Library of Pelion, 1050) for a complete listing of literary and artistic creations. Published as part of the millennium celebrations, it presents a detailed analysis of the best and worst works on the Agavean theme.

[2] The Nineteenth Mother, also known as The Preserver. For further information concerning her importance, see commentary in *Pelion Preserved*, Book Three of Maze.

[3] Commentary abridged from Astia/Gregor, *Chronicles of The Elder Days*, Volume II, Great Library of Pelion, 1091.

About the Author

Anna LaForge read Tolkien's *The Lord of the Rings* at fourteen, Asimov's *Foundation Trilogy* at sixteen, and LeGuin's *The Left Hand of Darkness* at eighteen, at which time she decided that she, too, wanted to create new worlds.

Born in Philadelphia, her work as an actor, director, dramaturg, and professor has taken her to San Francisco, Washington D.C. And New York City. Once an executive director of two not-for-profit theatre organizations, she now divides her time between teaching, writing, and seeing live performance.

The Marcella Fragment, the first book in her Maze series was published in June 2012. The second book of the series, *Agave Revealed*, followed in June 2013. It will be followed by additional novels in the series, including *Pelion Preserved* in 2014.

Anna's books are published by Newcal Publishing.

Connect with Anna LaForge online:

Twitter: twitter.com/annalaforge
Facebook: facebook.com/annalaforge
Her website and blog: annalaforge.com

CPSIA information can be obtained at www.ICGtesting.com
Printed in the USA
LVOW061730120513

333363LV00003B/18/P

9 780985 016845